A BLUESTONE LAKES NOVEL

JENN MCMAHON

Copyright © 2025 by Jenn McMahon LLC

All rights reserved.

Cover Design: Melissa Doughty | Mel D. Designs

Editing: Caroline Palmier

Developmental Editing: Amy Pritt

Proofreading: Erica Rogers

No part of this book may be reproduced in any form or by any electronic or mechanical means, including information storage and retrieval systems, without written permission from the author, except for the use of brief quotations in a book review.

Without in any way limiting the author's exclusive rights under copyright, any use of this publication to "train" generative artificial intelligence (AI) technologies to generate text is expressly prohibited.

This is a work of fiction, created without use of AI technology. Any names, characters, places or incidents are products of the author's imagination and used in a fictitious manner. Any resemblance to actual people, places, or events is purely coincidental or fictional.

A NOTE FROM JENN

Hello friend.

Thank you so much for picking up Finding Home. If you've read my Firsts in the City Series, you know I love writing men who will make you blush. I also love writing relatable women who we can see little pieces of ourselves in.

I'm so excited you're here to experience a whole new world with me. We're about to visit Bluestone Lakes, Wyoming! This little fictional town has become so real to me. The same way these characters hold a special place in my heart.

Through this series, you will find second chances and found family. Bluestone Lakes is an ideal location for those looking to escape everyday life or whatever problems you're facing back home. In our secluded town tucked between the mountains with a lake as far as the eyes can see, you will find peace and solitude during your stay. However long that may be..

If you want to see more, you can visit the town website. This will be updated regularly *wink wink* as the series progresses.

http://jennmcmahon.com

While this book was created to be light, funny, and easy to read —I understand there are some things that may be triggering to someone. My goal is to respect that before you dive into this story.

I wanted to make you aware that this book you has explicit language, alcohol consumption, and explicit sex scenes.

You will also find in the prologue, our girl Blair Andrews walks in to find her husband cheating on her. As cheating is such a sensitive topic, I wanted to ensure you knew about it before reading the prologue. There is also talk of her past as being manipulated to be someone she's not by her parents. Our girl really has a lot of struggles she faces before *finding home* in Blue-stone Lakes.

I hope I handled these topics with care and that you end up laughing, kicking your feet and swooning through this book the same way I did writing it.

As always, my Instagram DM's are always open for your reactions, favorite moments and to chat as you read!

Let the adventure begin, *sweetheart.*

xo, Jenn

Have you ever felt stuck? Like you're constantly wearing a mask to fit the mold of who you're supposed to be rather than who you want to be for the sake of others? This ones for you.

It's time to take the mask off, babe. It's time to be boldly, proudly, and unapologetically YOU.

FINDING HOME

BLUESTONE LAKES
BOOK 1

PROLOGUE

BLAIR

The kitchen fills with the irresistible scent of sugar, and a smile spreads across my face as the oven timer dings. The aroma envelops me as I open the oven, immersing myself in the baking process. The soft baked goodness, with its perfect golden-brown edges, is my favorite sight. The anticipation of its perfect consistency is almost palpable, and I can't wait to taste it.

Next to running, baking is one of my favorite hobbies and brings me the most happiness. It's also the only one I'm allowed to do often. Running, however, is a process of getting out the door and one of the many obstacles I face as a well-known politician's wife. The constant need for security—a reminder of my responsibilities—is a challenge I have to navigate every time I step out.

Experimenting with new recipes I find online keeps me busy since the days feel so long while he's in meetings for the better part of his days. Most nights are even longer when he's taken away for work or sleeps in his office because he needs to be there early in the morning.

But that's part of the job, right?

Sighing, I place the tray of cookies on top of the stove while

1

these thoughts flood my mind. Resting my hands on the counter next to the sink, I let my head fall. I haven't seen Theodore since early yesterday morning. The longing for his presence is a constant ache in my heart.

I miss my husband.

Based on our phone call earlier this morning, he plans to be in the office all day, which is why I'm baking his favorite cookies to bring to his office as an excuse to see him.

Even years later, I still find myself trying to adjust to this life since he was elected, despite having lived this lifestyle since I was young. I grew up the daughter of a powerful politician, so it should have been an easy transition. But it's much more complicated when you're actually in the spotlight at events. Something I was not used to as a child but have grown used to as a twenty-nine-year-old wife.

My sister, living in an apartment complex down the block from me, helps when I feel like I might go stir-crazy from loneliness.

Today is one of those days.

Unfortunately, Kodi is in meetings all day for her job.

Inhaling the smell of the oatmeal cookies once more, I pause, noticing a piece of dog hair on my sleeve. I roll my eyes but can't help the smile on my face.

Reginald.

I take a step away from the oven to avoid getting any small piece of corgi hair anywhere near the cookies before brushing any other pieces lingering along the fabric. When Theodore first proposed getting a dog to keep me company, I didn't love the idea because of our busy work schedule.

While I don't hold a traditional job, I've earned a substantial income through endorsements and television appearances outside of attending all events with my husband. These appearances typically revolve around sharing insights into my life as the well-known mayor's wife. It's enough to bring in extra money and gives me something I like doing. Something to keep me busy, hence being skeptical about bringing a dog into our home.

But that wasn't the only reason I was against it.

I want a baby and to start a family with the love of my life.

Theodore wasn't ready for that part of life as his career was just getting started. Because I love him as much as I do, I agreed to the dog because I felt it was the next best thing. Now I have a fluffy corgi that leaves hair on every black article of clothing I have. But has also brought so much joy into my life. I'd take the hair every day of my life knowing I have a mini best friend to spend my days with.

Making my way back to the oven, I remove the cookies from the baking sheet and transfer them to a cooling rack. I lift one up, fumbling it between my fingers while blowing on it to cool it down. Taste testing is the best part, and waiting for them to cool down is impossible when they look this good. My eyes roll the moment the flavor hits my tongue.

Perfection.

The perfect consistency of gooey goodness.

Removing my apron, I brush my black pencil skirt down and make sure there's no other dog hair lingering. Most people don't bake in an outfit like this, but since I will be heading into city hall soon, I wanted to ensure I was ready so the cookies are as fresh as they could be.

Grabbing my keys from the counter, the jingle of them sends Reginald running into the kitchen. His mouth is open and somewhat resembles a smile, making me laugh every time he looks at me.

"You're a good boy, aren't you?" I squat down to rub the top of his head. "Mommy needs to go see Daddy at work and bring him these cookies."

His ears perk up at the use of the word.

I give myself a mental facepalm, smiling as I realize what I've just done. I accidentally started calling his treats cookies when he was a puppy. Now he gets overly excited when he hears me talk about them.

"Fine. I'll give you one of your cookies," I tell him, reaching into the jar on the counter to grab one before I toss it to him. He catches it in the air without missing before running off to his bed, clearly satisfied with his treat.

Standing and righting my skirt, I take the opportunity to grab my handbag and basket of cookies and rush out the door to avoid him barking at me.

Once I reach my car, I take a deep breath because I hate driving in the city due to the never-ending traffic. It doesn't matter if I'm driving in the middle of the night or middle of the day, it's always busy.

Come to think of it, I never cared for living in the city, period.

It was never a dream of mine to stay here. I always thought this would be my sister's life—not mine. I had these visions of living in a small town in a white house with a wrap-around porch, giving way to views of the land in every direction. A vision of a lake on one side and mountains on the other. The best of both worlds in one place to call home.

Having never lived anywhere other than a city, the idea of small-town life was merely a fantasy, a stark contrast to my reality.

When I started dating Theodore in college, I didn't think he would be into politics like my father. I met him in one of my marketing classes. He wanted to be an accountant, and I wanted to get into advertising. Since my sister and I always had similar goals, she tried to get into business, starting a career with her love for interior design, and I wanted to work with her as her marketing director. But leave it to my dad to invite Theodore over for one family dinner early in the relationship, and his mind changed quickly. He changed his major to political science, a turn of events I never saw coming, and now here we are.

You can say my father is a very persuasive person.

I gave up that dream and the chance to leave San Francisco to live in a small town for Theodore. This is our life now, and while it has its downs, there are plenty of upsides as well.

I have an incredible husband who works hard to be the best mayor he can be, and I've made some really good friends through this life. Other wives who are in the same situation as I am where their spouses are busy and taken away for days on end for meetings. We often meet for brunch or early dinners to get out of the house. Most of them have personal drivers and are constantly trying to convince me I should get one too. But I hate the idea of inconveniencing anyone, despite knowing it would be their *job*. It still feels weird to me.

After a quick ten-minute drive, I find myself standing in front of his secretary's desk, looking around to see if anyone is here. She's nowhere to be found. Glancing down at the basket of cookies on my arm, I decide to walk in. If he's in a meeting, I can always excuse myself.

Once I turn down the hall leading to his office, I notice the door and blinds are shut.

Shit.

I guess he has a meeting in another part of the building.

Peeking down the hall, I still don't see anyone around before looking back at his door. An idea pops into my head that maybe I'll leave the cookies on his desk with a Post-it note saying I was here.

I open the door slowly, and I'm immediately taken aback. My feet don't move as my jaw drops open. Every part of me should want to turn away, but I can't.

My husband's bare ass faces me while he has a blonde bent over the chair in the corner of his office. The sound of wet skin slapping together fills the air. Mixed with the sound of this woman crying out his name.

"Oh, Teddy. That's it. That's the spot," she pants.

A gasp escapes my throat, and my basket of cookies falls to the ground with a light thud before my hands cover my mouth in shock.

5

He stops abruptly, and his head snaps to face me.

"Blair," he says quickly, frantically trying to pull apart from her while grasping at his pants in an attempt to hide his dick from me. "It's not what it looks like."

It's not what it looks like?

Are you joking right now?

There are so many things I want to say, but I keep my mouth shut. I'm sure if I were a stronger woman, I would scream and shout and beat the hell out of this woman. Instead, I straighten my spine like I've been programmed to do as the mayor's wife and fight like hell not to show any emotion toward this situation.

Anger rages through me, but I don't have the fight in me right now.

Even if I did, how do you find words to say to your husband after seeing him with another woman right in front of your face?

Turning around, I slam his office door and run for the parking garage without saying anything. He doesn't even deserve a reaction.

It's not what it looks like.

Once I'm safely in my car, I let my head fall back on the head-rest, forcing my breathing to steady and willing my body to relax in the seat. And I wait. I wait for the tears from years spent with this man to fall from my eyes. But they don't come. Even with every emotion surging through me, they don't because I'm so angry at giving up so much of my life for a man who can't even remain faithful.

I can't stay at our home.

I can't sleep in that bed again.

I pick up the phone and dial the one person who's always in my corner, praying she's in between one of her many meetings. She picks up on the first ring.

"Kodi, I need a place to stay."

CHAPTER 1

GO SET THE WORLD ON FIRE.

BLAIR

"I'm moving out," I announce as I enter the living room.

"What?" my sister asks, looking at me from the couch, both shocked and concerned. "Did you finally get approved for the place down the hall?"

Biting the inside of my cheek, I shake my head. "You know I've been searching for ten months now, give or take, to find a place in this same complex. It's been impossible, Kodi!"

"I know." She nods. "Even landing this spot myself was hard."

"I know, and you've been so supportive, letting me and Reginald crash in your guest bedroom after everything with... *Theodore*."

She holds up a hand. "We don't speak that name here."

My sister is my best friend and the person most protective of me, despite being a year younger. The night I found out what Theodore did, Kodi helped me pack as much as I could, including my dog, and left before he returned from work. It was impossible to take everything knowing I was moving into a single room. I sacrificed some of the luxuries as it simply didn't matter to me anymore. Those were all things that tied me to Theodore.

He didn't even bother trying to leave work early to fix what he broke. Which only made me wonder how long it had been going on, which sent my mind spiraling wondering if there were more women and how I missed all the signs.

"And I'm denied everywhere because I don't have verifiable income," I continue, taking a seat on the couch. "There's enough money in my bank account to buy the damn building, but without that steady income on paper, they don't give a shit."

"That's San Francisco for you," Kodi says.

The divorce did a number on Theodore's bank account. I didn't want a dime from him, but the courts ruled our penthouse in my name due to the nature of the divorce. A divorce that happened rather quickly, thanks to the fact he didn't try to contest it, and I didn't ask for anything. The only thing he begged to buy was our penthouse because there wasn't another one like ours available anywhere in the city. His only other option was a home in the suburbs, but he refused to travel into the city every day for work. He shocked me when he offered me more than double what it was worth.

I didn't—and still don't—feel guilty for a second selling it to him at that ridiculous price. Mostly due to the fact that he didn't put up a fight. He didn't beg for me to stay, only wanted his fancy place to live.

So no, I wasn't feeling guilty. Not after what he'd put me through.

"Exactly," I say before looking down at Reginald who jumps to sit next to me, resting his paws on my lap. "You're going to kill me, but I'm moving out of state."

"What?" Kodi jumps up from the couch. "You mean, like, just across the border, right?"

"Well...not exactly." I bite the inside of my cheek and force a smile to ease the blow.

"You're joking. Please tell me you're joking," she begs.

I look up and give her a knowing glare. "I want out, Kodi. You know this is what I need to do."

Her face falls, telling me she understands why.

"You know I haven't been able to go to the grocery store without having eyes on me," I say, feeling the heaviness fill my chest of everything that's happened. "I've been known for one thing, and that's being the mayor's wife."

"You were so much more than that."

I shake my head. "Then tell me why I can't leave the house without side glances and people whispering in their friends' ears when I walk by. They think I can't hear them, but I've heard mumbles of them saying, 'Oh, there's the mayor's ex-wife. He cheated on her. Poor thing.'"

None of it's a lie.

It's the sole reason why I have yet to actively seek employment.

"And do you remember that one time I tried to get back into running after letting my sneakers collect dust?" I continue.

"Yeah," Kodi draws out, brushing a strand of hair behind her ear.

"I couldn't make it down the block without seeing old billboards for ads I did for the local baking network, without seeing my eyes blacked out and whiskers on my face."

My sister grinds her teeth. "That still makes me rage. Like, are we okay? A cat? Who does that?"

"I feel like I need a fresh start from this life," I tell my sister. "You know, a place to settle down where no one knows me as the mayor's ex-wife. Where no one knows me, period."

Since the divorce, my emotions have shifted from hurt to anger. It's taken a significant toll on me, and I'm not sure I would have made it through without my sister's support.

Aside from Kodi, I don't have any friends or family to lean on. Once I was no longer married to Theodore, I lost all my old friends—who were mainly wives of his political friends. They have all proven to be fake because I thought they were friends with me for…me. Turns out, it was just being surrounded by my status that made them stay close to me.

I guess I was fake too for having no other friends outside of the political circle.

Kodi remains silent.

"Much of my life has involved doing what others tell me to do," I continue. "And I've never had a say in anything. My mind has been replaying all of this like a movie. I've realized that I've never really been my own person. I've been pushed and twisted into becoming someone I don't even recognize when I look in the mirror."

Since the day I discovered my husband's infidelity, I've undergone a profound transformation within myself. From feeling lost, helpless, and unable to get out of bed, to learning about the strength I've had within me all along that was simply masked by the person I was made into as his wife. I've shed the person I was and have embraced a new, more authentic version of myself. This newfound sense of self is the driving force behind my decision to move.

Don't get me wrong, I still have plenty of days where it hits me like a ton of bricks. The feeling of losing the one person who I vowed to spend my life with, for better or worse. I spiral just like any human and let the tears fall when my head hits the pillow and mourn the life I once knew.

"I get that. And I truly don't blame you," Kodi says. "But the idea of not being close to you isn't fun for me."

The reason I fought against moving is because of my sister. Kodi and I are close. She was born just one week before my first birthday. We're what they call "Irish twins." We could even pass as twins, with our only difference being she has long hair that's more natural brown, and I keep mine short with blonde high-lights mixed in.

Our mother is a lot like the person I was before the divorce.

A politician's wife who was the eye of the town. She has always been known for painting, baking, and wearing pencil skirts. It's all I've known growing up, which led me to live the same life she did, I guess. I don't know how she did it, because while I kept a happy face on at all times, looking back, I was miserable.

Well, that's only partially true.

I was miserable in the position I was in. But I loved my husband.

Or I thought I did.

There was always a part of me that thought my sister would have been the one to end up in the political spotlight in some way, shape, or form. But she got the better end of the deal, being a rebellious child who hates politics. She got herself a good social media gig doing interior design home projects until she graduated college and landed a job working for a company that does everything she was already doing.

She's damn good at what she does.

"The idea of it isn't fun for me either," I admit.

"How far away is it?" Kodi asks.

"Well..." I avert my gaze from her and continue to pet Reginald.

"Blair Andrews! I have to get on a plane to see you, don't I?"

I cringe at the use of my full name. Not just my full name but my full *married* name.

"I mean...you don't." I shrug. "But it's kind of a long drive. About sixteen hours long. A drive I'm actually planning to take next week."

"Did you say a sixteen-hour drive? And next week?"

Pulling my laptop off the coffee table, I open it to my recent tab. "Look how cute," I say as I turn the device to face her.

She looks down at the screen, and her eyes widen. "Wyoming?" she asks before scrolling through the page with her finger on the trackpad. "How did you even find this place?"

"I found it through an extensive search of small towns."

She leans closer, scrolling back up to the top of the page.

"There's literally one photo on that page that shows a lake and some trees. Show me more."

"That's actually the only photo I could find. The website is very basic, and the town seems to be off the map."

She stares at me unblinking before her fingers find her temples and begins to pace the living room. "Let me get this straight. You're moving out of state to a town you know jack shit about that has a half-ass website put together? And…" She leans down to look at the screen, poking the monitor with her finger. "One phone number with a pretty image of a lake?"

I nod. "Bluestone Lakes, to be exact."

"You didn't answer any of my questions."

"Yes, to all of them." I stand from the couch. "This is my chance to start fresh, Kodi. A town that's so off the map they don't even have a real website. A town where no one knows anything about me. Where I can be free from the chains of living how everyone wants me to. I already spoke to Nan and—"

"Nan?" she cuts me off, standing still in the middle of the room.

"The phone number on the page. It's connected to a woman named Nan."

She pauses, staring at me like I have two heads. "I wish you would stay here in California and just move out of the city or something. I understand your reasoning for all of this, I do. I just don't like it very much."

"She told me they have a house right on a lake for me. It's not Bluestone Lake, but a smaller lake in their town. The best part? It's a tiny home, Kodi. A TINY HOME," I exclaim. "I looked up what that was on an internet search, and I fell in love with the idea of owning one. How cool does that sound? And the second best part is that it's nestled on a street with only one other house. Hello, privacy."

Even with my excited tone, her face shows no emotion as she puts both hands on her hips. "Did she show you a picture?" she asks. "What if this tiny home you speak of is a dumpster on wheels?"

"Very funny," I deadpan.

"I'm being so serious right now."

"Me too. I'm going to do this," I say, closing my laptop and tucking it under my arms. "I'm leaving next week. I'm ready to start over and find my independence again instead of being known everywhere as Mrs. Andrews."

"You can have your independence here," she says.

Shaking my head, I turn to face the window overlooking the city. The same city where I grew up with Kodi. "You know I can't do that. You know this place will always have shackles tied to me, forcing me to be the person I've always been." I turn my body to face her again. "I need to get out of here to find that independence I've never had."

She offers me a soft smile. "You're right. And if you're happy, then I'm happy too. You know I'll always support you in anything you decide to do."

And I truly am.

I've never been more nervous in my life about this new adventure. Everything Kodi expressed in her concerns has me questioning whether this is the right move. But if this ends up being the biggest mistake of my life, it's something I can learn from.

Kodi begins to walk away. "But just know my spare room is always open for you when you learn it really is a dumpster fire and you need a place to stay," she says with her back to me.

"Thanks, sis."

"And, Blair?" she turns to face me from the hallway.

"Hm?"

"Go set the world on fire."

CHAPTER 2
YOU AREN'T A FELON, RIGHT?

BLAIR

A sixteen-hour drive turned into a two-day drive. A little more than halfway through, I decided it was best for me, my passenger princess Reginald, and all the drivers on the road if I took the night off. The anticipation of getting to this new town had us on the road before the sun began to rise to make good time.

Seeing the town's welcome sign finally coming into view, ignited a spark of excitement in every part of me.

Welcome to Bluestone Lakes.

It already feels like I'm putting the past behind me. The heavy memories, like the dense clouds that often hung over the Golden Gate Bridge, were finally lifting as the sign came closer to view.

I may be exhausted from the long trip, but seeing a fresh start for us right in front of me feels like I just shotgunned a venti cold brew and chased it with two espresso shots. Well, that might stop my heart. This view in front of me makes my heart race. The good kind of beating behind my ribcage. The kind you get when you know your future is about to change for the better. The fresh start outside the city that I so desperately crave.

That image on the website doesn't do this justice.

A small town nestled between towering mountains and crystal clear, blue waters stretching as far as the eyes can see. The water shimmers under the afternoon sun, with their clear waters reflecting the snow-capped peaks surrounding them. Tall, dense evergreen trees line the one-lane highway in clusters, their deep green hues contrasting sharply with the pale blue sky and muted tones of the mountains. It's a sight that leaves me in awe, the perfect end to this long drive.

It's unlike anything I've ever seen.

I continue forward on the bumpy road and see on the GPS that my destination is still another ten minutes away. I'm not sure how my little white sports car is going to handle the roads if they are anything like this in town. It's almost like they haven't been touched since they first asphalted them many years ago.

Up on my left is a small ranch, with at least a dozen horses of different shades and breeds lined up against a wooden fence that runs adjacent to the road. I slow down the car enough to take in the ranch. A wooden sign that reads *Barlow Ranch* hangs over the dirt road entrance.

I can't help but smile to myself.

Growing up in the city and in apartments, I've never been much for wildlife. I think you just become used to that because there sure as hell is no wildlife like this in San Francisco unless you're going to the zoo.

If the views in town are anything like this, I might fall in love.

I accelerate to the speed limit again for another half a mile before a cluster of buildings comes into view, forcing me to slow down again. I sit up higher in my seat, leaning forward on the steering wheel as if that's going to give me a better view. My grip tightens as nervous energy mixes with my excitement because the buildings in front of me scream old-town country. It already feels like a culture shock compared to what I'm used to.

There's a sense of stillness that contrasts sharply with the city's constant hum.

Entering the main street, I spot a second sign that reads *Heart of Bluestone Lakes*.

Remembering this was the sign where Nan told me to meet her, I scan my surroundings and feel the eyes of strangers on me already as they walk the sidewalks. Their glances are curious, yet kind—just a new face in a town full of possibilities.

The thought of that alone sends a thrill through my body.

As I pull my car to the side of the road, careful not to put it on the grass, Reginald barks in the passenger seat before poking his head up to peek out the window.

"We're home. That sounds weird, right?" I laugh, talking to my dog. "But this is our new home."

He barks again as I reach for the leash sitting on the back seat to attach it to his collar.

The crisp mountain air hits my lungs as soon as I open the door. It's different here—crispier, fresher, and filled with the scent of pine and earth. I inhale a deep breath and feel a profound sense of peace. As nervous as I am, I feel a spark of hope flicker. For the first time in a while, the future feels like something I can shape with my own hands. It's a strange feeling, but just breathing this air makes this all feel like it was the right decision.

It feels like the fresh start I've been so desperate for.

The sudden sound of an engine coming up behind me jolts me out of my reverie. I snap my head in that direction and spot an ancient-looking, dark red pickup truck coming from where I just came.

The truck slows down just enough for me to notice the person behind the wheel. A pair of angry eyes, hidden under the brim of a dark brown cowboy hat, lock onto mine, and it feels like time stands still. Everything around me slows down, and I hear nothing but my heart beating wildly as I stare back at the man. It only lasts a moment before the truck speeds away, leaving a trail of dust in its wake.

Great. Now I'm nervous again.

It's only been two minutes since I arrived, and already I've had a less-than-welcoming encounter.

I shake myself from the thoughts and realize I'm still looking in the direction the truck just disappeared to in the distance. That's when I spot an older woman sitting on a bench near the welcome sign. She has to be in her seventies with white hair that sits just over her ears. Not a speck of gray, just pure white. She's tiny, but doesn't look frail, even with the deep set of wrinkles around her eyes. Actually, she looks like she could kick someone's ass if she had the chance based on the stern look on her face.

Approaching her at the bench, I stop in front of her and clasp my hands together in front of me. "Hi. Good afternoon. Are you Nan by chance?"

"Depends on who's askin'." She raises a brow.

I force a smile and extend my hand. "I'm Blair Andrews." I regret the use of my full name the moment the words leave my lips. Not wanting anyone here to recognize the name. "We spoke on the phone," I continue, but the words come out fumbled.

She stands from the chair, taking my hand in hers and giving it a firm shake. "Well then, in that case, yes, I am." Her eyes scan me from head to toe and I instantly feel like I don't fit in. "You're quite the fancy pants, aren't you?"

I want to groan because I *feel* fancy. My entire wardrobe consists of pencil skirts and dress slacks. I couldn't even find a comfortable plain T-shirt mixed in my closet that wasn't a pair of silk pajamas, because all I own are blouses. I knew I would be overdressed but had no idea how much after seeing what Nan is wearing. She has on a pair of weathered jeans that look a size too big for her, with a long-sleeve T-shirt that shimmers along the collar and sleeves with even the smallest move. To some, that shirt might seem fancy for a night out, but it just looks...fun. The light blue, retro-framed glasses only add to the look.

"I know. I realized when I was driving in that I should probably get some new clothes," I say with a half laugh, trying to keep the embarrassment out of my tone.

"I can tell you just the spot," she says with certainty.

Reginald barks next to me, tail wagging in excitement.

"This is Reginald," I say.

She raises a brow. "That's…some name for a small dog like that. But who am I to judge? What kind of dog is he?"

"He's a corgi."

"Ain't got a clue about that kind."

She crouches down to give him a little pet on the head. He licks her hand wildly. His butt wiggles at a rapid speed and I can tell he's excited to meet a new friend.

I can't believe I was so nervous to meet this mysterious woman. I feel much more at ease than I did minutes ago. She isn't scary. Actually, she seems like she knows how to have a good time. She's that type of person, when you're in her presence, you just *feel* calm. Her confidence and demeanor have put me at ease. And she doesn't feel fake with her offer to help me, which is refreshing considering the friends I surrounded myself with back home in California.

"Ready to go?" she asks, standing up.

Scanning the area, I don't see another car. But Nan doesn't hesitate before grabbing Reginald's leash and walking to the passenger seat of my car. I remain rooted where I stand, and my eyebrows narrow in confusion.

"Where am I taking you?" I ask.

"To your house, girl." She barks out a laugh. "I'll direct you and this fancy rig where to go."

I hustle to the driver's side, slightly tripping over my feet as she gets in.

Once I'm seated, I buckle my seatbelt and open the GPS on the dashboard. "I can enter the address here."

She shakes her head, waving a hand in dismissal. "Unnecessary. I know this town like I know both of my tits."

I say nothing but stare at her before throwing the car into drive.

This should be fun.

She guides me to the outskirts of town, and I'm thankful the whole town isn't packed with dirt roads as you see on those TV shows about country towns. Then again, this doesn't seem like your typical small town.

"Turn here." She points to her left, putting me on a long, winding road. "What brings you to Bluestone Lakes?"

I turn the wheel as my head thinks over her question. I'm not ready to divulge my entire history to a stranger or bring up memories of the past. I'm not sure I'm ready for these people to know that part of me yet. A part of me worries they'll judge me the way people did back in San Francisco. Being that this is supposed to be a fresh start for me, I want to treat it as such.

I sigh. "I want to start a new life for myself. My old life…well, it was pretty shitty," I say, settling on a vague rendition of the truth.

"You aren't a felon, right?"

"No, ma'am."

She nods her head. "You know you're gonna want to do something about this car, right? It's going to be a mess," she says, before pointing to her right. "Turn here."

"Yeah?" I ask, turning the wheel right.

As soon as the words leave my lips, I realize why she made that comment.

Is this my street? Because if it is, I literally live on a dirt road.

"This is your street," she says, answering the question I asked myself in my head.

I look at the small street sign that's crooked and looks like it might fall off with the next gust of wind.

Barlow Drive.

Is this entire town named after someone named Barlow?

Another beautiful, much smaller lake sits to the right and spans from the start of the street to a cluster of trees a good distance away. I like that this place is tucked away in a secluded part of the town. It's close, but not too close.

After turning the car through a big bend around the lake, my eyes land on two houses. One of them is a tiny home, and the other is what looks like a gigantic estate-style home a quarter of a mile away.

Do they plan to build more on this road?

"There's your tiny home," Nan announces.

A smile splits across my face as I take it in. "Wow."

She says nothing more as I pull into a makeshift gravel driveway.

I exit the car quickly as the crisp air hits my lungs again. You couldn't wipe the smile off my face if you tried. A beautiful dock with two Adirondack chairs sits on the edge of the small lake. I can picture sitting out there late at night with a glass of wine, a blanket, and Reginald on my lap. And most definitely with a good book.

I glance to my left to see the bigger home. Evergreen trees surrounding it make it look tucked away at the north end of the street, while my home sits very much out in the open. It's far enough away that I can still have my privacy, but close enough that if we became friends, it's a short walk to each other's house.

I wonder if they are nice.

I hope like hell the entire town isn't as intimidating as that man driving the truck was.

How cool would it be to have a friend so close?

I turn back to face my house.

My home.

It's very small, but I expected that after doing some research on these types of houses. It's a simple design with a dark blue exterior with crisp white trim, giving it a modern but sophisticated appearance. It's a two-story house with a pitched roof, suggesting the upper level may be a loft-style room. Windows line the outside, which tells me that there is plenty of natural light to flood the interior.

20

"Needs some work," Nan says, coming to stand beside me with Reginald's leash in her hands.

"It's perfect."

"No one's lived here for years. But it's been kept up on the inside by the previous owner," she says. "The deck railing ain't too sturdy. Probably got a nail or two poking out somewhere, so careful."

The natural wood beams and posts of the porch truly don't look like it's going to last much longer. But realization hits me.

One of the biggest thoughts I had on the drive here is to learn who I truly am and gain some independence. So much of my life has been spent relying on others. Relying on a man to do the hard things for me. Once I moved into my sister's apartment, I realized I didn't even know who I was as a person anymore. Deep down under the polished exterior I had to maintain, I struggle to know who I really am.

This project might be something I can do to help me learn this independent lifestyle.

Emphasizing the word *"might."*

I don't know if I'll be able to fix a whole deck by myself, but what a project that could be, huh?

"Maybe one day I can build a bigger deck," I tell her.

"You need any help, you reach out to me. One of my boys will be right over to help you out with that."

I smile and nod.

That's exactly what I don't want, but I'm not about to tell her that. Besides, it's nice to know I will have a backup if it turns into more than I anticipated.

I turn to face her fully, taking Reginald's leash from her. "Thank you so much, ma'am. You know, for helping me get this place."

"It's what I do." She laughs. "We ain't got real estate agents here in town, so I make it my job to help sell some of these places. And you lucked out with this one. I never thought the owner would sell it."

"Wow," I say, chest feeling tight at the perfect turn of events. "It's going to be the perfect place for us."

She tosses me the set of keys to get inside and smiles before turning around to walk away.

"Do you want me to take you anywhere?" I ask before she can get too far.

"No, dear. One of my boys is probably up at the house." She points to the house I just had my sight on. "They can drive me back after they give me an ice-cold beer."

I laugh, shaking my head.

It's not even eleven in the morning.

"Thank you again," I shout as she walks away in the direction of the main house.

"Anytime. Welcome to Bluestone Lakes, Blair. I think you're gonna like it here." She winks and continues her walk.

I look down at Reginald, and he barks at the house.

"Oh, and Blair?" Nan shouts halfway to the road. I turn my head back to her. "Don't call me ma'am again. Makes me feel old. I still got a lot of life left in these bones. You call me Nan, just like everyone else."

I chuckle. "You got it, Nan."

I turn back to face my new home, letting the quiet embrace me as I smile to myself.

Bluestone Lakes is nothing like San Francisco, but maybe that's exactly what I need.

The fresh start I've been waiting for.

A place where no one knows who I am.

A place where I'm not associated with my piece of shit ex-husband.

A place where no one has sad, sympathetic eyes for the woman who was cheated on.

"I think we're going to like it here too," I tell Reginald.

CHAPTER 3

I'M NOT CUTTING HER GRASS.

GRIFFIN

"Helloooo? Is anyone home?" Nan bellows from the front door.

I round the hallway from the kitchen and find her standing in the foyer. "Sure, just let yourself in."

"I practically own this town, boy," she states with her hands on her hips and a scowl etched in her features.

I move to stand directly in front of her. She's a tiny thing, but she's got a lot of fire in her. Doesn't matter though, because I tower over her. "But I own *this* property."

"Oh, Mr. Grumpy Griffin," she says in a mocking tone, with my chin between her fingers. "Who pissed in your Cheerios this morning?"

Releasing an audible groan, I brush off Nan's stupid nickname—which she's been calling me for years—and walk back into my kitchen to pour myself a glass of ice-cold water.

Not that anyone in particular has pissed me off today. The bar I own here in town is just pure madness this week. We're short on supplies, and our trucks have been so late with the last couple of deliveries to this town in the middle of nowhere.

Well, that's a stretch.

It might feel like we're in the middle of nowhere, but we sure as hell get plenty of people passing through on a detour the moment they take one look at the crystal blue waters of the lake. Most see it while they're in the middle of a long road trip and decide this is where they want to stop for the night. I'm pretty sure the white Mercedes Benz I saw returning from the ranch earlier was someone passing through.

At least, I hope it was.

Taking one look at her, even if it was for just a few seconds, I knew she didn't belong here.

I knew she was from the city.

And I can't stand city people.

I'd rather have a secluded life. I prefer a quiet life with no one in my business. But I can't complain too much because they keep my bar up and running.

I lack patience for people who want to stay longer and destroy this place I call home with their piece of shit city attitudes and acting like they're better than everyone. I'm too old for the bullshit.

I finally reach my covered porch with glass in hand and swing the door open. I never know if I should call it the front porch or the back porch because it's all the same to me. It wraps around three sides of my house, with the front door tucked away on the right, covered by greenery.

The entire house is nestled away, just the way I fucking like it.

I'm the farthest house on the outskirts of town. If I walked a mile through the woods, I would cross the Bluestone Lakes border and into the next town.

"What are you even doing here?" I ask Nan, taking a seat on the rocking chair overlooking the lake on the porch. I realize there is no car in my driveway. "Did you walk here, you crazy woman?"

And that's not an exaggeration.

Nan is the craziest lady I've ever had the displeasure of

knowing. I might have called her Nan, but she's no one's Nan. She just makes everyone call her that. And she doesn't own the town, contrary to what she says.

Do you know who owns the town?

My parents.

I want to gag thinking about it. My dad's been the mayor of this place since before I was born. No one in town is crazy enough to go up against him in an election, either. Eventually, we just stopped having them. It's a small part of the reason I'm a grumpy bastard.

Among many other things.

They spent most of my childhood building this town into what it is. My dad now runs everything from the fire department to the police station to the zoning and planning board. While I love this town and will never leave, I resent it to an extent because it took away a piece of my younger years. Growing up the older brother of two sisters also led to constant aggravation. The only people I had were Poppy and Lily, until our cousin, Tucker, moved here for reasons he doesn't like to discuss.

I mean, I know why, but it's his story to tell.

Now, he's more like a younger brother to me.

Let's not forget the horrific work schedule I put on myself.

Since my patience is as thin as the ice on Bluestone Lake when it's barely below freezing temperatures, I can't stand the evening crowd at my bar.

Seven Stools—named after the seven original bar stools I painstakingly sanded and varnished—is my pride and joy. I built the bar from the ground up when I turned twenty-three. And it's turned out to be a really successful bar now that I'm older and wiser at thirty.

It's a place that's all mine and nothing of my parents.

They didn't want me to open the bar.

All the more reason to open it.

So, I signed myself up for a lifetime of working the lunch shift. Seven days a week. Because I would rather be miserable working seven days a week than work even one night shift with that crowd.

Hard. Pass.

My only issue is that it takes time away from the ranch. I've hired enough help to keep the horses fed and the acres of property from falling into disarray, but I hate not being able to spend as much time as I would like there. Owning Barlow Ranch and running a bar isn't for the weak, but the ranch was a gift from my parents. It's the only gift worth keeping because it's my serenity. I don't look at it as if it's *work*. I look at it as my escape. But the constant juggle between the two, the struggle to find a balance, is a challenge I face every day.

"I hold that title with pride, Griff," Nan finally replies, taking a seat next to me with a cold beer in her hand. "But I didn't walk here. I dropped off the new owner of your old home," she says before taking a swig from the bottle.

I narrow my eyes. "Did you carry her piggyback style down the dirt road?"

"Okay, Mr. Semantics. *She* drove *me*. I guided her where to go. Happy now?"

"No. Never."

"And that's why I call you Grumpy Griffin. Anyway," she continues with a grin, "she's here, and she's a lovely one."

Excellent.

I don't have the patience for this.

"I'm not cutting her grass," I state.

"Who said you have to do anything for her?" Nan laughs, and I don't miss the crinkle that forms around her eyes when she does.

"So, what's she here for?"

Nan rolls her eyes. "I just told you, she moved here. Clean your ears, boy."

Now it's my turn to mimic her. "I get that, but why here?"

She shrugs. "Hell if I know. I didn't ask too many questions.

But I asked if she was a felon. She said no." She shrugs before taking another sip of her beer.

"Anyone can tell you no and still be a felon."

"I went clearly off of vibes," she says, bringing her hand up the side of her like she's meditating.

"And hold on, rewind for a second. *You* didn't ask too many questions? Do I need to drive you to the hospital?"

"Fine. I'll tell you why she's here." She points a scolding finger in my direction. "But only because I don't want to sit in the car with your grumpy ass for over an hour to get to the nearest hospital."

"I'd get us there in fifty-five minutes," I state matter-of-factly.

"Do you want to know or not?"

"Proceed."

"She's here to start a new life."

My head falls back on the rocking chair, and I avert my gaze from Nan to the lake in my backyard. Do you know what's worse than someone taking away the quiet on my road? One who claims she wants a new beginning. One who's running from her so-called "hard life" to start over here. My last encounter with a female who wanted to start a new life was here in town. And she left me.

Did she do the same to someone back home?

I shake the thoughts from my head because I don't give a damn.

"This should be loads of fun," I say sarcastically.

"You're right, it should be," Nan confirms, not picking up on my tone. "And like I said, she seems like a lovely girl. So don't go scaring her away with all that negative energy you have floating around you. I'm going to get sick just sitting here with you."

My eyebrows furrow.

This woman really is certifiably insane.

I stand from the chair. "I'm heading to the bar for the lunch shift. Need a ride or not?"

"Well, since you asked so nicely."

With that, I move inside to grab the Chevy keys and head out the door. Right before I hop into my truck, I catch a glimpse of the tiny home out of the corner of my eye. *My* tiny home I've kept up all these years and was waiting for the right moment to put it on the market. A home that I love more than anything.

And that's when I see it.

A white Mercedes Benz in the driveway.

You have got to be fucking kidding me.

Not only is this woman moving onto my street and taking over my space, but she screams *City Girl*. And I'm normally not one to make assumptions based on the few seconds I glared at her as I was driving by, but there's no way she isn't from some big hub somewhere with how she's dressed.

"Some car, huh?" Nan says next to me on the top step. "That thing is going to be wrecked in a few days from these roads."

I don't answer her as she continues to descend the steps one at a time.

What I want to do is scream.

"Yeah," I finally answer, grinding my molars together. "Some car."

"It's not loud if that's what's got you all worked up," Nan says.

"I'm not worked up."

"You are, boy."

I roll my eyes and follow her down the stairs toward my truck.

Ready to get the hell away from one of the few places I've been able to find solitude.

Just that thought alone fills me with disappointment.

Guess I'll be spending a lot more time at Barlow Ranch.

CHAPTER 4

THE MAN HAS A PRETTY FACE.

BLAIR

I brought little with me for this move.

Not that I had much anyway.

Moving from my sister's spare bedroom to this tiny home that's already furnished for me is like the same thing as the apartments in San Francisco. Which is why I'm already heading back to my car to grab the last box.

Reginald barks on the porch, and my eyes land on where his attention is.

An engine rumbles before a pickup truck emerges from behind the trees.

Not just any truck.

Do not even tell me the angry cowboy lives next door to me.

I mean, this is a small town, so it's possible. But of all places for him to live, it has to be on the same road as me?

Or maybe he's just visiting family?

That could totally be the case and I'm just overthinking things.

The truck pulls onto the road, and I can't help but stand there with the box in my hand, unable to move. The truck looks like it's been through the ringer and might fall apart a mile down the road.

Woof.

No pun intended, since Reginald is barking his head off right now.

The truck slows down as it passes us in the driveway, and my heart rate skips a beat as it races in my chest. Nan is sitting up in the passenger seat, leaning over the center console as she waves her arms aggressively in a greeting as if she didn't just see me thirty minutes ago.

I can't help but cover my mouth and giggle before my gaze lands on the driver.

The same stormy eyes bore into me.

All the excitement I had looking forward to making friends with my one and only neighbor is gone with the wind. Kicked up like the dirt behind his truck. Because nothing about the way he's scowling at me, screams that he's a friendly neighbor.

He looks like...he hates me?

Already?

Jesus Christ, I just got here.

Reginald continues to bark at the truck, but his butt wiggles rapidly in true corgi fashion. Which tells me he's happy. He's usually a fantastic judge of character. So maybe I'm seriously overthinking this and reading his face all wrong.

The man has a pretty face. Is that a thing for men? I don't think so, but there's no denying that he has a pretty one even with the scowl currently plastered all over it. His sharp jawline is adorned with a thick, dark scruff, and his deep brown hair is neatly tucked under a backward baseball cap. He's wearing a black and white checkered flannel, which seems to be a popular choice in this area as I noticed a similar theme among people walking along the sidewalk when I first met Nan.

Despite the vibes I'm getting, I lift my arm in a friendly wave.

Forget what I just said.

With one greeting from me, he's peeling off down the road and disappears around the bend.

I sigh as I grab my last box.

"Let's get unpacked," I tell Reginald.

He barks in response and bolts through the front door ahead of me.

I enter the tiny house for the third time already and I'm still in shock that this is my place. The inside is even more perfect than the outside. Nan wasn't lying about it being kept up nicely while it remained vacant. In contrast to the dark blue siding on the outside, the inside is all light and neutral colors, allowing natural light to radiate through every inch.

The first thing I noticed upon walking into the home is how you can see from the front to the back easily with the open concept. That's the moment I knew it was perfect, which is weird, but I love the rustic yet contemporary feel of the space. The white cabinets, paired with the natural light through the windows only enhance the clean feel. The countertops are made of light-colored wood, extending into a small L-shaped counter that separates the living room with a single black stool placed at the counter.

I can't wait to decorate and really make this a home.

My phone rings on the counter and I realize I never called Kodi when I got here.

"Hello?" I answer.

"Oh good, you're alive. I thought you were lying in a ditch somewhere in the middle of nowhere," Kodi says, her tone laced with sarcasm.

"In the middle of nowhere, but not in a ditch."

"Hilarious," she deadpans. "Are you there or not?"

"I am. This place is seriously so cute and perfect, Kodi. You would truly have a field day decorating it. Every single wall is covered with shiplap. Your favorite."

"Oh my god, that's amazing. But get to the good stuff. What's the town like? Have you met anyone yet? Made any friends?" She rattles off the questions in rapid succession.

I roll my eyes even though she can't see me. "I've been in town for, like, less than an hour, so I don't have answers for you. I met with Nan, and she brought me to my place, and now I'm unpacking."

"That's boring."

I ignore her comment. "Nan is a riot. She reminds me of an older version of you."

"Is that really her name? This is still so weird to me, Blair. You're like states away now, with a random lady named *Nan* showing you your new home, and"—she draws out the word— "you're in the middle of nowhere!"

I sigh. I know my sister doesn't understand it. Hell, I don't either. This was a scary but exciting adventure for me. Crossing the town entrance did something to me. For the first time in as long as I can remember, a piece of me *felt* at home. I don't know why I feel that way just yet, but I'm eager to find out.

It feels right.

It feels good.

"I'm really liking it so far. It's quiet and secluded and the perfect place where no one knows who I am. I'm not associated with my past life, Kodi. I'm finally allowed to be myself and be who I want to be with no one telling me how to breathe. You know?"

"I get it," she resigns. "I just hope you end up finding a good friend. Do you have neighbors close by?"

"There's only one other house on my road. Which is a dirt road, for your information."

"Gross. Your poor car," she whines for me. "But have you met her yet? Did she see you and come over with a town welcome basket or some shit?"

"She is actually a *he*, and if I'm being honest, he doesn't seem super friendly. He definitely doesn't seem like the type to bring a basket of fruit over. Unless it's one of those poisonous apples."

"Ohhh," she emphasizes, curiosity peaking in her tone. "A male neighbor, huh? Just the two of you on the road. This sounds like a fun time written all over it."

"Kodi," I warn, "I didn't move here for that. It's the last thing I want to do while I'm here. I'm strictly here to focus on myself."

"You can do that and still get laid."

"Something isn't right in your head." I laugh. "After the shit I just went through with Theodore, I never want to get involved with anyone again. I refuse. My trusty vibrator is the only thing that will touch me down there for a long time."

That's only partially a lie.

It's not that I *never* want to be in another relationship, it's that I plan to be way more cautious before jumping into one. Being cheated on in the worst way possible does something to you. It changes you. It makes you trust less. It makes it hard to believe people's true intentions.

I want to learn how to trust again.

I don't want love in the dark.

I want big, loud, *can't live without me* love.

I want faithful love.

The memories of the day I walked into Theodore's office hit me like a truck. Emotions I fight so hard to keep down whenever the thoughts stir in my head, itching to break the surface. But I won't allow it. I can't allow it.

I won't let my past take away from my future here.

"Someday you will find someone, so you don't wear your batteries down on that thing," Kodi says. "Someday."

"I should get going," I say with thick emotions in my throat, avoiding the topic. "I want to unpack a bit. Then I really need to go find a store or something. My clothes do *not* fit the vibe here. I really don't want to look like an outcast any more than I already feel."

"Text me your new address. I have some perfect things for you."

I smile to myself. "You're the best. I'm going to work on getting a job next week. So I'll send you some money for them."

"Nonsense. I told you to go set the world on fire. You need to look good doing it."

I shake my head. "Bye, Kodi. Love you."

"Love you too."

I hang up and survey my surroundings.

There's still a lot to unpack. Mentally and physically.

But I've never been so ready for change.

CHAPTER 5

HAVE YOU SEEN THE NEW BENZ AROUND TOWN?

GRIFFIN

Everything is off.

And it pisses me off.

I'm having difficulty sleeping, knowing that my road is no longer just *my* road. Yes, it still has my name, but *she* occupies it now. It makes me uneasy. It makes me anxious. Especially knowing that it's someone who's never been here before.

She's not loud, but she just takes away my quiet.

Distracting my peace.

She moved here for what? To start a new life?

I don't buy it.

What I mean when I say everything is off is that *she's* off.

I've spent the last few nights sitting on my deck and peering like a creep through the trees in the direction of the tiny home. One night, I watched while she let her ridiculous ball of fluff outside to run around. Not only was it irritating that she let the mutt run free, but it came straight into my yard where I watched it piss on my rosebush.

What confused me the most was that she was dressed in business attire, like she was planning to go to town hall for a meeting.

I hate knowing someone is in that home now.

The bell for the door of the bar dings and I turn to face it.

My father. What a pleasure.

"Good afternoon, Griffin," my dad announces with a smile.

"Eugene." I nod in his direction. He takes one of the open seats at the bar and removes his cowboy hat. "What brings you in today?"

"I stopped by to have some lunch with my favorite son. Even though he can't call me Dad, I still wanted to stop in and see him." He smirks.

I raise a brow in his direction because I'm his only son.

Taking a moment to scan his features, he looks more like a cowboy than a mayor. He used to be one when he owned the ranch, before he ever got into town politics. This man did every job from cleaning the stalls to running the fences to repairing things that needed to be fixed. I've never once seen him wearing a suit and tie like a typical mayor. It doesn't fit the town vibes anyway. He prefers his Wrangler jeans, thick, brown outdoor jacket, and cowboy boots.

"And to let you know, you might get a little busier here by the end of the year," he adds with a raised brow, exaggerating the wrinkles around his face.

"Why's that?" I ask, placing a menu in front of him.

"I have a ton of meetings coming up with the zoning and planning board. We're working on getting that old ski resort on the west side of town up and running again."

"The one that's abandoned because Bluestone Lakes and Bonneville haven't been able to decide who's going to take ownership of the mountain?"

He nods. "We're going to work together with them. An improved resort to bring a bigger crowd into Bluestone."

Lovely.

"Wipe that annoyed look off your face." My dad laughs. "This is great for business, son."

I fight back a groan. Building up this town only means one

thing. Opening a ski resort would only turn this into a resort town. More out of town people coming here to treat us like the scum on the bottom of their feet. Rich investors would flock to my bar acting better than everyone because money lines their pockets. I can't wipe the annoyed look off my face because it doesn't sound fun. If I was someone who looked on the bright side of things, I'd be happy because it would bring in revenue for the bar.

It's really a catch twenty-two for someone like me.

"Do you want something to eat?" I ask, changing the subject.

He flips the brochure-style menu from front to back. "You should consider adding more to this menu. You only have like ten options here."

"It's a bar...with bar food. You get what you get with what we have to work with." I shrug.

He scans the small menu even though he gets the same thing every time he comes in here. "I'll take the chicken sandwich, extra bacon, and ranch on the side."

Yep, the same thing he always gets.

Nodding, I jot it down on our guest check before sliding it through the small window that leads to the kitchen. "New order," I shout to the two kitchen staff I have back there. The moment I turn around, the bell for the door dings again. The most annoying noise in the world.

"My man!" Tucker bellows, making his way to the bar when he spots my father, with his friend, Levi, in tow. His buddy from work right behind him. "Oh shit, hey, Pops. Didn't see ya there."

"Afternoon, Tuck. Staying out of trouble?" he asks.

"Always, sir. You know that."

I roll my eyes because Tucker Daniels lives and breathes trouble.

Even if he's just my cousin, I love him like a brother. But he sure is a smart ass, and always finds himself caught up in trouble he doesn't need. I blame it on his age. I can't discredit how hard of a worker he is, though. He spends all day doing construction, from building new homes to fixing up businesses in town, and then comes and works a few nights a week at the bar for me. For a twenty-three-year-old, he's probably the hardest-working guy around and will drop everything he's doing for his friends and family, without hesitation.

"Don't you get enough of this place?" I ask Tucker.

"Never in a million years, Griff. You know this." He grins proudly before taking a vacant seat next to my father, while his friend, Levi, takes the spot next to him at the same time the cook brings out Eugene's sandwich.

"Ohhh, the chicken sandwich with extra bacon? Good choice, Pops." Tucker nods in approval before facing me again. "Can I get the same?" I pull out the guest chest to take his order. "Oh, I'll take some of that spicy ranch sauce stuff you got on it too."

"Levi?" I say his name as if to ask if he wants anything before putting both of their orders in.

"Same thing," Levi says before I drop the guest check in the window, and I let the staff know we have another order.

Levi works with Tucker doing construction on the days where the workload is heavy, other days he tends to the Barlow Ranch and the horses for us. He's the best ranch hand we have.

I let them have a conversation over work and the weather, while I work on stocking what little we have behind the bar. It's been days since I heard things are going to be delayed, and guess what, it's still not here.

I pride myself on being able to carry a variety of things that guests would want to drink. Whiskeys and bourbons, flavored vodkas, and rums for mixed drinks. Beer isn't a common thing we sell here, believe it or not, but I always make sure to have it available for the few regulars who do drink it.

I like to think it's because of the atmosphere I've created here.

There are no windows, so it's kind of dark and weathered here. Everything on the inside is a deep wood color, including the tables and chairs. I think people associate the color scheme with a dark amber liquid. Whiskey and bourbon are most definitely our best sellers.

And guess which one is delayed right now?

Ding ding. My fucking bourbon.

I buy only the best and refuse to buy it from some cheap distillery. I import our bourbon straight from Fiasco, Kentucky.

Foxx Bourbon is our best seller. Rightfully so. I'd wait forever for it if I needed to.

"Hey, Griff," Tucker interrupts my thoughts at the same time the kitchen brings out the last two lunches. "Have you seen the new Benz around town? I saw it roll by the other day and I thought it was just a passerby but rumor has it they moved here."

My eyebrows knit together because I know exactly who he's talking about.

"What a stupid move on his part," Tucker continues. "A white car? In a town full of dirt roads? What a dumb ass." He laughs, shaking his head.

"Pretty sure it's a female," I tell him.

"Yeah, duh." Levi swats his arm. "You know, the whole white car thing. She's probably on the PTA somewhere and always has her shit together."

"Doubt it," Tucker scoffs with a mouthful of food. "You know small-town talk, we would totally know if she had a kid with her. So, PTA is off the table. But I wonder how she will survive here without that bullseye chain store."

Staring in disbelief, my gaze bounces between them. "What are you two even saying?"

Tucker shrugs. "It's a thing, apparently. White car versus black car. I think the saying is more SUV-related, but same shit. A black SUV usually means the person is messy and chaotic," Tucker explains.

"And white SUV means they are always clean with their shit together," Levi adds.

What in the world is wrong with these two?

"This is the dumbest thing I've ever heard. Which says a lot because half the shit out of both of your mouths is usually dumb."

Tucker holds up his hands in defense. "Hey, I didn't make it up."

Standing there in shock, I have nothing more to say.

I'm definitely not planning on telling them the owner of the white Benz is my new neighbor. I don't need to draw more attention to myself than necessary. Besides, I'm trying to avoid having any conversation with her if I can help it.

"You two have lost your minds," my father chimes in, standing from the chair and throwing down a twenty-dollar bill. "Thank you for lunch. Come over for dinner one day, yeah?"

"Am I invited?" Tucker's face lights up. "Please, say yes. Aunt Mary's cooking is heaven-sent, and I'll die if I don't get it soon."

My father laughs. "You're welcome anytime. You know that."

Tucker makes a fist and punches the air in success. "Uncle Gene is the shit."

He and Levi go quiet as they scarf down the rest of their sandwiches. I've never seen them eat so fast in my life.

Looking down at his watch, Tucker jumps from the chair. "Shit, we're going to be late. Our fifteen-minute break is over."

"You only had a fifteen-minute break?" I ask, confused, looking down at my watch. "But you've been here for at least a half hour by now."

"Yep. See ya, Griff." And he's out the door.

What…an interesting lunch crowd today.

CHAPTER 6

PLEASE USE SEXUAL REFERENCES TO EXPRESS HOW MUCH YOU ENJOY OUR TREATS.

BLAIR

KODI

Any new neighbor sightings? I'm waiting patiently for the text that you two are besties now.

ME

It's never happening.

KODI

It could if you left your house every once in a while.

ME

Who says I haven't left my house?

KODI

Blair...

ME

Kodi...

KODI

Get the hell out of the house and explore your new town a bit.

I didn't listen to Kodi.

I've spent the last week locked up at the house and loving every second. In my defense, I'm acclimating to the changing weather here. I spent one whole day unpacking and putting things where I want them. To my surprise, the kitchen was stocked with basics for me, which was enough to get me by for a few days. It's been raining on and off the last couple of days since then, which made me want to do nothing but lounge on the couch with a romantic suspense book and Reginald. He most certainly hasn't complained.

Aside from the rain, I didn't want to leave because I still don't have clothes that seem proper enough to wear around town.

Today, I'm exploring.

The sun is shining enough to take the chill out of the air.

It *feels* like a good day.

I settle on black dress pants, bootie heels, and the least fancy floral blouse and cover it with the lightweight cashmere sweater I find in my closet before making my way to the bathroom to refresh my hair. Pulling half of it back in a ponytail to keep it out of my face and letting the rest hang naturally because it's too short to pull the whole thing up. My natural waves are loving that the air here doesn't have a touch of humidity.

"Want to come with me, Reginald?" I ask in my puppy tone.

He barks in response.

"You have to be a good boy, though. I don't know what places are pet-friendly. But I need some clothes and maybe a job."

With a wag of his tail, he barks again. I smile before squatting down to pat his head.

Finding a job is probably the most important part of today's mission. I don't even know what's going to be available in a town that seems like everything will be full of locals. But I firmly believe in the motto "If you don't ask, the answer is no."

Pulling out of my driveway for the first time since the day I moved in, nerves skate across my skin because I'm not sure I even remember how to get out of here.

I *really* should have asked Nan for a town map.

"We got this," I say to Reginald. But it's more for me.

Once I round the bend on my road, a beautiful mountain landscape comes into view, forcing me to slow down. I didn't notice it on my drive in, but...wow. I remember dreaming of living in a place like this as a little girl, and now that it's a reality, I'll never take it for granted.

I don't know how I lived in the city for so long.

Knowing *this* is what's out there in the world.

My car jerks from a bump on the road. "Shit," I mutter. It's going to take some getting used to driving around here. These dirt roads that now have mud pockets all over them will destroy my car.

I should look into an SUV or truck.

I laugh. Me driving a truck. That's a hysterical thought.

The heart of town comes into view, and I sigh in relief that I found it on my own. I take note of a few places I didn't see the first day I arrived and send a silent thank you to the universe that there is an actual road in this part of town. It's not pretty and calling it a road is even a stretch. But at least it's not pure dirt.

Taking it all in, it reminds me of an old-town country movie. Park benches line the sidewalk with lamp posts every few feet. There are minimal parking spots lining the street, but it's just enough for a town like this. This town is more than any fantasy I've had growing up living outside the city. It's so tiny and quiet. I like the fact that no one here knows my story. I want to keep it that way for a while.

I turn onto the street called Main Street and immediately spot a general store called...General Store on one side of the road.

"Wow. So clever," I say out loud with zero surprise in my voice.

Reginald barks next to me.

I turn my gaze to the other side of the road and spot a bar, a coffee shop, and a bakery.

Bingo.

All three buildings are connected, with the bar called Seven Stools sitting on the corner. I fight back a laugh when I notice the neon sign over the sign is an actual bar stool.

Interesting name for a bar.

The bakery called Batter Up sits directly next to it. It's much brighter and more welcoming on the outside with two small windows covered in pale pink awnings and floral arrangements hanging on the ledges. I'm already in love with the place because baking has my heart. An adorable little outside sitting area is tucked between the buildings next to the bakery and the coffee shop called Cozy Cup.

It's genius marketing how it's set up.

A coffee shop on one side and a bakery on the other with a sitting area to enjoy a little something from each place? Chef's kiss.

Parking my car, I realize there are three job options in front of me. If these don't work, I can always try my hand at Barlow Ranch. I bet if they have any association with Nan, she will help me out.

I laugh at myself.

Could you imagine me working at a ranch?

At least I know I can still be funny. First, the truck thought, and now this.

As I stare at the quaint bakery, a wave of excitement washes over me. This is the dream I've always envisioned. The thought of combining my passion for baking with others while also earning a living from it feels like everything I have been searching for.

Cracking the passenger window of the car, I kiss the top of Reginald's head. "Stay here, buddy,"

Once I open the car door, a woman with long, copper-red hair spots me instantly.

44

"Hi. You're the new girl in town," she says without question.

I laugh. "What gave it away? The sports car in a town full of dirt roads?"

She looks from me to the car, covers her mouth with her hand, and snorts. The tiny woman snorts. "I mean, I wasn't gonna say it. Is that your dog?" She points to my passenger seat, and Reginald barks.

"Yes."

"What kind of dog is it?"

"He's a corgi." I turn to face him. "The best dog in the world."

"Were you planning to come into the bakery?"

"I was, actually." I face her again in confusion. "I don't know what's pet-friendly here or not, so I was going to leave him here."

"Nonsense." She rounds the car, opening the passenger side door and taking his leash in her hands.

People in this town are so bold but friendly about it.

"The whole town is pet friendly. If you ever want to go to Seven Stools for lunch, don't let the owner tell you otherwise."

"Are they mean?" I ask curiously.

I'm internally wondering if I need to cross that job opportunity off the list completely.

"He's not mean, but he's one of the few men in the world who can't stand dogs. Please, don't ask me why because I don't even know. And I've known him my whole life. It's a huge red flag I wanted to warn you about."

She crouches down, lifting Reginald in her arms as if he's a smaller dog and peppers kisses on his head. His little tail wagging back and forth tells me he's pleased with this attention.

"Are you sure it's okay if he comes in?" I ask. "He's kind of fluffy for a food establishment."

"We have the outdoor sitting area, silly. Which was my idea, don't let anyone else convince you it wasn't."

Wait, is she...

"Do you *own* Batter Up?"

She nods, and a proud grin spreads across her lips. "You bet. I'm Lily, by the way. I'm sorry. I should have said that earlier. Come inside."

I step inside after her, and as the door swings open, a warm wave of aromas hits me. The enticing scent of freshly baked goods fills the air, wrapping me in its embrace. My mouth waters at the rich, sweet smell of sugar and flour mingling together, creating an irresistible feeling that makes my heart race with joy. Not even the finest baked goods scented candle could ever compare to this.

"This is such a cute place you have here," I say, looking around and taking it all in.

A single counter sits nestled between two enticing display shelves featuring an array of treats. Showcasing specialty cookies with vibrant icing, rich and moist crumb cakes, and irresistible mini muffins in various flavors.

"I'm sorry, I never got your name," Lily says.

"I'm Blair. Blair Andrews." I want to take back the words as soon as they leave my mouth as I use my full name yet again. But I doubt people in town would know who the mayor is in a city that's states away. "And that little fluff ball in your arms is Reginald."

"Nice to formally meet you both," she says with a small nod before she rounds the counter to stand on the other side with Reginald still in her arms. "Can I interest you in something?"

"Everything looks amazing," I say, scanning the cases displaying everything available for the day. Stopping my scan, and my eyes widen. "Is this a crumb cake?"

"Cinnamon swirl crumb cake," Lily answers with a nod.

I lean down to get a closer look. "I've never mastered baking a crumb cake. It seems too easy, but I could never make it work and come out this good."

"You bake?"

I nod. "It's my favorite hobby."

"I knew we were destined to be friends." Lily beams, putting Reginald down and letting him explore the place freely.

The word "friends" feels so foreign to me.

The same way everything here feels.

As I look at Lily, I'm speechless. She's nothing like the people I know in the city. Instead, she's warm and inviting, with seemingly no hidden agendas. In my past, friendships have often felt transactional, with people befriending me for their own gain. But with Lily, it's different. She's genuine.

"Do you know anywhere in town hiring?" I finally ask.

"I'm sure we can find you something," Lily says, pulling a slice of crumb cake from the tray and placing it on a small paper plate for me. "Between my friend, Autumn, next door at Cozy Cup or the bar, we can find you something."

"Thank you so much. That would be so helpful and really appreciated."

"Here." She pulls her phone from the back pocket of her jeans. "Put your number in here. I'll shoot you a text message, so you have mine. I'll talk to them this afternoon, and we can find something for you. Don't worry. We take care of each other around here."

Warmth fills me with her comment as she places her phone in my hand.

In just a short amount of time, Lily successfully makes this feel one step closer to this town being home. Making me feel like part of this community just days into moving here, despite not knowing a thing about me.

"Hey, Lily," a female voice calls from the front door.

"Speak of the devil." Lily grins. "Autumn, come meet my new friend, Blair. She just moved here and is looking for a job."

Autumn offers me a welcoming smile, and I get the same friendly vibes from her as I did the moment I met Lily.

"Tell me you got this dressed up for a job interview and not just to explore the town." Autumn laughs but covers her mouth quickly. "I'm sorry. That was rude. I tend to be a little blunt."

I can feel my cheeks turn crimson red.

Reginald takes that moment to let out a bark. As if he's telling them "yes."

Traitor.

"Well…"

"Oh, my dear sweet Blair," Lily exaggerates. "Moved here from the city?"

I nod.

"Which one?" Lily asks.

"San Francisco."

"Well, I'll take you to the General Store and help you pick some stuff out," Lily says with certainty.

"My sister is also mailing me some stuff," I add.

"That will take forever with how our postal service works," Autumn says, rolling her eyes. "At least let us take you to get some stuff to hold you over."

I smile at both of them. It's a genuine one that feels strange. I can't remember the last time I felt like this. "I'd love that," I say, finally taking a bite of the crumb cake. "Oh my lord. This is orgasmic."

Lily extends her arm like a showcase display but looks at Autumn. "See, Autumn. *This* is the reaction I want from all our customers."

"If you want that so much, put a sign on the door that says, 'Please use sexual references to express how much you enjoy our treats'."

"I just might," Lily says confidently, with her hands on her hips and chin held high. "I take pride in my baking."

"I know the feeling," I jump into the conversation. "I mean, I don't do it for money or business, but baking has kept me sane most of my life."

"I might have to hire you before anyone else can." Lily winks.

"Listen, I'll be happy with whatever you can set me up with

to get my feet on the ground here," I say. "But if you gave me a choice, this bakery might be number one on my list."

Lily waves a finger in the air like she's drawing. "Noted."

It *feels* like a good day today.

And it most definitely is.

Because I think I've made a friend.

Something I need if I want to survive here all alone.

CHAPTER 7

DON'T CURSE IN FRONT OF LITTLE EARS.

GRIFFIN

Tucker got stuck on a job site longer than expected and ended up being later than usual for work. In true Tucker fashion, he came barreling into the bar like his ass was on fire, apologizing profusely for being late.

It didn't help that I had a sour attitude.

But what else is fucking new?

It wasn't because he was late, though; the evening crowd decided today was the day they wanted to celebrate happy hour a whole hour earlier than we have scheduled.

So yeah, I'm driving home with a piss-poor attitude.

Only to pull into my driveway and become more aggravated than I was five minutes ago because Nan is sitting on *my* porch.

And she's not alone.

Exiting the car, I take the steps two at a time up my front steps. "What are you doing here with that thing?"

"Oh, hello. Good evening to you too, Grumpy Griffin," Nan jokes.

"Stop calling me that."

She shrugs. "I just call it like I see it."

"If I'm so grumpy, why do you keep showing up at my house?"

"It's a nice one. Pretty views. Lovely neighbors. Quiet. You know." She rattles off each thing while counting with her fingers.

I narrow my eyes. "You have the same views on your side of town. See that mountain." I point in the distance. "You can see that same one from your porch."

She lifts a shoulder but says nothing.

"What are you doing *here*, Nan?"

Her face lights up as she pets the mutt's head. "I'm dog sittin'."

"The neighbor's dog?"

"Yep." She holds the dog up by its front paws, and I take a step back.

"Come on. Isn't Reggie so cute?" she coos.

"That fucking dog's name is *Reggie*?"

"Reggie is short for Reginald." Nan covers the dog's ears as if it has feelings. "Don't curse in front of little ears."

I throw my head back and groan in frustration.

"His mom got a new job in town and is attending a brief orientation. You know how we work around here," she emphasizes. "We offer little training and like to throw newbies right into the flames. So I offered to watch this little cutie for a bit."

"That thing is not cute."

"Ignore Mr. Grumpy Griffin, little guy," she says to the dog with a cutesy tone. "He's the meanest on the block. And you're the cutest thing here."

"I'm the only one on the block."

"Not no more," she huffs.

"So why are you here and not on her porch? Or sitting out by the lake?"

"What if the dog drowns, Griffin? And besides, she doesn't have a large porch. And I counted about seven nails sticking out on the railing while the dog took care of his business. No, thank you. But don't you worry"—she squiggles a finger in the air—

"she's planning to fix her up real good one day. She's going to make it bigger too."

I raise an eyebrow. "Can she do that?"

Nan barks out a laugh. "I doubt it. She's a city girl through and through. I mean, did you see the Benz? Whoa, nelly. Fancy pantsy," she jokes before her laughter dies down. "But hey, I'm interested in seeing her try."

I roll my eyes.

"You gonna let us in or not?" Nan asks. "We're hungry."

"Fine. But that thing stays out here."

"He's hungry too," she whines.

"No."

She groans but lets the dog off her lap. "You're the worst."

Opening my front door, I allow Nan to walk in first. I might live in an aggravated state, but I'm still a gentleman. I look down at the dog one more time. He's a ball of fluff staring at me with what looks like a smile. Which is freaky for a dog. His ears stick straight up in the air as he cocks his head to the side.

"Stay," I order.

The dog plops down on his belly, his back legs kicking out behind him while he lays flat like a pancake on the porch.

What a weird creature.

"You got nothing in this fridge," Nan announces as I make my way into the kitchen.

I close my eyes and shake my head.

Is this happening right now?

This damn woman truly thinks she lives here.

"I haven't had a second to get to the General Store. I have enough stuff to make two sandwiches, though."

"That will do." She beams, taking a seat at the counter while I pull out lunch meat and the bread. "How was work today?"

"Work was work," I answer as I throw together the sandwich for her.

"You consider adding to that menu yet?"

"Nope," I say, sliding a plate across the island to her.

"You're a real pleasure to have a conversation with."

"Yep."

I take a bite of my sandwich and ignore the topic at hand. When I get home from work, the last thing I want to do is have more conversations. I just had to play nice for hours through the lunch shift, which turned into some of the evening shift.

I'm always professional, but I'm done with that when I get home.

The dog barks excessively on the porch.

"Oh." Nan jumps from her chair. "Blair must be back."

Blair.

A scowl involuntarily forms on my face as I hear my neighbor's name for the first time. Nan rushes to the front door, her excitement palpable. Until now, I hadn't bothered to learn more about the woman living next door, but hearing her name sends a jolt of surprise through me. It's not one I expected, but it is a name that would be associated with some uptight, rich girl.

I take one more bite of my sandwich and follow Nan.

Nan is on the steps, waving her down. Whistling and pointing to the dog and then waving her over again before shouting her name. You know, to make sure she gets the point.

Blair notices and starts walking this way.

Great.

Perfect.

More conversation.

It's getting darker as the minutes pass. The moon reflects off the lake, while the sun hides behind the mountain peaks. It's not until my porch light illuminates her that I finally get a good look at the woman who's annoyed me since she moved in. For no other reason than existing.

Now I'm fucking pissed.

She's not supposed to be this beautiful.

From the nights I've watched her letting her dog out from a distance and the time I drove past her in the truck, I never once got the view I do right now.

Her hair is a natural blend of light brown and blonde that falls just above her shoulders, with subtle highlights that I bet catch the sunlight when she stands in it. She has some of it pulled back in a petite bun on top of her head, pulling the hair away from her face to allow me a good look. The tiny bun makes her look young, but...fuck. Absolutely breathtaking. It's hard to distinguish her eye color from the setting sun, but if I had to guess, they're amber.

The color of my favorite whiskey.

With long lashes fluttering around them.

She's smiling at me. Jesus Christ, she's smiling.

I take a moment to scan her from head to toe. That's when I notice she's wearing a dress. What is with this woman and her dress clothes? It's a deep maroon, long sleeve to match the weather for the night and stops just above her ankles, showing off a pair of boots with a low heel.

My eyes trail back up her body, and I notice her hand extended to greet me.

"I'm Blair. It's nice to meet my neighbor finally," she says softly.

Looking at her hand and back up to her, I have nothing to say. The soft smile on her lips falls at the same time her arm drops to her side when she realizes I'm not shaking her hand in return.

She's rendered me speechless, and I want to scream because of it.

The last time I saw someone the way I see her right now, she left.

She walked out of my life and this town like it meant nothing to her. Not that this would be the same, but I can't remember the last time I even looked at a woman and thought she was beautiful. It's a new feeling that brings back way too many bad memories.

She's my neighbor. That's fucking it.

I settle on, "Keep your dog away from my rose bushes," then turn on my heel and walk back into my house.

I feel like an asshole, but I don't regret it.

Even catching the brief feeling of hurt in her face, I can't regret it.

She's a city girl and doesn't belong here.

Keeping my distance is the best thing for me.

But I have a strange feeling that my new neighbor is an angel who's going to drag me through hell.

CHAPTER 8

YOU'RE FIRED.

BLAIR

"When is your first official day of work?" Kodi asks through the phone speaker sitting on the end table next to the couch.

"Today!" I beam.

Kodi and I have been trying to find a happy medium for updating each other without disrupting each other's lives—not that we would be. We've settled on the regularity of weekly phone calls, always for a minimum of an hour at a time, to keep each other informed and up to date about life.

"Lily allowed me another week to get acclimated to the town more after my orientation session. If you even want to call it that."

"How much training do you need in a bakery, Blair? Honestly," she asks seriously. "I've had your baked goods, and they are the best. Plus, you know how to work an oven."

I laugh. "That's why I made that comment. It was really just showing me the industrial size oven, and how to work the cash register."

"Okay, that makes more sense."

I pick up the phone and turn the speaker off, putting it to my ear as I let Reginald out the door to take care of business. The act sparking a memory from last week I'd forgotten to share with my sister.

"Oh my god. Did I tell you I met my neighbor last week?"

"No! Are they nice?"

"It's a man, and he's definitely solo in that large house."

"Oh, wow," Kodi says, shocked.

"I didn't catch his name because he was kind of rude. And let me tell you, I'm not a hundred percent sure, but I don't think Nan is actually his Nan. I can't figure out who she belongs to yet."

"Maybe she's one of those meddling town folk." Kodi laughs. "You know, the wanderers who are always in everyone's business, but keep theirs private."

"Not sure. But I kind of love her."

"She sounds fantastic. But can we get back to your hot and single male neighbor?"

All I heard was the word *hot* come out of her mouth.

But I don't tell her she's right.

My nerves were on high alert when I saw Reginald sitting on his step waiting for me and Nan waving me down with a grin on her face. I almost turned around to go back home, telling myself she could bring my dog back when she's done. Except, my neighbor walked onto the porch with the same *I can't stand you* look etched all over his face. The closer I got, the more the hairs on my neck perked up. He is totally one of those burly mountain men. Born and raised in the dirt and woods. Scruff dusting his jawline. The one clenched so tight as he stared at me while standing on his property, I thought he was going to snap a tooth.

His hair remained tucked under a baseball cap, but from what I saw when I finally got close, it's dark. Matching the color of his facial hair and dark brown flannel shirt. A stark contrast to the stormy blue color of his eyes. It should actually be illegal for a man who comes across *that* mean, to have such pretty eyes.

"Did you not hear me when I said he was rude?" I ask her.

"No. All I heard was he's hot."

"Those words never left my lips."

"But you thought it," she says in a playful tone.

I groan out loud. "He's okay. But that doesn't take away from the fact that he's ugly on the inside."

"Well, what did he actually say to you?"

"Nothing at first. I even extended a hand to shake in a very friendly manner, and he looked at it like touching it would poison him. Then he told me to stop letting Reginald pee in his rosebush."

She gasps. "Oh no, not the rosebush. Let me play Switzerland for a second. Maybe dog pee isn't good for them. Maybe he takes pride in his gardening abilities and likes to keep things looking nice."

I roll my eyes even though she can't see me. "It's not what he said, it's how he said it. His tone was just mean. Demanding. Ugly."

"Okay, whatever you say, Blair." She laughs.

Looking at the clock on my microwave, I realize I'm about to be late. "I have to head to work. I'll text you later."

"Wait, before you go. Did you get the clothes I mailed?"

"No! I could knit my clothes faster than the postal service around here."

"Jesus. Okay. Well, have the best first day at the bakery. Proud of you. Go set the world on fire, just not the bakery."

I snort at that. "Thank you, Kodi. Love you."

And I hang up the phone, tossing it to the couch before letting Reginald back inside.

Looking down at my outfit, I know it will have to do. It's the least dressy thing I could find. The store didn't have any pants in my size. Being as short as I am, it's hard to find pants that don't drag along the floor. But I found a sweatshirt that I'm choosing to wear today.

A little corny, if you ask me.

It's two cartoon geese fist bumping, and it says "goose

58

bumps". But it's better than showing up at the bakery with a button-down blouse.

It will have to do.

It's time to do my favorite thing ever.

Bake.

"You just *whipped* these together?" Lily asks, taking another bite of the oatmeal cookies that I made.

In an attempt to hide my emotions, I give her a reluctant nod, feeling the heaviness in my chest. Simply because I loathe the thought of making these cookies again. They were Theodore's favorite and the memories of the last time I made them came rushing back as soon as I started mixing the batter in the oversized bowl. This is a new kitchen for me, and my thought process wasn't to bring up my past, it was to find the most basic recipe I remember so I can learn my way around the kitchen and how the oven bakes.

If you're a baker, you know that not all ovens are the same. One you might only need twelve minutes, while another might need fifteen.

It's a real thing.

"You all right?" she asks as if she's picked up on my mood.

"Yeah. I'm all right. Just…this type of cookie sometimes stirs up old memories for me. Not the good ones."

Swallowing past the knot in my throat, I turn away from her. I'm definitely not trying to unload my trauma on her during my first day. But there's an undeniable sense of comfort in Lily. Kind of like a need to talk to someone about what's on my chest. Someone who isn't my sister.

"My parents were intense growing up."

She scoffs. "Same, girl."

Turning to face her, I continue. "I've always had to be someone *they* wanted me to be. I've always had to live up to the standards in place for me. My dad was a powerful politician in California who ran the entire state basically. I hated that life. My aunt got me an Easy-Bake Oven when I was younger. It sparked my love for baking. Whenever I had the chance, I would offer to make cookies for the family just to do *something*. Half the time my parents didn't care because they sat on their laptops." I roll my eyes. "The only thing they asked of me was not to burn the house down."

Lily pushes to sit on the small counter next to where I stir together a new batter for chocolate chip cookies.

"When I tell you I know that feeling, I do. My parents are heavy into politics too. It's not big like California, but my dad is actually the mayor here in town. He runs it like it's a city, though," she huffs. "Baking was also my escape."

I offer her a weak smile.

"Do you have someone back home? Like dating or married or whatever?" She laughs but quickly covers her mouth with her hand for a pause before continuing. "I'm sorry. That's a really personal question. I mean, if you were married, he would be here too. Or you could be and he's coming later." She stops herself, looking down at her feet. "I really just put my foot in my mouth, huh?"

I chuckle in response to her rambling. "No one is back home, and no one is coming here for me."

It feels like I'm lying, but the truth is, the only person I care about back home is my sister. There's no one else there for me. Not anymore. I'm just not ready to share that part of my story yet.

She breathes out a relieved sigh. "That was embarrassing."

Shaking my head, I offer her a reassuring grin. "Nonsense. It's a valid question when getting to know someone."

Placing a hand on my shoulder. "I'm glad you're here, Blair."

I'm not entirely sure how I got *this* lucky to have one of the first people who accepted me as their friend in this town relate to me on such a personal level. If I didn't think she was going to be a good friend before, she sure is now.

"I feel like a broken record when I say this, but I can't thank you enough, Lily. The opportunity to do my favorite hobby and earn some money from it means everything."

A friendly smile crosses her face, and she jumps off the counter. "I'm just happy I found someone who has a love for baking the way I do. It's scarce."

"It's funny." I giggle nervously. "When I first saw my new house, I wasn't sure how I would find the space to bake in it. This feels more of a relief because of that than the money."

She holds her arms out to showcase the kitchen. "You have plenty of space here, don't worry. And here." She reaches into her pocket and pulls out a set of keys, taking one off the ring before tossing it in my direction. "Whenever you want to bake, you're welcome here."

Looking down at the brass key in my hand, my eyes widen. "Seriously?"

She nods. "I know what it's like to love this hobby. It's in my heart. It's in my blood. Something I got from my late grand-mother. One day she told me a story about how she was mocked for being thirty and her job was in a bakery. People found it hard to believe that a thirty-year-old wouldn't have a better job, you know? But she told me to always follow my heart. That if you do what you love, it will never feel like work. That's why I opened Batter Up. It's even etched into my skin. I mean, see?"

She lifts her arm to reveal a tattoo on her inner forearm. It's a black-and-white stamp with a cupcake right in the middle.

"Anyway," she continues before I can ask more about what it means, "I know what it's like to need to get away from reality and get lost in a recipe. You can do whatever you want when-ever you want and use what we have here."

The emotions I held back moments ago, fight to come to the surface. Lily barely knows me, aside from hiring me and having a few conversations with her. Yet she just trusted me with the keys to her business, allowing me to use it freely.

"Thank you," I say, thick with emotion.

"I'll do you one better," she says with a hand on my shoulder. "If you come up with something new, we can put it on the menu. Or, *oh my god*, we can start weekly specials." She jumps up and down, flapping her arms as if she's a bird at the ideas flowing through her head. "Marketing at its finest. Bring people back for something new every week."

"I don't see that being an issue for you. This place is perfect."

Her excitement dies down, but she still keeps a smile on her face. Something tells me that no matter what mood she's in, she's always smiling. She seems like the person constantly trying to keep it together, while inside she's falling apart.

"Not to get into too much detail, but I've been struggling a bit to keep this place alive. I'm barely making ends meet here."

"But you hired me?"

"My brother owns part of this place with me, as well as the bar next door. That's all his, though. He thought the idea of hiring someone would help me free up some time so my head doesn't feel like it's going to explode."

"He seems really nice," I tell her honestly. "I hope to meet him someday."

"Today's the day!" She does a little country line dance looking move in place and we both laugh. "Lunch is on him so he can meet the new employee."

"That sounds amazing. I'm starving."

"Me too. Let's go."

Stepping outside, I take a deep breath before following Lily into the bar. Something shifts inside of me as we cross the front door. I can't tell if it's because it's dimly lit and a new atmosphere for me, or something else.

But it feels…off.

That's when I spot him.

He walks out of the kitchen with a crate of glasses fresh out of the dishwasher. His baseball cap is backward on his head, a dish rag over his shoulder, and he's wearing the same black and white checkered flannel I saw when I first made eye contact with the man driving past me in the old red truck.

His sleeves are rolled up just above his elbows, and the flannel is unbuttoned, showcasing his white T-shirt underneath. Holding the crate in both arms only accentuates the muscles and tendons in his forearms, which can be seen from a mile away.

As soon as he spots me, he stops in his tracks.

A wrinkle forms between his eyebrows, and I can already tell I'm not welcome in this bar.

Did he not know that Lily hired the "new girl" in town? There can't be someone else who just so happened to move here the same time I did.

"Griff." Lily smiles, skipping to a seat at the bar. "This is Blair, the new girl I hired."

My skin burns as his eyes trail my body.

I want to crawl under the bar and hide.

"You're fired."

CHAPTER 9

LEARN HOW TO BE NICE OR LEAVE HER ALONE.

GRIFFIN

"You can't fire me."

Blair stands tall with her hands on her hips and her chin held high. Being more at her level, I realize just how small she really is.

My gaze bounces between her and Lily. Come to think of it, I might just be large because she's actually the same size as my sister seeing them standing next to one another.

"You don't own the place," she continues.

"Actually, I do," I deadpan.

Blair turns to Lily, waving a hand in my direction. "This is your brother?"

Lily nods, her mouth agape. Clearly shocked by this exchange.

My sister told me *nothing* about the new girl she was hiring. Then again, I didn't ask many questions myself. When she told me about it, I didn't even think about how we have a new girl roaming around town. My head went straight to a trustworthy local.

I'm pissed at myself for not thinking it was the *city girl* she hired.

"Did you know your brother was an asshole?" Blair asks her.

"Did you just call me an asshole?" I want to laugh, but aggravation is the only thing flowing through my blood right now.

She faces me, stepping into my space. Which only pisses me off even more, because the buzz in the air when she's this close is undeniable.

I want to turn away. I want to run off into the kitchen. Because I don't want to feel like this with anyone new.

Especially her.

"I call it like I see it," she says with a shrug.

"How do you two know each other?" Lily asks.

But I can't take my eyes off Blair, who's giving me the death stare. The evil eye only makes her look that much hotter and sends chills down my spine. And fuck me for even thinking that.

Also...I was right.

The whiskey color in her eyes burns worse than when drinking it straight from the bottle.

She should come with a warning.

"She just moved here. To *my* road."

"Barlow Drive is not *your* road. Just because you were the only person who lived there before I got here, doesn't mean it's yours. It's town property."

She's got a backbone; I'll give her that. I extend my hand in front of her, void of emotion. But all she does is look at it like its poison before her eyes lock with mine again. "Hi, Blair..."

"Andrews," she says, crossing her arms over her chest.

"It's nice to meet you. I think." I shrug. "That part is still up for debate. But, I'm Griffin Barlow."

I watch as everything in her changes. Her shoulders relax while her eyes widen, taking a few steps away from me before her hand covers her forehead. I feel the air change around me from just moments ago.

Almost like I can breathe again.

"This can't be happening right now," she murmurs under her breath. "I'm going to the restroom," she tells Lily.

I want to laugh, or hell, even smile with satisfaction.

But that's not who I am.

It's kind of comical watching as the wheels spin in her head, putting the pieces of the puzzle together.

I lied when I told her I owned Barlow Drive.

Even though it has my name on it, it's not *mine*. But I own the property on the road. Including the house she lives in now. It was mine before Nan helped me sell it. I just didn't think she would sell it to some city girl when she knows exactly how I feel about them.

Knowing the shit I've been through.

"Be nice, Griff," Lily says, swatting my forearm. "She's still trying to get acclimated and, whether or not you like it, she's my new employee. It might be too soon to tell, but she might actually be one of my new friends. I like her a lot, and I know she's going to be an amazing addition to Batter Up."

I glare at her, not caring about any of it.

"Besides," she continues, "despite her tough exterior, I think she's been through some shit. I don't know all of it, but she briefly told me about her parents, and I feel bad for her."

"I truly don't care, Lil," I answer quickly, ignoring her comments about Blair's past. "Her dog runs around my property all hours of the night. Not only do I have to live next to her, but now I have to work next to her? It's just grating on my nerves."

"Why?"

"Because I hate the city. You know this. That woman reeks of it. Her stupid car and her clothes. She's not fucking from here."

Lily throws her arms out. "Neither are half of the people who come through here. The difference is, she's here to stay. You have to give her a chance, just like everyone else who's ever moved here."

I know my sister's right. I do.

But it's hard for me to accept it.

Lily was my voice when I went through the greatest heart-break of my life, so she should know how hard this is for me.

66

Blair coming back from the bathroom forces me to turn my gaze in her direction, pushing back the feelings of my past.

Hurt replaced with anger that she's still here.

"I'm going to head back to the bakery," she tells Lily, glancing at me before looking back to Lily. "I have an idea for a cookie."

"But you didn't eat anything," Lily says.

"I'm not that hungry. I'll grab something when I get home after I'm done."

With that, she's out the door.

Lily glares at me with rage. "Do you know what she told me before we walked over here?"

I cross my arms over my chest, keeping my chin held high. "I don't. But I know you're going to tell me anyway."

"She told me she was starving," Lily says, throwing her arms out. "I can't even believe how rude you were to her."

"I told you. I don't want her here."

Lily's shoulders relax as if she's admitted defeat.

Or she just completely gives up on me. I don't blame her.

"You really need to get over your past. You need to learn how to be nice or leave her alone. She's a good fucking person and likes it here."

And then she's out the door.

"Fuck," I curse, pulling a bottle of whiskey from the shelf and pouring a glass. I down it in one gulp.

I never drink when I'm on the clock.

But I'm losing my mind.

It turns out whiskey isn't enough to numb the past or the present.

CHAPTER 10
WHAT, LIKE IT'S HARD?

BLAIR

"He's my boss's brother, Kodi," I groan.

"He's your *friend's* brother. Start rewording that because she really sounds like a good friend to you so far."

That's exactly why I didn't wait a week to call Kodi and tell her what happened yesterday. I need her voice of reason. Even if she can be a little out there sometimes.

After excusing myself to the bathroom, I overheard Lily stand up for me with her brother. Something I didn't expect was that she and my grumpy neighbor are blood-related. It was the words he said to her that rang in my ear and had all night while I tossed and turned in bed.

She's not fucking from here.

The old me would have run back to San Francisco so fast.

The person I'm trying to become only wants to work harder to prove I'm here to stay.

I didn't uproot my entire life to be treated like this.

"It doesn't matter who he is. He was a total jerk. It sort of takes away how pretty he is." I shrug.

"At least you're finally admitting he's pretty." She laughs.

"Don't even start."

She giggles to herself. "I'm just saying."

"I just don't understand what makes him think he can act like that. He went on and on about how he owns the street and it's irritating him that I'm there. How was I supposed to know that? Nan is the one who sold me the house. I didn't actively seek it out." I pace my small space, growing frustrated with every word out of my mouth. "And in my defense, I didn't even know his name, let alone last name, to figure out he owned all of this."

"*You* own the house, Blair," Kodi reminds me. "So, he can't kick you out or run you out of town."

I scoff. "Trust me, I'm not planning on going anywhere."

I'm not letting the short incident with him take away from the best day I had at the bakery. I went back into Batter Up with my head held high because a bad attitude can't break me. I've already hit rock bottom in my life and felt completely broken in the cruelest way once before by a man. I won't let this man, who I barely know, bring me down to that dark place.

I spent the rest of my shift putting together an apple crumb cake. My first attempt was a success. It actually came out better than I could have expected. Lily even said she might put it on the weekly specials next week.

"Now," I tell Kodi, "no more negative shit. Tell me what *you* have planned today?"

"I have a consultation about twenty miles outside of the city for an indoor rustic design. Let me tell you, I am *really* enjoying the farmhouse style so many people have been looking for. It's a challenge for me which I like."

"That sounds amazing. You're so good at what you do. Even if it is a challenge, it's one you will nail."

"Thank you." I can feel her pride through the phone. "What about you? What are you doing since you're off today?"

"You're never going to believe me when I tell you," I say with a wide smile that I'm sure she can feel through my tone.

"I'm scared."

"I'm going to the General Store to buy a power washer."

"I'm sorry…what?"

"You heard correctly." I begin to laugh. "I don't know what the hell I'm doing, but I'm going to figure it out."

"I'm still over here trying to visualize you using a power washer. I can't see it. Now the question is, what do you plan on washing with this thing?"

"What, like it's hard?" I scoff. "And I'm going to power wash the outside of the house."

She laughs incredulously.

"Don't laugh at me," I tell her, despite me actually laughing as well. "This is me finding my independence, remember? I have to learn how to do this. I *want* to learn how to do this. I own a home now. I think this is part of that process."

"You're right. I have full faith in you, sis."

"Thank you," I say proudly. "I'm going to let you go so I can get this project started. I'm confident it's going to take me most of the day just learning how to turn the thing on."

She barks out a laugh. "Have fun."

The General Store is a lot less busy than it was last time I was here. Probably because I made it here early in the day. I don't know why more places don't have something like this. It's truly the town's one-stop shop. It stretches the whole block. One side of the store is where you can shop for groceries, the middle of the store is apparel, while the other side is all household supplies. Including paint, hardware, and those types of things that I wouldn't even know the names of.

It's weird and foreign to me, but I don't hate it.

I'm used to having to go to one place for groceries, another for clothes, and then a specific spot for household supplies. Then again, I've never had to shop for household stuff.

Stopping by the clothing racks first, I realize I need something for today because the weather is on the warmer side. It's wild how different each day is here.

Even the clothing here is different from the city. Most of the stores in the city were filled with designer things or outfits for people who worked in offices. None of this is what I'm used to wearing.

But I'm here to embrace the changes.

I see a cute pair of jean shorts, and the first one on the rack is my size, which is a total sign I need them. Next to it is a light blue crew neck that reads *Bluestone* on it.

Would it be weird to buy a shirt with the town name on it?

It feels kind of touristy, and that's the last thing I'm trying to feel here.

Lifting it up to assess the front and back, I spot a familiar face and pause.

Griffin Barlow.

My eyebrows pinch together, and I feel a sense of annoyance course through me as I lift the sweatshirt to hide myself and hope he doesn't see me. I won't let him ruin this already positive day.

When I find the guts to peek over the hanger again, he's gone.

In his place I see a strange man staring at me as if he were here for me. At least that's what it looks like with the way he doesn't move or look away. My insides flutter with nerves and the uneasiness of his posture. It's stiff, as if he's saying "got ya" in his head. After three seconds too long, he looks away and walks out of the store.

Breathing a sigh of relief, I decide I'm getting the crewneck. It's light enough to wear during these crisp days, but not thick enough that I'll sweat if the sun peeks out.

Making my way to the hardware side of the store, my eyes land on a pair of rain boots. The cutest pair of high-top pink boots. I can't help it when my eyes light up.

These would be perfect for today's mission.

Different than what I'm used to, but perfect.

The moment I cross the threshold to the hardware section, I feel overwhelmed. I find myself questioning if I'm getting in over my head here.

A clerk walks by, and I stop him.

"Excuse me, sir, I'm looking to buy a power washer."

Greeting me with a warm smile and assessing the items in my arms, he nods. "Right this way, ma'am."

He guides me to the back of the store after silently grabbing me a cart for my belongings. I hope he's not judging me. Not that there's anything to judge. But I'm an outsider.

Walking to the back, I almost trip over my feet and lose my grip on my cart when I see Griffin again. He's with…a woman.

Thankfully, he doesn't see me.

But I keep staring like a creep.

He wears a signature scowl look on his face and for a reason I can't quite comprehend, it makes my heart rate spike. I feel the thunder in my chest and will it to slow down while I wonder if that man ever smiles. I'm thinking absolutely not. Is that his girlfriend or wife? I feel bad for her if that's the case.

She's beautiful, though; there's no denying that.

She has long, strawberry-blonde hair that cascades down her back in loose curls. She also looks very young. Freckles line the apple of her cheeks. She doesn't seem like his type.

Then again, is anyone his type?

He's probably into the *Cruella de Vil* type of woman since he hates dogs too.

Big red flag. BIG.

The clerk is telling me about the three different power washers, but there's something about watching Griffin with this woman that I can't seem to focus on anything the clerk's telling me. My curiosity's piqued and I wish I knew why.

The words coming out of the clerk's mouth drown out in the background as I watch Griffin lean in and hug her. It does nothing to help slow the pounding in my chest as I watch. The corner of his lip lifts just the smallest amount when he pulls away. If I blinked, I would have missed it. It's not a real one, but still...does that count as a smile? It's enough that it shows he appreciates her to some extent.

Now there's a pang of jealousy in my chest.

Not because I wish he would hug me like that.

Hell no.

I'm not looking for a relationship in Bluestone Lakes. It's too small of a town to get wrapped up in that. Nor do I want one with that man.

It's a type of jealousy from watching him be nice to her.

Being his neighbor, I wish he would be nice to me, too. I'm not planning to go anywhere, and clearly, he isn't either. It's a shitty feeling walking on eggshells in your own yard because the person who lives on the property next to you can't stand you.

I sigh, realizing I didn't hear a thing the clerk told me.

"I'll take whatever one you think is best for a beginner," I tell him.

"You got it."

I brush away the thoughts of what I just saw and check out with all my items.

Let's do this.

CHAPTER 11
LOOKS LIKE WRESTLING TO ME.

GRIFFIN

"You know, showing up thirty minutes early doesn't mean you get to have drinks on the house before your shift."

"I know," Tucker says with a shit-eating grin plastered on his face. "You're giving me exactly one on the house because I'm your favorite cousin."

"You're my *only* cousin," I deadpan.

"Good point."

I move to pour him a beer on tap. I know Tucker isn't stupid enough to get drunk when he's at work. Not once has he even accepted a shot when the ladies come in and beg him to take one with him. But I know he's been outside working all day and could probably use this.

"How was work?" I say, sliding the glass in front of him.

He shakes his head. "Annoying. I feel like we're moving at snail's speed to build those houses up on the east side of town."

Bluestone Lakes has a ton of empty land. We're in no rush to grow it, even if he wants the projects to move quicker. Even if I hate the idea of more people coming into town and moving here, our businesses need it.

I need customers.

Lily needs customers.

Tucker needs construction work.

"I give it another year before Poplar Street is done," Tucker says after taking a sip of his beer.

"Poppy will be happy when she gets her street back."

"I don't blame her. I'm ready to tackle Redwood Avenue, though. In my opinion, that road has the best views in town. I can only imagine the houses we can build there. If I can afford it before we start, I'm definitely building my dream home there."

He's not wrong.

Redwood Avenue curves around the side of a mountain. If you find just the right spot, you can see a spectacular view of the mountains on one side and the heart of Bluestone Lakes on the other. But the best part—our actual lake—sits right in the middle. If I wasn't already building my home at the time where I was, that's the exact spot I would have chosen too.

"You will do it," I say. "Slow and steady."

"You know I'm way too antsy of a person for slow and steady, Griff. I need to move." He lifts his hands in front of him, wiggling his fingers. "My hands need to work their magic."

I stare at him, unblinking.

"They are magic hands, Griffin Barlow. You should know this," he defends.

"No, I shouldn't."

"I can show you someday." He winks.

"On that note, I'm heading out," I say, tossing the dish rag on the counter.

"You got it, boss." He salutes.

Rolling my eyes, I grab the keys to my truck from the kitchen. Whenever it's time for me to leave, I always rush out of here as fast as I can before I get stuck talking to a customer or listening to issues about something.

Not many people rush to leave one job to go to another.

But not many people own a ranch like mine.

The anticipation of spending the evening in my own personal

serenity to relax and unwind forces me to hustle out of there. Even if it's not a relaxing job, it's quiet for me. Feeding the horses, taking them for a ride, and catching a glimpse of the sunset is what I live for. Today is no different. The skies are blue, and the weather is on the warmer side. Rolling my windows down, I let the breeze hit my face on my quick drive home to drop off the stuff I picked up from the General Store before heading to work.

It's moments just like this that make me wonder what my life would be like if I left and moved to the city.

Imagine missing this?

No fucking thank you.

I turn onto my street, eager to get changed, and head to the ranch.

I purposely avoid looking at Blair's house. But something catches my eye, forcing me to do a double take and slow the truck down. She's standing on the side of the house in a pair of hot pink rain boots, jean shorts, and a sweatshirt. Some of her hair pulled to the top of her head and the rest flying in every direction.

"What in the world is she doing?" I ask myself.

My eyes scan the area, and I spot her mutt sitting on the grass near her. He's got his legs out, head resting on the grass and his eyes closed. Clearly unfazed by what's happening, as if he's used to this type of behavior.

Movement causes me to snap my head back in her direction.

Is she…is she fighting a hose?

She's wrangling the hose like she's a firefighter on her first day. Water is flying in every direction while she attempts to straddle it between her legs.

Throwing my truck in park in the middle of the road, I sit there for a moment wondering if I should even bother. I should keep driving straight home and not help her. I don't need her to think I care more than I do.

76

Reluctantly, I decide to get out of the truck before I march over to where she's fighting the water.

I can't believe this is happening right now.

That's when I notice it's not *just* a hose, it's a power washer. Blair is power washing her house. Or, at least trying to. I'm now glad I got out of the truck because she's going to ruin the siding on the house if she keeps this up.

"What are you doing?" I shout over the loud buzzing of the power washer.

It's a piece of shit one if you ask me.

Where the hell did she even get this?

"What does it look like I'm doing?" she shouts back, using every part of her body to get it under control. Water sprays in every direction, and across my flannel causing me to startle from the sting of pressure. She even manages to get the dog wet. Of course, it doesn't move because it's far enough away to avoid the force of it.

My arms fly out as I look down in shock at my now drenched shirt before looking back up at her.

She finally lets it fall to the ground, stomping a pink boot on it to keep it down, and flips the power off on the machine. She looks up at me, brushing her hands over the top of her head and schooling her features. "I'm power washing," she says casually.

Crossing my arms over my chest, I shoot her a skeptical glare. "Looks like wrestling to me."

She shrugs a shoulder. "Just getting used to it. That's all. I've…uh…never done this before." Her gaze trails my body. "Sorry about your shirt." She shrugs again, but this time without an ounce of remorse in her tone.

Rolling my eyes, I stomp toward her. The same damn energy from the last time I was this close to her rips through me. The sting from the force of the water is quickly replaced with a burning feeling behind my ribcage. I don't have time to register the feeling completely because her eyes widen at my sudden movements when I reach down between her legs to rip the hose from under her boot. My forearm brushes against the bare skin sitting above her boot and I almost fumble the hose between my fingers from the electric zing I just felt along my arm. I fight like hell to ignore it despite the way my heart begins to race, holding the hose up in my hands with ease.

She looks from my face to my arms where I hold the hose. The way her eyes burn my skin worse than the water pisses me off, forcing me to grip the hose tighter. Her lips part slightly before she brings her bottom lip between her teeth.

"That's really annoying how you got control of that so easily," she says to me but is still looking at my grip on the hose.

"It's not hard."

"Oh, yes, it is," she mumbles under her breath, still not meeting my stare.

Turning around to assess the machine she got; I notice rather quickly that it really is a hunk of garbage. I can't believe she bought this. I shake my head as I tighten the hose and turn it back on.

"Give it back," she demands. "I need to finish this before the sun sets."

White knuckling the hose between my fingers, I want to be a dick and let her fight this hose for all hours of the night. I really do. But I'm a selfish bastard and don't want to hear the machine buzzing, along with her screams, all night long.

"I got it," I tell her.

"No," she practically shouts. "I want to do this."

"Why?" I ask, curious about the quick change in tone.

"Because."

One word before something washes over her, I can't quite figure out. It looks like pain and hurt. Lily told me she's been through some shit. I never asked Lily more because I don't want to know. It's not my right to know.

It might just make me want to be nice.

"I just want to do this, okay?" she adds. Her tone is much softer and less demanding.

The rapid change solidifies my theory.

Something has definitely happened in her past. But what?

Fuck. Now I'm here and I want to know.

"Now, if you'll excuse me," she says, ripping the hose from my hand. "I need to wrestle this hose some more and get this side of the house done."

I look from the hose to her face, unable to say anything back while the aching in my chest intensifies. But her whiskey eyes plead with me to give her this chance.

"If you insist."

"I do." She nods.

Avoiding further conversation, I turn around and make my way to the truck. I refuse to look back at her house as I put it in drive, ready to get back to my house.

Everything about that doesn't feel right.

It feels off.

Which is making *me* feel off.

I'm not someone who's supposed to care like this. I'm not someone who's supposed to be curious about the city girl.

I skip going to the ranch for the first time in as long as I can remember to sit on my porch and wonder more about her as she successfully gets control of the hose and finishes the one side of her house.

I give up when the sun hides behind the mountain.

But when my head finally hits the pillow at night, my only thoughts are of her.

CHAPTER 12

SEVEN MILES.

BLAIR

It may have taken me a whole week, but my house is done and sparkling clean. One would think that being such a small home it would be a quick project.

Wrong.

I found my strength when I felt like I had to prove to not only myself but to my grumpy next-door neighbor, that I could handle this. I saw the look on his face when he noticed me struggling. I stayed awake all night playing it on repeat in my head.

Along with the muscles flexing in his forearm that were staring me in the face.

Guilt consumed me as those thoughts flooded my brain. Thinking of another man the way I thought about Griffin only churned in my gut. Theodore was all I've known for so long, and while we're divorced with no chance of us ever getting back together, it's still hard to process that my brain is thinking about how hot another man's forearms are.

All of this only sent me down a spiral of crying myself to sleep.

Not from missing Theodore.

But because of feeling more alone than ever.

I miss my sister back in San Francisco. And I miss...there's no one else. It's just Kodi. Because I have no one else. I was alone then, and I'm alone now.

I can do this, though.

When all is said and done, there's a peace I've found here in Bluestone Lakes. A sense of belonging even if it's only been a short time. A feeling that tells me this is where I'm meant to be and to learn who I was all along.

When I finally got a handle on the power washer, I flew through the rest of the house. I'm thankful I didn't strip any of the blue from the siding. I say that because I accidentally stripped the stain from the deck. *Whoops.*

The deck project is not something I am ready to tackle anytime soon, so I'm just embracing the natural wood while I figure out a plan.

Someday I hope to extend it, creating enough space for an outdoor seating area. I picture one of those comfortable outdoor sofas, and next to it, on each side, a glider. I picture making more friends here and someday hosting them at my home, enjoying drinks and good company on *my* porch.

Those thoughts helped ease the tears I shed as I looked to the bright side of the future.

There was plenty of time for me to sit around and envision my porch the following days because my body was sore from head to toe. It's a shame because I really wanted to go for a run the other day.

It worked out though, because the next day my clothes finally came from my sister, and everything fit me perfectly. They don't *scream* country, and some of them are way too risqué for my liking. But the outfits work for someone who works in a bakery. Which is all I asked for.

Kodi knows me well enough to know I need to get out and run too. Her throwing in a pair of biker shorts was like winning the lottery when I opened the box.

Today's the day I finally set out in town on a run. I'm definitely nervous, but I've missed this part of me. Even if I'm working on a new and improved Blair, this part of me can never leave. It's my peace. It's my calm. It's my time to shut the world out around me.

My only hesitation is that I don't know the town completely, and I'm intimidated by all the mountains surrounding me. Which also makes me afraid that the altitude will take me out before the incline of the hills do.

But I'm doing it anyway.

Early evenings have become my favorite part of the day here, so why not incorporate my two favorites at the same time?

Once my feet hit the dirt road, I do my normal stretching routine before I take off. My phone blasts some playlist I made last week when I was mentally preparing to get back to running.

It's not as bad as I thought.

I keep an easy pace, and once I leave Barlow Drive, I decide to explore a little deeper. Focusing on where I just came from so I can get myself back home. I find myself in a new area of town I've never seen. There are very few houses and definitely no businesses. I run past a ton of construction sites, which must mean the town is still growing.

My guess is that I ran around the heart of town.

Continuing down the road, I find myself coming to a stop when I realize it's a dead end. I take a moment to lean forward with my hands on my thighs to catch my breath before surveying my surroundings.

"Where the hell am I?"

I don't think I ended up on any *real* road this entire run. I got a little caught up in the music for a while to pay attention.

Am I lost?

Great. Just what I need.

I dial Lily's number.

"Hello?"

"Hey, Lily."

"Why does it sound like you're in the middle of running a marathon?" She laughs.

"Not a marathon," I choke out. "But definitely running. Barely."

"What? Where the heck are you? Who's chasing you?"

"No one is chasing me that I know of. But you know…you ask a fantastic question," I get out through my ragged breaths. "There are no signs or houses anywhere. But if I have to guess, I'm on the opposite side of town. Actually, I may not even be in Bluestone Lakes anymore. Maybe I'm in another state."

She laughs. "How far did you run?"

"I don't know. I kind of got lost in my playlist. And I don't track my distance with those fancy apps or anything. Made a few lefts, and a few rights, and now I'm on a dead-end road."

"Shit. You're probably on the east side of town. You said there are no houses?"

"No houses, but I passed some new construction about fifteen minutes ago."

"I'm going to have Griffin come get—"

"No!" I cut her off. "Please, no. I'm good. I'm great actually. I was really just calling to see how things were going. And to maybe give me a general direction I should go to get home. You know… East. West. Up. Down? Anything will work."

"If you give me…" Her voice trails off and I hear the sound of wind through the speakers as if she just stepped outside. Quickly followed by the front door to the bar chiming in the background. "Griffin. Are you off yet?"

No. No. No.

Please don't tell me this is happening.

"Can you pick up Blair on the east side? I think she's on Redwood," she says to him.

"No, Lily! He doesn't need to—" I attempt to stop her, but they continue having a whole conversation in my ear.

"Griffin is on his way," she tells me. "Stay where you are."

And then she hangs up.

I groan. So loud that I think I heard it echo in the mountains.

Realization dawns on me and I feel my heart rate reach running speed again.

What if a bear found me out here? Or even worse...a moose.

Do they have those in Wyoming?

I should have looked that up.

I know moose aren't known to be mean like bears, but those are some scary looking creatures with those big antler-looking things. I'm picturing one of them bull rushing me and impaling me right in the chest. I do not want to die at the head of one of those things.

I contemplate figuring out how to get back myself before *he* can find me. One, I don't want to wait around and see if there are really bears or moose around here, and two, I don't want to see Griffin.

I already feel weak after the way he saw me with the power washer.

He thinks I can't handle myself.

I can't stand that feeling.

Turning around in the direction I came from; I send a silent prayer up that something will spark my memory.

Just three minutes later, a truck barrels down the dirt road at a high speed, leaving a cloud of dust in its wake. Griffin comes to a halt right in front of me. The beat-up Chevy must have some power behind it, which surprises me because it looks like it's about to fall apart right in front of my eyes.

He turns off the engine and in no time, he's already on the other side of the truck, standing right in front of me.

"Okay, Batman. That was quick. But you really didn't need to come."

"I wasn't leaving you out here by yourself with the sun going down soon."

I feel my eyes wanting to widen in shock as he pretends to care, but I make a conscious effort to keep my gaze level and steady on him. At the same time controlling my breathing in an effort to bring my heart rate down to normal.

"I would have found my way back."

"Or you would have found yourself in a ditch," he replies a little too quickly.

I look around us. "I don't see a ditch anywhere."

"You also don't even know where you are," he says, crossing his arms over his chest.

"Touché. But you didn't have to save me. Because this is two times now." I hold up two fingers to emphasize my words. "Granted, I turned down your heroic measures with the power washer thing. I got that done, by the way," I add with a wink and a finger gun in his direction.

I feel myself rambling and wanting to continue, but he cuts me off.

"Can you just get in the truck?"

"Oh, yes. I can do that. Even if I feel guilty that you had to go out of your way."

"It's fine."

For the first time, he doesn't sound annoyed at all. His body language tells me he's probably irritated from either my rambling or having to come out here to get me, but the way he talks doesn't reflect that. It's hard to figure him out though, because he never smiles.

I hustle to the passenger side, but he beats me to it. Opening it before I can put my hand on it.

Did he just...

"Thank you, kind gentleman."

Oh my god, Blair. Stop it.

I think the altitude is getting to me.

I jump in the truck and watch as he rounds the hood. Looking at the dirt road with each step he takes. My stomach does a somersault with nerves that I'm putting him out for coming to get me.

Once he gets in the truck, the tension grows thicker just being in such a small space with the man. The truck is small, and on the inside, it's well kept, like he cares for it often. The smell takes over my senses and forces me to turn and look at his side profile. I can't pinpoint exactly what the smell is, but it's a mix of spice and earth. Whatever the hell the earth smells like, it's right here in this Chevy.

I stare at him longer, wanting to know more about it, but also not wanting to pry into his life when he's clearly a private person. His facial features are flat while he focuses on the road ahead of us. One hand on the wheel and the other hanging out the window. Wearing his signature look of a flannel rolled up at the sleeves.

I'll never stop wanting to see that.

Okay, but I have to stop.

He clearly has a girlfriend. I saw her with my own two eyes at the store.

"Thanks again. I'm sorry about all this," I tell him honestly.

"Do you run a lot?" he asks, gaze still locked on the road.

"I used to. Back in the city." The way his jaw hardens when I say the word city makes the hairs on my arm stand tall.

What is that all about?

"This was the first time I've been running since I got here," I continue. "I don't normally run with a GPS tracker. Which is why I got lost. I don't even know how far I ran. It feels like a lot. Maybe my longest run in years."

He nods but doesn't respond.

Now I feel like I'm rambling again. My hands feel sweaty on my lap and my chest feels tight. There's something about him that just sends a nervous frenzy through my blood. Maybe it's how rude he is. Maybe it's that I'm afraid he's going to go off on me in a fit of rage.

I'm nervous, but I'm not scared.

Griffin Barlow doesn't scare me.

He sort of intrigues me. I think under that grumpy exterior is a man who's hurting from something...but what?

"So, you work every day?" I ask; in an attempt to make this drive less awkward.

He nods again.

"Can't you hire some help?"

"I enjoy working the lunch shift," he says. *Finally, some words.* "It's always regulars and it's a shorter shift. I'm better off not dealing with the evening crowd. They are a bit too rowdy for my liking. Basically, I avoid being there if I'm not scheduled to be. If I can help it, at least."

I think that was the most consecutive words I've heard him say at once before.

Impressive.

Hot.

His voice is smooth and sexy.

Stop it, Blair.

"What made you name it Seven Stools?"

"Next time you come in, count how many stools you find at the bar," he answers with a straight face.

"Did you just crack a joke, Angry Cowboy?"

He still doesn't laugh.

Tough crowd.

"I, for one, thought that was funny and will be visiting your establishment *very* soon to confirm this."

I really believed my sense of humor would make him laugh or, hell, crack a smile. But no success there.

Next thing I know, we're pulling up to my house.

By pulling up, I mean he stops in the middle of the road to let me out. I'm not mad about it because not only did he pick me up, but he actually had some kind of conversation with me. It's all a good start.

"Thanks again for the ride," I say with a smile just before slamming the door, turning on my heel, and walking across the driveway.

Just as my foot hits the first step of my deck, he beeps the horn. Whipping my head around, he leans over the center console to shout out the passenger window.

"Seven miles."

"Huh?"

"You ran seven miles today."

A grin spreads across my face as he drives away.

Leaving my heart beating faster than it was on my run. Because Griffin Barlow does have a heart.

CHAPTER 13

WE CAN PUT A PIN IN THAT FOR NOW.

GRIFFIN

> **EUGENE**
>
> Your mom would like to know if you'd like to come over for dinner one day this week.
>
> **EUGENE**
>
> It's been a while.

> **ME**
>
> I know. Tell her I'm sorry. Work has been busy.

> **EUGENE**
>
> Still doesn't answer my question, son.

> **ME**
>
> Yeah. Soon.

"You really need a day off, man. You're getting more miserable by the day. I take that back. The hour."

I glare at Tucker sitting across the bar, amused by the words coming out of his mouth.

I, for one, am not.

I would love to have a day off, but this bar won't operate on its own like the ranch does if I'm not there. If I take an afternoon off here, it means either hiring someone else or paying someone more to cover my shift. Plus, the bar has been keeping me busy and out of the house.

And I've needed to fucking get out of the house, so I'm not sitting on my porch and watching my neighbor go for her morning runs.

I've been spending more time at Barlow Ranch just to get off my property. The issue is, when I'm taking one of my horses out on the trail, all I think about is Blair and the way she felt sitting in my truck last week when I picked her up.

I wish I had never gone to pick her up.

"Or, you could start an exercise routine," Tucker suggests. "It's a good way to relieve stress. There are many types of exercise you can do," he says with a wink. "You seem tense and stressed out."

"I agree. Is this seat taken?" Nan says, taking a seat next to Tucker.

"No, ma'am." He smiles at her. "But even if it was, there's five other stools to choose from. This place is deader than dead."

"Hilarious," I deadpan.

"I like to think so." Tucker laughs.

"Did you both come in today to annoy me?"

Tucker raises his hand like he's in school and has an answer to my question before nodding his head. Such a child.

"Yes and no," Nan says.

"What's up?" I tip my head toward her.

"I have a total of two questions for you," she says, holding up her thumb and pointer finger to emphasize her case.

"I have time for one," I tell her, wiping the counter in front of them.

Nan looks around, surveying the bar. "By the looks of this place, you'd have time for an entire interview. But I'm gonna keep it to two questions."

"Get on with it."

"One"—she holds up a pointer finger—"how would you feel about karaoke night at the bar?"

"No. Next."

"Great. We can put a pin in that for now. I'll circle back in forty-eight hours."

This woman.

"Two. How do you feel about your new neighbor? Are you two getting along nicely?" She waggles her eyebrows. "She's a really sweet girl."

I'm actively trying to keep my new neighbor out of my head, and Nan has to come in here and bring her up.

In front of Tucker, no less.

I can't answer her question because I don't know how I feel about her.

I want to say she's growing on me, but I don't know enough about her.

What I do know is that she's got thighs for days. A body I would love to consume myself with. I want to explore every curve and run my hands along her bare skin. Admittedly, I've undressed her in my head every night before going to bed since having her in the passenger seat of my truck. Losing my mind every time my head hits the pillow.

She's bringing up feelings I wish I never felt.

It's been years since I've slept with anyone.

This is a small town. I don't want to get involved with anyone for the risk of everyone knowing by morning. I know how we operate around here. Everyone talks because no one knows how to keep their mouths shut.

And that's just a fraction of the reasoning.

I never want to make myself feel vulnerable enough to allow them to break me the way I've been broken. I've been doing just fine believing that I'm better off alone for the rest of my life.

My routine works for me.

My life works for me.

"Wait, wait, *wait*," Tucker says. I watch as the wheels in his head spin and he puts two and two together. *Great.* "Is the new city girl your new neighbor?"

I stare at him unblinkingly.

Lovely. Now he knows the truth.

"And you've been holding out on us since she got here? It's been, like, a month now?"

I've been holding out because of this exact reaction.

"My neighbor is none of your concern," I tell him.

"She lives in your house!" Tucker says.

"My *old* house," I correct.

Nan turns to face Tucker, elbows on the bar, resting her chin on her knuckles. "Don't you think it's about time that Griffin here got over Sleazy Sierra?"

"I do, Nan." He nods his head repeatedly. "But can we pause this for just one second?" he asks, turning his stool to face her. "How come you don't have a fun nickname for me? I'm supposed to be your favorite."

"I don't know what you're talking about." She narrows her eyes.

"I know you have nicknames for the Barlow kids. And now I'm learning you have one for Sleazy Sierra. What am I, chopped liver? I may not be a Barlow, but I'm a Daniels."

"I'll give ya one," I chime in. "Annoying Tucker."

He turns to face me. "That's the dumbest thing you've ever said."

"Talkative Tucker," Nan answers.

He pauses while his face wrinkles in thought. "Actually…I'll take it. Now, back to what we were saying." He brings his fingers to his chin to remember.

I shake my head because these two together are a recipe for mayhem.

"Oh yes, the bitch ass ex. It's been years now. It's time for him to find someone new."

"I was thinking the same thing, Tuck. The moment I laid eyes on Blair, I knew she would be perfect for him." She beams.

I swear, if hearts coming out of eyes was a real thing, I just witnessed them coming from her.

"I can't confirm that because I haven't seen her with *my* eyes yet," Tucker says to Nan. "But I trust your judgment."

"I am a pretty good judge of character, aren't I?" Nan asks him.

"I mean, you call this guy behind the bar *Grumpy Griffin*. So, yes."

"You two know I am still standing right here, right?" I interrupt.

"Oh, yes." Nan smiles at me. "Welcome to our conversation about your life."

I groan.

This is why I can't confide in anyone about the thoughts I have for my neighbor. Tucker would only feed off it. My sisters would push me harder in her direction. And Nan's meddling only encourages others to do the same.

She's pulling Tucker into her influence right before my eyes.

"Nans got a point," Tucker says, pointing at me. "She's hot, and she lives close to you. Easy access." He shrugs.

"You just said you haven't seen her."

"Like I've already said...I trust Nan's judgment."

"I have an idea." I raise a finger in the air as if a lightbulb just went off in my head. They both turn their stools to face me completely, waiting to hear what I have to say. "How about we put a pin in *this* conversation and *don't* circle back? Ever."

"That's a shitty idea." Nan wrinkles her face in disgust.

"I second what she said. Worst idea. Next." Tucker grins.

"Or you two can get the hell out of my bar." I shrug.

Tucker barks out a laugh. "You're not very good with ideas here, Griff. I'm concerned about you." He takes a sip of his drink. "Oh, my turn for a better idea. How about you bang your neighbor?"

"Good one." Nan nods, lifting her hand toward Tucker.

The two fucking high five in front of me.

"Now we're discussing my sex life? Excellent." I run a frustrated hand through my hair. "Love this for me."

"It's a healthy conversation," Nan adds.

"We're done here," I say, grabbing a clean dish rag before turning away to dry some glasses.

"We're just saying you should think about it," Nan says from behind me. "She's not planning on leaving. She's here to stay, which is why she *bought* the house and didn't ask to rent one."

I stare at the glass in my hand while my mind travels to the time Sierra left.

She told me she was never planning to leave. Yet she did.

Her buying the house means nothing.

I'm content with my life. I wouldn't say I'm happy, but I'm content.

That's enough for me.

I don't need to let anyone in, because they always leave anyway.

CHAPTER 14

OKAY, I'LL SHUT UP NOW.

BLAIR

I've settled into a good routine here now.

I'm slowly becoming obsessed with all of Bluestone Lakes.

I can say this confidently because I've learned my way around through my early morning runs. The weather when the sun rises is my new favorite time of day. There is runner's high and there is seeing the sun peak over the mountain early morning high. Both of which I experience daily now. If I time my runs just right, I get to see that view when I get back home after each run.

Of course, Reginald is always waiting for me at the front door.

I've picked up some shifts to help Lily out at the bakery too since the crowds were picking up, and she needed the extra set of hands.

"It's crazy how busy you guys get with very little information on the website for this town."

Lily rolls her eyes. "Tell me about it. Nan has no idea how to work technology. If she would just accept the help I've offered over a dozen times, it would be a much cleaner and more inviting website."

"I heard that," Nan interrupts.

Our heads snap to the front door, and she stands there with her hands on her hips, but a smile stretched across her face. It hasn't been that long since I last saw Nan, but whenever I do, I feel like she ages backward. As if each passing day she's a year younger than she was. Nan is goals, honestly.

"Speak of the devil." Lily laughs.

"Who, me?" Nan gasps with a hand to her chest. "I'm no devil. Now come here and give me a hug, Lovely Lily."

Lily shakes her head but offers her a smile before she embraces her.

"What brings you in this afternoon, Nan? It's later than usual."

"I'm making my rounds to see if anyone would be interested in starting a karaoke night at Seven Stools."

"Oh." Lily claps her hands together and bounces where she stands. "Yes. I love that idea. Let's do it."

"We just need to work on the details," Nan says, rounding the counter like she works here and taking a seat by the register. "We can't do Mondays because that's when the book club meets."

"Oh, the town has a book club?" I ask, cutting her off.

She nods her head. "I'm not sure you'd like it, Blair. We don't read the kind of books you'd tell your grandma about."

I cock my head to the side in question.

"We read those romance books," Nan adds. "With every single descriptive detail someone could want."

"Wait, I read those too!" I tell her.

"Well then." She smiles widely. "You're invited. I'll tell you more about it later, but let's get back to karaoke. It's very important. Now, Tuesdays we can't do that night because that's pickleball night."

"You play pickleball too?" I ask. "Damn, you're a busy woman."

"God, no. But I like to watch." She winks. "And then Wednesdays are the night I catch up on my soap operas."

I giggle behind my hand.

Nan is a unique woman. I really admire her. I'm sure she keeps everyone in this town entertained and active as much as possible. She's like the unofficial mayor of the place. Even with her Wednesday night activities, it seems like she doesn't like to sit still for long if she can help it.

"We *could* possibly do Thursdays or Fridays, but I know both nights are short staffed at Seven Stools," she continues.

See? She even knows what the staffing looks like at the bar.

"I don't see why Griffin wouldn't stay late to help." Lily shrugs.

"Grumpy Griffin *hates* the idea," Nan says right before she rolls her eyes.

I can't help the laugh that I practically choke out. "Did you just call him *Grumpy Griffin*?"

"Yep. I have nicknames for all my town's children."

"If you don't mind me asking..." I raise a brow in question before I speak, knowing this might be a personal question. "Who exactly are your children?"

"No one." She chuckles. "But everyone."

"That makes...no sense."

"We have Grumpy Griffin, Lovely Lily, and Pretty Poppy," Nan rattles off as she counts on her hand. "Oh, and newly added...Talkative Tucker."

Lily blushes. "Nan is the best."

I pause, thinking about the names she just mentioned.

I've obviously met Griffin, but who are Poppy and Tucker?

"You have a sister?" I ask Lily.

"Yes. You just haven't met her yet. She's the youngest of all of us and a first-grade teacher in town." Her smile grows as she continues talking about her. "She's so good with kids. She has the patience of a saint."

"Why is Griffin the only one with a negative nickname?"

Nan lifts a shoulder. "I call it like I see it."

"And she's not wrong," Lily adds. "He wasn't always like that, though. I'd give anything to have my old brother back. The happier version of him."

My curiosity piques. I wonder what she's talking about. I want to ask more, but I don't want to invade his privacy. I'm usually good at reading people. Call it growing up around politicians, and from the first few interactions with Griffin, I knew there was a deeper meaning to his burly, grumpy exterior.

"Thursdays really would be ideal," Lily continues. "It's a perfect day for it and a good marketing tactic for the bar. If we pitch it that way, he can't say no."

"My thoughts too." Nan jumps from the stool. "Thirsty Thursday. My only issue is that he needs some convincing. He shut me down an hour ago."

"Between you and me, we're very persuasive." Lily laughs, bumping shoulders with Nan. "Let's go talk to him quickly." She turns to face me. "Are you good holding down the fort for a little bit?"

"Yep." I nod. "I got this handled here."

Lily and Nan leave to go next door.

I start to organize the display of baked goods to make them look less empty, and I keep replaying that conversation in my head, wondering what happened to him to make him that way.

It makes me want to talk to him more and get to know the deeper version of the man. Only because I *know* there's a heart in there somewhere. I know he's not truly that big of an asshole. I mean, he did barrel down the road to pick me up when I was lost.

The bell chimes for the front door and I look up expecting to find Lily and Nan already back after being shut down with their ideas. But my gaze lands on the pretty woman Griffin was with at the General Store.

"Oh, hi." She smiles at me. "Lil told me she hired a new girl. It's so nice to finally put a face with the name."

"Hi, yes." I stumble over my words slightly. "I actually saw you last week with Griffin at the General Store. Sorry if that sounds creepy. It's just nice to meet a girl who can actually put up with my neighbor. Sorry if that's offensive. I tend to talk too much. Okay, I'll shut up now."

I don't know what the hell just came over me.

Am I nervous to talk to this woman?

I don't get nervous, but maybe it's the fact that I've been thinking not-so-friendly things about her boyfriend. It's hard to help with the way he wears his baseball cap backward and the sleeves of his flannel rolled up, showing off his really freakin' hot forearms. When I'm letting the dog out late at night, I find myself looking in the direction of his property. Wondering what he's doing. Wondering if this woman standing in front of me is over there. Then I question if he smiles behind closed doors with her.

"Wow. I like you." She laughs.

"That makes…" I pause to count on my fingers. "A total of three people in town so far. I'm doing excellent."

She extends her hand to greet me. "But I'm not dating Griffin. He's my brother."

"Well…" I draw out, taking her hand in mine. "Foot in my mouth, I guess. You must be Poppy. It's really nice to finally meet you. I can't wait to remember this interaction for the rest of my existence."

She waves me off, laughing to lighten the mood. "Oh, please. Don't stress about that with me. You're funny. It's nice to have a bright face around here. I was just coming by on my lunch break to grab some treats for the kids."

I move to the back counter, grab the bag Lily left out, and pass it to her. "I heard you're a teacher. That's really amazing."

She beams with pride. "It's the greatest job in the world. I hate to cut this short, but I need to head back. Maybe we can get together for lunch one day to chat more."

"I-I'd love that," I practically stutter, in shock that she's a stranger who actually wants to get to know me more.

"Perfect! I'll get your number from Lily after school and text you. Have a good rest of your day," she says with a wave.

"You too," I tell her and watch as she walks out.

I can't help but admire her for being able to do what she loves and for having nothing holding her back. It's a feeling I can relate to, as I'm also finally doing what I love.

It brings an intense feeling of contentment, peace, and fulfillment I never thought I could achieve after my divorce. Maybe it's the joy of being in a place where no one knows my past. No one's seen me on a billboard with whiskers painted on my face. No one's seen me on the news besides my ex-husband waving and looking perfectly put together.

If I hadn't made this decision to come here, would I still be curled up in my sister's apartment with no leads on a place to live?

Emotions are fighting to break through to the surface, but I will not cry over him right now. I am choosing happiness, and I am damn proud of myself for holding my head high. It's not easy, but I've found that focusing on the things that bring me joy —like my new job and the friends I've made—helps me stay positive.

It feels like I am becoming the person I have been deep down all along, the person who was buried under the weight of a failing marriage. I'm rediscovering my passions, my strengths, and my independence, and it's a truly liberating feeling.

I have new friends, a new town, and a job that I am obsessed with.

The past feels so far in the rearview mirror that I can't even see it anymore.

I think I like who I'm becoming.

CHAPTER 15
A MOOSE?

GRIFFIN

I had the longest day for the first time in a while today, and my body is really feeling it.

After the lunch shift, I ended up staying later than intended, feeling frustrated as I tried to finish some work in the back office. The bookkeeping, scheduling, paychecks, and sourcing supplies seemed to come at me faster than I could handle. The little things I need—like the paper roll for receipts, napkins, and other essentials—didn't arrive on time, adding to the feeling of being overwhelmed.

It's exhausting.

The weather is making everything feel even more challenging. It feels like a monsoon with relentless rain that has been ongoing throughout the day. I wish I was exaggerating. This weather is truly wearing me out, and I'm feeling more exhausted than I have in a long time.

I pull a cold beer from the refrigerator and make my way to my porch. It's completely covered and all I want is to enjoy this drink and listen to the rain.

My mind travels to the conversation I had with Tucker and

Nan at the bar a few days ago. Only for that same conversation to be brought up an hour later when Lily showed up at the bar with Nan persuading me to start a karaoke night.

In what world do they think I would be okay with that?

It's bad enough we have our annual Founder's Day creeping up on us. A day when almost the whole town congregates at the heart of town to celebrate Bluestone Lakes. There's food, drinks, activities for the kids, and an epic display of fireworks to end the day. There's absolutely no tired like the tired you feel when that day is done.

Not even how I feel now holds a candle to that.

Hence why I don't feel like hosting a karaoke night at my bar anytime soon.

Nan brought up Blair in conversation in front of Lily, and I fought the urge to groan. It's not a topic I wanted to talk about because I don't know her well enough.

The question is…do I want to know her more?

Lily seems to think I'm a miserable fuck because I'm lonely.

Am I? No way.

Do my sisters want me to find someone to make me happy and finally get over my ex? Yes.

Joke's on them because I've been over her for a while.

I just don't have a heart inside me anymore. Sierra took it with her when she left, probably tossed it out the window on her drive to the airport for another car to run over.

Now, I'm here.

Making a life for myself.

A life I fucking love, thank you very much.

I lean my head back on the rocking chair, close my eyes, and allow myself to relax after this long day when a piercing scream comes from Blair's house.

Jumping from my chair, I clutch the neck of the beer bottle as I scan the area as best I can. The rain is falling hard, a relentless curtain that obscures any danger that may lurk in the shadows.

But if there was an intruder or something running from the house, I think I would see it.

Then I hear her dog barking excessively and another scream. It's *her* scream. It has to be. This time, it's louder and more painful? I drop my beer on the deck, not bothering to grab a jacket, and run through the rain toward her house.

I don't know why I care, but I'm not having someone die on my road.

I don't bother knocking or kicking off my boots when I storm inside her place.

But I immediately regret my decision.

Blair stands in the tiny hallway at the back of the house in nothing, but a dark gray towel wrapped around her body. Water droplets cascade down every inch of exposed skin and her wet hair flies around when she turns to face me.

"*Ahhh! Griffin!*" she screams in the same tone I heard moments ago.

I turn away from her, bringing my hands up to cover my eyes. "What the fuck are you screaming about?"

"You're in my house!"

"Because you were screaming!"

"I know!"

We're both just standing here, shouting at each other while I fight the urge to turn and look at her body in that towel. I finally give in and turn toward her again as I scan around to see what has her in this state of panic. The dog is unfazed by the whole thing and sits next to my legs, looking up at me with its tongue out like it's waiting for me to pet it.

Good luck, buddy.

"A moose!" she shouts again. Her voice is not dying down at all.

My eyes snap to her, landing right on her chest. The swell of her breasts pop as she hugs the towel tight around her body.

Jesus Christ.

"A moose?" I question.

"Out of my bathroom window!" She points through the door that leads to the bathroom.

I nod, realizing it's the side of the house that doesn't face mine. Which is why I didn't see anything when I first heard the scream.

Without another word, I walk to the bathroom.

She's going to keep shouting, anyway.

Water drips from my boots with every step, but she's already made a mess in the hallway herself. Another decision I regret instantly is walking into the bathroom, because the smell of her honeysuckle shampoo or body wash or whatever the hell she was using hits me right in the face.

That's when I spot our friendly neighborhood moose staring right through the window.

I want to laugh, but now I'm just annoyed that I ran here, got drenched from the rain, and she's not actually hurt. I almost wished it was an intruder, not because I want her hurt, but because I'd love a face to smash in to let out the frustrations of the day.

"A moose," I confirm, walking back into the living space.

"Yeah, I said that," she replies, her voice many decibels lower than it was seconds ago but annoyed nonetheless.

"That's a nice change. You're not yelling."

"Sorry for fearing the wild animal outside of my window," she says defensively.

One arm flies out as she talks, and her towel slips a little bit before she catches it. My eyes snap to where it just fell a few inches. Almost giving me a full show of her perfect breasts.

Fuck me.

I'm not supposed to find her attractive, but my dick has a mind of its own as I stare at the beautiful woman standing in front of me, dripping wet. It just needs a minute to catch up to my brain that she is supposed to aggravate me.

"I'm glad you're okay," I say quickly and turn away.

As I'm about to walk out the door, something that sounds

similar to crying comes from behind me, forcing me to turn around to face her again. Except it's not tears. She's laughing.

I furrow a brow, and she notices. Only making her laugh that much harder. She holds her towel over her chest with one hand, while she bends over and rests the other on her thigh. The move causes the slit to open even more, exposing her bare side to me. If she moves even an inch, I'm going to see everything.

"A moose," she repeats again, before laughing uncontrollably.

God, her laugh is *almost* contagious. I want to laugh with her, but I can't find it in me. This whole situation after the day I've had is not amusing.

Only a true city girl would scream like this over wildlife.

"I can't believe I just overreacted to a moose in my window. It was staring at me naked in the shower. I mean, you know that's a glass shower, right?" she says, catching her breath. "It just watched me touch myself."

My jaw practically falls to the floor in shock.

What in the fuck?

This is *not* an image I wanted in my head right now.

Her hand covers her face, the towel almost slipping again. "Oh my god. Not like that. Oh my god, foot in my mouth. *Again.*"

"Again?" I tilt my head in confusion.

"Your. Uh. Sister. Poppy. She came into Batter Up. I totally thought she was your girlfriend."

My lip curls in disgust.

"You thought my sister was my girlfriend? What kind of sick shit do you think goes on in Bluestone Lakes?"

"I don't know," she groans, throwing both arms out, letting the towel completely fall to the ground.

Oh. My. God.

I should turn away. I should. I shouldn't be staring at my neighbor's bare-naked body in front of me. I know she runs, because, like an asshole, I watch her leave every morning through the kitchen window above my sink, but she has a toned body showcasing how much she does.

It's been so long since I've looked at woman the way I'm looking at her.

It doesn't help that she's constantly been on my mind, now I have to think about this to go along with it.

"Oops. Sorry about that," she says frantically, picking it up and wrapping it tight around her again. "What's one more wildlife creature seeing my tits, huh? The moose, and now you. I'm on a roll here." She fist-bumps the air.

I groan in frustration and turn away from her, adjusting the strain against the zipper of my pants the moment I do. "I'm leaving."

"For what it's worth…" She pauses, making my steps halter. "Thanks for checking on me, Angry Cowboy. I take back my statement about you being a meanie. This was very nice of you. Unnecessary, but nice."

"I wasn't having you die on my street, Blair."

Her name rolling off my tongue for the first time out loud feels different. Foreign. Good. Bad. I don't know, but I want to say it again.

"Very noble of you, sir."

And now my cock is coming back to life.

"I will make sure I keep the screaming to a minimum on Barlow Drive."

I'd prefer if you were screaming for other reasons.

Jesus Christ. I need to get out of here right now.

I open the door and step out onto the deck but stop myself with my hand still on the door handle when I look down and see the wood.

"What in the world did you do to this deck?" I ask with my back to her.

"I got into a fight with the power washer." I can hear the smile behind her words without even looking. "Don't worry, I'm removing that old deck soon and building a new one."

I nod but don't turn around and look at her again.

I can't.

I need to get the hell out of here.

I need to get the image of her in a towel *and* naked out of my head before I wake up in the morning. Or else her being my neighbor is going to be a slow, dangerous torture.

CHAPTER 16
HE'S AFRAID OF THE NEIGHBORHOOD MOOSE, TOO?

BLAIR

"You were naked?" Lily's laughter howls from the other side of the kitchen.

"Lily, it was not my finest moment."

She only laughs harder at the seriousness in my voice. "To be a fly on that wall to see Griffin's face."

I was just catching Lily up on the exciting evening I had when I met the diverse wildlife of the town. To my surprise, I learned we have a friendly neighborhood moose that occasionally wanders into my yard. You'd think Nan would have given me a heads-up about that. I make a mental note to touch base with her on that minor detail she left out.

I giggle as I mix the batter of cookie dough. "It's just hysterical to me looking back that a moose watching me shower scared me more than walking in on my husband banging his secretary in his office."

When I don't hear her laughing with me, I turn to face her.

Her face is sheet white, and I definitely just ruined the mood of the morning.

"What?" she asks, barely above a whisper.

Shit.

I tried to avoid talking to people about this. I got caught up in the moment with her and just let the words fly out of my mouth.

I sigh, knowing it had to get out at some point. "I was married before I came here. It was the reason that I moved out of the city. I was married to the mayor and learned of his infidelity when I was bringing him a batch of oatmeal cookies."

"You can't be serious? Oh my god," she says, covering her face with her hands. "You should have said something when I asked you about being married. I'm so embarrassed now."

"Don't be. I guess you can say I am trying to run from that life. I said nothing because I don't want to be known as the girl who got cheated on anymore. Ten months after my divorce, I had enough. The chatter behind my back just going to the store, and the friends who ghosted me when I was no longer his wife...it was all too much for me. Not to mention, I wasn't able to be myself anymore. I was hiding at my sister's apartment to avoid the criticism."

"Jesus. I'm so sorry that happened to you," Lily says sympathetically.

"Don't be. I'm really okay."

And none of that is a lie. Since the divorce, I've had my moments. I've still shed some tears. However, things have never been better than my life today. I'm happier and feel at peace with this new atmosphere and friends.

It's actually the first time sharing this story out loud with someone other than Kodi, and I didn't cry.

That's huge for me.

"Was the divorce recent?" she asks.

I shake my head. "It was quick, actually. I moved out the evening I found him. Taking Reginald, a few belongings, and myself to live with my sister. He didn't beg me for anything other than out penthouse we owned together. He said he would be 'politically fine without me.'"

"What a jerk."

I scoff, letting out a scoff. "Tell me about it. I haven't asked my sister for an update on him either. I don't want to know how he's doing, if he's running for office again, or hell, if he's already married to that secretary now."

"You think he will want you to take him back if he needs it? You know, for political exposure."

The thought never crossed my mind.

"I doubt it," I tell her. "He knows where my head was at when we ended. I wanted nothing to do with him. Besides, he probably has no idea I even moved out of the city."

"Good."

"It's why I'm just focusing on my life right now. I'm learning more and more about myself and how to be independent without being in a relationship. Like this is my first *real* job as an adult," I tell her.

"No way," she says shocked.

I nod. "I know that sounds really out there. A twenty-nine-year-old who's never had a real job until now. But like I've told you before, I grew up with overbearing parents. I had life handed to me on a silver platter."

"I know what you mean," Lily says. "It's why this bakery is my pride and joy."

I offer her a soft smile. "After everything I went through, I realized I never want to settle again. Not in any part of life, including a job or a relationship. If it happens again, I know I want that big, loud type of love when it comes around."

"And you deserve that, Blair. Between the story you told me the first day I met you about your parents, and now this? No one should ever have to go through that."

I nod, unsure how to respond because she's right.

"You know, you and Griffin are a lot more alike than you think."

"You mean he's afraid of the neighborhood moose too?" I joke to ease the tension forming in my gut.

She laughs lightly. "No, but his ex left him. And...I guess it's his story to reveal. I don't want to dip into my brother's laundry and share more than he's willing to tell people."

"I understand."

And I do, because I would rather hear it from him.

If he's ever willing to tell me.

I've been feeling like there's more to Griffin than meets the eye, and it intrigues me but also makes me feel bad for him in a way. I'd hate the thought of him being the way he is because of some pain from his past. I wouldn't wish that on anyone.

"The reason I think you two are a lot alike is that you each have created this rough exterior on the outside. You've both built up these walls around you..." She pauses, deep in thought. "I always knew something was up with you. Not in a bad way, no offense."

I raise my hands in the air. "None taken."

"It's just," she continues, trying to find the words, "no one just moves to a town they know nothing about. I had a feeling it was for a deeper reason."

"And how is Griffin like that?"

"I wish I had an answer for why he's the way he is," she explains nonchalantly. "I understand people handle their emotions differently, and that's absolutely fine. I once felt the overwhelming feeling of being head over heels for a man myself, only to be left here alone..." She pauses, delicately running her fingers over the tattoo on her forearm. "We all face challenging times. It only serves to strengthen us. Just look at you now," she says, beaming with pride. "You're so fun and you look so free. This new divorced life— even if I didn't know you before now—looks fucking good on you."

Her words hit me right in the chest.

While most of my life has involved others doing things for me, growing up with the life I had posed its challenges. Everything I've ever been through has truly led to where I am today.

Here in Bluestone Lakes.

"I feel free. I feel *good*." I emphasize the truth coming out. "I allowed myself to sulk after catching Theodore in the act. I wanted to rage. I wanted to fight. I almost stayed."

"What?" she gasps.

I shake my head. "I didn't know any better. I walked out of his office and called my sister to see if I could stay with her. Only to be hit with guilt for leaving."

"Oh, Blair." She sighs. "I'm so happy you didn't stay."

"I'm happy too." I nod repeatedly. "The idea even crossed my mind that I could be foolish enough to forgive him for what he did. I never can and never will."

"That's where you and Griffin are different. He processed his pain by keeping a wall up around his heart. Hell, around his life to the point he doesn't trust anyone anymore. He doesn't let anyone in and has made his entire life his bar and the ranch."

I can totally see that.

She offers me a warm smile. "I immersed myself in baking. I know that he's never coming back."

"I didn't say anything to your comment before because I don't want to bring up a sore subject, but I'm here if you want to talk about it."

She laughs. "I didn't even date the guy, Blair. I know that sounds so stupid, but we grew up to be the best of friends. He was actually more Griffin's friend than anyone else's. The day after graduation, he just left town without another word. No one has heard from him since."

"I can't even imagine. Are you seeing someone now?"

She shakes her head, letting her eyes land on her tattooed skin again. As if it holds all the answers for her. "I'm better off being on my own. I'm told I have way too much sass and work too hard. Besides, outside of this bakery, being at the ranch is my lifeline. Riding horses keeps me sane, and I would be lost without it."

"I don't see *any* issues with that. I can't believe you ride horses. That is seriously so cool."

She smiles widely. "It's the most freeing, and exhilarating

feeling in the world." She takes a step closer to me, placing a hand on my shoulder. "I'm really happy you're here, Blair. It's nice to have a good friend in town."

She has no idea how nice it is to have a good friend in town too.

"And since you're such a good friend, I'm going to let you in on my secret spot in town," she says.

I raise an eyebrow in her direction.

"Barlow Ranch," she says, nodding her head. "Okay, maybe it's not a secret spot. But it's *my* secret spot. A place I go to when I need to clear my head, allow myself to feel feelings alone, or just need to breathe."

"I saw it briefly when I drove into town but haven't been that way since. It sounds wonderful," I say.

She looks down at her watch before looking back at me with a grin on her face. "Since we're closing up here soon, why don't you head out now? If you're going to visit my spot, you need to go at just the right time to see the most perfect views."

"I can't just leave. My shift isn't over."

"I'm the boss," she says, pulling at my apron to bring it over my head. "And what I say goes." She successfully gets it off me before swatting me with it to get out of the kitchen. "Now, go."

"Fine. Fine." I hold my hands up in defense before turning to leave. But I stop myself and turn around to face her. "I'm really lucky to have met you, Lily."

"Right back at you, sister."

I haven't been toward the main entrance of town since the day I got here. It's out of the way of everything and truthfully, everything I need is in the heart of the town.

My car rolls to a stop as I see the sign come into view.

I scan the surroundings, remembering that Lily said the best spot is the far south end of the ranch. I speed up a little more until I reach the spot where the wooden fence curves at almost a ninety-degree angle. I park off to the side of the road, round the front of my car, and step up to the point in the fence.

Two horses that were standing near the edge of the fence start to make their way toward me. A stunning white horse and a deep chocolate brown one. Both are draped in what appears to be blankets. I wonder if one of these horses is Lily's.

I don't know a thing about horses to even know what it's called.

As I stand there, the sky undergoes a breathtaking transformation, shifting from a vibrant blue to a palette of pale orange and pink.

Looking up, I finally grasp what Lily was trying to convey about this spot.

The way she described it doesn't do it justice.

I inhale the smell of fresh cut grass, closing my eyes to really take it in.

I let my mind wander to every single step that led me to this moment. That led me here. A single tear escapes, and I let it fall freely as I sit here in the open with no one around.

But it's a happy tear.

Laced with the profound feeling of pride that I fucking did it.

I escaped the chains of my life to start a new one, breaking the mold that was put in place for who I was supposed to become, and let myself fall into the person I was meant to be all along. While there are still some rough edges and I feel lost at times, I don't feel the pull to remain poised and presentable every hour of the day.

I'm free.

Kodi was skeptical, and I don't blame her, I was too.

As the sun crests more over the mountain, I inhale and exhale again before leaving for my car.

The whinny of a horse in the distance causes me to turn around again.

A dark black horse gallops in the distance with someone on its back. The horse's tail sticks out straight off the back and the rider bounces almost gracefully on its back as they both move with speed across the pasture.

They finally slow in the shadows of the stable and that's when I realize the man riding the horse is Griffin.

I thought he looked good the last few times I've seen him.

Right now, even from a good distance away, he looks downright hot.

But in a burly cowboy type of way. Gone is the flannel I always see him in. This time he's wearing his signature dark wash jeans with a solid white T-shirt that looks painted on him with sweat, likely from working around the stables.

The cowboy hat on his head covers his hair, but the thick scruff of his beard is on full display.

Slowly, I watch as he dismounts the horse, carefully petting the top of its head before he presses a kiss to the side of its face. My heart leaps watching him interact with the horse and doing what he seems to love.

Is this his escape?

What really happened to him to make him the way he is?

As if he can feel my presence, his head turns in my direction. The sun hits his face at just the right angle, allowing me to see it entirely. My breath hitches in my throat, but I don't move.

He doesn't look angry for the first time since I've arrived in town.

He doesn't look like he wants to run me out of here.

He looks...like the pretty man I know is deep inside of him.

I lean forward, resting my arms on the wooden fence, but don't take my eyes off him the same way he doesn't take his off me while he wraps the reins of the horse around his wrist, tugging the horse in the direction he wants him to go.

Side by side, I watch as he walks the horse into the stable putting even more distance between us than there already was.

Only then does he turn to break the stare.

There's something about Griffin Barlow that draws me in, but I'm torn. His silence and short, clipped answers to things drives me crazy. Would he allow me in? Getting closer to him would only lead to falling for him. I know in my heart, I can't. But sometimes the heart has a mind of its own.

It falls without warning.

The last thing I want to do is fall for the angry cowboy.

CHAPTER 17

REMEMBER, WE ONLY HAVE SEVEN STOOLS.

GRIFFIN

TUCKER

What's the town buzz about a possible karaoke night?

ME

Not happening.

TUCKER

Sounds kind of fun.

ME

Not. Happening.

TUCKER

Noted.

The bell to the front door chimes.

I really hate that damn thing. I should get rid of it.

Lily, Autumn, and Blair come walking in. My eyes immediately land on Blair. She's laughing with the girls as if someone in the group had just told a joke before they entered. She has the type of laugh that can light up even the darkest of hearts.

There's something about her that always has me on edge.

A feeling that's driving me fucking insane.

Ever since I caught her watching me at the ranch from a distance, I can't get the image out of my head. I fell asleep with the vision of her whiskey eyes on me while I led Storm into the stable.

They walk toward the bar; each step she takes lulls me into a trance. Jean shorts rest high on her thighs, which isn't helping my urge to run my hands over every inch of her legs. Today, she's wearing a light brown sweater, and I'm convinced she wore it because it brings out the color of her eyes that much more.

I want to get her out of my head.

She's entirely my type if I were looking. And I'm not looking.

Shaking myself out of my daze, I turn to face Lily. "Just because your brother owns the place doesn't mean you can come here and eat for free all the time."

"Oh, Mr. Tough Guy," Lily says, "when have I ever asked for a free meal?"

"We're always paying customers," Autumn adds. "Not that I'm your sister or anything. Gross."

I turn to face Blair and she's just smiling at the interaction, forcing me to back down from the made-up fight.

"Find a booth." I gesture toward the sitting area. "I'll bring over some menus."

Rounding the bar, I grab the menus from where we keep them next to the register. Every single one flies to the floor, and I groan. Letting out a string of curse words under my breath, I before bending down to pick them up.

Seeing Blair laughing with the girls has flipped my world on its axis. Clearly.

I grab three menus and make my way to the table. When I get there, I notice it's just Lily and Autumn.

"Why do you get so flustered when she's around?" Autumn asks.

"I don't," I answer quickly.

Of all people, Lily is in my business more than Poppy is. Being that Autumn is her best friend; she goes along for the ride and knows everything that Lily does and thinks. She's not my sister, but she might as well be with how much she knows about my life and how many family dinners she's attended. I just don't need them knowing they're right at this moment.

"We know you pretty well, big brother. And you most definitely do," Lily scoffs.

Dammit.

"It's just annoying that you keep bringing her around," I lie.

"I think she gets under your skin because you have the hots for her," Autumn says.

She's always been the blunt one.

"She's my neighbor and nothing more," I affirm.

"There can always be more." Autumn winks.

"Cut it out," Lily tells her. "She's been through enough shit."

I'm taken aback by her words, and my eyes narrow at Lily.

"What do you mean by that?" I ask.

"Have there been any visitors at the ranch lately?" Lily asks with a wink, ignoring my question.

"No?"

"You know, someone just sitting on the south end of the ranch where the land ends to…watch the sunset?"

Lily is clearly nudging for information right now. Leading me to believe she sent Blair down there that evening I saw her. I knew Blair wouldn't voluntarily go to Barlow Ranch, knowing it's my name attached to it. I also know Lily frequents the ranch in the same spot to catch the sunset and get her mind off things when she isn't riding.

What she needs to find peace from…I'll never know.

Before I can ask more questions, Blair chooses that moment to come back to the table.

I don't need an answer because it will only make me want to talk to her that much more, and I don't need the small talk that comes from staying at their table. I leave them alone without another word. But I find myself glancing in their direction more and more, wondering what it is about her.

Why am I so triggered by her?

She *bought* a home here, is friends with my sister now, and works next door. The least I can do is actually be…nice.

I internally groan.

We don't need to make this a whole ordeal. I can be nice, but we don't have to be friends.

I'm not even making sense in my head.

Every time I see her, it alters my brain chemistry even more. It's like my mind and body have this pull closer to her. One that I can't control.

And I like being in control.

Perhaps it's been too long since I've felt this way about a woman—the way I feel about Blair. I want to see all of her and discover what she's concealing beneath her tough exterior. She makes me want to open up, which I never do. And most of all, I want to know what led her to Bluestone Lakes in the first place.

But can I learn to trust again?

The bell to the front door chimes again, forcing me to throw my head back in aggravation. I'm ready to rip that thing from the door frame right now.

Despite my better judgment, I look to the door, and in strolls Nan.

"I'm here to remove the pin," she says, standing tall.

"Excuse me?" confusion etched in my tone.

"Karaoke night."

I roll my eyes. "Would you give it up already?"

"Never," she says, with a fist in the air and a deep gravel in her voice. "I'm old and persistent. Besides, what if I die tomorrow?"

"You can't die tomorrow. You haven't caught up on your soaps."

"It's unbecoming how you know the status of my soaps."

"And *you're* over dramatic. You should consider medication for your psychotic behavior," I tell her.

"The only medication I take is for the headache you give me. Now, hear me out," she says, hands in the air like she's painting a picture. "Karaoke."

"You said that. So far, you're not selling me on it."

"Because you didn't let me finish, Grumpy Griffin." Nan laughs at herself.

"Continue." I wave a hand in front of me, signaling that she has the floor to speak.

I wipe the counter, not wanting to hear a minute more about an idea that could make this place packed. Because it just means I'd have to stay here longer than I want to be here.

"We make it a weekly thing," Nan starts.

"Nope."

"You can choose Thursdays or Fridays," she persists. "They're my only free nights."

"I was going to say yes, but it would have to be Tuesday," I joke, without so much as a smile.

"That would inconvenience the pickleball team because I'd have to move their day to Thursday," she groans.

My eyebrows pinch. "So then, Monday."

Her hands fly to her hips. "You know that's book club night."

"Okay?"

She throws her arms out, shaking her head. "Griffin! I can't have the town moving everything around for me."

Staring at the most persistent woman I know, my features harden. I don't want to concede and do this. Not here. Not at my bar. While more people would mean me working more, it would also mean more money into the place to keep it alive. More money I can use to stock up on better supplies and drinks.

But would Blair come?

I hate myself for caring if she would come or not, but the idea of seeing her here, drinking drinks I make for her, and laughing with her new friends is something I most definitely want to witness.

Don't ask me why.

She irritates me, remember?

"Fine," I finally say.

"Fine as in…we can do it?" Nan says, her tone full of hope.

I nod. "Under one condition." I hold up my index finger in front of her.

She shrugs. "Can't make any promises."

"You do the marketing for it. I don't have time, nor do I want any part of it. If you can drum up interest, I will stay late and help behind the bar that night."

"Yes," she cheers.

"One night!"

"You won't regret this," she sing-songs, turning to walk away. "You should already know I'll have this place packed to the brim."

That's what I'm afraid of.

"Remember, we only have seven stools!" I shout.

"You're going to need more!" she says just before exiting the bar.

I don't have time to think before my sister raises her hand from her booth.

She did not just raise her hand to beckon me over to their table.

Shaking my head, I reluctantly make my way there.

"We're ready to order." Lily smiles up at me.

They all order grilled chicken sandwiches. My eyes don't leave Blair when they each tell me what they want. Wouldn't. No matter how hard I tried to look away. I even fumbled with the menus when they handed them back to me, even though Blair said little her entire time here other than to order. This only gives Lily more ammunition to harp on me over the fact that I do indeed get flustered when she's around.

122

I've never seen someone as beautiful as her come through this town.

But her being here is driving me insane.

She annoys me equally as much as she intrigues me.

I still can't help but want to explore it more.

I'm consumed by the desire to unravel everything about her.

CHAPTER 18

YOU KNOW, JUST LEANING OVER TO SEE THE BIRDS.

BLAIR

"I really feel like the worst sister," I say, maneuvering the phone on my shoulder to adjust Reginald's leash before we continue our walk.

"What?" Kodi exclaims. "Never think that. You're just busy with your new job. Besides, I've been swamped with interior design work."

I've been following Kodi's adventures on social media and with every design project she does, it just gets better and better. She's the true definition of the more you do something, the better you get at it.

"I guess. I just feel like it's been forever since we caught up," I say.

"It's been a week." She laughs.

"Listen, I just miss you, Kodi. Okay?" I admit.

Reginald barks at the mention of her name and stops his walk to jump up and down on my leg.

"See, Reginald misses you too." I chuckle. "He stopped his walk at the mention of your name. You know how much he loves walks."

"Tell that fur ball I miss him too," she says, and I can feel the smile in her words.

Reginald spots a squirrel and forgets all about why he was just jumping up and down. We turn the corner on our street, and he practically pulls me toward our house when he sees it come into view.

I really believe he loves it here.

"You should come visit if work slows down," I say through ragged breaths, trying to keep up with my twenty-pound dog.

"I promise," Kodi draws out. "I will absolutely come visit soon."

"You know how I feel about promises," I say seriously. "You can't break them."

"I know, I know," she mutters. "A promise is a promise only if it's kept. Otherwise, it's a lie. Trust me, I always remember your words."

I smile to myself because I love how she knows me so well.

It's something I've said all my life growing up.

I've had many promises broken in my life from people who swore they would never hurt me or break them. I know with certainty that Kodi isn't one of those people. I know she will come visit when time allows, but it feels good knowing she remembers.

The problem at hand is that the biggest promise someone made to me destroyed my trust in people.

We took vows.

We said through thick and thin. In sickness and in health.

Promises broken for a sleazy lay with a secretary.

I push down the memories because this isn't the time nor the place for it.

Just as I push them down, I spot Griffin in his yard doing yard work. I practically fall over my feet when I notice he's wearing nothing but jeans, work boots, and a backward baseball cap.

Oh. My. God.

"Hello," Kodi says. "Are you still there?"

"Yes. I—uh," I stutter. "I have to go. Love you." And without another word, I hang up the phone knowing I'll explain everything to her later.

I can't help but continue to stare at the beautiful species of a man working in his yard. Suddenly, I'm sweating. And it's not like it's one hundred degrees out. It's cool enough for me to be wearing my lightweight Bluestone Lakes sweatshirt and a pair of biker shorts.

But to wear no shirt…

I hustle into the house, hoping he didn't catch me staring the last few feet of our walk. I pace my living room before trying to find a window facing his yard to watch him some more. But none of them provide me with a good enough angle.

Who the hell am I right now?

Realization dawns on me that this man stood in my tiny living room and watched me freak out over a moose in nothing but a towel—and saw me naked.

I can totally creep on him shirtless. Right?

I scan the area, looking for something that will make me look busy outside. My eyes land on a feather duster I bought at the General Store and have yet to use. This is probably the most asinine thing, but it's not like he can really see what I'm doing over here.

I make my way outside and start dusting the beaten wood on the railing as if there's actually dust on it.

This is absolutely crazy.

I look in the direction of his house, and I still myself when I watch him rip out an entire bush next to his house with his bare hands. My mouth parts, watching the way the muscles in his arm morph with each move he makes. The ridges in his back flex when the bush is out of the ground while he walks it over the area of brush he has piled to remove.

Griffin is built like a brick wall.

Once he tosses the bush into the pile, he claps his hands

126

together to remove the dust before removing his baseball cap and wipes a sheen of sweat off his forehead. He shakes the hair out of his face before replacing it right where it was.

I can't take my eyes off him as he reaches for a water bottle, throwing it back to take a long chug. I have to lean forward more just to really get a good view of this.

Why is that so hot?

I don't realize how much my body is pressing into the railing until I hear wood breaking, and I'm tumbling headfirst into the bushes skirting the bottom of the deck.

"Ahh," I squeal.

I lie on the ground, unmoving, with my hand over my face. I'm terrified I just brought attention to myself and now he's going to know I was creeping on him.

I reluctantly turn to face his house and lock eyes with Griffin.

This is absolutely mortifying.

That's when I see him move toward my house.

Shit. Shit. Shit.

I attempt to move, but a pain in my knee causes me to move slower than I want to. I find enough energy to roll over on my stomach to make it look like I'm just casually resting in the yard. I'm clearly not thinking properly right now.

Did I hit my head that hard?

"You okay over there?" Griffin asks a few feet from my house, still walking full of swagger and hotness.

"Yep. Great," I stammer, locking eyes with the grass in front of me. "Just checking out the grass. It's really fine and green. Soft too."

He comes to a stop next to me, and I fight the urge to look up at him.

Of course, my eyes betray me when they decide to turn up in his direction. They lock right on his bare chest. Painted with muscles that might as well smack me right in the face where I lie on the ground. My gaze trails down to the dips and curves of his abdomen, where I finally get a close view of how built this man really is.

I avert my gaze to his face before drool forms in the corner of my lips. He raises a questioning eyebrow, stopping right next to where I lie.

"Did your deck railing just break?" he asks.

I don't answer right away, because I can't stop watching as he takes off his baseball cap, allowing me a full view of that gorgeous hair he keeps hidden under all the hats he owns. He wipes the beads of sweat from his head using his forearm and then combs his hair back with his fingers. My mouth hangs open on its own accord as he flips the hat backward, adjusting it on his head.

"No. Yes," I admit, feeling my words stammer. "You know, just leaning over to see the birds."

Griffin looks up in the sky to scan the area.

"I don't see any birds," he says.

I look up, trying to find one single bird, but he's right. Nothing.

"I must have scared them away." I attempt to laugh. "But, hey, good thing I was planning to get rid of this deck and build a bigger one, huh?"

I'm still on the ground, because I refuse to get up.

With Griffin standing this close to me, I don't want him to witness me feeling weak or in pain. I want him to believe I can handle my shit. There's a good chance my leg is actively bleeding right now.

The adrenaline from the whole interaction is quickly wearing off, though.

I feel myself wince when I try to move, but I hide my features as best I can.

"Whatever you say," he finally says.

I look up at him one more time and notice his eyes trailing my body. Likely assessing the situation. Hopefully, if I'm actively bleeding, I've hidden it well enough by lying on my stomach.

"Be more careful," he tells me, right before turning on his heels and walking away.

I don't take my eyes off him as he retreats to his house.

My mind is swirling with this entire situation.

Did Griffin Barlow just show that he cares about me? Am I reading too much into it?

Once he's out of eyesight, I find the strength to lift myself off the ground. I look down at where the pain is slicing through my leg and see my entire lower right leg covered in blood.

Great.

I move to take a step, and the pain slices through me.

I'm not entirely sure, but I wouldn't be surprised if there's a piece of wood stuck in there.

I hobble inside and realize I don't have a single thing to help me right now. I never once thought to grab a first aid kit at the General Store when I was filling my house with supplies.

I grab a clean dish towel before turning on the water to let it run warm, knowing I'm about to ruin a solid white towel with my own blood.

The knock on the door causes me to snap my head in that direction and I spot Griffin standing on the other side of the glass with a first aid kit in his hand.

He put on a shirt too.

That's a shame.

Okay, I definitely hit my head.

I wave a hand, signaling for him to come in. Once he crosses the threshold into my home, I feel him everywhere. This house is tiny, and he's just too much man to be taking over this space. He makes it feel smaller, more confined.

His presence makes it hard to breathe all of a sudden.

"I saw your leg," he says, lifting the kit to place it on the counter next to me. "Brought you some stuff to clean it up and make sure you don't have a splinter."

"Oh, I'm fine," I say, waving him off.

He gives me a skeptical glare as if he doesn't actually believe me.

"Sit on the counter, Blair."

Lord. The way he says my name has me ready to obey his every command.

Except the moment I try to pull myself to sit on the ledge of the counter, pain slices through me. Griffin is there instantly with his hands on my waist, helping me up. My body trembles from his touch. He pulls away quickly, but the touch is now branded on my skin. The heat spreading to every part of me.

Griffin opens the case next to me. His eyes bounce between the cut on my leg and the first aid kit to see what supplies he needs. I watch his eyes with every movement. In them, I can see a man who deeply cares, even though he pretends to not.

As if he can sense me staring, he keeps his head down, lifting only his eyes to meet mine. Goose bumps pebble over my skin even though I still feel hot all over, but I brush my hands over my forearms to hide the effect he has on me right now.

He clears his throat before averting his gaze back to my leg.

His large, calloused hand rests on my opposite thigh from where the wound is, and it only makes me realize how big this man really is.

"This might sting," he warns, lifting a bottle of antiseptic.

I nod, because I can't find a word to say back, even if I tried. Because Griffin Barlow is standing so close to me, in my kitchen, with his hands on me. Him being here is turning my brain to mush. It's distracting me from the pain enough, but it's causing me to fumble any words I dare try to say out loud.

I shouldn't feel turned on by this. I shouldn't be thinking about my neighbor this way. I shouldn't want to kiss him right now.

It's not why I came to Bluestone Lakes.

I didn't come here to find a new relationship or get involved with anyone.

But the way he's so close right now sends my brain into overdrive.

He pours the antiseptic on it, and I hiss from the pain. My hands fly up to grip both of his biceps on their own accord, while I wait for the burning sensation to pass.

"I'm sorry," he says softly.

My hands release their claw-like hold on his upper arm, and our eyes meet. Stormy blue eyes bore into mine and capture all my attention.

"Are you?" I ask, the corner of my lip twisting in a half smile.

I watch his throat bob as he swallows and then nods before grabbing something from the kit and looking back down at my leg. I can't help but keep watching his face. Assessing every feature and fighting the urge to run my hands along the thick scruff on his jawline or remove his baseball cap and run my hands through the hair he keeps hidden.

"Got it," he says, lifting the tweezers in the air with a large chunk of wood between them.

My lips part in shock that he pulled that out without me even noticing. I expected to feel the pain when he did, but clearly, I was so transfixed by this man that it took away any pain I was just feeling.

"How are you feeling?" he asks me.

"Lightheaded," I answer quickly and honestly. It's not just the splinter removal that's making me feel lightheaded, it's his presence. "But okay."

He places the tweezers down next to the first aid kit before taking half a step back and resting both hands on each side of my thighs. He leans down until his face is eye level with mine. My heart pounding rapidly in my chest with each passing moment of him staring at me with uncertainty. As if he's afraid I'm going to keel over any second.

If he keeps looking at me like that, I might.

"I'm okay, Griffin," I assure him.

He clears his throat, breaking whatever the hell that just was between us before looking down at the ground and taking a step away from me. I already feel cold at the lack of his body.

I want him in my space.

I don't want him to leave.

"Are you sure you're going to be okay?" he asks.

I nod. "I'm fine. I have Reginald here to keep me company," I say, gesturing to where Reginald lies on the floor, deep in sleep and unfazed by this whole thing.

He raises a quizzical brow, looking from me to the dog.

"Don't look at him like that," I scold. "He's a good dog."

Griffin says nothing as he packs up the first aid kit he brought and heads to leave through my front door.

I stay on the counter, watching every move he makes.

He wouldn't just walk out of here without a word, would he?

There's no way what I just felt was one-sided.

"Thank you," I say to his back. "You know, for cleaning this up and helping me. You didn't have to, but I want you to know that I appreciate it."

Just as he reaches for the door handle, he turns around to face me, void of emotion per usual.

"Next time you want to watch me work in the yard, just walk over. I don't bite," he says, and then leaves without even waiting for a response.

Oh, but I think you do, Griffin Barlow.

I think you do.

CHAPTER 19

OH, MAYBE SHE'S A RUNAWAY BRIDE!

GRIFFIN

> ME
>
> U up for a task this afternoon?

TUCKER

You're getting better at texting. Who are you and what have you done with my Griffin?

> ME
>
> Are u going to answer the question?

TUCKER

Does it involve working at the bar?

> ME
>
> A construction project.

TUCKER

Sign me up.

TUCKER

Also. Asking for a friend...what do you do with all that extra time you have not spelling out the entire word: Y-O-U.

TUCKER

Do you save a lot of time only using one letter?

ME

Fuck YOU.

I'm not sure what I was thinking when I decided on this project.

I haven't slept in two nights, and I've spent every minute of sunlight at the ranch or the bar. Trying like hell to stay off Barlow Drive, and away from the temptation living next door to me.

I call Blair that because after I stupidly showed up at her house with a first aid kit, everything shifted. My brain spiraled, and thoughts I never wanted to have again in my life came back with a vengeance.

I started thinking about a relationship.

Something I swore I would never have again in my life.

When insomnia struck the first night, I found myself with my head face down, screaming into the pillow out of frustration. All because I put my hands where they don't belong.

I put my hands on *her*.

And it sparked something I had buried so deep down that it would never see the light of day again. I felt the electricity through my palm when it made contact with her bare leg, shooting through every part of me. And I didn't want to leave.

Tucker walking through the front door of the General Store forces me to stuff these thoughts back down.

"Are you in a better mood?" Tucker asks immediately.

"Who said I was in a bad mood?"

"You always are. And your profanities via text message almost had me putting on body armor for this project, just in case you try to kill me," he jokes.

"Hysterical," I deadpan.

"What in the world are we doing now? Isn't your house done?"

I don't answer him but turn around and head for the hardware side of the store. I meet with the clerk, who sets me up with slabs of pressure-treated wood. I built the deck myself years ago, so I already know it has a solid base. But I went cheap on the wood, which clearly has deteriorated over time.

Once I'm ready to head to the checkout, I scan the area and can't find Tucker anywhere.

"Tucker," I shout.

"Right here," he says, hustling to the register with an armful of snacks.

I narrow my eyes. "Are you kidding me right now?"

"What? I get hungry on the job site." He shrugs. "I got you some trail mix."

I shake my head. "I don't want trail mix."

"You will, Griff. I'm confident in knowing what your stomach needs."

I stare at him unblinkingly before looking back at the clerk behind the counter. "I guess you can add this mess to the total."

The clerk laughs before lifting the bag of seasoned pretzel twists. "Good choice here," he says to Tucker.

"Right? I can fuck up some pretzel twists," Tucker says.

I shake my head. I can't believe the one person I trust to help me finish this project before the sun sets today is the one person who loves to waste my time over snacks.

I hand the clerk cash and leave before we can engage in any more conversation.

I already know this is going to be a long day.

I didn't tell Tucker what we were doing today.

The entire ride back to my place, he kept asking questions about why I wanted to redo my deck so soon when we just did it last year. I just stayed quiet because I didn't want to explain anything going through my head. After the railing broke on Blair's deck, I hated the thought of her getting hurt again.

When I pull the truck into her driveway instead of mine, I look out of the corner of my eye and see Tucker realizing everything.

He scans the deck, the broken pieces from when she fell still scattered along the grass. Blair cleaned nothing up, and I wasn't surprised. After that wicked gash in her leg, I doubt she wanted to subject herself to another one by touching it.

"Ready to explain?" he says.

I turn to face him from the driver's seat, his arms across his chest and a shit-eating grin plastered on his face.

"Nope," I say, popping the p and exiting the truck.

"Are you building your hot neighbor a deck?" he asks, rounding the front of the truck to meet me.

"Have you met her?"

"Nope," he mocks me, popping the p the same way I did.

"Then don't fucking call her my hot neighbor," I warn him. "Do you see that broken rail over there?" I gesture to the deck.

"Yeah?"

"She fell a couple of days ago. I'm simply helping her out by fixing it for her. But also making it a little bigger since she mentioned she wants to expand it," I explain, trying my best to hide any feelings I've been fighting in my chest.

"Dang." Tucker huffs out a laugh. "If I didn't know any better, I'd say you're falling for the girl."

"Never fucking happening," I grit out quicker than I intend, pointing a finger in his direction. "And I don't want to hear it out of your mouth again."

He holds his hands up in defense. "Sore subject."

I turn on my heel and start to unload the supplies from the bed of my truck, while Tucker silently grabs the tools we need from the back seat.

For the next hour, we successfully tear off the old wooden pieces, leaving us with the concrete base I poured that's still in excellent condition. I wipe the sweat from my forehead and assess the next steps, while Tucker pops open a bag of his stupid pretzel twists.

I roll my eyes and work to set up the buzz saw for the wood, so each piece is the same length.

Once we lay down the first few pieces, I look over at Tucker, the conversation from before running through my head with each minute that passes.

"There's something about her," I say out loud.

My words cause Tucker to stop what he's doing, sit back on his heel, and waiting for me to say more.

"I think Blair's been through some shit. That's why she's here," I say.

"Maybe she's trying to start over." He shrugs before his eyes widen. "Oh, maybe she's a runaway bride! Could you imagine?" He laughs.

"You're delusional."

He scoffs. "Says the guy building his neighbor, who he barely knows, a whole ass deck."

I don't respond, because he's right.

For the first time in his life, Tucker Daniels is right.

As we get back to work, I think about what would happen if I tried to pursue something with Blair. If I tried harder to find out why the hell I'm so drawn to her as much as I am. Why I want to learn more about her and her life back in the city.

She's quirky, stubborn, and…real.

Fear creeps in, mixing with these thoughts, because what if I finally decide to open up to her, and she doesn't stay? What if I let myself fall and she goes back to wherever she came from? What if she decides the bakery isn't enough for her and she opens one up back in the city just to go home?

These are all the reasons I can't let it happen.

But, dammit, she makes me want things again.

I need to get out of my own head.

I lose track of how long we've been here when the sky morphs into an orange glow as the sun crests over the mountain. I stand back with Tucker and assess all the work we've put in for the whole day.

It's done, and it's fucking beautiful if you ask me.

"All that's left is to stain it," Tucker says, standing next to me with his hands on his hips.

"I'll find out what color she wants before we do that."

"You got it." He nods. "If you need help with that, call me. Don't text. I get bad vibes from your messages."

I scowl in his direction, ready to rebuttal when a white sports car pulls into the driveway behind my truck.

Blair jogs in our direction and her eyes widen before it quickly morphs into a scowl as she crosses her arms over her chest. "What did you do?" she hisses.

"Oh, she seems pissed," Tucker whispers next to me, before straightening his spine. "It was his idea," he defends.

"Who are you?" she asks him.

"I'm Tucker," he says, shuffling in her direction with his hand extended to her. She eyes it before taking it to return the greeting. "Unfortunately, I'm related to this guy." He hikes a thumb in my direction.

"My condolences," she says to him, but is now looking at me.

"Whoa." Tucker beams. "Even pissed off, she's got jokes. I like this one."

I keep my gaze locked on her angry eyes and refuse to laugh at this entire interaction. Not until I know she's not actually mad.

Okay, I mean…she's mad. Her body language is screaming it right now.

Tucker looks between both of us. "Well, I'm going to head up to your house and make a sandwich. I'm starving again. Those pretzel twists just weren't enough," he says, before making his way across the lawn.

Blair and I stand where he left us, still looking at each other. The tension I feel radiating off her, even from a decent distance away, is so thick that I can barely breathe right now.

"What did you do?" she asks again, this time crossing her arms over her chest.

Still mad, I see.

"I wanted to fix your railing," I say honestly.

Her arms fly out, gesturing to the deck. "This doesn't look like fixing my railing. The entire thing is new. I can fit an entire ten-piece patio furniture set on here."

"Didn't you want it bigger?" I question. "I remember you saying that. I was just helping make your life easier."

She groans. "I don't want it to be easier," she shouts, throwing her arms out before muttering *"fuck"* under her breath. She turns away from me, kicking the rocks around in the gravel driveway. "You wouldn't understand."

"So, make me understand," I say, my voice louder than I expected.

She turns to face me quickly, shocked that I even care.

Me too, Blair. Me too.

"You really want to know?"

I nod.

"My husband cheated on me."

The words leave her lips so fast that I don't have time to fully register what she just said.

Her husband?

Are they still married?

Did he fucking hurt her?

I remain silent, hoping like hell that she keeps going.

"That's why I'm here," she continues. "I want to start over. I want to find my independence again and learn who the hell I really am." She pauses, looking down at the ground. "I've spent my entire life having other people do things for me. I've always relied on my parents or my husband for things. I don't want to do that anymore. I moved sixteen hours away so that I can make something of *myself*. To get out of the city and finally be...who I'm meant to be."

My heart thunders in my chest with every word out of her mouth.

I knew she'd been through some shit, but I never expected this to be it. And I fucking hate myself for thinking about my past in this moment because that's what she did to me.

I take slow steps toward her, and every part of me wants to wrap her in my arms.

She's not my ex.

I know this with every fiber of my being.

When she refuses to look at me, I take her chin between my fingers and force her to look at me. The same electric buzz flows through my body with just one touch again.

"Regardless of trying to find your independence or not, there's no way in hell I was letting you build a deck on your own to find it."

She blinks but says nothing. Keeping her eyes locked with mine.

They burn the way they always do.

"How about this," I start, keeping my tone level, releasing my hold on her chin and stuffing my hands in my pockets to calm the fire I feel on them. "Next week, we go down to the General Store and you pick out the stain you want, and we finish it. You're in control of it."

Just like she's slowly gaining control over me.

"We?" she asks with a raised eyebrow.

I nod.

She looks from the deck and back to me, thinking about it.

"Okay," she finally agrees.

I want to smile. I want to acknowledge that her agreeing to this actually makes me happy for the first time in a while, but I can't get my head to cooperate.

I move to load the tools in the back of the truck and finish cleaning up the loose pieces of wood, tossing them into the truck's bed. Once I slam the tailgate shut, I turn around and Blair stands there, staring at her new deck, delicately running her fingers along the new railing in place.

The corner of my lip twists up, but I turn around before she catches me.

Just as I'm about to make it to the driver's side door, she stops me.

"Griffin," she shouts.

I snap my head in her direction and find her rushing at me. Next thing I know, she has her arms wrapped around my neck. Her body pressed into mine only causes every part of me to stiffen. I feel tense at this new feeling rushing through me.

"Thank you," she whispers into my neck.

I relax under her touch, wrapping my arms around her waist delicately. Not wanting to release her from my hold, but I know I need to.

"You're welcome," I choke out, releasing our hold and turning to get in my truck and leave as fast as I can.

Her words against my bare neck confirmed every desire I've had.

The feel of her body against mine just changed everything.

Even though I barely know her, I'm definitely falling for the city girl.

CHAPTER 20

SEE YOU AT 9, ANGRY COWBOY.

BLAIR

> **UNKNOWN**
> General store. 9am. Stain.

> **ME**
> Griffin?

> **UNKNOWN**
> Yes.

> **ME**
> First, how did you get my number? Second, are all of your texts always this short and abrupt?

> **GRIFFIN**
> Nan. Yes.

> **ME**
> Great. See you at 9, angry cowboy.

"You're kidding!" Kodi practically shrieks through the phone.

I laugh. "I wish I was. Angry Cowboy actually built me a whole deck. And I'm not going to lie, it's a *really* nice one too."

"What a turn of events." She emphasizes each word. "And hold on, is he *actually* a cowboy?"

"Truthfully...I don't even know," I say with a chuckle in my voice. "But he has this look about him that definitely screams cowboy. It's like he showers and tosses some dirt on his jeans or something to finish the look."

"I thought he owned the bar in town?"

"He does. I don't think Bluestone Lakes has cattle and shit. Or whatever you call those creatures on ranches that they herd and stuff. But he rides horses and *definitely* looks good in a cowboy hat."

"I'm glad you're finally admitting it out loud." Kodi beams, likely nodding her head in approval.

"And...I told him about Theodore."

Kodi gasps on the other end of the line.

"I was mad at first about the deck because I didn't want to rely on a man to help me with anything unless I asked. Once I got over myself, I was like, *this is actually nice*, and I thanked him." I pause, seeing if she will say anything more. "With a hug."

"Blair!" she shouts my name so loud I have to pull the phone away from my ear. "You hugged the grumpy neighbor?"

"I know, I know." I find myself pacing my living room telling her the story. "It just happened. And it felt so weird."

"Like a good weird, or a bad weird?"

I stop pacing. "Kodi, the man was stiff as a board, like he hadn't been hugged ever in his life. But it was a good kind of weird. He felt good." I sigh. "Griffin is *all man*. Rugged and broad and it was... He felt strong."

"Ha! There you go. Someone to fulfill your *needs*," she coos.

"Not everything needs to be about sex."

"But it helps." She laughs, and I just roll my eyes even though she can't see me.

"This is a really small town. The last thing I want to do is ruin my reputation around here," I say.

"Ohhh, big reputation."

"Now's not the time for jokes," I warn her.

Don't get me wrong, I've thought about it.

For an entire week.

I played every scenario in my head and the consequences of falling for my neighbor. The list of reasons I want to get to know him more, be around him, and just talk to him was long. Only the short list of reasons I shouldn't that holds me back.

The biggest being my fear of heartbreak again.

Because of what I went through, I now just assume all men are the same.

I conjured up a whole fake scene in my head of me dating Griffin. He would kiss me goodbye in the morning before going off to ride his horse at the ranch. He didn't come home before going right to the bar. He then called me to tell me he was going right back to the ranch. Only for me to head there to the spot Lily told me was her favorite to watch the sunset and find him with someone who works on the ranch, riding him like a horse in one of the stalls.

The scene is so irrational and out there.

But seeing something as horrific as I did with my own two eyes has ruined me. I cried myself to sleep a few nights ago with the thought that I may never be able to love again. That I may never be able to open myself up completely to allow someone, even the *chance* to hurt me.

Dammit. I want to, though.

I crave that big, loud love.

"Fine." Kodi's voice shuts down my runaway brain. "But I think you should just let him help you. You can work on growing your independence while still accepting help. Isn't that a part of it?"

I release a long exhale. "I guess you're right."

"I know," she scoffs. "I always am."

"Whatever." I laugh at her antics. "I have to go. I'll text you later. Love you."

"Love you big," she says just before hanging up the phone.

I check the clock on the stove and realize Griffin should be here any minute now, and I'm still in my sleep set. Opening the front door, I assess the weather for the day. You know how you stick an arm out to feel the temperature to decide your outfit choice? Yeah, it's the only way to do it around here.

Shuffling through my closet, I find a pair of biker shorts and settle on an old, oversized T-shirt since I know we'll be staining the deck today. Not that I'm even sure how *staining* a deck works. It's got to be the same thing as painting, right?

I hustle into the bathroom and quickly throw my hair up in a half bun and let the rest fall in its natural waves to keep it out of my face for this project. Just as I throw the last bobby pin into the small bun, I hear a knock at the door that startles me and spikes a nervous energy through me.

I'm spending the day with Griffin.

He's staying here to help me finish the deck.

It's just strange, considering when I first got here, I thought he couldn't stand me. I swear he was avoiding me for so long by spending his mornings leaving the house, working during the day, and then still not coming home until the late hours of the night.

Uh, yeah. I'm embarrassed by how much I watched him.

Finally answering the door, I'm greeted with the unfazed face he always wears, paired with his signature flannel rolled up at the sleeves. I feel warmth spread through my body instantly because he makes flannels look so damn good. I almost want to tell him to never roll the sleeves down.

But what really makes the whole ensemble is the dark brown cowboy hat that only brings out the deep blues of his eyes. A combination I could find myself lost in if I'm not careful.

I clear my throat, breaking myself from the trance he's put me in already. "Morning."

"Good morning," he replies with a nod. "Ready to stain this thing?"

My hand flies to my chest, and I gasp. "Did Griffin Barlow just say more than one word? *In a row?* I feel blessed, and it's only nine in the morning."

I swear I see the corner of his lip faintly twist in a grin, but it's hard to confirm because I've yet to see the man actually smile with anyone. Not with his sister when I spotted him at the General Store and not the times I've gone to Seven Stools with Lily for lunch.

"Let's go pick out a color for this deck," he says, looking down at the wood.

"I'm ready," I say, grabbing my cross-shoulder purse and bending down to pet my dog's head. "Reginald, be a good boy. You can't come with me today, so stay here."

Reginald barks in response.

"You take him everywhere with you?" Griffin asks from just outside the front door.

I smile in his direction while still petting Reginald's head, and I nod. "He's really not as bad as you think."

Griffin looks from me to the dog before looking back at me.

"You want to bring him with us?"

I stand up, mouth open in shock that he's even offering when it seems like he can't stand dogs. Lily has mentioned it and the way he demanded Reginald stay off his property told me every-thing I needed to know.

"You…want me to bring him? Like, in your truck? And to the store with us?" I rattle off the questions while my heart thrums in my chest.

He gives me a curt nod.

Without reading too much into it, I reach for Reginald's leash, and he barks in response.

"You want to go for a drive, buddy?" I ask my dog, using my best puppy voice.

That earns me another bark and a rapid wag of his tail before he jumps up on my leg and starts spinning in circles in excitement.

A laugh bubbles from my chest. "Okay. Okay. But you have to be an extra good boy."

Reginald sits and opens his mouth, sticking his tongue out and panting in response before I hook the leash up to his collar and guide him out the door.

Once in the truck, Griffin's manly scent envelops me, and I feel dazed and lightheaded at the wild turn of events. Mostly because I never expected this man to do any of this. Not only offering to help me but being so welcoming to allow my dog to come with us for this mini adventure.

If that's what you want to call it.

Reginald sits up tall on my lap, resting his paws on the armrest of the door, looking at the views out the window. Griffin surprises me yet again when he rolls the window down for him. Mostly because I'm shocked this ancient truck even has power windows.

His tail wags a mile a minute, and his little ears fall back from the wind in his face. I can't help the laughter that I allow to come to the surface despite feeling nervous in Griffin's space.

I look over at Griffin, who has one hand on the wheel and the other resting on the gear stick. His head snaps straight ahead as if I just caught him staring at me and he didn't want me to notice.

Little does he know, I notice a lot about the man in the driver's seat.

He isn't who I thought he was.

I regret silently wishing to myself that someone would put marbles in his gas tank. I know it does nothing, but he would have had to spend thousands of dollars trying to fix the problem.

I never said that aloud to anyone, but I definitely wished it after he scolded me for Reginald pissing on his rosebush.

And now here we are, both me and the dog that I thought couldn't stand, sitting in *his* truck.

I finally stop staring at him and bring my gaze back to the view outside. But my heart rate refuses to settle, and neither do the butterflies in my stomach that warn me I could fall for this man.

The trip to General Store was filled with a strange, awkward energy. Almost everyone we saw greeted Griffin. I couldn't shake the feeling that all eyes were on me during our brief trip. The fear of being judged by the townspeople, of them thinking I'm just a city girl trying to lasso a cowboy, sent my nerves into overdrive. I was thankful Reginald was with me because something about the presence of him keeps me calm.

These are irrational thoughts, but something I can't help but wonder.

I settle on a dark gray stain that I feel would perfectly contrast the shade of blue on the outside of the house. To my surprise, Griffin agreed with me. But now that we're back at the house, and prepping what we need to start the project, he's back to being the quiet man I knew before.

"You're going to want to test a small area first," Griffin finally says after getting everything set up for me. "And then you start with the railings and vertical surfaces before doing the base of the deck."

"Me?"

He nods.

I stare at him for a few heartbeats and realize he's letting *me* take control of this. He wants *me* to do it.

Because he knows.

He knows, even from our brief interaction, how much doing this project means to me even if it is absolutely insane.

I look away from him, down to where he has the can of stain open with the supplies next to it. I feel overwhelmed and extremely out of place. A part of me even feels stupid because I know I'm way over my head thinking I could have done this on my own.

"Can you...show me?" I ask hesitantly.

"Yes," he says, moving quickly to where everything is set out on the grass for me. "First, you need to put these on." He hands me a pair of gloves and I put them on the same time he puts his on. "This is a bristle brush," he tells me, lifting a wide-looking brush in my direction.

I crouch down next to him and take it from his hands, our fingertips brushing when I do, and I suck in a quiet breath, hoping he didn't notice how the small touch affected me.

I swallow, holding it up and dipping it into the can without further instruction.

"See. You got it," he praises. "Make sure you brush it along the side of the can so you don't have too much stain on the brush."

I nod, brushing it against the can before bringing it to the railing of the deck closest to the house for the test spot.

"Like this?" I ask him, moving the brush in languid strokes against the wood.

"Go with the grain," he says.

I look up at him before looking back down where I have the brush against the wood. "I don't know what that means," I admit.

Griffin takes a few steps toward me until his body crowds every part of mine. I lift the brush to hand it to him, but he shakes his head.

"I'm going to teach you," he says, his voice deep and gravelly, forcing my insides to do a full somersault.

His body is so close to being pressed against my back that if one gust of wind blew into me, it would push me against him. His large palm moves to cover my hand wrapped around the brush handle and his other cages me in, resting against the railing.

"See these small lines in the wood, the ones that travel

through it?" he asks, and I nod in response. "That's the grain of the wood. You want to stain in the same direction as those lines."

"Okay," I breathe out, unable to even control what's happening in my head right now, let alone say more words than that.

His fingertips apply light pressure against mine as he moves the brush with me in the direction of the lines. I can barely register what we're doing because the only thing I can think of is how good it feels to be doing this with Griffin.

How good his hand feels around mine.

Everything that's led to this moment only confirms the idea of *something* with him swirling in my head. He's shown me that behind that rugged exterior, he cares.

He ran to my house in the rain when he thought something was killing me, when it was really just a moose.

He came back to my house after I fell off my deck, tending to my knee when I didn't even realize I needed it.

And he built me this entire deck.

As we move farther down the deck rail, a rock catches on my sneaker and I lose my footing, forcing my back to collide with his chest. My breath hitches as I feel his every muscle against me, his arms preventing my fall. My body freezes in his small embrace, and I turn my head to meet his gaze. I'm taken aback by the intensity of his gaze, a kaleidoscope of blues that seems to pierce through me. He looks down at my lips, then back up, holding my attention.

Is he going to kiss me?

Does he want to kiss me?

Do I want him *to kiss me?*

Yes. I want all of it. I want to know what it would feel like kissing Griffin Barlow in the worst way possible.

His throat bobs before he lifts my body to a full standing position, averting his gaze to the deck. When he steps away from me completely, I feel cold and embarrassed for even thinking he wanted to kiss me.

"This color is going to look good on this," he says, refusing to look at me.

"It is," I say, pushing down my flustered thoughts.

I move to pick up the second bristle brush and get to work on some of the vertical pieces of the deck while he moves to work on another area of the deck, putting distance between us.

The faster this project is done, the faster I can get inside and away from this intense feeling of being around him.

I'm not sure what I was thinking.

CHAPTER 21
ARE YOU ASKING ME ON A DATE, GRIFFIN BARLOW?

GRIFFIN

What the hell was I thinking?

For the past two hours, I've been wrestling with the idea of leaving Blair to finish the deck on her own.

Like a fucking coward.

Because I've allowed myself to get too close to the woman and skip out on work this afternoon—which I never do—to do this with her. I've allowed myself to feel something I didn't want to feel with her. That I wish I *never* felt.

My pulse has been in overdrive since coming back from the General Store. It didn't help that I decided to show her by pressing my body against hers, keeping her hand in mine as I showed her stroke for stroke how to properly stain the deck before she tripped on a rock and fell right into my arms.

The urge to kiss her was overwhelming.

Right then and there, I wanted to lean in and claim her lips.

And because I'm so fucked up in the head, I only thought about how kissing her would open me up to the potential heartbreak when she decides that Bluestone Lakes isn't where she wants to spend her life. Nan claims she's here for good, but none of us know that for sure.

I haven't run off to my house because I don't want to.

Ask me to understand the turmoil in my brain and I won't have an answer, because *she* is my turmoil now.

Every laugh.

Every light touch.

Every word she speaks.

I can't stay away from her, even if my brain tells me I should.

Just as I finish up the last board of the horizontal base, I look up and see Blair standing in the grass. She has her hands on her hips with stain splattered on her oversized T-shirt. Her eyes scan the entire deck as if she's assessing the work we've put in today.

It's not the way she's standing that sends chills up my spine.

It's the smile on her face.

It's vibrant and full of life, even after everything she's been through. I don't know enough to know when her life changed or when her husband cheated on her. She wears a contagious smile that has me ready to mimic it for the first time in years.

She turns to look at me as if she can sense me staring.

"We did good," she says, the smile growing wider.

I swallow past the lump in my throat and give her a nod. "*You* did good," I tell her. "You did most of the work here. I just simply showed up as an assistant."

A laugh bubbles out of her as she looks to the ground, shaking her head before walking in my direction. Those same chills race through every part of me. I'm not so sure I can hold off and not touch her if she gets too close to me again.

"Can I offer my *assistant* something to drink, then?"

Looking from her to the house and back to her. "It's going to be hard to get inside as it needs a little longer to dry since we started closer to the house. It shouldn't be long, though."

"Right." She giggles. "Guess I forgot about that little tidbit."

I feel my lips twist into a lopsided grin as I follow her. Thankful she can't see me right now to know the effect she has on me. I'd like to keep up my reputation as the grump in town.

Simply to keep anyone from talking to me longer than I want them to.

"Rain check," she says as she takes a seat in one of the porch chairs sitting on the grass.

Without thinking, I take the vacant seat next to her.

I should really just go home.

My work here is done.

"Have you ever been told you can't do something, and it only makes you want to do that something even more?" she asks.

"Huh?"

She stares at her home as if the answer to all life's questions is inside.

"Peach iced tea," she says.

"I'm still not understanding."

She laughs before turning to face me again. "The deck is wet, and all I can think about now is how the peach iced tea I mixed up earlier this morning is sitting in my fridge waiting to be consumed. It's truly the superior flavor of iced teas. Something about the peach flavor, and the coldness, and…okay, I'm talking way too much and making no sense. Maybe the fumes from the stain are getting to me."

I shake my head, a grin forming on my lips without even thinking.

Leaning forward in her chair with her lips parted. Gone is the contagious smile I've seen since she was standing outside admiring the work we've put in.

"What? Do I have something on my face?"

"Yeah…" She pauses as if she's trying to collect her thoughts. "A…you have a smile."

Yeah, because of you, Blair. Because of you.

"It was the peach iced tea ramble." I shrug.

"I think I might have to ramble about it more often, then." She laughs.

And there it is again.

If she keeps doing that, laughing the most perfect laugh I've ever heard, I might just have to wrap her in my arms and take her home and—

"Have dinner with me tonight?" I ask, the words flying out of my mouth without even a second thought.

What am I doing?

She stares at me, unblinking.

"My place," I add.

The words are flying out of my mouth on their own accord at this point.

She leans back in the seat, her eyes stay fixed on mine, but an eyebrow raises in question.

"Are you asking me on a date, Griffin Barlow?"

I narrow my eyes and instantly regret it the moment her eyes widen, and her hand comes up to cover her face.

"I—Uh—I'm sorry. That just came out of me." She trembles over her words. "I didn't mean it like that. Uh—*Shit.*" She says the last words under her breath, turning away from me so I don't see the embarrassment.

It's not that I react the way I do because of what she asked me, more so because I can't remember the last time I've even been on a date. I swore off women and anything that would remotely open me up to that type of life a long time ago.

"I figured since you don't have any food in your house..." I say.

She turns back around to look at me, but this time there's more hope in her eyes.

"Also, I'm a mean cook," I add.

Thank fuck, the smile is back. I feel like I'm getting to the point of needing to see that smile on her face at all times. I can't *not* see it. It's becoming the sole thing that's bringing me joy lately.

"I'd expect nothing less, Angry Cowboy."

Blair is in my house.

Not only is she in my personal space, but her scent is taking over every square inch of my spacious kitchen. Overpowering the smell of chicken parmesan in the oven.

It's not a meal I love to make. I'd prefer steak and potatoes over this. But I wasn't sure what she would want, and I felt too nervous to even ask. I'm not sure how I went from being annoyed by her presence in this town to being nervous about having her in my home.

The oven timer dings and I wish like hell I could get the smell of some kind of flower I can't pinpoint, mixed with honey, out of my nose. It's a wild combo, but it fits her.

It's a consuming scent that I'm getting lost in.

"Your house is really nice," she says, breaking the silence stretching between us.

I pull the baking dish from the oven and place it on the hot plate in the center of the island separating us. "Thank you. I built it myself."

Her eyes widen. "You're joking."

A smirk plays on my lips, unable to control the urge to smile any longer. "I wish I was. I have the chronic back pain to prove it."

"That's…impressive." She nods repeatedly.

"Thank you," I say, before passing her a plate. "Did you want to eat here? On the table? Outside?" I rattle off the options in nervous succession because I want to make her comfortable.

I want her to enjoy the company and the time here.

I just don't know how to act around her.

"Outside?" She raises a brow with her suggestion.

I nod, grabbing the plates, and try to juggle everything to bring it outside.

Her hand reaches for my forearm, and I freeze, snapping my head in her direction. Our eyes lock and I feel like time stands still.

"Let me help," she says in a calming tone.

I hope she isn't picking up on my nerves here. I'm probably ruining this entire thing.

She grabs the plates from my hand before picking up napkins and utensils, and I grab the dish of chicken parmesan with pasta.

Once she steps on the porch, I remember I don't actually have a table back here on the covered porch. It's just me, and I never have guests here unless they are uninvited ones like Nan or my sisters.

"Do the rocking chairs work?" I choke out, my voice thick with nerves.

"Oh my god, yes." She beams with a giggle. She places the plates down on the oversized side table I have sitting between the two chairs. "Something about rocking chairs...they are so therapeutic."

She takes a seat as I place the trivet down and the dish from the oven on top. Her head falls back as she rocks back and forth on the chair.

Her comfort eases my nerves.

She has her eyes closed and rocks back and forth slowly as if she's taking in the moment the same way I am staring at her.

She's truly so captivating.

She might have gotten on my nerves when she first arrived, but this right here is a nice reminder why I shouldn't judge people before I get to know them. While my nervous system is still in overdrive because the last thing I want is to fall for her when I don't know what her plans for the future are, I can't help but *want* to enjoy this time with her.

Would it be so bad if I let someone in?

Let someone see the parts of me I keep hidden from the world?

She breaks herself out of her trance when a loud rumble

comes from her stomach. She clutches it with wide eyes and her head snaps in my direction.

"Guess I'm hungrier than I thought." She laughs.

I'm a goner if she keeps laughing like that.

"Dig in," I tell her, gesturing to dinner as I take a seat in the other rocking chair.

She makes herself a plate before I do and we both sit in silence, with nothing but the sound of utensils hitting the plate, eating dinner, and enjoying each other's company.

I want to ask her about her life in the city and learn everything about her.

What city did she even come from?

Is she divorced or still married?

"So, you own a bar in town, you ride horses into the sunset, you built this house with your bare hands, *and* you can cook a mean chicken parmesan." Blair chuckles. "Any more surprises for me?"

Tilting my head in her direction, I smile. A full-on smile at her, and the way her face morphs tells me even she's shocked, but she masks her features quickly.

"Ride horses into the sunset, huh?"

"That's all you heard from all of that?" she asks.

I shrug. "I didn't realize you've been watching me enough to know I've been riding off into the sunset on my horse."

She scoffs. "I don't watch you."

I raise an eyebrow in her direction, shifting in my chair to lean in her direction. The smallest move just created the biggest energy shift. There's still a table between us, but I've seemed to lean into her space *just enough* that I can smell her all over again.

Flowers and fucking honey.

Honeysuckle. That's what she smells like.

"Need I remind you; I rescued you when you fell over your deck watching me?"

Her lips part for just a moment, and she locks eyes with mine. She zips her lips shut quickly, looking from my lips back to my eyes. A shiver racks my body at the idea of her lips on mine. Feeling those soft, pink lips, and tasting the air she breathes.

I'm losing all control.

"And I've seen you at the ranch," I add.

"I—Uh," she stutters, fidgeting with her hands. "I didn't go there for you. Promise. Lily recommended that spot to me to just get away and feel some quiet peace for a little bit."

I nod, keeping my focus on her face. I can't look away even if I tried.

"I get that," I tell her honestly. "That's why I ride."

"Yeah?"

"Yeah." I sigh, adjusting myself in my seat so I'm leaning back, resting my head against the chair to lightly rock back and forth. "Seems like we've both been through some shit."

She remains silent and I can't tell if it's because she doesn't want to pry into my personal life, or she's waiting for me to continue. I close my eyes, inhaling the crisp air of the night before releasing it.

"I was in love once," I say.

I hear a gasp come from her direction, but I don't turn to look at her.

I want her to know this part of me.

I want her to know why I've become the *angry cowboy* she likes to call me.

"It was the first and last time I've ever loved a woman," I continue. "We had a future planned out. I built this house for her. We were going to spend our life together." I pause, swallowing past the anger and emotion stuck in my throat. "And now she's gone. She apparently had this dream that she never told me about—of living in the city and becoming a writer for some fashion magazine. In my head, I thought she could do it from anywhere. It's writing, for crying out loud, but she was determined to move." I shake my head at the thought because it still pisses me off. "She asked me to go with her, but I was just opening the bar. I wasn't ready to give up my small town life here for the high rises and traffic jams. Well, she left the next day as if our relationship meant nothing to her. As if...I meant nothing to her."

"I'm so sorry you went through that," she says on an exhale. "You didn't need to tell me all of that."

"Don't be sorry, and yes, I did," I say, turning my head to look in her direction. "I guess I needed you to know why I'm the way I am. Why I can't stand the city, and why I hated you when you first got here."

Her hand flies to her chest and she gasps. "You hated me?" she asks before her shocked face turns into a smile.

I offer her a lopsided grin, because that was cute.

"In all seriousness, I appreciate you telling me all of this," she continues. "Seems like we both have terrible people in our past."

The way she just put her husband—or ex-husband or whoever he is to her—in her past causes my heart to race in my chest.

Is she *really* here for good?

Is that what that all means?

I can't even find the words to reply to her, but Reginald barking in the distance snaps Blair out of this bubble we've created.

"I should probably head back and let him out." She stands from the chair, picking up her plate.

I stand quickly to take it from her. "I got this."

"Are you sure?"

I nod before gesturing over my shoulder toward her house. "Go let Reginald out."

Her face lights up with a warm smile before she takes a few steps toward me, stopping only inches from me, which forces her head to tilt up to keep eye contact with me.

"Thank you for dinner," she says.

I swallow, letting my gaze travel from her eyes to her plush lips.

Would it be so bad if I kissed her right now?

She shocks me when she wraps her arms around my waist while the side of her face presses into my chest. I suck in a breath and still my body just before I wrap my arms around her neck. Holding her into me as if I don't want to let her go. She doesn't move to leave either. I swear we stand there, holding each other for hours when in reality, it's only been a minute.

I rest my chin on the top of her head.

"You're really not such an Angry Cowboy, are you?" she asks against my shirt.

"Not anymore."

And it's got everything to do with her.

CHAPTER 22
HOW GOOD DOES BLAIR LOOK TONIGHT?

GRIFFIN

> **LILY**
> Are we invited to the party tonight?

> **ME**
> Not a party.

> **LILY**
> Karaoke night. Party. Same shit.

> **ME**
> It's not my event.

> **LILY**
> That's what I thought you would say. See you soon, brother.

> **POPPY**
> I'll be there tonight guys!

> **LILY**
> ALERT THE MEDIA. POPPY IS COMING OUT.

> **ME**
> Are we done here?

I can't believe I agreed to do this karaoke night knowing how much I hate the evening crowd around here. But this makes Nan happy.

Come to think of it, I don't think she's ever been happier.

Okay, that's a stretch.

I think she's happier at pickleball on Tuesday nights.

Nan has the place decorated from top to bottom. I'm pretty sure she put confetti poppers and mini strobe lights in the fucking bathrooms too. The karaoke machine sits in the corner with a full projector screen to display the lyrics and a small table for people to sign up. I have no idea where she got all of this stuff, but I've got to give it to her, she did a great job putting this together.

The bell for the front door chimes and I already know that's going to piss me off all night.

In walks a man I've never seen before. He's wearing dress slacks and an ivory-colored button-down shirt. He looks all business, which tells me he's definitely not from here or a regular. Looking down at his watch, he moves to take an empty seat at a high-top table along the back wall.

The bell chimes again, and Tucker walks in followed by Levi.

I snap my fingers before pointing in his direction. "Tucker."

He stops mid-step, throwing his hands up in defense. "I didn't do it. Whatever it is, I didn't do it."

I shake my head. "I didn't say you did anything. But can you, please, for the love of God, unwire that fucking bell over the front door before I lose my shit."

He turns to look at where the bell sits before looking back at me. "You mean this is what's going to piss you off? How is that different from any other thing in life that makes you lose your shit?"

"Don't start."

He chuckles before heading into the back to grab the small ladder to reach the wire. Tucker has it disconnected in a matter of seconds before putting the ladder back and taking his place behind the bar with me.

"I still can't believe you agreed to do this," Tucker says.

"Same," Levi says from the other side of the bar, sipping water.

"Tell me about it, but Nan sure knows how to plan things, though," I tell them.

Tucker moves to set up the bar and pulls the glasses I just washed out of the dishwasher rack to display them on the counter behind us. "What are you serving tonight?" he asks me.

"The usual." I shrug. "But I pulled out some Foxx Bourbon I had stashed in the back and some top-shelf whiskey."

Tucker gasps. "Are you feeling okay?"

I scowl in his direction just as the loud piercing sound of a speaker forces me to wince.

"Sorry, y'all," Nan shouts.

I look in her direction and find her setting up the machine. I drop the dish rag in my hands and make my way to her.

"Need any help?" I ask her.

She shakes her head. "I don't know shit about these wires and where they go, but I saw some videos online, so I'm good."

I narrow my eyes. "Is the bar going to blow up?"

"Maybe." She shrugs.

"Great," I mutter under my breath before turning to leave her to do her thing.

Just as I turn, I see my sisters walking through the door. I look past them, hoping Blair came with them. No one said for sure if she was coming and I didn't have the guts to text her myself and ask.

Knowing Lily, she probably made her come out.

It's so good to see both my sisters together. I feel like it doesn't happen often because each of them has their own personalities that often clash. Lily is the happy and outspoken one, with occasional sass mixed in. And then Poppy is just the opposite. She's innocent and a rule follower. She loves her job, teaching and working with kids. It's her entire life and personality. She never gets out much for fear of being judged as a teacher in a bar, but she's working on becoming more social.

I continue making my way to the bar and Tucker must spot the girls too.

"My favorite cousins!" Tucker beams.

"We're your only cousins, Tuck." Lily rolls her eyes.

"Which makes you my favorites, duh." Tucker looks around. "Where's your new friend?"

My chest tightens at Tucker asking the question I was afraid to ask, but I step closer to him, acting like I'm wiping the counter to make sure I can hear their response.

Lily turns to look at me, a wicked grin crossing her lips. "She'll be here."

"Why are you looking at him like that?" Poppy asks.

"No reason," Lily brushes her question off.

Poppy's gaze bounces between me and Lily. "No. No. I need to know. What have I been missing?"

"Lily is waiting for Griffin to get his head out of his ass and realize he's got a thing for the new girl in town," Autumn chimes in as she makes her way for the girls.

Poppy gasps. "No way."

I shake my head. "It's not fucking happening. So drop it."

Just as the words leave my lips, I feel a pull to look toward the front door. The way goosebumps pebble my skin tells me exactly what's about to happen. I quite literally *feel* her before I see her.

Holy. Shit.

Blair looks like a goddamn smoke show tonight. It's the first time I've ever seen her looking like she fits in here.

Looking so…country.

Looking like she could stay here.

She's wearing a dress that reaches the floor, but it's not overly fancy. It's pink with deep pink and red flowers etched through the fabric. As I continue scanning her from bottom to top, my eyes land on the swell of her breasts. It's a strapless dress, show-casing her perfectly tanned skin that I'd love to trail my fingers over.

I feel all the blood rush to my cock the longer I stare at her. The part of the outfit that's making me feel a primal need to claim her is the black cowgirl boots peeking out under the hem of the dress that matches her black rhinestone-studded cowgirl hat.

I'd love to see her in nothing *but* those boots and that hat.

I can't help that she looks so fucking good right now. To the point it's painful to keep staring at her.

I shouldn't be looking at her like this.

I can't allow myself to go there with her.

I clench my jaw and look in Tucker's direction. Only to find his face laced with satisfaction that he was right about her the day we built the deck. That there's something there with her.

I throw him the middle finger and place the last of the glasses on the counter behind us.

I'm here to work.

An hour later, Seven Stools is the busiest I've seen in years.

All the stools we have are occupied—which isn't saying much. I mean, there's only seven.

The entire town came out tonight for this event. Including my father and some out-of-towners I don't recognize, who must be staying at the Inn and heard about this event.

I'm impressed with what Nan has put together.

The singers tonight are questionable, but everyone's having fun.

"Griff, this place is packed," Tucker shouts over the music

and chatter of people talking. "Looks like you'll be keeping this on the schedule, huh?"

I groan, rolling my eyes.

"And, looks like City Chic finally fits in." Tucker smirks.

"Call her by her name," I scold, pointing a finger in his direction. "It's Blair."

Tucker holds his hands up in defense. "Oh, sensitive subject. But after seeing her tonight, I definitely need to stop calling her that." He turns to look at her.

"Don't you dare look in her direction," I warn.

Tucker chuckles. "I love possessive Griffin. You've gone from Grumpy Griffin to Give-me-her Griffin. Wait, no…" He pauses, hand to his chin. "That's too many syllables."

I stare at him, unblinking. "Something is wrong with you."

"Hey, Tuck," Poppy interrupts, coming to the bar.

"Ahh, my favorite cousin," Tucker says, leaning his elbows on the bar.

"I heard that," Lily says from Poppy's side. "And it's such a shame, because you *were* my favorite cousin."

"I'm your only cousin, Lil." Tucker laughs.

Lily sways side to side with the beat of the music, not responding to Tucker, and takes a sip of her vodka and cranberry. "This is epic, Griffy."

Well, she's drunk.

"You're cut off," I tell her.

"I drink to dull the pain." She emphasizes with the back of her hand on her forehead in dramatic fashion.

Poppy rolls her eyes at her but laughs.

She acts like she has a long-lost love out there somewhere. It's wild to me.

"How good does Blair look tonight?" Lily winks at me before turning to face Blair, watching the singers and dancing in the middle of the room. "I think she's succeeded in her mission tonight."

"What was that?" Poppy asks.

"She's trying to find herself," Lily says, still looking at Blair and smiling before turning back to face us. "You guys know her parents were a lot like ours, but less cool."

I cock my head to the side.

"They were politicians," she continues. "But, like, big city ones."

"You don't say," Tucker jokes.

"Shut up." Lily leans on the bar and smacks the side of Tucker's head. "All she's ever known is people hovering over her, telling her what to do and how to dress. Her life was black and white, and she was never able to just be herself. And look at her," Lily says, and all of us turn to face her.

Nan stands next to her, both of them laughing hysterically before she grabs Nan's hand and does a twirl with her before they rock side to side with the music again.

She never stops laughing.

She never stops smiling.

If Lily hadn't told me that, or Blair hadn't told me a little about her life back in the city, I would never believe the shit she's been through.

Right now, she lights up the dark bar.

And it's not just the vibrant colors of her outfit.

My eyes trail her body, the same way I did when she first walked in. Her hips sway and I want my hands on them more than my next breath. I want my hands on every single part of exposed skin I see.

I'm suddenly finding it difficult to catch a breath, because *she* has taken it from me.

Staring at her right now…

Blair fucking looks like *mine*.

CHAPTER 23
THIS WOULD PROBABLY TASTE WAY BETTER ON YOU.

BLAIR

"Are you gonna sing a song?" Nan asks me while we dance.

I shake my head. "Oh no. I don't need to embarrass myself."

She waves a hand. "Nonsense. You can't embarrass yourself here, girl. This is a place for us to be ourselves. Fun and full of life," she says with her hands in the air as she closes her eyes and moves with the music.

This woman never ceases to surprise me.

She slows her dancing. "I'm goin' up there. What should I sing?" she asks me.

My eyes widen. "Oh, I am not good at picking out songs."

"Noted." She nods. "I'll just close my eyes and let these little fingers land on something. How fun does that sound?" she asks, full of mischief before leaving me to head to the table to put her song in.

Next thing I know, Lily is swaying her hips into mine from my side with a drunk smile on her face. "I love watching you have the time of your life, babe."

She continues dancing next to me, my smile matching hers.

I'm so glad she convinced me to come out tonight. I wasn't sure if I was going to come after having dinner last week with

Griffin. It's not that I didn't enjoy myself, it was because the tension I felt walking back to my place followed me until I climbed into bed.

I hugged him goodbye.

My body moved on its own and I stayed there longer than I intended to. Only for him to return the hug and hold on as long as I did.

It made me want to look up into his eyes.

Beg him to kiss me.

I've replayed it in my head several times since while lying in bed.

Is that what I really want, though?

How have I gone from swearing off men and relationships, to wanting the angry cowboy next door to kiss me like his life depends on it? Wanting him to touch me in places I haven't been touched in so long.

Out of the corner of my eye, my gaze lands on the weird man I saw at the General Store when I was buying my power washer. Once again, nerves swarm my gut because he's got his eyes locked on me. Staring at me with such intensity that it almost knocks me off my feet.

"Hey, Lil?"

"Ya."

"Don't look now, but over your shoulder, like two o'clock, there's a man staring at me. Do you know him?"

She casually does a search around the bar as if she's looking for something before she looks where I guided her to look. To keep the act up, she keeps looking around for another second before shaking her head. "No, he looks like an out-of-towner. But I don't blame him for having eyes on you. You look hot tonight." She winks.

The scratch of the speakers draws our attention to the mini stage set up for the karaoke party. There's a full black backdrop with twinkle lights cascading in rows down the middle along with multicolor strobe lights that rotate throughout the whole bar.

"Good evening, Bluestone Lakes," she shouts into the microphone like she's the main performer at Coachella. "It's my turn to give this karaoke shit a try."

The room laughs because they know her.

The music plays, and Lily and I still our dance moves, turning to look at each other with wide eyes.

"She did not," Lily gasps.

Nan dons a pair of black sunglasses, putting one hand in the air and holding the microphone in front of her face. Clearly ready for the most epic performance of her life.

And then she sings. *"I've been drinking. I've been drinking."*

"She did not choose 'Drunk in Love' to sing at a karaoke bar," I say to Lily.

"She so did," she replies, eyes on Nan as she sways her hips in a seductive motion on stage, bellowing every word into the microphone as if she's the main character.

We watch fascinated as she gets into the moves. Using the whole stage as her platform to let everyone know that she's "drunk in love" tonight, it seems.

Lily and I turn to each other and both of us curl over in laughter.

Neither of us can believe this is happening right now.

"I need another drink for the rest of this show," I tell her.

"Go see Griffin." She gestures to the bar. "He will take good care of you."

I keep laughing, but it comes out more nervous. Because the idea of Griffin Barlow taking "good care of me" sends shivers down my spine.

And I'm not talking about him making me a drink.

I turn to head toward the bar and my eyes land directly on Griffin, who's already looking at me. Poppy and Tucker are smiling and engaging in conversation.

But he's not.

His eyes remain locked on mine in the fiercest way possible.

In a way that makes me feels like I'm the only one in the bar tonight.

And, damn, he looks so good tonight. I noticed when I first walked in, but it's hitting me all over again right now. He's wearing a baseball cap, shadowing his eyes. He ditched the flannel for the evening, only giving the entire bar a show of his abdominal muscles. And I say that because the solid black T-shirt he's wearing hugs every ridge and curve of his body.

Making me want to trail my fingertips along—

"One day he will smile again," Lily says into my ear.

Little does she know, I've seen it. Just enough to tell me that there's a heart somewhere deep inside of him.

Ordering an actual drink from him has me on edge. I don't know if it's because I can't get my mind to stop thinking about him in very inappropriate ways, or because I want him to lean over the bar and kiss me, or because I need to keep my distance before I end up screwed and falling for the guy.

I see Tucker behind the bar and remember him from the day they rebuilt my deck.

I decide to head in his direction, hoping to avoid feeling awkward.

Tucker spots me as I step up to the counter, resting my forearms on the edge. He offers me a welcoming smile. "Hey there, City Chick. How's the new deck holding up?"

"It's great." I laugh. "Thank you again. For, you know… helping and all."

He raises a hand. "No thanks needed. Construction work is kind of my thing."

"Good to know," I answer before looking in Griffin's direction to find him no longer looking my way.

It's now my mission to get a smile out of Griffin while in public tonight.

"You'll get used to him," Tucker cuts through my thoughts. "He's an acquired taste."

Just as I'm about to order a drink from Tucker, Autumn, and Poppy spot me and make their way to me with their drinks in hand. Autumn has some type of light beer in a glass, and Poppy is drinking ice water.

"So happy you could make it," Autumn says at the same time she wraps her arms around me for a hug.

"A night spent with you girls?" I raise an eyebrow. "Never in my life would I miss this."

"I think you just became one of my favorite people." Autumn chuckles, pressing a kiss to my cheek as I join her in laughter.

I meant it when I said I would never miss this because of them.

They've welcomed me and invited me into their lives, quickly becoming my people here in this small town. A group of girls I didn't know I needed until I met them. It's a complete 180 from the "friends" I had back in California. They genuinely care about me and it's not a one-sided type of friendship.

The song changes, and I hear Shania shout "Let's Go Girls" through the speakers. The girls look at each other with wide eyes and open mouths.

"It's our song!" they shout in unison.

They grab each other's hands and hustle out to the middle of the dance floor.

"Whoa," Tucker says, rounding the bar quickly. "It's my song too. Wait for me."

I follow his movements until he reaches the girls, jumping up and down like an excited teenage girl at the high school dance ready to tear up the dance floor. I can't stop smiling at how fun this group is.

I turn around to face the bar and see Griffin standing right across from me.

His face is all work, no play.

I almost feel the smile on my face fall, but determination wins, and I refuse to let him know I feel nervous around him.

"What are ya drinkin'?" he asks.

"A martini?"

His eyebrows knit together. "We don't have those here."

I tilt my head in confusion. "You mean to tell me you're a bar that doesn't serve martinis?"

I've already noticed the ingredients needed to make it line the counter behind him but decide to play this little game he seems to want to play right now.

He shakes his head. "Beer or whiskey. It's what we're known for."

"I thought it was the seven stools?" I smirk.

He nods his head repeatedly, as if he's proud of my response. "You're catching on."

I scan the bar behind him, trying to figure out what to order. One thing I can't stand is beer. I've never liked it. It's gross and makes me feel like shit after just one drink.

But I've also never had whiskey before.

"Fine," I say, lifting my chin to find the confidence I didn't know I had in me. "I'll take a whiskey."

"You sure about that?"

The corner of my lip tips up. "It's all you got, right?"

He pauses, staring at me for just a brief moment before he nods.

I can't take my eyes off him the entire time he works behind the bar pouring my drink. He grabs a short glass, skips the ice, and reaches for a bottle of whiskey that sits on the top of the three-tiered liquor shelf he has set up.

"Whiskey neat," he says, sliding it across the bar in front of me. "On me."

I look from him to the glass and back to him, lifting the glass in the air for a toast even though he has nothing in his hand.

I take a small sip and crinkle my face in disgust.

People actually drink this? What the hell? It tastes like I'm drinking something straight off a tree. Oak mixed with spices? This can't be something people actually enjoy.

"That's disgusting," I say, sticking my tongue out repeatedly, as if moving it around my mouth will actually remove the taste. I lift the glass in the air and look at the amber liquid before looking back at Griffin. "This would probably taste way better on you."

His eyes narrow, and I don't back down.

I kinda, sorta mean it. This drink is gross, but, damn, it'd probably taste way better on him.

"What did you just say?" he says, flatly.

"Oops," I say, covering my mouth with my hand, forcing the words to come out all muffled. "Did I just put my foot in my mouth again?"

He leans one forearm on the bar, bringing himself closer to me and I suck in a breath. "What did you just say?" he repeats.

I remove my hand from my mouth and straighten my spine. "I said...this would probably taste better on *you*. It's certainly got an interesting taste."

"Explain," he demands.

I rest my elbows on the bar, leaning over, and watch as his eyes trail to the swell of my breasts before looking back into my eyes. This outfit isn't something I normally settle for, and it's very outside my comfort zone with how vibrant the colors are. But it sparkles. It makes me feel sexy. The combination of the boots with the hat makes me feel like I belong somewhere again.

Something about the way this man looks at me, even without a smile on his face, turns me on so damn much.

This is my chance to crack a smile.

I want to see it in the worst way possible.

Not to mention, the shitty wine coolers I had earlier are definitely making me feel bolder than I normally am.

"It means that if you took this glass and slowly poured it down your chest, letting it drip down your body for me to lick off, it would probably taste better," I say, finishing my sentence with a smirk. "Is that a good enough explanation, Angry Cowboy?"

He stares at me, unblinking, before he moves his gaze to my

mouth. He doesn't stop staring so I take the moment to let my tongue trail along my bottom lip. The same tongue I just told him I would use to lick whiskey off his bare skin. His pupils widen, telling me he's absolutely thinking about it. But then he surprises me by walking away without even acknowledging a single thing I just said.

Shit. I screwed that up.

Now my very good-looking, grumpy neighbor thinks I'm a freak in so many more ways than just screaming about a moose standing outside of my window watching me shower.

I leave the full glass of whiskey at the bar and head to where the girls and Tucker are dancing.

"Where's your drink?" Lily asks.

"Whiskey isn't my thing." I shrug with a laugh.

"I couldn't help but watch that entire thing go down," Tucker says, leaning into me. "You seem to have gotten him fired up, huh, City Chic?"

"City Chic?" I question.

"That's my nickname for you," he says with a proud smile.

I smile in his direction, resting a hand on his shoulder. "Hey, it's better than 'freak show.'"

He rears his head back. "Who calls you that? Let me find out, City Chic. I'll throw some elbows."

"Relax," I joke. "I'm just guessing that's what his nickname for me is."

"Griffin is an acquired taste," Poppy chimes in, adding an eye roll.

That's the second time someone's said that, and now I'm definitely thinking more and more about how he actually tastes.

"Don't stress about it," Tucker says. "He's just set in his ways and will come around. You're not so bad, City Chic." He bumps my shoulder with a grin.

I can't help but wonder if he ever will.

But I also want to know why the hell I'm so drawn to him.

CHAPTER 24

LET'S SEE IF WE CAN CHANGE YOUR MIND ABOUT IT.

GRIFFIN

Thank fuck it's the end of this night.

All tonight did was solidify all the reasons I can't stand working evenings, and these late nights only confirm more that I'm too old to be dealing with this shit.

More than half the crowd has left, minus a few stragglers and Nan cleaning up the karaoke stuff.

Lily saunters over to me, tripping over her feet before both hands find the top of the bar to help balance herself. She's totally drunk, and I don't have the energy to care right now as long as she gets home safe.

"How are you getting home?" I ask her.

She turns, pointing to Poppy. "She didn't drink, so she's driving."

"Good."

"Hey," she says, leaning on the bar with a mischievous grin on her face. "Think you can take Blair home? I mean, you literally have to pass her house." She pauses, a hiccup escaping her. "This way, no one has to go out of their way."

I roll my eyes.

"Oh stop." She giggles. "You can tell me if you like her."

"You're too drunk for this conversation, Lil."

"Am not," she slurs with another hiccup. "But it's about time you gave it up already. Forget your stupid piece of shit ex-girlfriend." The volume of her voice rises with each word that spills from her mouth. "Blair is smokin' hot. And the best part is, she's not your ex!" she shouts.

I'm taken aback by the tone of her voice.

I know she's drunk, but this isn't a side of Lily I'm used to.

"Did you just raise your voice at me?"

"I did." She nods. "And I will again. Blair is a good person. She's not going anywhere. She *bought* the only house on your block, and you're stuck with her. I'm stuck with her." She smiles widely. "I love her so much and I'm lucky to have a friend like her in my life. So I can't have you chasing her out of town."

I stare at her in shock, knowing she's right.

It's been on my mind constantly since having her over for dinner. Blair's not the person I thought she would be. She might have moved from the city, but she isn't like the rest of them. Not only is she downright beautiful, but she's smart and funny. She's witty and I like that she's always keeping me on my toes.

"Fine," I tell Lily. "I'll drop her off, but she's going to have to hang out for a bit while I finish closing up."

"Good," she says through a hiccup. "Get her home safe."

"I can get myself home," Blair interprets.

I glare in her direction. "Are you going to walk?"

"Yep," she states, popping the p, flipping her hair behind her shoulder, and rolling her eyes.

That sass.

After our little interaction earlier at the bar, she had me wound up tighter than usual. And now I'd love nothing more than to shut her up with my cock in her mouth after her little stunt earlier. I haven't been able to stop thinking about it. I *had* to walk away from her before she saw the effect she had on me. There's no doubt that if her eyes trailed my body, she would have noticed how hard she made me.

She boldly told me the whiskey would taste better *on me.*

Now it's a vision I can't get out of my head.

This isn't who I am, but Blair seems to bring out the inner beast in me I never knew existed.

Or hasn't existed in years.

"I'll be done here in twenty minutes. I'm taking you home whether you want me to or not," I tell her and turn to walk away.

I *can't* get close to her. I know this. Then I find myself in these positions where we're alone. She's in my truck, she's in my bar, she's in my house. All of it has only built up these feelings I'm fighting. The thought of being alone with her again makes my chest feel tight, like I'm having difficulty breathing when she's around.

I make my way to the kitchen, bringing the glasses back to get washed in the morning because it's too late to deal with this right now. Standing there for a moment, I work on controlling my breathing. Being around Blair is not good for me. I'm on the verge of breaking at any second with her. Doing something I'm afraid I'll regret or something that will inevitably break my heart in the end.

I keep myself busy for the next fifteen minutes, making sure the ovens are off, and the back door is locked before grabbing my flannel from the hook behind the kitchen door and replacing my alcohol- and food-scented T-shirt with it, but keeping my baseball hat on because I know my hair is a disaster under this cap.

I don't bother buttoning it up, yet as I make my way back out to the bar, everyone has left but Blair.

This time she's standing behind the bar where only the employees are allowed. She's holding up a bottle of liquor that could have made her a martini earlier in the night.

But I wanted to test her.

See if she was really ready to fit in here…with me.

"This looks familiar," she says, lifting it in the air for me to see.

I shrug a shoulder, but keep my face straight, emotionless.

"Well," she says, placing the bottle back where she found it. "Are you going to make me a drink before we go?" She grins.

"I cleaned up all the glasses already, and I'm not making a martini right now."

"I noticed." She smirks before scanning the shelves of liquor lining the back wall. She reaches up to grab a bottle of whiskey off the top shelf. As she does, her dress gets pulled down ever so slightly, exposing more of her breasts, but not all of them. The dim lights only draw out the sparkle of her skin, if that's even possible. My cock strains in my jeans, thinking about what she plans to do with that, knowing damn well she hates the taste of it.

Half of me is hoping she lives up to her words.

The other half is hoping she lets it go so I don't go down this road with her.

"I'd love to acquire a taste for this." She holds up the bottle.

I drop the dishrag I'm holding and take slow, tentative steps toward her until I'm only inches away from her. My body buzzes without a single sip of alcohol in my system. I feel drunk just from being so close to her and staring into those eyes.

"You want a taste of whiskey on me, sweetheart?"

Her eyes light up, and the smirk on her face grows.

"Like I said...I'd love to build up my taste for it. Maybe I can learn to like it."

I feel weak staring at her. My reserves are crumbling with every word out of her mouth, and I don't know how much more I can take. I told myself I wouldn't give in to the temptation of her. The pull I have with her.

How far is she willing to go?

I lean down, lips grazing the shell of her ear, and just this touch sends a shock through my system. My lips burn from the light contact.

"Then take off my shirt," I whisper. "Let's see if we can change your mind about it."

Without hesitation, she drops the whiskey bottle on the counter before reaching for the lapels of my already unbuttoned flannel, keeping her eyes locked on mine. In a painfully slow motion, she pushes it over my shoulders.

The same way she's unraveling me minute by minute.

As she fully exposes my chest, I feel my cock strain ever harder against the zipper of my jeans as my flannel falls to the ground.

I'd give anything at this point to feel her fist wrap around it for even a second.

The moment her hands make contact with my chest, fire erupts across my skin, and I just about lose it, but maintain my composure.

"Jesus," she mutters under her breath. "Is there a gym in town I don't know about?"

"It's called the outdoors."

She smirks. "Noted." Then she reaches for the bottle of whiskey and hands it to me. I take it from her hands and watch as she lowers herself to her knees in front of me.

Fuckkkkk.

She smiles up at me, knowingly. I uncap the bottle of whiskey and angle it at the top of my chest, making sure I watch every single move she makes because I don't want to miss a moment of this.

I angle my upper body back slightly, and then slowly pour down the middle, letting it trickle down. Her hands reach for the belt of my jeans, and the contact of her hands on my skin makes me jump, but not enough for her to notice. She lifts herself up, her tongue connecting just above my navel, and she licks up every drop of whiskey I just poured.

The feel of her tongue on my skin brings out the feral side of me.

Licking the corner of her lips she gives me a light shrug, not bothering to stand from where she's crouched down in front of me. "Better. I think. Maybe I should try it again, though."

Curiosity for how far she's willing to take this is now laced with desire. I can't believe she even did this in the first place, let alone wants to do it again. Never did I think something that wasn't sex could turn me on this much. Then again, I'm beginning to believe everything she does turns me on.

That statement alone tells me she has to be equally turned on by this as I am. I want to feel her tongue on my body again and then repeat it on her to see how whiskey tastes off her bare skin.

"If I didn't know any better, I'd say you're liking it," I grit out.

"Maybe I am." She winks.

I line up the bottle the same way I did before, and let it trickle down my chest. This time, she uses more force against my belt, tugging my jeans down as her tongue makes contact *below* my navel this time.

Fuck. That feels so good.

She lifts herself, using more force against my skin as she licks all the way up to my chest. Her eyes never leave mine and it's so fucking hot to see this side of Blair.

Just when I think she's going to pull away from me, she releases her mouth from my body and stands tall in front of me. Looking up at me with whiskey-hazed eyes.

She wants me to kiss her.

Hell, I want to kiss her.

But not here. Not right now.

I take her chin between my fingers, letting my lips linger dangerously close to hers. I can feel her breath pick up against mine.

"It's my turn for a taste, sweetheart."

CHAPTER 25
THE BOOTS STAY ON.

BLAIR

I don't know who this version of me is, but no part of me cares. Because the way Griffin has been looking at me tonight—even if he was scowling before—has me needing to release some of this built-up tension in my body.

It doesn't help that he's standing in front of me, shirtless, and telling me it's his turn for a taste with my chin in his hands.

I want him to touch me more than this, though.

Even if it doesn't bring me to a release, I know that when I get home, this whole thing will be the center of that fantasy while my vibrator gets some serious use.

"You want me to take this off?" I gesture to my dress.

He nods, releasing his hold on my chin. I take a step back, watching him as his eyes track my every move. I turn around, brushing my hair to the side as I look over my shoulder, silently begging him to undo the zipper for me. His throat bobs and my body shivers with desire as he reaches for the zipper with one hand. His knuckles brushing my skin only intensifies the buzz coursing through my body.

And it's not from the alcohol.

It's all him.

Turning to face him again, I notice his grip harden on the whiskey bottle still in his hand. White knuckling the neck of the bottle while I let the dress fall to the floor beside me. I'm not wearing a bra under this outfit, so the feel of his eyes on me and the chill in my body causes my nipples to harden under the weight of it all. My heart thunders in my chest with anticipation for what's about to happen.

"On the bar," he orders, gesturing to the spot behind me.

I take a step back, hiking myself up until I'm in a seated position. He takes slow steps in my direction, his attention fixed on my exposed legs. I feel goosebumps trail over the top of the skin the longer he keeps looking.

He runs the bottom of the bottle from my knees up to my thigh until he reaches the apex of them. It's so light that it does nothing to stop the pleasure forming inside of me, forcing me to clench my legs together. The wetness I feel in my panties is proof that this is turning me on even more than before.

"Now lie down," he says.

I lower my upper body down and bring my legs up until I'm laid across the bar for him.

His bar.

The thought makes me smile, and I can't help it.

"You're enjoying this, aren't you?" Griffin says. "On top of *my* bar, with the front doors unlocked for anyone to come back at any moment and see you like this."

"The thought crossed my mind," I answer honestly.

He growls, stepping closer to me before angling the whiskey over my chest, letting it pool between my breasts before he pours some in the middle of my stomach around my belly button.

The cold liquid causes my back to arch slightly off the bar top, but his opposite hand presses me back down.

Jesus, that was insanely hot.

I watch him as he twists his baseball cap to the back of his head.

That move alone could send me straight to orgasmville.

184

He doesn't say anything as he lowers his head to the lower part of my stomach, letting his tongue trail from the hem of my panties to my naval where he licks the whiskey clear off me. His eyes close and I swear I hear a moan come out of him. He doesn't remove his mouth from me but continues to trail his tongue until he reaches the lower part of my chest. He pauses and opens his eyes while looking up at me, just before he glides his mouth between my breasts to drink the whiskey right off of my skin.

I suck in a gasp, and my nipples harden even more while I fight the urge to dip my hand inside my shorts and touch myself.

He lifts himself up, but just enough so that I can still feel his breath against my skin. "You're right. Whiskey tastes better this way."

He picks up the bottle again and pours, this time pooling it only between my breasts. Placing the bottle down, he lowers himself to the whiskey he just poured before letting his tongue make its way to my nipple.

The contact makes me cry out. "Griffin."

His mouth covers the hardened bud, sucking on it before releasing it and repeating the move on the other side. This time, he reaches across my chest to cup my breast. His hand covers it entirely and squeezes, but it feels so good right now.

My thighs clench together with desperate need.

A rush of pleasure courses through me—one I've never felt in my life. I've had plenty of orgasms, but never have I come with a man like Griffin playing with my nipples.

I refuse to come from just him licking whiskey off my skin and playing with my nipples. How embarrassing would that be?

But Griffin notices my thighs moving ever so slightly in his peripheral.

He releases my nipple from his mouth and his hand from my body before lifting me up into a seated position. He nudges my knees apart with his hips as he steps into me, placing a large palm on my thigh and the other on the bar beside me. He's so close that I can feel his labored breaths against my mouth as if he's going to give in and kiss me.

I want him so badly that I can barely breathe.

"Tell me what you want," he says, keeping his voice barely above a whisper. But his whisper is deep and raspy, enough to drive me over the edge of insanity.

I shake my head, not ready to speak aloud all the things I want him to do to me.

Just when I think he's going to step away from me, he turns his head and leans down, bringing his lips to my collarbone, pressing them to my skin before trailing his way up to my ear. My back arches at the delicate way his lips touch me. My hands grip the edge of the bar on each side of my thighs.

"You're aching to be touched," he whispers against the shell of my ear. "Your body is begging for a release, and you're so turned on right now you can't even think straight." He pulls away, staring at me as he waits for a response.

My lips part, and I'm at a loss for words.

"Tell me I'm wrong," he continues.

"You're not wrong," I answer quickly and more out of breath than I was before. "You're way too hot for your own good, Angry Cowboy."

He reaches between us, fingers grazing my stomach as he plays with the hem of my panties. I rest my arms back on the bar top, silently telling him to have his way with me.

I cannot believe this is really happening right now.

Who the hell do I think I am being this bold out in the open like this?

"The boots stay on," he tells me, brushing his fingers delicately from the shaft of the boot, along the inner part of my leg until he reaches just outside of my panty line. "Now spread your legs for me, sweetheart."

I do as he says and instantly feel vulnerable because I know there's a spot on my panties drenched in my arousal from him touching me.

It's been there half the night from the way he was looking at me.

Never did I think moving here would lead to something like this.

Moving to a small town, meeting a man like Griffin, and being practically naked on top of his bar.

But here I am, and, dammit, do I want this.

"I knew you wanted this," he says, admiring me open in front of him. "Your pussy is soaked for me already."

My head falls back, and I fight to keep my legs open for him, craving friction even more than before at the way he looks feral for me. I know that a man like him who works as hard as he does knows what to do with those hands.

He places one hand on my thigh, inches from the most sensitive parts of my body, and I lift my head back up to watch him. He reaches over to grab the neck of the whiskey bottle before lowering himself behind the bar. He hooks a finger into the side of my panties, moving them to the side, which only makes me open up wider for him.

My eyes never leave his as he lifts the bottle to his mouth, taking a long pull before lowering himself between my legs. His lips connect with my pussy and everything around me blurs. I fall back on my hands, gripping the other side of the bar while electric shocks fly through every part of me.

The cold of the liquid, mixed with the warmth of his tongue, forces me to release a long, drawn-out moan. "Mmm."

My hands tighten their hold on the edge of the bar as he opens his mouth, taking my clit between his teeth before flicking his tongue up and down. Fireworks explode through me, and I nearly lose it already.

"Griffin, you're going to make me come," I pant.

He releases his hold on me for just a moment. "That's the fucking goal," he rasps. His hot, rapid breaths do nothing to ease the buildup.

His deep voice, mixed with the way he's back to devouring me, licking and sucking like his life depends on this right now.

It all sends me right over the edge.

"Griffin, oh god." I'm barely able to get the words out through my moans. "I'm coming. Jesus. I'm coming."

My orgasm rocks me like an earthquake. My legs tremble around him and before I know it, I see stars. I don't think I've ever seen stars or had it hit me *this* hard before. In all the years I was married, it's never felt like this.

He doesn't let up and doesn't slow down.

Riding out my orgasm, sucking every drop of pleasure from me he can as if I'm his last meal on earth.

Griffin Barlow can devour me any day if this is what it feels like.

As soon as I come down from my high, he unhooks my panty from his hand, lifting to stand before me. Bringing himself eye level with me, he runs his tongue along his bottom lip. My eyes track his tongue before looking back at him. Stormy blue eyes boring into mine.

"Now, *that*…tasted better than any drink in this bar."

Then he turns around and grabs his flannel off the ground before making his way back into the kitchen.

I sit there, shocked and exposed.

I'm practically naked out here alone.

But I'm not mad.

He has to come back out here to take me home.

I'm actually partially thankful he left me here alone to think about the hottest thing that I've ever experienced in my life. I really wouldn't be mad if that happened again.

But also…that didn't even get a smile out of him.

CHAPTER 26
WE LOOK OUT FOR OUR NEIGHBORS.

GRIFFIN

I'm living in hell.

And next door to the only woman who has ever twisted my head in a way that's driving me absolutely insane for the last week.

I know I should have stopped myself. But she was tempting me.

I'm not delusional. She's absolutely breathtaking.

But now that I've had a taste, I want more, even though she made it clear on the awkward car ride home that it can't happen again. It's what she wanted to happen though, isn't it? She was behind my bar when I came out from the kitchen, ready to leave. She had the whiskey in her hand.

The ride home told me otherwise.

She wasn't herself in a way. Her constant need for questions and talking non-stop used to annoy the shit out of me because I didn't want her talking to me, and then the one time I do want it, she shuts down on me.

Needless to say, my poor dick has never been so worn out. That night, and every night since, the only thing on my mind when I lay my head down at night is the way she looked lying across *my* bar top. The way she looked in nothing but those panties and cowgirl boots.

Fuck.

The thoughts consuming me are too much to handle.

I've tried to come up with a reason to walk over to her house and do something about it. I've stopped myself every single one of those times. Instead, I've just been working and spending more time at the ranch. I've moved my morning porch coffee inside to avoid seeing her leaving or returning from her morning runs. A few of the days, I even left early for work just so I didn't have to see her watering her plants outside.

One fucking taste, and now I'm a ruined man.

Blair threw me off my schedule this morning when she went for a run later than usual. It's disgusting that I've memorized her routine. It makes me want to pull my hair out.

While I was doing dishes in my kitchen sink shortly after watching her leave, I spotted something out of the corner of my eye, and it was Blair coming back from her run.

She seemed off.

She didn't look the way she normally does when she gets back. She's usually gone for much longer and always has more of a pep in her step. I've learned she's one of those people who gets a high from running and comes back more energized than before she left. I'll never understand it, because if I were to run down the block, I would need to take a nap at the street sign.

Today, she was slouched over, dragging her feet and a frown on her face. She didn't even bother to sit on her deck and enjoy the new patio furniture she set up a few days ago. Telling me something wasn't right, and I make a mental note to possibly check on her when I leave the bar today.

I say possibly because I don't know what the hell I'm doing here.

The bell over the front door chimes, and I groan. I could have sworn I had Tucker disconnect that ridiculous thing before karaoke night.

"Hey, Griff," Poppy greets me with a smile.

"Hey, Pop. What brings you in today?" I ask, turning to look at the clock on the wall. "Aren't you in the middle of the school day?"

"I am, but I stopped by Batter Up to grab some treats for the kids this afternoon because we have a birthday in the class."

She was *made* to be a first grade teacher. Every single one of her students is lucky to have her because she doesn't just teach. She cares about them with everything inside of her. If one of them is sick, she stops by their house, brings them soup, and makes sure they are okay. She has the most caring heart I've ever known. I've always looked up to *her*, even with her being five years younger than me.

"That's nice of you," I tell her honestly. "I know I say this all the time, but they're lucky to have you as their teacher."

"I'll never tire of you telling me that." She laughs. "But I appreciate it. You know how much I love my job and these kids. Some days, I feel like all eighteen of them are mine."

I nod. "So, what brings you in here? I know you didn't come in for an afternoon cocktail."

She shakes her head with a laugh. "I had a reason for this quick visit..." she starts, but pauses, looking down at her hands before clasping them together on top of the bar. "I was wondering if you heard anything about the new rumor in town?"

"Rumor?" I ask, feeling my heart rate pick up.

Is she about to ask me about Blair?

Did someone see us at the bar that night and word got out?

She looks back up at me. "I don't know if it's Nan trying to stir up the rumor mill, but she claims someone new is coming to town. Someone with a big name. And I saw her walking the property next door to me. I'm not sure I want whoever it is on my street."

I roll my eyes. "You know her, it's probably nobody."

She laughs, but it comes out more nervous. "You're probably

right. Oh, by the way, did you see Blair at the house when you left?" she questions.

My nerves shift instantly the second I hear her say Blair's name.

Why is she bringing her up?

"Yeah? Why?" I abruptly spit out.

Why do I sound all nervous and guilty about something?

Oh, maybe because my head was between her legs a week ago on this very bar.

Poppy's face wrinkles in confusion. "Is she okay?"

I shrug. "How would I know? I don't stalk her or watch her," I lie.

Maybe I have been.

She's turning me into an addict. She's a drug I want more of but shouldn't have—can't have.

"Okay, Mr. Defensive." She smiles widely. "Is there something you need to tell me? If there is, you know your secret is safe with me. I know Lily can be a little overbearing about things."

I should tell her.

I need to tell someone to get this off my chest.

And between my sisters, I trust Poppy the most.

I open my mouth to confess, but the bell over the door chimes again, and I turn to see Nan walking in.

"Anyone know where I can hide a dead body?" she shouts, making her way in our direction.

Tucker walks in right behind her.

"Who did you murder?" I ask flatly, rolling my eyes.

"It's 'bout to be this one," she states, hiking a thumb over her shoulder where Tucker stands.

"I didn't do shit," Tucker defends.

Nan cranes her neck and glares at Tucker.

"Is that Nan's angry face?" Poppy whispers to me, keeping her eyes on the two of them.

"I think so," I whisper back.

"You bought the last three bags of the seasoned pretzel twists," she snaps at him.

He holds his arms out wide. "You know they're my favorite."

"Mine too! You only left me with those honey mustard ones. I can't eat those. They leave my fingers all messy," Nan explains.

Tucker rolls his eyes. "God forbid. That's what napkins are for."

Nan grits her teeth, rearing her arm back as if she's actually going to punch him.

"Hold on," Poppy interrupts, stepping between them before she actually throws a fist in his face. I wouldn't put it past her. "This argument is over pretzels?"

"Yes," Nan and Tucker shout in unison.

Poppy turns to face Tucker. "You bought three bags, right?" He nods. "Why don't you give her just one? And when more come in, we can get you some bags for your stash."

"Why must you be so reasonable?" Tucker whines, stomping a foot on the ground like a petulant child.

I lift my hands to rub my temples. "I can't believe this is happening right now. Is anyone here for lunch, or are we just here to bullshit?"

Poppy looks down at her watch. "Actually, I have to get back to the school." She grabs her purse to leave, but she stops before she reaches the door and turns around. "Can you just check on Blair for us when you leave here, Griff?"

Tucker's gaze bounces between Poppy and me. "What's wrong with my girl?"

"Your girl?" I question.

"She's sick," Nan answers, saving Tucker's ass from getting beat by me this time.

"She is?" I ask Nan.

I think about how I saw her this morning. Something definitely wasn't right with her, and this might explain it. I didn't even consider that she might have been sick. I guess I just assumed she ran a little too hard.

Nan takes a seat on a stool. "Yeah, she called out for the day at the bakery. She's got the flu, or the stomach bug, or the plague. Hell if I know, but Lily said she didn't sound good."

I turn to look at the clock on the wall.

Another two hours before I'm out of here.

I'm fighting the urge to run out of here to make sure she's okay. I don't understand why, because she's not mine to worry about.

"That's a shame," I finally say.

A knowing grin spreads across Nan's face, but she says nothing.

Tucker notices and looks back at me. "Anything you want to tell us?" he asks, only adding fuel to the fire. But before I can respond, his eyes widen. "Wait a second. Are you finally getting some action with City Chick?"

"Stop calling her that," I snap. I pick up the dishrag and start wiping down the already clean bar top to keep busy.

Nan snaps her fingers before pointing toward me. "He's not denying it!"

I drop the rag on the counter, place both palms down in front of me, and stare at Nan. "Nothing is happening between us," I say, before turning my gaze on Tucker. "And nothing will," I lie again.

"Why did your voice just sound all squeaky with those last words." Nan laughs.

"I'm fine," I say as I grab the discarded dishrag to wipe the counter again.

"Something's totally happening," Tucker barks out a laugh. "That came out squeaky too."

"Nothing is. Now, both of you drop it. I'm not having this discussion again," I snap. I look at the clock again, and then at Tucker. "Aren't you supposed to be at work anyway?"

He looks down at his watch. "Shit. Yeah."

I shake my head. "Let me guess, a fifteen-minute break?"

"Yep." He turns on his heel to make his way out the door.

"Going on thirty-five minutes," he shouts over his shoulder and is out the door.

Leaving me alone with Nan.

The one person in the world who never lets anything go.

I finally face her, and she just sits there with her hands crossed on the bar, staring at me. In all the years I've known her, I know she can read someone like a book.

"You care about her." She breaks the silence.

"She's my neighbor," I scoff.

"And?"

"*And*...we look out for our neighbors."

She tilts her head to the side, staring at me like I'm full of shit. "But you care about her more than that."

This time, I have nothing to say.

Because I think I do—No, I *know* I do.

Nan reaches across the bar, resting her small hands on top of mine.

"I won't say anything, Griffin. I may be the town gossip, but this is different."

"How so?"

"I can't explain it, but it's different. And listen," she says, sitting up taller in her chair with her hands up in defense. "You don't have to tell me or admit anything. I'll drop it right here if you want me to. But I just need you to know that it's okay if you care about her."

I remain silent, only offering her a curt nod.

Part of me wants to drop this conversation quicker than a bad habit, but I know she's about to keep going.

"I might be a smart ass one hundred percent of the time," she continues. "But I mean it when I tell you it's okay to have these feelings. It's scary and probably feels new. You're unsure because of your past. And you *know*"—she points a sharp finger my way—"I can tell when people are bad. I call it out immediately with no regrets and no bullshit. I don't get those vibes from Blair."

Hearing her name only makes this conversation feel more real.

"I believe she's fuckin' good, Griff," Nan emphasizes. "I knew the moment I laid eyes on her and got to talkin' to her that she would be good for *you*."

"So, this was all a setup?" I ask, slightly offended.

She shakes her head quickly. "No. Absolutely not. I promise you that. But I knew when you were ready to give someone a chance again, to get over your past and finally move on, that she might be a good fit for you."

I stand there shocked, unable to speak.

Nan stares at me for a moment longer before standing up from the stool. She pats her hand on the counter.

"I'm gonna head out. Think about what I said," she says before turning to leave. "Oh, and call your mother," she shouts as she walks away with a pointer finger swirling in the air. "She wants you over for dinner sometime this century." She laughs, pushes the doors open, and walks out.

Leaving me alone in my bar.

No customers. Just me and these thoughts consuming me.

I can't shake the thought that Nan is right that this might be the time to give someone a chance again.

CHAPTER 27

I'M KNOCKING ON DEATH'S DOOR.

BLAIR

LILY

How are you feeling?

ME

I'm knocking on death's door.

LILY

Is this my dramatic best friend, or my serious best friend?

ME

Both.

LILY

Do you have soup?

ME

No. And I can't even think about food right now or I will be sick again.

LILY

Noted. Well, I love you. Go to sleep.

ME

Love you too.

I can't remember the last time I was ever this sick.

I wish I was exaggerating when I told Lily I felt like I was dying.

When I woke up this morning, it wasn't terrible. I felt drained, but thought it was because I didn't sleep well. I was tossing and turning all night long. I didn't want to miss going for my run, so I pulled it together, put my big girl pants on, and hit the road.

Only to have to turn around not even five minutes in because I thought I was going to vomit on the side of the road.

Spoiler alert: I did.

Right next to the beat-up *Barlow Drive* street sign.

I wanted to sit down and wait for a passing car to take me home. *That's* how shitty I felt. I didn't even think my body would make it another five minutes to get home.

As soon as I got back, I stripped out of my running clothes and replaced them with an old pair of sweatpants and an over-sized T-shirt before making my home on the couch for the entire day. Only time I got up was to get sick. Not like I had much inside of me after the first two times.

I can't sleep because when I close my eyes the room spins.

I can't eat because it just comes right back up.

I can't read because trying to focus on the words induces a headache.

The worst of it all is the guilt I feel for calling out of work and leaving Lily alone to tend to the bakery. I know she said she could handle it—she always did before she hired me—but I hate the idea of missing work.

Reginald barks on the floor next to me, lifting his head toward the front door. I follow his gaze, and standing on the other side of the glass doors is Griffin with a bag in his hand. He stares at me through the glass, unmoving. He doesn't knock or lift the bag. He just stands there, and he looks...distraught.

"Go away," I shout, pulling one of the many pillows out from under my head and covering my face. "I have germs and you're going to get them," I add, hoping it's loud enough for him to hear through the door.

I hear the click of the door opening but refuse to remove the pillow from my head. I *can't* let him see me like this. I probably smell like vomit, my hair is full of knots, and I know I look white as a ghost.

Oh my god, what if I puke on him?

"Go away," I repeat, my tone much softer.

"I heard you were sick." His voice sounds so close as if he's standing right over me.

"I'm warning you, Griffin. You're going to catch my germs."

"I don't care."

I remove the pillow from half my face, exposing only my eyes to him.

That's when I'm met with his piercing gaze standing over me as I lie there—vulnerable and not feeling like myself at all. The last time I saw him was karaoke night, where I felt bold, confident, and beautiful in front of him. I don't feel that right now.

I feel sick and small.

I feel like I might break and cry at any moment from lack of sleep.

Griffin crouches down next to me, and Reginald rushes up to him, placing both paws on his broad legs and reaching his head up to offer him some face kisses.

To my surprise, Griffin places a hand on Reginald's head, petting him and greeting him by allowing my dog to soak his cheek with dog licks. I'm thankful for the pillow covering my mouth because right now it's open in shock.

For a man who hates dogs, he's being super nice to Reginald.

"Down," I tell Reginald, and he listens. He backs up and circles himself a few times before curling into a ball on the floor by my feet.

"He's fine," Griffin says, looking from him and back to me. "Are you okay?"

Three simple words; and the dam behind my eyes is ready to explode.

"No," I admit. "I want to die."

He reaches for the pillow and my hold on it tightens, but it's no use because there isn't a single ounce of energy in my body to fight it. Griffin takes the pillow and tosses it at my feet. I attempt to hide my face in the other pillow under me, but he stops me when his hand comes up to cup the side of my face, his eyes looking at me as if he's memorizing my every feature.

Even sick, he's looking at me in a way that sends tingles up my spine.

"Don't do that," he whispers, brushing the hair out of my face.

I almost ask *"Don't do what?"* but I remember what I just told him.

A single tear breaks free, dripping on my pillow before I blink the rest away. "I don't feel so good."

"I know."

My eyes flutter closed, while my heart beats so hard in my chest causing me to feel hot all over. I can't tell if it's from my fever or Griffin being here, caring about me in a way no one ever has before. My sister has taken care of me more times than I can count, but with my ex-husband, I can't even count on one hand the times he's been there for me when I was sick. Even if all the times before this didn't feel as bad as this, he was never there.

The thought alone makes me want to break out in a full sob.

I refuse to do that in front of Griffin.

It's bad enough he's seeing me like this, at my worst.

I open my eyes and he's still staring at me, assessing me.

"Why are you here?" I ask, my voice thick with emotion.

He stands, reaching for the same bag he had in his hands before. "I brought over some stuff to make chicken noodle soup."

"Joke's on you. I can bake, but I can't cook." I huff out a laugh. "Nor do I have the energy to do so."

200

"I didn't say *you* were making it," he replies, making his way to the kitchen. "You're going to lie there and try to sleep while I make the soup."

It's almost laughable that he thinks I can fall asleep with him taking over my small space.

I track his movements and that's when I notice there's something different about him. I scan him from head to toe and realize it's his clothes. A new side of Griffin. He's wearing light gray sweatpants and a solid black T-shirt that hugs every muscle on his upper body. And, of course, his signature backward baseball cap.

Dammit.

He's dressed the most casual I've ever seen him, only making me want to curl up next to him. To let him hold me and take away the pain of this sickness. Not that it would work, but I bet it would feel so good to have his arms around me, ensuring me I'm not actually dying here.

Even if I were, what a way to die.

I reposition myself on the couch so I can watch him move around the kitchen, but the sudden movement startles something in my gut. I leap from the couch and run past Griffin in the kitchen to the bathroom, slamming the door behind me.

There's nothing left in me! Why the hell am I still dry heaving?

The door to the bathroom opens, but I don't look. "Turn around, please," I beg, face in the toilet. "Please, just get out."

He says nothing, but I hear the door close. I let out a relieved sign into the toilet that he actually listened to me while my hands rest on the seat before letting my eyes fall closed.

Griffin's fingertips brushing along both of my shoulders in unison startles me. He pulls the hair out of my face and gathers what little I have in one hand, while the other rubs my back in slow, steady circles.

I choke out a cry; the sound echoing in the toilet.

"Shhh," he whispers. "You're okay. I got you."

I lift my head now that the nausea is passing. I lean my body back to sit on my heels, but Griffin's hard body is there. I melt into him without a second thought. His arms fall around me, holding me, keeping me up when I feel like breaking.

"Griffin?"

"Yeah?"

"Why are you here?" I ask again, resting my head back on his shoulder. "I thought you were avoiding me this past week."

He releases a sigh, angling his head over my shoulder so he can see me. The move forces me to turn my head to face him. We sit there for one...two...three heartbeats. He drops his gaze to my lips for a beat then back up to my eyes. There's no way in hell he wants to kiss me at this moment after I just dry heaved in the toilet.

"I don't know why I'm here," he admits.

My eyes close, but I don't turn away from him.

His hand comes up, holding the side of my face in the most intimate way. I lean into his palm on instinct, wanting this feeling to never go away. It's a small move that only confirms everything I've been thinking about him for so long. Feelings I've been denying.

I want to believe it's the lack of sleep or the fever forcing me to think this way. But it's all him and the way he's caring for me.

The way he showed up for me.

"But I can't stay away from you no matter how much I try," he continues.

My eyes open. The corner of his lip curves up the slightest bit.

"You care about me, huh?" I smirk.

"More than I wanted to, sweetheart," he says, shaking his head as if he doesn't even believe he's feeling this way too.

I don't know what to even say back to that.

This isn't what I came to Bluestones Lakes for.

This wasn't my plan.

It's a twist I'm content with if Griffin keeps looking at me the way he is now, despite how much of a mess I am.

202

Realization hits me, and I quickly bring my hand up to cover my mouth. He rears his head back in confusion. "I need to brush my teeth. Oh my god," I say muffled behind my hand, and scramble out of his hold. "This is so embarrassing. That probably smells so bad. I'm sorry."

I stand and make my way to the sink, putting the toothpaste on the brush before bringing it to my mouth. Lifting my head to look at myself in the mirror and now I want to cry all over again because I can't believe how bad I *really* look.

But Griffin takes his place behind me, watching my every move like he refuses to take his eyes off me. Staring at me through the reflection while I brush my teeth, and I can't stop staring at him either. He puts his hands in the pockets of his sweats, and I swear there's a smile on his features. It's just too damn small to even make out if it's real or not.

I spit into the sink.

Why is brushing teeth so unladylike?

"That was really gross," I say into the sink. "Sorry you had to see that." I stand and keep forward, looking at him again through the reflection.

"Nothing gross about it. You're brushing your teeth." He shrugs.

I turn around to face him fully.

"Feel at least a little better from that?" he asks.

I inhale and exhale slowly, trying to see if the nausea rips through me again at the mention of it. "I think...I'm okay."

He nods. "Let's try to get some food in your system."

He walks out of the bathroom, and I follow him into the kitchen space. He goes directly for the stove, where he already had everything thrown into a giant boiling pot. He must have had everything pre-cut and ready to throw on the stove before he came here, or he's just really that good at making soup.

The smell hits my senses, and I expect to feel sick, but I don't.

I feel everything *but* sick with Griffin here taking care of it.

I don't know what his intentions are. Maybe he's just being a friendly neighbor.

My heart can't seem to stop believing that this could be leading to something more, though.

I've learned I really enjoy his company.

From him helping me with my deck, to having dinner at his house, and the out of this world orgasm he gave me at the bar. Each instance has been different, but good. Not to mention the way he listens to me and understands what I want, the way he makes me laugh even when he can't laugh himself, and the way he looks at me—all these things are leading my heart to feel something for this man standing in my kitchen.

"Thank you," I tell him, taking a place next to him at the stove.

He looks at me while he stirs the pot but remains silent as he assesses my features. I can feel the energy around him and the way the muscles in his jaw tense as if he's just as nervous to get too close. His upper body leans in. Is he finally going to kiss me? I've been wanting to kiss him since the moment he played doctor on my knee. But I pull back, turning my head and walking away. "I should probably get changed."

And like a coward, I head up to my room to get changed and freshen up. I pace my room back and forth, wondering why the hell I just did that when I *want* this man to kiss me.

Am I scared of kissing someone other than my ex-husband?

I shouldn't fucking be.

He's in my past.

This is my home now.

For the first time since moving here, I don't feel guilt for thinking about another man.

I stop pacing and shuffle through my closet. I'm not looking to get dressed up, but I know I need to just change my sweat-pants and T-shirt for a cleaner one so I can stand in the same room as him and not smell like sickness. *If that even has a smell.*

Then I run a brush through my hair before making my way downstairs again.

Once I make it to the last two steps, my body slows, and I watch Griffin setting two placemats with spoons and bowls on my kitchen island for both of us to eat.

He steps back, eying the setup to make sure it's good enough.

I clear my throat while taking the last two steps. His head snaps around, facing me.

"I had to change. I think I smelled like too much sickness," I say, feeling a blush creeping up my cheeks. "I really need a shower, but I *need* food more."

He gestures to the kitchen counter. "Have a seat. The soup is ready for you," he says. Then grabs each bowl and scoops the soup into them.

"Seriously, thank you. For all of this," I tell him honestly, making my way to the small stool. "You truly didn't have to do this. I feel so bad because whatever this sickness is, it's fierce. And gross. And I don't want you to get it."

"I won't," he assures me. "I have the immune system of a moose."

I cross my arms over my chest, smiling for the first time all day. "Is that supposed to be a joke?"

"It made you smile."

Now I know for sure, my pale face is crimson red with that statement. I look down at the bowl he placed in front of me, smiling at it and tucking a strand of hair behind my ear.

"Don't do that."

"Do what?" I ask, looking up at him.

"Hide your smile from me. When I was standing at your door when I got here, that's what pained me the most. You looked so miserable, and I hated that."

"You…" I pause, feeling confused. "What?"

"You're growing on me, sweetheart."

I blink a few times in his direction before looking down at my soup, swirling the spoon around the hot mix of chicken and vegetables. I can feel the smile begin to form on my lips. No matter how much I try to fight it off, I can't.

Silence stretches between us for a few minutes, only increasing the tension in the tiny home.

"What city exactly are you from?" he asks out of nowhere.

I feel my stomach churn; this time it's not from the sickness. This conversation was inevitable. Bringing up my past was something that eventually people would want to know.

"San Francisco," I answer honestly.

"What made you move here?"

He's getting to know me. That's all this is. He doesn't know my husband.

Concentrating on maintaining an even heart rate at his question, I inhale and exhale slowly to calm my nerves. "My life back home was far from ideal. As I told you before, my husband cheated on me. Betraying my trust in the worst way possible..." I pause, swallowing past the emotions of my past. "It left me feeling lost. I realized I needed some space to rediscover myself. It wasn't that I didn't love the city. However, I felt as if I was simply lost in the masses. I lost sight of who I was as a person."

He nods repeatedly as if he understands.

"I come from a life of politics. Always in the spotlight and was molded into this person who was supposed to be professional one hundred percent of the time."

"And that's not who you are."

I shake my head. "I don't think it ever was. Being here, in Bluestone Lakes, I've learned a lot about myself. Who I've always been under the mask I had up."

"You're free."

Two words. Hitting me square in the chest.

A feeling that's grown on me in my short time here, only confirmed by hearing it from Griffin.

Nodding, letting the smile crest my lips. "I am."

Griffin's features soften, averting his gaze to the bowl of soup in front of him. His smile matches mine, but it's cut short when he lets out a yawn.

"Did you work today?" I ask, trying to keep the conversation going without feeling awkward after the discussion of my past.

"I did, and it was an interesting crowd today."

I eye him in confusion. "Isn't it normally, like, the same people around here?"

He scoffs. "Yeah, usually it is. But it was Nan and Tucker. Both of them came in arguing over pretzel twists."

I throw my head back and laugh. "Nan and Tucker would fight over pretzels. Tucker seems so funny."

"You think so?" he asks, but the shift in his tone sounds all gruff and feral. Like…he's jealous?

Oh, this could be fun.

"Yeah. The few times I've seen him, I could tell he has this charm about him. All laughs. All fun. Serious when he needs to be, you know?"

He stares at me for a heartbeat before looking down at his now-empty bowl of soup and picking it up to take to the sink. I watch his every move as he rinses the bowl, placing it in the sink and resting both hands on the edge of the counter as if deep in thought.

Picking up my bowl, I meet him at the sink. He steps to the side, allowing me to put mine in the sink as well. Turning to face him, I place a hand on his forearm.

"I'll finish the dishes later," I say. "Seriously, thank you for all of this. I already feel so much better from you being here."

He nods but remains silent.

He heads toward the front door as if he's going to leave without saying anything more. After opening up to him and showing my vulnerable side, there's no way he's going to just walk out of here.

"Hey," I call after him. He stops, turning to face me. "Are you just going to leave without a goodbye?" My hands find my hips in annoyance.

For a brief moment, I think he's going to say goodbye and turn around and leave, but he doesn't. He eyes me up and down, taking a few steps toward me. Close enough that I have to angle my head to meet his stare.

"There's a lot more I want to say than that single word."

I cross my arms over my chest. "Okay?"

He cups the side of my cheek with his calloused but gentle hand and brushes his thumb over the apple of my cheek. His stare is so intense, my body shivers and I want to throw myself into him.

"But if I say all the things I want to say, I'll never leave." He pauses, eyes scanning my face. "And if I say it, it changes everything."

"Let it change everything," I whisper, letting my eyes flutter closed from his touch. "I can handle it."

"Get some sleep, Blair."

He leans down and presses a soft kiss on my forehead. I've never wanted to feel those lips on mine more than I do right now. Soft and warm, awakening a feeling inside of me so foreign.

He pulls back, his gaze never leaving my face.

Then I witness the most beautiful thing I've ever seen.

Griffin Barlow's smile.

CHAPTER 28

YOU'VE BEEN DRIVING ME CRAZY SINCE I GOT HERE, ANGRY COWBOY.

GRIFFIN

> **ME**
> Feeling any better?

> **BLAIR**
> I was able to get all that sleep you told me to get.

> **ME**
> Funny.

> **BLAIR**
> I thought so.

> **ME**
> You didn't answer my question.

> **BLAIR**
> Two full days of sleep helped. I'm feeling much better.

> **ME**
> Good.

The more time I spend with Blair, the more I realize how good it feels to be around her.

I can't explain it because I'm trying to wrap my head around it myself.

She has a way about her that can evoke a smile from even the grumpiest soul. She came into town and brought the sunshine with her even after everything she's been through.

She still manages to smile through the pain.

Even the other night, with how sick she was, she still wore a smile on her face.

It's only made keeping my tough exterior in place that much harder. She broke me down. She made me smile. I think she's been doing it for a while now. I just haven't been able to let it see the light of day.

I fought the good mood at work yesterday and today because I wanted to avoid questions from everyone. If she doesn't feel the same, I don't need people knowing and turning it into something it's not.

Just as I'm about to leave to head home for the evening, Lily walks in.

"Oh good, you're still here," she says, shaking off the rain from her jacket. "It's gross out there."

"What brings you in? I was just heading home."

"Perfect timing." She beams, lifting a bag of treats in front of me. "Can you bring these to Blair? Since you're going that way."

I narrow my eyes. "Is this a trick?"

"Nope." She shakes her head, chin held high.

"Why don't I believe you?"

"You should. I'm your sister," she scoffs. "Unless there's something you're not telling me, Griffy," she says in an accusing tone.

"Don't call me that."

"You didn't answer my question," she says with her hands on her hips.

"You didn't ask one."

She rolls her eyes and groans. "You're so annoying."

"I'm your brother. That's my job." I wink at her and feel the corner of my lips tip up in a grin.

Her eyes widen and lips part.

I quickly realize she just caught me feeling something other than miserable. I school my features, snatching the bag of baked goods from her hand and sidestepping her to leave.

"Oh no, you don't," Lily says from behind me. "You don't just smile for the first time in years and not explain yourself."

I stop, closing my eyes and lifting my head to the ceiling before turning to face her, unsure of what to say and definitely unable to hide any sort of expression from my face.

"Maybe it was just because I think you're funny," I lie.

"You never think I'm funny," she says, her tone serious. "Is there something going on I should know about? This is kind of a big deal."

"It's really not, Lil. Please don't make it into something it's not. Yes, I smiled. Barely. No, I don't want to talk about it because I don't need the whole town knowing my business within the hour."

"Is that what you think I would do?"

I shake my head, immediately feeling bad for accusing her of telling everyone about my business. I know she wouldn't, but how can I even explain it when it's not something I'm even sure of myself?

"I know you wouldn't," I tell her honestly.

"Is this about Blair?" She grins mischievously.

I remain silent, averting my gaze to the floor between us.

Lily smacks my arm, and I snap my head back up and meet her shocked features. "I knew it! I've been waiting for this moment," she cheers.

"Like I said before, don't make this into something it's not. Do I like her? Sure. She's growing on me. But we've both been through some shit. I have no doubt her guard is up just as much as mine is. I can't let what happened before happen again. I will not jump into something unless I know she's really staying. Unless she wants this."

Lily's smile softens. It feels weird to share this piece of me with someone. But this is my sister, and if there's anyone I can trust, it's her.

"I can't speak for her future plans, but it sounds like she's staying, Griffin," Lily says. "But as you know, I'm someone who believes in gut feelings. If something is off, it's off. If something feels right, it's right. I understand the need to protect yourself here..." She pauses, swallowing as if emotions are getting the best of her, but she doesn't want to show it. "I've grown to love Blair. I've never been so happy that someone landed in this town, of all places. It's like she was meant to come here when she did. The universe always works in crazy ways."

The universe always works in crazy ways.

And she's right.

My tiny house sat vacant for a long time before Nan finally sold it for me. I didn't expect the new owner to be an out-of-town city girl, but life put her in front of me when I least expected it.

And now I can't get her out of my head.

"I'll get these to her," I tell Lily, and turn around to leave. Stopping before I walk out the door, I turn to face Lily again. "And keep this between us for now."

She zips her lips shut with her fingers. "My lips are sealed."

I nod and turn to leave.

I guess I'm going to Blair's house to drop off these treats.

The rain has completely stopped in the short time it takes for me to leave the bar and turn onto my road. The sky is still ominous and filled with clouds, but it might hold off for a bit.

Maybe after I drop this off, I can spend some time at the ranch, go for a ride, and try to process some of these things I've been feeling.

Pulling into her driveway, I spot her car and park behind her. My nerves spike for an unknown reason. The more I think about her, the more unsure I am about being around her—I don't want to screw this up before it's even something to screw up.

I take a deep breath before I step onto her porch and tap on the glass. No response, not even from the dog. I turn around to double-check her car, just to be sure. It is indeed hers.

I run back to my vehicle and grab a piece of scrap paper from the glove compartment to leave her a note with the bag of treats from Lily.

I stopped by to drop these off from Lily. If you need anything, you know where to find me.
- Griffin

After leaving them on the small table she has set up, I jump back in my truck. Sitting there for a moment, my eyes stay fixed on her house.

Her home.

I allow my mind to wander to places they haven't been in a long time—visions of the future dance around my head. Someone to come home to after a day at the bar, filling a home with laughter. I can't remember the last time I sat and thought about where I saw myself in the future. I'm someone who takes everything one day at a time. I don't think about yesterday—just today and what's in store for tomorrow.

I shake my head because I need an open field to clear my head of this.

I reverse from her driveway, not bothering to stop at home, and head for the ranch. The minute I cross the entrance archway;

I already feel at peace. I'll never get over the feeling of this place, this area, this field.

I spend the next thirty minutes getting Storm ready to ride, ensuring the tack is secure before I mount him. Once I do, I lean down and offer him a pet on the side of his face, and then we take off out of the barn.

The skies don't look promising, but I've been in worse weather.

I know I need this time, though.

The same thoughts I had sitting in Blair's driveway come back. I find them eating me alive every time she's in my head, which is more times than I can count.

Storm sets into a steady gallop through the field, sending us in the direction of the trail I always go down with him. I call it *my* trail. I found it by mistake and have never seen anyone else on it. It brings me just to the outskirts of town with a private view of the back end of Bluestone Lake.

I've come here so often that I've built benches for myself and a small fence for Storm to secure him when I need more time to sit with thoughts.

Today, my adrenaline is too high to sit.

I need to ride. And fast.

Everything about Blair is driving me wild.

I want that wild.

I want the freedom she has.

I want more with Blair; it scares me, and that fear holds me back. There's this need inside of me wanting to know if she's genuinely staying. The confirmation that this is her home forever and she won't be running back to the city or her husband.

It sounds ridiculous, but I wouldn't survive another heartbreak.

Can I make her stay?

No, that's even crazier.

Storm picks up speed as if he's sensing my mood, but my mind doesn't stop spiraling.

I wonder if she feels the same way I'm feeling right now.

Is she holding back too?

I wouldn't call this love, not this soon. But there's chemistry there. Something is brewing in my gut, and the thought of anything with her makes my heart race at the speed of light.

I pull the reins on Storm, slowing us to a stop when we enter the open fields that lead us back toward the barn. My arms fall to my side as I close my eyes and lift my head to the sky.

"I need some guidance here. A sign. Anything that tells me what I should do," I say to the sky, hoping the universe is listening to my plea.

Small raindrops land on my cheeks, and I open my eyes to see a wall of rain in the distance. That's the fascinating thing about this open land and weather.

This overwhelming urge to go back to her house hits me.

She wasn't home, but maybe she is now. Is that why I'm feeling this pull?

I nudge Storm forward in a slow trot to the barn before we get caught in the downpour headed our way.

I want...no, I *need* to know how she's feeling about this, us, what's happening here.

And there's only one way to do that.

Something catches my eye off to the side and I have to do a double take to see, but a white car sits at the corner of the property. The same spot I once caught Blair sitting. A spot I know Lily told her about because it's an ideal spot to catch the views of the sunset across the fields.

I pull Storm's reins again to a stop, turning us to face her direction.

As soon as I stop, Blair exits the car.

I watch intently as she walks up to the wooden fence, resting both arms on top. I scan her from head to toe and notice she's wearing a blue and white floral skirt, and a skintight white shirt tucked inside.

Fuck, she looks beautiful.

It takes me a moment to realize she's also wearing a...cowgirl hat?

Tingles erupt all over my skin with the need to touch her, hold her, *brand her,* and make her mine.

I dismount my horse—right here in the middle of the open field.

Blair wedges her way between the horizontal posts of the fence and steps into the property. Standing there for a pause before taking slow steps in my direction.

She didn't come here for the view today.

There's no way, because it's obstructed by clouds and rain.

I begin walking in her direction, and when I do, she picks up the pace into a slow jog toward me through the long grass. A smile stretched across her face as one hand holds her skirt up and the other keeping the hat in place on her head.

Now it's my turn to smile.

She slows to a stop in front of me, but it doesn't feel close enough.

Neither of us says anything.

Looking down at her hands, she fidgets with them as if she's nervous about being here. Then she brings her bottom lip between her teeth as if she wants to say something. Anything.

I want those lips on mine.

I want her to breathe life into me.

"I came to say thank you for dropping off the treats from Lily," she breaks the silence, finally meeting my gaze.

I nod.

My throat can't even form words looking at her.

I've never known the feeling of someone taking your breath away. I always thought it was a corny saying people would use to describe a feeling they couldn't put into words.

Standing here in front of Blair, I understand it now.

"You left me a note," she continues. "You said if I needed anything, I would know where to find you."

"You found me." I grin.

"I, uh," she starts, looking from me to the ground again. "I guess I just wanted to say thank you for the other night. In person. You know? Needed you to know that it was appreciated. And, uh…yeah," she rambles.

My smile grows because she's just as nervous as I am and it's cute as shit.

"You came all the way out here to tell me that?" I ask.

She tightens her lips and puffs her cheeks out, looking around us. "Well, when you put it like that…" She takes a few steps back, hiking her thumb over her shoulder. "So, I'm going to head back now. Yeah. Thank you," she says quickly before turning around.

Just as she starts a jog back toward her car, I stop her.

"Do you feel it too?" I shout.

She stops and turns to face me with her hands at her sides, tilting her head to the side in question. "The rain? Yeah, it feels like it's going to pour any second."

I look down at the tall grass, chuckling to myself before walking toward her, closing the space between us. She didn't get far, but I need this confirmation.

She doesn't move an inch.

She allows me to take over her space.

My reach up to cup the side of her face. Her eyes fall closed when I bring my other hand up, removing the hat from her head. I trail my eyes along every delicate feature of her face I've already memorized. The light freckles that line the apple of her cheek, and the barely noticeable dimple on the left side of her mouth when she smiles. Her soft pink lips part, and her long, thick lashes sweep up as she opens her eyes, silently pleading for me to kiss her.

"Do you feel this too?" I ask again.

She nods. A silent understanding that she knows exactly what I mean now.

My hand moves, letting my knuckles graze her jawline until I'm angling her head up to face me. I pause, giving her the chance to back away, but she doesn't. So I lean down and press my lips to hers.

The world around me stops spinning as raindrops hit the back of my neck. I feel weightless; like I'm standing on a cloud.

Kissing Blair feels like coming back to life.

I close the gap between us, wrapping one hand around her body to pull her into me, needing to feel her close. My other hand drops the hat to the ground before I wrap it around the back of her head, tangling my fingers in her hair.

The rain only falls harder around us.

But she doesn't push me away.

She moves her head to the side, opening up for me and allowing my tongue to dance with hers. Her arms fly around my neck while she presses up on her toes as if she can't get close enough to me.

I never want this kiss to end.

I could die a happy man if this is the last taste on my lips.

But Blair pulls away, taking half a step back before her fingertips touch her swollen lips.

"I'm sorry," I tell her, watching as she tries to determine what that was all about. "I...just—"

She cuts me off by leaping back into my arms and crushing her lips to mine. She's feral for this, the way I am with her. I'd give anything to take her back home, bring her to her room, and do this all night. But I won't. I can't.

She moans into my mouth, and I swear I lose it right there.

My hands grip her hips, hard, holding her body against mine, and I'm sure she feels what she's doing to me with just this kiss.

I pull away. "Blair," I say breathlessly. "The rain is really coming down."

"Yes. The rain. Lots of it," she pants.

A smile plays at my lips, because she's so cute when she's flustered.

"And there you go again," she groans.

"What?"

"You smiled. And I really like when you smile. Which is a new development because you don't do it enough. But now I want you to kiss me again because of it. But this weather is getting worse and I'm sure we're both going to get sick now from the wet, cold clothes," she rambles, and it only widens my smile.

My hand holds her face, urging her to look up at me. When she does, the rain blurs her vision, and she has to blink away the raindrops. I can't help myself; I brush the wet strands out of her face.

"I'm glad you showed up today," I tell her honestly.

"You are?"

I nod, using my thumb to wipe the rainwater from her cheek. "You're driving me absolutely crazy, Blair. In a good way," I assure her. "I can't stop thinking about you. I can't stop wondering what you're doing. I want to be near you any chance I can. And most of all, I needed to feel your lips on mine to see if there was any part of you that was going just as crazy as I was."

She stares at me, her breathing faster than before, and my stomach does a somersault when she doesn't immediately answer. She brings her hands up, cupping both sides of my face, letting her thumb graze the scruff lining my jaw.

"You've been driving me crazy since I got here, Angry Cowboy."

The biggest smile I've had in years stretches across my face with her words, and I lean in for another kiss. Her hands hold my face there, telling me she wants this as bad as I do. Her body trembles, and I realize we can't stay out here forever.

I release the kiss reluctantly, but hover just over her lips.

"Let's get you home and warmed up," I say.

I drape an arm over her shoulders as I walk her back to her car, realizing we didn't come here together, so I can't actually take her home.

But I fucking want to.

I also want to tread lightly and not dive in too quickly.

"This is me," she jokes as if I don't know her car by heart now.

"Yeah, you have to get some better wheels for these roads."

"I know, I just don't have it in me yet to give up this baby," she says, patting the hood of the car.

I offer her a smile. It comes on instinct with her now.

Blair has this power over me now that I can't even help it.

She opens the door, getting in, and looking up at me before closing the door. With one hand on the hood of the car, and the other on the door, I say, "You know where to find me if you need me."

"I guess I do, huh?" She lightly laughs.

With that, she pulls her car door shut. I step back and watch as the engine turns on and she backs it up out of the grass before driving away. I don't take my eyes off the car or move from where I stand until it's completely out of sight.

Everything just changed.

And later that night, for the first time in a long time, I fall asleep with a smile.

CHAPTER 29

ONE KISS AND YOU'RE PART OF THE FAMILY.

BLAIR

"I feel like it's been longer than a week since we had our check-in calls," Kodi says through the phone speaker. "I'm feeling like you're forgetting me already."

"Never." I laugh. "I've just been so busy here."

And distracted, if I'm being honest.

I have been bouncing around my house as if I live on an actual cloud since yesterday. Because Griffin Barlow kissed me.

I'm not ashamed to say I came home, threw myself on the couch, and kicked my feet in the air like a dead bug in excitement over it. I felt like a high school girl all over again whose crush just admitted feelings for her. I can't remember a time I've ever felt like that before.

The kiss was electric.

It was fire.

It was hot.

All things it shouldn't have been considering it was cold and raining out.

"*Hellooo?*" Kodi bellows through the phone. "Did you hear anything I just said?"

"In an effort to maintain honesty between us...no."

"I was telling you I saw Mom yesterday. She was asking about you," Kodi says softly.

Just like that, my happiness bubble pops.

I scoff. "That's funny. She has my number. She could, you know, pick up the phone and call me."

"You know how she is."

"Yeah, I do. I know she's not happy about me leaving the spotlight and the political life *she* wants me to live. She doesn't care at all about our happiness."

"Why do you think I avoid her myself?" Kodi laughs. "She's a lot. *A lot.* And that says something coming from me."

"So, what did she want?" I ask reluctantly.

"She wanted to know when you were planning to come home. When you were done playing the victim. But don't worry," she says quickly. "I told her it's justified because that twatwaffle cheated on *you*, not the other way around. In her eyes, everyone deserves a second chance. Blah blah."

And she's right.

That's exactly how my mother is. She's manipulative and will toy with your emotions so that it always looks like she wins at the end.

"She's actually crazy," I tell Kodi. "I don't plan to come back."

Kodi remains silent on the other end, and I know instantly that my words hurt her. She wants me to come back. I miss her just as much as she misses me, if not more. Not having my sister here is painful. She's my rock, my sounding board.

"I don't mean it like that, Kodi."

"I know what you mean. I get it. Sometimes I just get sad because I really miss you so much. These phone calls aren't enough. She might have...brought up Theodore too."

I wince at his name being brought up.

"I know," she continues as if she heard me. "He's not doing good, Blair."

"What do you mean?"

"His life is quite literally crumbling since you left."

"Me?" I gasp. "This has nothing to do with me. Our divorce was over long before I decided to move out here."

"No, no, no. I'm not saying *because* of you. I'm just saying in general. He's been plastered all over the news with scandal after scandal. His approval ratings are shit, and there's no way he's going to get reelected unless he gets his shit together."

There's a really small part of me that feels bad for him. A *really small* part. Because no one deserves to be going through shit. But in this situation, Theodore brought it on himself. He's the reason behind the scandals she's telling me about because he can't keep his dick in his pants and remain faithful.

I wait for the hurt he put me through to hit my chest.

But it doesn't come.

For once, it doesn't come.

I knew prior to moving here that I'd moved on from him, and there was no chance of ever giving him a second chance. I knew the emotions would come to the surface, every once in a while, as it's part of the healing process. The memories of my past will always be there as it was part of my life for so long.

At one point or another, they stop hurting.

They stop being painful memories and they turn into just... memories.

"In an effort to change the subject," Kodi interrupts my thoughts. "I hope you know how happy and proud of you I am for getting out of here and starting a life you deserve."

Now the emotions fight to come to the surface.

Just as I'm about to respond a text comes through my phone. Looking down, I see it's Griffin.

GRIFFIN
Hey.

ME
Hey.

"This man," I whisper to myself out loud, shaking my head.

"Huh?"

"Oh, I'm sorry. I just got a text from Griffin," I tell her, clicking out of my texts and back to the phone screen. "He's the superior one-word texter."

"Is he now?" she coos. "Is there something happening with this neighbor friend of yours?"

Guilt flashes through my head for not filling Kodi in on everything that's happened here. I don't know why because she's in another state and there's no chance of people in town finding out from her.

Another text comes through, and I switch screens.

GRIFFIN

Dinner. Parents' house. Tonight.

ME

Is this a question or demand?

"For starters, I think he just asked me to dinner at his parents' house tonight," I say.

"You think?"

"He's not good at texting. He gives one word for things and said *dinner*. Period. *Parents' house*. Period. *Tonight*. Period." I laugh.

"Thank you for spelling that out for me and including punctuation marks."

"I wanted you to get the vibes."

"Back to what's really happening here. He asked you to his parents' house for dinner? What the hell is happening out there in Bluewater Rivers?"

I nearly choke on my own words. "Bluestone Lakes is a very fun place. They have horses and hot neighbors. One of whom is an exceptional kisser."

"*What?*"

My phone chimes again.

"Hold please," I tell Kodi, switching to the text app.

"You can't tell me to hold after dropping this information," Kodi snaps while I read through the message.

GRIFFIN

Question.

ME

You're asking me to go to dinner at your parents' house tonight? Just so I'm understanding correctly.

GRIFFIN

Yes.

ME

Well, you should have just said that.

"I'm three seconds from screaming," Kodi practically shouts.

"Yesterday," I start, pausing to allow the smile to stretch across my face, thinking about the kiss again. "I went to the ranch where he usually rides after he left me treats Lily sent for me from the bakery. I don't know why I went there, but when I arrived, I felt silly and off. Almost like I was making the wrong choice in being there."

"Valid. Continue."

"So I rambled and thanked him for making me soup when I was sick. He stopped me as I was going back to my car, and I can't remember a single thing that happened seconds before his lips were on mine."

"I feel like I'm listening to a movie."

"It felt like I was *in* one. The rain was coming down so hard. My hair was soaked, and by the time we got back to my car, both our clothes were sopping wet. But it didn't matter because that man can kiss, Kodi. I've never felt a kiss as intense as that."

"This is...I...don't know what to say," Kodi says, clearly at a loss for words.

"I feel the same way right now. I don't know how to process

225

it," I tell her honestly. "One minute I'm trying to get my life together for me, and the next I'm falling for my neighbor."

"Rewind. *Back up!*" she stops me. "So, this is serious. You're really falling for the guy. Are you sure you want to get into something so soon?"

"I'm not sure about anything anymore." I scoff. "But what I do know is there's something between us. I can't seem to shake it either. And now, he's inviting me to his family's house for dinner."

"One kiss, and you're part of the family. Way to go, Blair," she cheers.

My phone chimes with a text again.

GRIFFIN
I did.

ME
No, you demanded.

"I wouldn't go that far," I continue with Kodi.

"I would. No man invites you to dinner with the family unless it's serious."

I roll my eyes, even though she can't see. "You don't know this town. It's small and everyone here is close. But I won't deny myself of something if the universe keeps pushing me in his direction. I totally get butterflies every time he's around too."

"How very high school of you." She laughs.

"I'm being so serious." I chuckle, even though I really am being honest. "I want to fight it off. But like I said, the universe, gravity, some outer space pull, keeps shoving me his way."

"Did you pull that off the internet?"

"I can't stand you."

"You know I don't do the sappy love bullshit," she says with humor in her tone.

That's the one area of life where she and I are opposites. I'm a hopeless romantic and she's good at being alone and working on growing a successful business. If I could have half of her independence in life, I would make it anywhere. I know it.

"Listen," she continues before I can respond. "I love you more than anything and I just never want to see you hurt the way Theo-fuckface hurt you. It was the most painful thing to witness, knowing I couldn't do anything to fix it for you. So just be careful with your heart."

"I will. I love you, Kodi."

"Love you too. Have fun at dinner, but not too much fun." She giggles before hitting end on the call.

I mull over her words as I stare down at the open text conversation with Griffin that he didn't respond to.

I know deep down I need to protect my heart.

But I can't deny this.

I can't deny him anymore.

I decide to add to the previous message.

ME

But I'll admit, it was kind of hot.

GRIFFIN

Blair...

Dinner tonight should be very interesting.

I look at the clock on the microwave and realize Griffin should be here any minute.

I make my way to the bathroom to give myself a once-over.

I settled on a flowy skirt with a tucked-in sweater. It's been so long since I've done this. The whole "meet the parents" thing. I'm not even sure what to make of this whole thing, which puts me that much more on edge.

Hearing the sound of truck tires in the gravel driveway, I inhale slowly and release before making my way outside to meet him. I step onto the porch at the same time he closes the truck door.

He lifts his head to find me already standing there and stops dead in his tracks. An intense look bores into me as he trails his gaze up and down my body before he swallows. He catches himself and averts his stare to the ground, then continues walking until he's on my porch.

Nervous energy flows through me.

He lifts his eyes to meet mine again. Heat dances along my skin, but at the same time, shivers rack my body, and I fight the urge to not visibly shake where I stand.

"You look beautiful," he says. "You didn't need to get dressed up for my parents."

I smile. "This is actually one of my more casual outfits. But do you think I'm overdressed?"

He practically chokes on air. "Yes," he says before swallowing. "I mean, no."

The grin on my face only grows as I place both hands on my hips. "Are you flustered, Griffin Barlow?"

"Are you always this forward?"

I shrug. "New town, new me."

But is it still considered a "new town" if I've been here a few months now? I don't know, but I'm rolling with it.

Griffin doesn't move. He opens his mouth to say something but closes it quickly as if to stop himself.

"Ready?" he settles on.

I nod before he guides me to his truck.

Like a true gentleman, he opens the truck door for me, letting me get in before he closes it and rounds the hood with a little pep in his step. I watch every move as if I can't take my eyes off of him. He hops in the truck so easily, twisting the key in the ignition. With one hand on the wheel, and the other resting on the back of my seat, he maneuvers out of the driveway and onto the road.

There's something about the way a man does that.

Specifically, him.

"I just want to warn you before we get there," he starts, pausing to take a deep breath. "My parents can be overbearing. They want what's best for me, but sometimes I don't think they really know me that well and what I actually want in life."

I turn to look at him while he stares out the front window, keeping his eyes on the road.

"I understand that. I used to feel that way about mine too. Except, mine had a sprinkle of manipulation in there." I laugh lightly to ease the tension. "No matter what I was feeling, they would make it about themselves and how *they* felt. They never failed to make me feel like my feelings were invalid. I cut them off years ago because of this. Now I just talk to them on my own terms," I say, but realize I haven't stopped talking. "And now I'm trauma dumping on you and I'm surprised you haven't dropped me on the curb."

"Are you done?" he asks.

"Yes."

"Good, because I have no plans of dropping you off on the curb," he says, bringing the car to a stop at the stop sign and turning his gaze on me. "I want you there tonight."

I nod in understanding before he accelerates the truck, turning on a new road.

I want you there tonight.

His words ring in my ear like a song I can't stop singing.

He wants me there.

He wants me to meet his parents.

Fear pricks the back of my head that this is too good to be true. There was a time when I first met Theodore's parents, and he wanted me there. It all changed so fast and quickly, though. We settled into a "normal" that I don't think was very normal

229

now that I look back. We got comfortable and forgot about wanting each other. *Needing* each other.

The only long-term relationship I know is my broken marriage.

So, is that what it's supposed to be like?

Okay, not that I'm marrying Griffin or anything, but will he get bored with me and find someone new?

I hate that my brain is doing this to me right now.

"We're here," Griffin says, breaking the silence as he throws the truck in park.

"That was fast."

"Small town." He winks before exiting and hustling to my side to open the door for me.

I can't hold back the smile on my face even if I tried.

Touché.

I face the house, and my jaw falls to the ground. The house resembles a log cabin-style home nestled between trees as if we're in the middle of the woods. The surrounding view is nothing like the ones on our street, but it's beautiful. Cozy and secluded.

"Will your sisters be here?" I ask him.

He shakes his head. "Just us tonight."

I nod, following Griffin up the wooden porch. The door opens before we even reach it and Nan greets us.

"What are you doing here?" Griffin asks her, confused.

"Your mom said she made that chicken recipe I love so much." She giggles. "You know how much I love that shit, so I invited myself."

Griffin simply shakes his head, and sidesteps her to enter the home.

"Hope you're hungry, Blair." Nan winks.

I offer her a soft smile and follow her inside.

Here goes nothing.

A beautiful woman enters the hallway, holding a dishrag, drying her hands, and stops when she notices me.

"You didn't tell me you were bringing a guest?" She beams at Griffin.

I feel my cheeks heat up with embarrassment because the last thing I want to be is a burden and overstep my welcome.

I open my mouth to respond, but Griffin beats me to it.

"She's my neighbor."

My head snaps in his direction, and I force a smile.

That hurt way more than it should.

I know my brain has been so back and forth for a little while now, wondering if this is what I want. Do I want more? Kind of. No. I *do* want more.

"I'm Mary," his mom says.

"I'm Blair," I say, taking a few steps to greet her with my hand extended. She takes my hand in hers. "I've heard nothing but good things."

Nan chokes on her drink somewhere beside me.

"You don't have to lie to us," an older man says, entering the hallway to greet us. He extends his hand in front of me. "I'm Eugene. Everyone calls me Gene."

"It's nice to meet you too."

"You two are just in time," Mary says, guiding us to the table set up for dinner already. "Dinner is ready."

I follow Griffin, wrapping a hand around his thick bicep and stopping him before we enter the kitchen. "You didn't tell them I was coming?"

"I'm a man full of surprises, sweetheart." He winks. "If I told them I was bringing someone she would have broken out the fine China. This is casual."

"Okay."

It's all I can think to even say. I mean, when it comes to his family, he knows better than me, that's for sure.

Mary sets up an extra table setting. "I'm sorry I didn't have time to bring out the fancy dinnerware for you, Blair. This one" —she tilts her head toward Griffin—"didn't think to tell us you were coming."

I find Griffin smirking in the corner of the room.

"Don't be sorry, ma'am. I appreciate you making a spot for me," I tell her honestly.

"None of that 'ma'am' stuff," she says, waving me off.

Mary and Eugene bring dishes to the table while Griffin pulls out a chair, extending his arm to show me my seat.

"Can I get you something to drink?" he asks.

"Whatever you're having is fine."

He nods, retreating to the kitchen with his mom and dad right behind him.

Nan takes a seat next to me, resting her elbow on the table and turning her body to face me. I look at her, confused, while she keeps an evil smile written all over her face.

"Are you okay?" I laugh at her.

"I'm so happy you're here, Blair."

Griffin enters before she can say more with two glasses in hand. One with an amber liquid and the other a white wine, that he places in front of me.

"So, Nan," Gene says, taking a seat while everyone fills their plates with food. "Tell us about this new guy coming to town."

She runs her fingers across her lips, signaling that they are sealed.

"Apparently, he's a celebrity," Mary says, cutting into her chicken. "Nan knows who it is but refuses to tell us how and why he's a celebrity."

"Maybe he's into politics, and that's why he's considered a celebrity," Gene says. "How fun would that be?"

My stomach flips at the thought of a male politician coming to town.

Did Theodore find out where I live?

He's most definitely considered a celebrity back in San Francisco.

"All I can tell you is he's moving to Poplar Street next door to Poppy." Nan laughs with a mouthful of food before pointing her fork in Eugene's direction. "And don't bother looking up the record, because it's off the book."

"Is that legal?" I ask, curious.

"The marijuana I smoke ain't legal either," she barks out. "But no one's going to get me in trouble. I have a shank."

"A shank?" Griffin asks, choking on his chicken.

"Yep. A weapon of mass destruction." Nan nods.

Griffin rolls his eyes. "You can't call a steak knife a weapon of mass destruction."

"You. Shush," she cuts him off. "Don't give away all my secrets. I like people to fear me."

My hand comes up to cover my mouth as I laugh into my palm.

"Well, that's enough violence for one dinner," Mary says. "Let's talk about Blair. Where are you from?"

My stomach does another somersault. Griffin knows where I'm from, but being his father is the mayor of this town, I wonder if he's in contact with others. Like there's some special hub online of mayors connecting with each other.

I'm definitely thinking too much into this.

I just don't want my past to be brought into my future when I'm in such a good place right now. I feel good, and things are going really well for me.

"I'm from San Francisco," I say.

"Wow," Gene says. "That's a long way away. It's a whole new world here compared to there, huh?"

"You could say that again," I scoff.

Nan clears her throat. "It's a whole new world—"

"Nan," Griffin cuts her off.

"Oh, right." Nan nods, before cutting into her meal again.

"What made you move out here?" Mary asks. "Do you have a job that allows you to work anywhere?"

"Well…" *Inhale. Exhale.* "I didn't have a job. I was married to the mayor."

I answer Mary's question, looking in Griffin's direction, when something flashes in his eyes. I can't find it in me to look away from him as he stares at me blankly.

A look full of questions.

But also full of desire.

It's as if something shifted in that one sentence.

I replay my own words in my head while Nan continues a conversation about lord knows what. It's drowned out the longer I keep my gaze locked with Griffin.

I *was* married to the mayor.

Confirmation for both of us that I'm no longer that person.

I'm not married.

I don't have a husband.

I'm free.

That's when I finally realize I don't want to be free anymore.

I want to be claimed in every way possible by Griffin Barlow.

CHAPTER 30
CAN'T HELP IT WHEN YOU'RE AROUND.

GRIFFIN

Dinner goes by in a blur.

Of course, my parents found the opportunity to bring up small-town politics. Blair even seemed annoyed by the entire conversation, making me fascinated by her. Showing me she can't stand the life she used to live, the same way I can't stand the politics surrounding my family.

My mom starts serving dessert. Even if it's just my sisters and me here, she always makes a show of things by going over the top and making sure we leave here extra full.

"So, Blair," my dad starts again. "What got you into politics?"

She scoffs. "I was never into politics."

I narrow my eyes at my father, and he notices, but refuses to back down.

"Well, a big-time mayor like that in San Francisco should have a wife who's into that sort of thing."

"Eugene. That's enough," I snap.

He extends his hand out in Blair's direction, but stares at me. "Son, I'm just trying to get to know her."

"You're not," I say, my tone growing more frustrated. "You're finding an opening to continue a discussion about politics by insinuating Blair is a part of it. She's not like that. She got out of that life for a reason, and I'd appreciate it if you didn't bring it up at the table."

My dad pauses, staring at me before taking a bite of his pie.

"With all due respect," Blair cuts in. "Just because I was married to him doesn't mean I was happy. I left for a reason. I cut my parents off for a reason. Both because of politics and a life I no longer wanted to be associated with. I mean…" She pauses, twirling her fork in her hand. "Leaving my husband was a mix of that and his *appreciation* for his secretary." She laughs lightly. "But it all boiled down to living a life I wasn't happy with. I don't say this to disrespect you in your home. I say this because it's not who I am."

I stare at her in shock and admiration.

No one ever stands up to my father like that.

"I know things are different here," she continues. "I'd love to know more about this town, this family, and what you do for work…but my past is my past for a reason."

My past is my past for a reason.

One short sentence causes my past to flash before my eyes.

What's my reason?

Is Blair my reason? Did I have to go through devastating heartbreak because life knew something better would come my way? Maybe Sierra leaving was a way to protect me from getting any deeper with her and being hurt worse.

"Do you plan to go back?" my mom asks.

I hold my breath because this is what I've been wanting to ask her.

I almost asked her when I picked her up tonight, and she brought up the whole new town comment.

Blair turns her head to face me, a soft smile stretched across her lips.

"I still have a lot to see and learn here," she says before turning to face my parents again.

It's not a yes, but it's not a no.

The same question I keep asking myself comes back up. Can I make her stay? Because, fuck, I want her to.

"I know I'm biased," my dad starts. "But...even though this is a small town there is certainly a lot to see. The reason I love this town as much as I do is because no matter where you are, there's always a view somewhere. Three hundred and sixty degrees of scenic beauty. I'll never get used to a single square inch of this place."

"I'm starting to understand that myself," Blair says.

I remain silent for the rest of their conversation. My dad fills her in on the plans he has for the town. Even though she seems like she couldn't care less, she entertains the conversation, keeping a smile on her face and nodding in approval for all his crazy ideas.

Once we're finished, I help my mom bring the dishes into the kitchen while my dad has her ear.

Placing the dishes in the sink, I feel my mom's eyes on me. Turning to face her, I give her a look silently pleading not to say anything more.

But she doesn't pick up on it.

"She's lovely, Griffin."

I nod, because she is. She's a lot of things, but lovely wouldn't be my first word choice.

She's breathtaking.

She's funny.

She's...*perfect*.

"I think she's going to stick around," she continues.

"You think?"

"Just from my short encounter with her, I can tell this town is everything she didn't know she needed."

I swallow past the lump in my throat and focus on cleaning the dishes in front of me.

Blair has been everything *I* didn't know I needed.

The short drive home is quiet. It feels as if both of us have so much to say, but neither of us wants to be the one to say it. I almost have to crack a window in the truck because the tension floating around us was almost too much to bear.

"I'm going to drop the truck off at my place and I'll walk you back," I say, breaking the silence before pulling into my gravel driveway.

"Okay." One word is all she says as she fiddles with her hands in the passenger seat.

Is she nervous?

Throwing the truck in park, I round the car and catch the door at the same time she opens it. I watch as the smile on her face brightens with one small gesture. Little does she know, I'm at her mercy and would do anything she asks me to do at this point.

Taking a few steps into the open grass, she tips her face toward the sky. Her shoulders rise and fall with each deep breath she takes of the evening mountain air.

"It's so beautiful out," she says.

I say nothing back. I don't know *what* to say back truthfully.

Can I make her stay?

Not just tonight, but for good?

"Do you want to sit on your porch for a little bit?" she asks, turning to face me.

I almost stumble back from where I stand, because every time I come face to face with her, a new wave of adrenaline flows through me. Emotions hit me in the face like I've been punched repeatedly.

Yep, I'm 100 percent at her mercy.

Extending my hand to my side, signaling ladies first, I follow her up my porch steps. She takes the same seat she did when she came over for dinner, crossing one leg over the other and her gaze locked on the stars in the sky.

She's not wrong.

It's fucking beautiful out tonight.

It might even be the clearest night we've had in a while.

The only thing blocking my view is the tension that has followed us from the car to the porch. It's thick and almost suffocating.

Her phone chimes three times consecutively in her small handbag on the table and she reaches for and takes a moment to read the texts before putting it back without replying.

"Everything okay?" I ask.

She nods. "Lily is texting me to remind me that tomorrow is the day I have to be at the bakery super early for work. Founder's Day?" She looks at me from her chair.

"Biggest day of the year in Bluestone Lakes."

She lightly chuckles, looking back out to the sky.

"Did you want me to take you home now to get some sleep?"

A selfish part of me hopes the answer is no. I don't want this time with her to end.

Shaking her head, she keeps her stare out beyond the porch.

"I'm sorry about my parents and how much political talk they brought to the table tonight," I say, trying to ease whatever is floating around us.

The moonlight causes a glow to her features as she turns to face me and the urge to get up and kiss her is stronger than it's been all night.

"Don't be sorry for them, Griffin. I'm used to that kind of talk. It's all I knew growing up and the past however many years I was married to that life."

I swallow, and it burns. A painful reminder of her past.

"Was married," I repeat her words.

Confirmation I've already received, but needing again.

She stares at me for one...two...three heartbeats before she stands from her chair and moves to stand directly in front of me.

I adjust myself in my chair, extending my legs and tilting my head to meet her stare.

She leans down, one hand on the side of my neck and the other resting on my thigh. The contact forces my eyes closed and I suck in a deep breath, inhaling the smell of honeysuckle radiating off her. Her hands on me successfully put me at ease while burning me right to my core.

"Griffin," she whispers.

Opening my eyes, I burn all over as her whiskey eyes bore into mine. Even in the moonlight, they fucking burn with desire.

"Was married," she repeats with confirmation, her hand that was on my neck coming up to the side of my cheek. "I was divorced long before I moved out of the city. That was my past. It's staying there and I have no plans on ever bringing it into my future."

My head leans into her touch before turning to face her hand and kissing the inside of her palm. A silent answer from me that I understand.

I do.

She moves to sit on my one thigh, and I keep my eyes locked on hers the same way she does mine as she removes my baseball cap and rakes her hand through my hair.

"I've always wondered what you have under this hat of yours," she says with a light laugh.

"Have you?"

She nods. "I mean...the cowboy hat is hot. And the way you wear this thing backward is definitely hotter. Mostly when you do that move where you flip the visor to the back. Mm-hmm," she practically moans, bringing both hands up and running them through my hair.

"Blair," I warn, shifting in my seat because her words are stirring even more inside of me.

"Yes?" she asks in a challenging tone.

I take my hand off the armrest of the chair and place it on her knee where the hem of her skirt sits. "You're sitting on my lap." I slowly move my palm under her skirt and up her leg, giving it a squeeze when I reach mid-thigh. "You're on my porch." My hand travels farther. "Telling me things I've wanted to hear from your lips for a while now."

"You've been wanting to hear that I've thought about what's under your hats?" she jokes.

"Your past," I say, leaning close enough to her lips that if she moved an inch, they would touch. "And the fact that it's staying there."

Her breath catches in her throat.

"It is," she whispers against my lips, repositioning herself on my lap and forcing my fingertips to graze her wet panties. "And, in case you needed to hear it one more time... It's staying there and I have no plans on ever bringing it into my future."

I exhale whatever I was holding it and let my head fall to her chest. Her arms wrap around my neck as if she's holding me up when I'm the one sitting under her. I feel her head move before I feel her breath on the shell of my ear.

"Are you going to touch me or not, Angry Cowboy?"

I groan into her, using one hand to tug the neckline of her light sweater down to expose her collarbone to me before pressing my lips to the sensitive spot. She practically moans, and I take it as an invitation to hook a finger into the side of her panties, and I can already feel my cock hardening with the one small move.

Blair is soaked.

I lift my head to meet her stare. She brings her bottom lip between her teeth and I don't stop watching her as I swipe one digit through her slick pussy lips before landing on her bundle of nerves. Her back arches while her head falls back, and I take the opportunity to bring my mouth to the pounding pulse in her neck, forcing a moan out of her.

"This what you wanted, sweetheart?" I say against her skin, putting pressure on her clit with languid circles. "My hands inside this dripping tight cunt and claiming you out here on this porch?"

"Jesus," she breathes out, her hand moving to rest on my shoulder as if she needs to find her balance.

I work my finger quicker against her clit, putting more pressure on it because there's nothing I want more at this moment than seeing her fall apart for me on my lap. Her hips buck against my hand as if she's chasing her pleasure. My cock throbs in my jeans, begging for a release as it's been far too long since a woman has had this effect on me.

"Answer the question," I practically growl out.

"Yes," she pants. "Yes. This is what I want. My god, this feels so good."

I move my hand quickly and shove two fingers deep inside of her. Her hand on my shoulder claws at my skin as she fists my shirt. She repositions herself, allowing me full access to fuck her with my fingers while I sit up taller for a better angle.

"Just me and you here, sweetheart. When you tell me this feels so good, you better be screaming my name and *only* my name. Understood?"

She nods in agreement, bringing her bottom lip between her teeth again as if she's fighting the pleasure. I take it as a sign to move faster. My palm is dripping with her arousal as I work my fingers in and out in rapid succession. As soon as I slow down, hooking them inside of her, she loses it.

"Griffin. Fuck," she cries out. "I think I might come. I've never come this fast, so I don't know for sure, but *fuuuck.*" She draws out the last word.

Her admission does something to me I can't even explain.

It makes me borderline feral.

"I recall you coming quick for me at the bar," I say, working my fingers inside of her, letting my thumb make contact with her clit, hoping it's enough to send her over the edge.

I need to see her.

I need to feel her.

I need every fucking thing she's willing to give me.

"Oh my god," she moans louder. "That's it. Don't stop."

"Didn't plan on it," I rasp.

I move faster, harder. Fucking her with my hand and pressing my thumb against her clit, moving in circles. I hook my finger again and that does it. I feel her pussy contract around me. At the same time, I feel like I'm about to come in my pants. I fight the urge so I don't embarrass myself, but Blair is so hot with the moans coming out of her mouth and the way her body responds to me.

"Fuck," she screams. The sound echoing in the distance.

I don't let up as she rides out her orgasm on me. Her breathing is fast and erratic as she wiggles her hips on my lap, lost in her pleasure. I don't stop staring because I want to memorize every single thing about this moment.

Watching Blair come for me is my new favorite thing.

She's my new favorite thing.

And just like that, I absolutely come in my pants.

"What the hell was that?" she asks, coming down from her high.

"That was a real man making you come with just two fingers in record time."

Her eyes widen, and I know my words hit her.

Because it's the truth.

A real man wouldn't need anyone other than her.

She repositions herself on my lap, wrapping both arms around my neck as I wrap mine around her waist. My eyes fall closed. I can't help but realize what I'm holding in my arms.

"Griffin?"

"Yeah, sweetheart?"

"Can you kiss me again?"

I don't waste a second before my lips are on hers. She doesn't need to ask me twice for something like that. If I had it my way, my lips would never leave hers.

She melts into me as my hand moves up her back and around

the nape of her neck, holding her in place and ensuring she doesn't pull away too soon. Even though she wanted this, I wanted this more.

Reluctantly, she pulls away.

She looks down at me with lust-filled eyes, and I can't help the smile that spreads across my face.

"You're going to force me to have to come up with a new nickname for you if you keep smiling like that," she says with a giggle before pressing her lips to mine again for a quick kiss before she stands from my lap. I have to adjust myself in my jeans before standing with her.

"Can't help it when you're around," I admit.

"And if you keep talking like that, you're going to make me fall for you."

I shrug, because little does she know I've already fallen for her. She broke down my walls even before all of this happened on the porch. Before I even touched her intimately.

"Would that be a bad thing?" I ask, my voice laced with hesitation.

She smiles up at me, pressing to her toes and kissing me one more time before turning to walk down the steps of my porch to head home.

She doesn't need to answer.

Because that kiss was confirmation enough that it wouldn't be the worst thing that could happen.

"Good night, Griffin," she says over her shoulder.

"Night, Blair."

And I stand there on my porch and watch every single step she takes across the grass to her place.

Wishing like hell she wasn't walking away from me right now.

Can I make her stay?

CHAPTER 31

PUT THE BEST FRIEND HAT BACK ON.

BLAIR

"It's entirely too early in the morning to be baking." I yawn.

Thankfully, Cozy Cup even opened earlier than usual today. Lily grabbed us caffeine, but it still isn't enough to wake me up.

Lily laughs as she puts a tray of chocolate chip cookies in the oven. "I know, I'm really not a fan of early mornings either. Especially when the sun hasn't even peaked over the horizon yet."

"Tell me again why we had to be up three hours earlier than normal to do this?"

"It's Founder's Day," she exclaims.

"That's right. I remember you briefly telling me about it," I say, pulling a tray of cookies from the oven just to put another in.

From what I've heard through Lily and customers coming into the bakery over the last few months, the town festival is the biggest event Bluestone Lakes has every year. It's a tradition for them to celebrate the town through a little market set up on Main Street, a carnival set up in front of the school, and ending the night with a fireworks display over the mountains.

I mean, that's just what I've heard through the grapevine.

"It's the best day of the whole year." Lily beams with her

arms out wide and a smile so big, you could probably see it from outer space.

I can't help but laugh.

"It sounds like it. And from the look on your face, I can already tell it's going to be a great day. I don't think I've ever seen you smile like that—ever."

She blushes at my realization, but the happiness in her features doesn't waver.

"Tell me more," I practically beg.

She jumps up on the counter next to where I mix the batter for an apple crumb cake.

"So it's an all-day event, basically. People from all over come into town just for this day. Mostly it's just the neighboring towns, but we're certainly busier than usual," she says. "We have tents set up right outside here where people set up tables to sell their homemade crafts and things. We're going to set up right on the sidewalk."

"That explains the extra early morning and triple the amount of baked goods." I laugh.

"Yep." She nods. "And even with all of this, we'll sell out by ten in the morning."

The bell over the front door chimes and Lily leaps off the counter. We both check the hole through the kitchen door and find Poppy walking toward us.

"It's Founder's Day," she practically yells in excitement with her hands in the air, doing a little dance in the kitchen with Lily.

"Where are you going to be today?" Lily asks her.

"I'll be at the school for the carnival rides this afternoon. But I have some time to kill and couldn't sleep due to excitement, so I came to see if you needed an extra hand to set up your stuff."

"Duh," Lily replies, reaching for an extra apron and tossing it to Poppy. "We need those cookies on the table over there packaged up in the cellophane bags for individual sale."

"On it." Poppy salutes, before getting to work. "Oh, has anyone talked to Nan to find out who's moving onto my street?"

"Someone's moving to your street?" Lily questions.

She nods. "She told Mom and Dad that it's some kind of celebrity. She won't give up a name. She won't even tell us how or why he's popular. Started throwing out some lies about how she had to sign a nondisclosure agreement, and everything is being done off the record so no one can even look it up."

"That's...strange," Lily replies.

"I know. I thought the same thing," Poppy says, turning to face Lily. "Like if this guy is a 'celebrity'"—she uses air quotes to emphasize the word—"is it because he's some type of criminal? I don't want a criminal living on my street."

"Have you asked Griffin if he knows anything?" Lily says.

The sound of his name causes me to fumble the whisk I was using. Enough that it crashes to the ground, sending batter flying everywhere.

"Shit," I mumble under my breath and hoping they ignore me.

"Are you okay?" Poppy asks first.

"Yep," I choke out nervously.

I turn to face both of them and I know my cheeks are bright red right now. For no reason.

Okay, maybe for a reason.

And it's definitely not embarrassment.

"Have you asked Griffin if he knows anything?" Lily repeats her question to Poppy but looks at me curiously.

I feel the corners of my lips twist into a smile, so I quickly turn around, grabbing a new whisk to get back to work.

"Blair!" Lily shouts with excitement.

"Don't do it, Lily," I warn over my shoulder with a whisk in the air. "Don't. Do. It."

She grabs my shoulders, spinning me around and I'm met with the stares of both Lily and Poppy standing directly behind me.

I groan, letting my head fall back and closing my eyes.

"I said my brother's name twice." Lily holds up two fingers. "And both times you got flustered. Explain."

I look from her to Poppy and notice a knowing look on Poppy's face already. Like she knows exactly what happened last night.

But how could she? I'm overthinking it because there is no way Griffin called his sister after that to talk about the things we did on his porch.

Just the memory of last night stirs something in my stomach.

Butterflies? Sure. Let's call it that.

From the start of the night when he picked me up, until the very end before I went home, I felt everything building inside of me for him. More than ever before. I didn't expect him to give me an orgasm while on his lap. It was my intention to stay and enjoy the beautiful night.

Truthfully, I just didn't want to go home yet.

I enjoy his company.

I wanted to be near him, which is an entirely new revelation. Maybe it was that epic first kiss at the ranch. Maybe it was meeting his parents.

Maybe it's just him.

It's definitely all Griffin.

Lily snaps her fingers in front of my face. "Earth to Blair."

I roll my eyes. "Fine, but you can't say anything."

She narrows her eyes.

"You can't," I say, pointing a finger in her face. "I know he's your brother, but you have to hear what I'm about to say as my best friend."

"Okay," Lily says flatly, straightening her shoulders before she takes a hand and waves it in front of her face like she's a character in a theatrical performance. "Tell me everything, bestie," she adds in a more chipper tone.

I stare at her for a moment longer before I break out in laughter from her rapid change in tone and new personality in a matter of seconds.

But I stop myself quickly, realizing I'm about to admit this out loud.

"So...I think I've developed feelings for Griffin. No, scratch that, I *have* developed feelings." I say everything at record speed. "And fast. I don't know how, when, or why, but I did. Now I can't stop swooning over him." I get the last word out and quickly inhale a breath because I'm pretty sure I used only one to get all of that out.

"Did you just say swooning over my brother?" Lily deadpans.

"Best friend, Lily," I groan, reminding her of what I said only minutes ago. "Put the best friend hat back on."

"Fine." She pretends to take off a hat, throws it across the room, and reaches for another pretend had to put back on.

"Is this the right one?" I laugh.

She rolls her eyes. "Yes."

"And something happened last night." I waggle my eyebrows insinuating the words I don't want to say out loud. "On his porch. Just us. Well, of course it was just us, duh. But something happened." Another string of words and sentences I said at rapid speed.

Lily says nothing as she stands there with her mouth parted in shock.

I turn to face Poppy, and she has a similar look on her face, but her features quickly morph into something that resembles happiness.

"I knew it," Poppy breaks the silence first. "I freakin' knew it. This makes me so happy," she says with a fist bump in the air.

"Everyone having sex makes you happy," Lily deadpans, turning to face Poppy. "Because you're a virgin," she whispers the last words.

"Whoa," I say, hands out in front of me. "What?"

"Yes," Poppy groans. "I'm a twenty-five-year-old virgin," she tells me before turning to face Lily, crossing her arms over her chest. "It's not something the entire world needs to know, *Lily*."

She turns back to face me. "I'm a hopeless romantic, and this is a small town. It sounds boring, but I want to make sure it's the right guy that I give it to."

"I've been telling you, just give it up already?" Lily barks out a laugh.

"Can we not discuss my non-existent sex life and get back to Blair, please?" she asks Lily.

Lily turns to face me completely, arms relaxing at her side as she stares at me curiously. Like she has so much to say but doesn't know how to even start. My stomach does a full somersault with nerves, wondering what she's going to say next. Will it be my best friend talking? Or will this be Griffin's sister talking?

"Can I ask you something?" Lily finally says, in a tone so soft I would have missed it.

I nod.

"Are you planning to stay?"

I almost rear my head back in confusion. Does Lily think I plan on going back to the city? Does she think I would go back to the life I tried so hard to get away from?

Does *Griffin* think I plan on moving back?

"Yeah, I do. Why do you ask?" When she doesn't immediately answer, I continue. "I had planned to stay here for good. Unless something terrible happens, that would make everyone in this town hate me to where I have to leave because I wasn't comfortable."

"Well, lucky for us. Everyone in this town loves you," Poppy says first, smiling from ear to ear with encouragement. "Nan never stops talking about you."

"She's been so great to me. From the moment I came into town and met her," I answer Poppy before turning to face Lily again. "I don't plan on leaving, Lil."

"Does Griffin know how you feel?" she asks.

"I think so?" I answer in a questioning tone. "I'm not entirely sure how he feels. I mean, we've kissed and done thin—"

"Don't go any further," Lily stops me, covering her ears. "Even with the best friend hat on, I don't need to know."

"Noted."

"Listen, Blair," Lily starts, placing a comforting hand on my forearm. "I ask these questions, because if you really want him to open up to you and gain a better understanding of exactly how he's feeling, he needs to hear you say that you're not going anywhere. He needs to know that you're in Bluestone Lakes to stay." Lily pauses, and I see anguish flash in her eyes. "I don't think he will survive being abandoned again."

Then she turns and walks out of the kitchen without another word.

I know about his past and how his ex left him in such a terrible way. I'd never want to hurt him like that.

But I didn't realize the effect it had on his sisters, too.

Or maybe just Lily.

Has she also been through something similar?

I definitely consider Lily one of my best friends here in town, but have realized in this interaction that I know little about *her* past. I can't fault her for it though, because when I came to town, I didn't want anyone to know about mine. I wanted to keep it under lock and key.

But everything she's said rings true in my ear.

She's right.

I need to tell him exactly how I feel and my plans, so he knows where I stand. I already know I want more with him. Even when I thought I didn't, I did. Even when I tried to talk myself out of it because that's not what I moved here for, I did then too.

"Everything Lily said was true," Poppy breaks through my running thoughts. "He won't survive another heartbreak like that, so you have to assure him. With that being said, I know he has feelings for you. I just didn't want to say it in front of her." She gestures toward the kitchen doors.

"He does?"

She nods. "He confided in me recently about it. Said he needed to let it out. I don't blame him. Sometimes when you feel something, it's necessary to talk it out. Just like we did here today."

"I appreciate you two so much," I tell her honestly. "I definitely needed to get that out, and I know I need to tell Griffin all of this, too."

"Good." She nods. "Now, let's finish up here so we can have the best day ever."

I get back to work with only one thought in my head.

I need to see Griffin at some point today.

CHAPTER 32

IS GRIFFIN BARLOW A ROMANTIC AT HEART?

GRIFFIN

As much as it pains me to say this, Founder's Day might be my favorite day of the year we have here in town. It's our busiest day at the bar. Likely, the only two places someone can drink are here or buying something from the General Store to bring back home with you.

When it comes to Founder's Day, though, everyone always wants to be in the heart of the town. I don't blame them, because we go all out. They set up a live band in the middle of Main Street and balloons are set up on every streetlight.

Schools and construction sites are even closed.

Thank fuck, because it's a day where I *need* the extra hands behind the bar for the afternoon shift. Tucker could spend the whole day here without a single complaint. His coworker, Levi, also volunteered some time for the evening shift since they both know I hate the crowd.

However, tonight...part of me wants to stay.

A totally new revelation for me.

My sisters are planning to come by, and I hope that Blair is coming with them. I'm finding myself consumed by her every minute of the day. I wake up to thoughts of her, go to sleep with thoughts of her, and everything in between is *her*.

If she comes in with Poppy and Lily, I'm not so sure I'll be able to tend this bar. I know I won't be able to keep my hands off of her. They crave to touch her. The desire burns inside of me to always keep her nestled in my arms and protect her. From what? I don't know, because there's no need to protect her from anything in this town.

Just as the thoughts race through my mind, the bell chimes for the front door.

"I thought I told you to disconnect that shit," I shout across the bar to Tucker, who's delivering drinks to a table.

"Did you?" He smirks.

That smug son of a bitch.

I shake my head, but don't have time to respond because my sisters are standing in front of me. I scan their features and they each have shit-eating grins on their face.

"What's wrong with your faces?" I ask, my tone laced with question.

"My girls." Tucker beams before they can even respond to me. "You finally made it."

"Hey Tuck," they both say in unison.

"You ready to turn up?" Tucker asks them.

"Are you a teenager?" Poppy barks out a laugh. "No grown adult says that these days."

"I'm forever young at heart," Tucker says with a hand to his chest like he's proud of himself.

"But you're twenty-three," Lily scoffs. "Let's act like it."

Tucker pouts. "You're no fun, Lil."

The conversation is cut short when shouting starts from the other side of the bar. "Hey, Seven Stools!" Nan commands the room. We all turn our heads to find Nan standing on a chair. "It's Founder's Day!" Nan screams with a bottle of beer in each hand, raised in the air. "Best day ever!"

And the crowd surrounding her follows her cheers.

"Do you think she knows any of those people?" Poppy asks.

"Nope," Tucker, Lily, and I all say in unison.

"See, Lil?" Tucker points to Nan. "I aspire to be as cool as her all my life. Young at heart."

"Give it up, Tucker. There's no one out there like Nan."

Tucker huffs and wrinkles his face in disgust. "Again...no fun."

I can't help myself, looking around during this entire conversation happening in front of me, hoping Blair is going to walk in behind them any minute.

"Hey, Griffy." Lily beams, forcing me to look at her. When I do, she looks down at her wrist as if she has a watch on, but doesn't. "You're here later than usual."

I shrug. "It's a busy day."

"Tell me about it," she says, fighting a yawn. "I feel bad because I worked Blair to the bone this morning. She had no idea what to expect for the day when I texted her last night, telling her we needed to start a whole three hours earlier than usual." She laughs.

Memories from last night flood my brain.

I look around again, mostly to avoid looking at my sister and giving away any thoughts I have about her at the moment. Like the way she was on her knees with a mouthful of my—

"She's not here," Poppy cuts through my thoughts.

When I snap my gaze to hers, she sends me a wink.

She knows.

Of course, she does.

These two know me better than anyone else.

"She was exhausted from the day and said she was just going to watch the fireworks from her deck," Poppy adds.

The idea of Blair watching the greatest fireworks the country will ever see from her deck hits me in my chest. Maybe I haven't seen any in other places, but I'm confident we have some of the best because of the wide-open space that stretches the horizon. I want her to experience the beauty of them from the only spot I know won't be littered with town folk.

My spot.

"You know...Levi is here to help for the evening shift," Tucker says beside me. His elbow is on the table, his knuckles are resting under his chin, and the look on his face is telling me everything. It screams *get the hell out of here and go get your girl.*

"You guys have everything covered?" I ask him.

He nods knowingly, grabbing the dishrag from the bar top in front of me, and begins wiping down the space where I just stood.

"Get outta here, old man." Tucker laughs.

Grabbing my flannel off the hook by the kitchen door, I round the bar to leave, but Poppy stops me before I can make it to the door.

"Hey, Griffin?"

"Yeah?"

"Make sure you're sure about this...with Blair," she says, locking sympathetic eyes with me. "I don't want to see you... well, you know."

I give her a quick nod and offer her a smile. I love that my sisters worry about me. Hell, I worry about me too.

But this is different.

"I've never been more sure of anything."

I pull up to Blair's house and every single light is shining through the windows of the tiny home. I exit my car quickly because the anticipation of seeing her for the first time since yesterday forces a little pep in my step.

As soon as I step onto her porch and see what's happening inside through the glass door, my footsteps slow.

256

Blair is bouncing around her living room, her hair flying in every direction, and she has a broom in her hand. Some kind of loud music blasts through the walls and the vibration of the beat thrums in my body as I come to a stop right outside of the door.

She's using the stick of the broom as a microphone, and a smile stretches across my face.

She looks so free.

She looks like everything I want in life.

Visions of coming home from work just like this and finding her in my kitchen dancing, laughing, and loving her life to the point she can let loose like this float around in my head.

I can't remember the last time I let loose like that myself.

I've never been more sure of anything.

I open her front door because there's no way she'll hear me knocking over the beat, and to my surprise, it's unlocked. As if she can sense the presence of someone in the room, she stops and snaps her head in my direction.

Running a hand through her hair to smooth it down, she smiles wildly at me, holding the broom next to her in her hands with her other hand on her hip.

"Hey there, Angry Cowboy."

I shake my head at her for still calling me that.

Doesn't she know that she's replaced every bit of anger that once consumed my life with something new? Something bright. Like sunshine on a rainy day. Blair has stormed into my life—my town—like a hurricane.

And we don't fucking get those here in Wyoming.

Her eyes scan my body, and I can't help but do the same.

"Did it hurt when you fell from the vending machine?" she asks. I eye her curiously, wondering where the hell that came from. She moves to the counter to take a sip from the glass of wine sitting there. "Because you're looking like a snack tonight."

Feeling the corner of my mouth tip up, I make my way to her. Stopping only inches from her and resting the back of my finger under her chin to lock her gaze with mine.

"Are you hitting on me?"

She swallows, but her grin matches mine. "Have been since I got here."

"No, you haven't."

"Okay, fine," she says confidently. "Maybe not since then, but eventually I was."

I shake my head. "You're insane, you know that?"

"And yet, here you stand," she mocks.

"Guess I should leave then," I say in the same tone.

"Wait." She pushes away from me, hustling down the hall. "I'll bring out my other personality. Hold on."

She runs into the bathroom and comes back out seconds later with her arms wide in the air, laughing as if it's the best joke she's ever told.

"Here I am."

I bark out a laugh, bending at the waist and resting my hands on my thighs to hold me up because I can't believe her right now.

Everything I thought before walking into her house, I think about again. This. This right here is what I want for the rest of my life.

The laughter.

The antics.

This *feeling*.

I look up through my fit of hysterics and find her standing there, eyes wide and very much *not* laughing with me.

"Success," she breathes out, barely loud enough for me to hear.

"Huh?" I ask, letting myself relax from that. There's still a chuckle in my tone, but not as much as before.

Her signature smile hits her face again and I would give anything to press my lips to them and taste the joy she radiates.

"I've been trying to make you laugh since I got here," she admits.

Stalking over to her, I twist my baseball cap backward and

refuse to waste another minute. My hands grip her waist, pulling her flush to me and I crash my lips to hers. Instantly, her arms are around my neck while her body melts into mine.

This kiss is fierce and passionate.

Like we've both been waiting for it to happen again since the first time.

She tilts her head to the side, moaning and allowing me access to deepen the kiss to taste everything she's willing to give me.

Kissing Blair is like waking from a deep sleep to the rumble of thunder. A lightning strike to the chest that I would *gladly* let hit me repeatedly if it meant getting to do this for the rest of my life.

Maybe it's that I don't run around kissing women.

Maybe it's just *her.*

Reluctantly, I pull away, keeping my lips hovering over hers. "Get changed. I want to take you somewhere."

"So bossy," she says playfully, before locking her lips with mine one more time and retreating up the small stairs to the bedroom.

"Something warm," I shout up to her.

"You mean you won't be keeping me warm?" she shouts back with a giggle.

"Blair," I warn, waiting for a response, but it doesn't come. "I'll be right back."

She mumbles something in response, but I'm already halfway out the door. I rush back to my place to grab a few things to load into the bed of the truck. I said I wanted Blair to experience these fireworks at my spot, but I also crave this time with her. Do I want it to feel like a date of sorts? Yeah, I do.

She has to know I want her in every sense of the word.

She makes me want to go above and beyond to show it.

When I head back to her house, I find her already standing on her deck, waiting for me. She's wearing a pair of bootcut jeans and an oversized sweater. It looks so big on her that it's bunched at her wrists. She brings one arm across her stomach, with the other elbow resting on top of it while her thumb plays with her bottom lip. It's cute, and sexy, and, fuck, she drives me wild just standing there the way she is.

Opening the truck door, I pull myself to a standing position with one hand on the door and the other on the roof of my truck.

"Bring the dog," I tell her.

"What?"

"Bring the dog," I repeat, gesturing to the house. "He will love it."

She stands there, shocked for a moment, before retreating inside to grab Reginald. She emerges with him on his leash, and he offers me a bark before descending the steps with her right behind him. I jump down from the car and try to reach my passenger door before she does, but fail.

"It's my job to open the door for you, sweetheart."

"Always such a gentleman," she says, stepping back and allowing me to do it. I watch her intently as her eyes track every movement. Almost as if she's not used to this type of treatment.

Once she's in, I jump back in right after. Reginald nestles himself in the middle of the bench seat, and I already hate the space between us.

The ride is quick.

Likely because I gunned it here to make sure I could get set up before the fireworks start.

I don't head for the same trail I use to get there by horse, because it's too small for the truck. Instead, I pass the ranch and make my way down a wooded path I carved out for myself. I created it with just the right amount hidden at the entry of the road so that people didn't get curious and try to explore back here.

Not that many people explore outside the heart of town.

But it's my private getaway in Bluestone Lakes.

"Wow," Blair says from the passenger seat, lifting herself up to see the trail the headlights illuminate for us. "I had no idea this was all back here."

"I made sure of that."

We hit a few bumps that cause Reginald to startle in his seat, but when we finally reach the space, Blair's eyes widen.

She's seen this lake before.

Everyone has.

It's the reason people visit.

I'm just showing her from a completely new viewpoint on the outskirts of town. The opposite side of the lake that tourists visit. I whip the truck around to back it up into the space I created, angling the truck to where I know the fireworks will go off.

After throwing the truck in park, I jump out, rounding the back of the truck and opening the bed hatch. I set up the array of blankets I loaded in, as well as pillows along the back.

"Is Griffin Barlow a romantic at heart?" I hear Blair ask from behind me.

I turn to face her, sitting back on my heels and sending her a knowing smile. One that tells her *this is all for you, sweetheart.'*

"I wouldn't call myself a romantic, but there's this new girl in town—"

"There's a new girl in town?" she feigns shock, cutting me off. "Well, I must meet her. She and I would hit it off perfectly since I know what it's like. I can probably show her around. Make sure she knows to stay off that one dead-end road that apparently has a ditch. Share what it's like around here as a former new girl. Urge her to stay away from the angry cowboy who lives on Barlow Drive."

I shake my head, standing before jumping off the back of the truck and coming to a stop in front of her. My hand comes up, cupping the side of her face, and she leans into my touch.

"You want the new girl to stay away from me, huh?"

She nods, unable to respond.

"Why's that?"

She lifts a shoulder but doesn't immediately say anything back. Her eyes fall closed as my thumb brushes the apple of her cheek. "Because I don't want her seeing this side of you," she finally says, barely above a whisper.

Bringing my other hand up, I hold her face as I tilt her head up, urging her to open her eyes and look at me. When she does, the world around me goes quiet. A feeling I'll never get used to, because it happens every single time. A burning whiskey through my blood with just one look from her.

"There's only one girl I want to see this side of me."

Silence stretches between us at my admission.

It's out there.

My heart is on the line, and it's up to her to hold it and protect it or stomp it on the ground and put me in my grave.

I just hope it's the first of the two.

CHAPTER 33
WHAT ARE YOU GOING TO DO ABOUT IT?

BLAIR

Griffin holds my face as if he never wants to let go.

My hands come up, delicately wrapping around his strong forearms, ensuring he doesn't let go. Or maybe it's because his admission makes me feel weak in the knees. Like, if he were to let go I would fall to the ground in a puddle at his feet.

Reginald barking pops the bubble we both just found ourselves in. We step away from each other, and Griffin walks to the passenger side door to let him out of the truck.

I lean down, willing him to run to me, and his short little legs hustle him over. He rests his paws on my thigh and presses his face into mine to lick my cheek before scurrying around to smell the new space.

"Stay," I order Reginald.

"He won't run off, will he?" Griffin asks, concerned.

I shake my head. "No. Even though this is a new area for him, he never goes far from me. He knows not to wonder."

"Good," he says before patting the bed of the truck. "Hop on up. The show is going to start any minute."

In the least graceful way possible, I climb into the truck bed and Griffin hoists Reginald up to sit up there with us.

He was right in telling me to dress warmly. The night air mixed with the breeze from the lake sends a shiver through my body. I look down at my dog and even he shakes where he sits. He jumps right off the back of the truck, and my eyes widen because it's a steep drop for his little corgi legs.

Leaning over the side of the truck, I sit up on my knees and watch where he's heading. And the little shit sits right by the truck door, looking from me to Griffin for someone to let him in the warm cab.

I let out a laugh.

"He wants to sit in there when all of this is out here?" Griffin eyes him curiously.

"He's not a normal dog," I reply, with a giggle.

"I can see that." Griffin opens the truck door and Reginald's tail goes wild before Griffin picks him up and places him on the bench. I move to look through the back window and watch him curl himself into a ball right where he was for the drive.

"Maybe we should have left him home," I tell Griffin, following his movements as he closes the door before rounding the truck and joining me in the blanket mess he laid out for us.

"He's fine."

Griffin props a few pillows up and settles himself with his back against them and his legs stretched out in front of him. With blankets layered under us, I crawl next to him. He lifts an arm, allowing me to curl into his side. The warmth of his body—even through the clothing—would be enough to get me through anything if I was stranded out here with him.

A loud bang echoes in the distance, forcing my palm to land on his thigh before looking out over the lake and into the wide-open space where fireworks light up the sky. His arm draped over my shoulders gives me a light squeeze.

I watch as colors dance with the stars.

A loud, beautiful display reflecting on the glass-like water.

He's right, this is the perfect spot.

I sit up taller, unable to even look away for a second. The fireworks throw random shapes in the sky. Cascading willows, comets, and rings spread across the mountains. Not just in one particular section, but everywhere. As if people are sitting on different mountains setting them off to create this show just for us.

"This is...wow," I say, but I can't turn away from them. "I know you all said this is the best show of fireworks in the country, but I was skeptical. Because fireworks are fireworks. It can't be *that* different, but this...it's amazing. It's beautiful."

Griffin doesn't respond. After a moment, I finally turn to face him and he's already looking at me. Wonder in his features, and his signature smile all over his face. If that's even what I should call it. It's new to me. It's new to him.

The bang continues to echo in the distance, and the light in the sky reflects off his eyes. I sit up on my knees in front of him, taking his face in my hands before I straddle my legs over his thick thighs, refusing to sit down completely because I don't want to take this further if he's not ready.

"Blair," he says on an exhale, so low I almost miss it.

My name coming off his lips like a plea.

Begging me for more.

Slowly I lean in. Letting my lips graze his, and I feel the sharp intake of his breath. I press my lips to the corner of his before grazing back to the middle.

"I want you," I whisper.

His one hand grips my thigh, holding me in place, while the other comes up, brushing a strand of hair out of my face before tangling his fingers through the hair at the back of my head.

"Now you know how I feel," he says, his breath hot on my lips. My heart pounds in my chest as I settle down completely on his lap. I feel his already hardened cock between my legs, and desire burns through my blood. I don't pull away. "I've never fucking wanted anyone the way I want you, Blair."

His words come out with conviction.

He means everything he's telling me right now.

I smile against his lips. "What are you going to do about it?"

He pulls his head back for a better look into my eyes. Boom after boom echo, while lights flash around us. Each one lighting up the space, showing me every feature on his face. Every feeling.

It's want.

It's need and desire.

"Not here," he grits out, bringing his hands to my hips and holding them tightly in place. "The first time I have you completely, it won't be out here."

I'm so turned on by the way he talks to me. Even if it's not meant to come out dirty, his change in tone just makes me want it that much more. It's a burly and demanding voice, begging me to go against everything he's saying.

Grinding my hips once against his erection beneath me, he groans. I realize instantly, I've made a mistake because if he truly tries to stop me, I don't think I'll survive. He's thick and hard, I don't even have to see it with my eyes to know this.

"Sweetheart," he growls. "Don't start something we can't finish."

I rest both hands on his shoulders and grind my hips again, chasing the friction between us. But he stops me by lifting me off his lap. I let him, but I scoot down his legs and let my hands find the buckle on his belt.

This time he doesn't stop me.

I unclasp it, pulling it from the loops before looking up at him. He watches my every move as he pulls his bottom lip between his teeth. Unbuttoning his jeans and pulling the zipper down, he lifts just enough to allow me to scoot the jeans down to his thighs. When I reach for his boxer briefs, I hook a finger into the waistband, but he stops me with a hand around my wrist.

"You don't have to do this," he says.

The only answer I give in response is dipping my hand into his briefs and wrapping it around his length. I moan in pleasure. I *freaking* moan from just the contact because Griffin Barlow is huge. Without even looking down, I can feel the veins in the palm of my hand.

Reluctantly, I release my hold on his cock. Using both hands, I slide his briefs down and then his jeans, bringing them all the way down to his ankles to allow me space between him. I look down, my eyes widen, and my breath picks up speed. I have never been this turned on before when we haven't even done anything.

I sit back on my heels between his legs, letting my hand glide up his length and over the tip. Precum coats my palm, and I moan quietly again. A vision of him inside of me as I stroke up and down.

He might actually break me.

"Fuck, that feels good," he hisses, letting his eyes close and head fall back.

Taking the opportunity to really give him pleasure the way he did me last night, I lean down and swipe my tongue across the tip of his cock, watching as his eyes fly open and he stares down at me. I open my mouth wide and slowly take him in.

Holy. Shit. This is so hot.

He moves the hair out of my face before holding it at the top of my head for a better view.

"I've had thoughts about this," he breathes out. "Thoughts of you sucking my cock and taking me deep in the back of your throat with that pretty little mouth of yours."

His dirty words fill the air and I bob my head up and down at a faster speed. Letting my tongue drag up the shaft slowly before attempting to take him completely.

"But this right here," he pants out. "Never did I envision you would look this fucking perfect doing it."

I hum around his cock, the vibration causing him to hiss and tighten his hold on my hair. I don't let up. I want him to feel everything he's made me feel. The way he made me come so hard I saw stars, figuratively and literally, on his back porch. I grip the base of his cock with my hand, keeping it in motion with my mouth.

My legs squirm, aching for some kind of friction to release what's building inside of me, and he notices.

"Reach your hand inside your jeans, sweetheart," he orders. "I want to know how wet you are right now."

I release him from my mouth, but keep my mouth hovering over the tip. "I'm *soaked*, Griffin." I moan the word as if saying it out loud is painful. I want his hands on me. I want *him* to feel it for himself. "I told you I want you."

"Fuck," he murmurs under his breath, letting his head fall back.

I slide my hand up and down his shaft before taking him in my mouth again. The way his body flinches at my touch, and he hisses at the contact tells me he's enjoying this as much as I am.

Bobbing my head up and down, keeping a quick rhythm, I know he's close. I want to see him lose control for once. *Only for me.*

"Blair," he warns. "I'm close."

I hum in response, twisting my hand at just the right angle to elicit a gasp from him. His body tightens and his head falls back against the truck as pleasure races through him.

"Shit. Off. I'm going to come," he rasps.

With one hand on his cock, I press the other to his abdomen before opening the back of my throat and letting him in completely. Silently telling him that I will absolutely not be releasing my mouth from this moment. In seconds, his cum is pouring down the back of my throat while he simultaneously releases a string of curse words under his breath. His voice is deep and raspy, igniting every nerve ending in my body. Wanting—no, needing—more from him.

Once he stops pulsing and his body goes slack, I sit up on my heels, wiping the corner of my mouth with the tip of my finger. His gaze locked on the small movement as he sits there in silence.

268

Something flashes in his eyes, and he moves quickly to hold the sides of my face, pulling me in before he crashes his lips to mine. Never in my history of dating or being married has a man kissed me after something like this. I hesitate, keeping my lips tight to avoid him cringing.

He pulls away, only a breath from my lips. "Open up for me. Let me in. Let me kiss you the way you deserve to be kissed."

My eyes bounce between his for just a brief second before my lips are back on his. I pull my body forward to straddle his bare legs to deepen the kiss. His mouth suctions to mine like he needs this more than air. Like he wouldn't survive without this.

I've never been kissed the way he kisses me.

It's primal, mixed with sweet and soft. If that's even possible.

His hands tangle in my hair, but he pulls away again, "I wasn't planning on fucking you out here," he starts, while his other hand trails down my back before landing on my ass. He gives me a tight squeeze. "But I'm not sure I could resist you if I tried."

"Lose control with me, Griffin," I whisper against his mouth, letting my forehead fall to his. "I want everything."

He moves quickly, sitting up while I move to the side, letting him reach for the pocket of his jeans bunched around his ankles and pulls out his wallet to grab a condom. Tearing the packet with his teeth before sliding it on.

I think he's going to reach for the button of my jeans, but he kisses me again. I melt into him because I can't help it. I want it just as much as he does.

He releases his hold on my face, but I don't pull away.

I let my lips linger over his as he reaches for the button on my jeans, undoing them in record time and pushing them down to my ankles, allowing me to kick them off.

I straddle his legs to sit, but he stops me *again,* and I can't fight the groan I let out. Holding me over him, he takes a finger, slides it through my pussy, and my back arches at the sensation. My annoyance is out the window with just one light touch.

"Fuck. You're dripping for me," he draws out.

I rest my hands on his shoulders again, hovering over his thick erection. I don't know how he's even this hard, this quick. He has one hand on my waist, and the other wrapped around his shaft lined up with my entrance. Just as I'm about to slide down, he swipes the tip across my clit one, two, three times, forcing my hold on his shoulders to tighten at how good it feels before he presses the tip of his cock inside of me.

"I—Shit," I stutter, unable to find the words for the pleasure that's currently taking over my body. "I don't think it's going to fit."

"You can take it, sweetheart."

His voice reverberates in my body, and I stare at him. My breathing feels rapid and labored the longer I keep eye contact with him. Knowing I've never wanted something the way I want this with him.

"Breathe for me, Blair," he whispers. "Relax for me."

I refuse to avert my gaze as I settle on him, pushing him deeper and deeper into me until he's as far as he can go. My mouth opens at the sensation, feeling him through every inch of my body as his cock stretches me.

"Holy shit," I breathe out.

I can't move. I can't even see straight because Griffin Barlow has taken every single part of me and turned me into a puddle on his lap.

"Are you okay?" he asks.

I swallow, my throat feeling dry, before giving him a tight nod. "I'm good."

"You feel so fucking good, Blair. Your pussy is so tight, like it was made for me."

"Mm-hmm."

"You haven't even moved, and I already know that I'm going to come again, harder than I ever have before."

"If you keep talking like that, I might too." I laugh, but the way my body shakes when I do, I suck in a sharp breath because I feel him everywhere.

I allow my hips to roll on top of him, bringing my lip between my teeth. Him inside of me, the friction on my clit, it's almost too much. It's overwhelming in all the right ways.

This feels right.

His hands grip my waist as I pick up speed, rocking back and forth on him, chasing the pleasure. Neither of us stops staring at the other, and I know by the look in his eyes this isn't about sex for either of us.

It's more.

It's a feeling that used to scare me, because the idea of being with another man after the greatest heartbreak in life was the scariest thing. I swore I wouldn't let another man inside my heart. He's broken down those walls over time to the point this only feels that much more powerful.

I reach for the hem of my shirt, lifting it over my head as my hips continue in a back-and-forth rocking motion. As soon as I toss it to the side, cold air hits my chest and I'm finding it difficult to breathe. Griffin reaches behind me, unhooking the clasp of my bra and letting it fall to the side as he cups both breasts in his large hands.

"You're fucking perfect," he draws out before peppering kisses along my collarbone, sending even more chills down my spine. My body arches into him as my hands intertwine in his hair, pulling him close to me, only deepening the connection that's already happening between us.

"This feels so good, Griffin. Fuck," I pant, picking up speed. "I don't think I'm going to last."

"You need to last," he spits out.

I draw back, eyes connecting with his dark ones. "Huh?"

"I don't want this feeling to end," he admits. "The feeling of you riding my cock like this is...it's heaven. You are fucking heaven on earth, Blair. A storm that's taken over every part of my life and I don't want this to end. I need you to last a little longer so I can feel everything you're willing to give me."

He grips my breasts harder. Then fingers toy with one nipple and his mouth comes to suck on the other.

"If you keep doing that, I won't be able to," I moan into his hair. "I'm struggling to hold back here. You're so big. I feel so full."

"You're doing so well, sweetheart."

I reposition myself on him, allowing myself to bounce on his lap. Feeling his cock drive in and out of me.

"That's it. Ride me," he growls.

I won't stop. Instead, I move harder and faster with his words until I reach a breaking point. Bringing both of us closer to the edge than I've ever been before, fighting like hell.

"Give it to me," he groans as if he's right there too. "Give me fucking everything."

And I do.

"Fuck," I cry out as I allow myself to go over the edge with him at the same time the grand finale of fireworks explodes in the surrounding sky, lighting up everything surrounding us. My orgasm is so powerful that my vision blurs. My body shakes around him as he holds me close to him, and I do the same with arms around his neck, pulling his face to my chest.

"Oh my god," I moan through it.

"Fuck," he grits out at the same time.

Both of us ride out our orgasm, holding each other close as if neither of us wants to let go. Our chests rise and fall in unison as we sit there, unmoving. Thoughts racing through my head as I wonder what the hell that was. It wasn't like anything I've ever experienced before.

Reginald barking from inside the truck forces us to snap out of our haze. We pause, staring at each other before we both let out a laugh and we move to gather our things to get dressed. The sky around us is dark, and the only sound is crickets in the distance and the light breeze blowing the trees.

272

Griffin jumps from the bed of the truck as I finish putting my shirt back on. The chill in the air, and losing contact with his arms, has left me feeling colder than before.

Once I finish, I look over at him and he has his hand extended for me, guiding me out of the truck to the ground. My legs feel weak, and I almost lose my footing, but he catches me with strong arms around my waist before his fingers grip my chin, urging me to look up at him.

"I'm sorry," he says. "This wasn't how I wanted to do that. Not out here. It's not why I brought you here."

I grip the edges of his flannel that's still unbuttoned, lifting on my toes to press my lips to his. We both melt as he hums into my kiss.

I don't want to stop kissing him.

I think about what Lily told me. How she said I need to assure him I plan to stay here if I want him to tell me how he's really feeling about all of this. How I need to tell him that this isn't a temporary home for me to escape the city life.

When I first moved here, I wasn't sure.

Before I fell for Griffin I fell for the town charm. I knew this place was it for me.

Finding home wasn't what I expected, but it happened.

I pull away from the kiss, smiling into his lips. "Everything was perfect, Griffin."

"Did I officially lose the nickname?" He smirks.

I laugh, stepping out of his hold and leaning back against the bed of the truck. "I guess." I shrug.

"Good," he says. I open my mouth to tell him what Lily told me I should say to him, even though it feels cliché after a moment like this, but he continues. "Come to the ranch with me tomorrow," he asks quickly.

"The ranch?"

He nods. "I want to show you something."

"Okay, cowboy," I say with a grin, knowing it's the same nickname, but different.

He shakes his head in disbelief as he makes his way to the passenger door to open it for me. I don't miss the smile on his face, even if he is trying to hide it from me.

I spend the whole drive home replaying the night in my head.

Thoughts of a possible future with the man who has one hand on the wheel and the other resting his on Reginald's back, lightly petting him.

I want it.

I just hope like hell my past never creeps into my future.

CHAPTER 34

DON'T MAKE ME TELL YOU WHY.

BLAIR

ME

I have news.

KODI

You're coming home? Finally!

ME

I'm not coming home. You know this already.

KODI

It was worth a shot.

ME

Kodi, I've absolutely fallen head over heels for my neighbor.

KODI

This isn't new information.

KODI

But I'm glad you're finally realizing it, sis.

My body aches in all the right places this morning, and I

haven't been able to wipe the smile off my face since I opened my eyes.

I'm alone in the kitchen of Batter Up, with music blasting and making a new recipe I found scrolling the internet last night when I couldn't fall asleep.

Cowboy cookies.

Clearly, Griffin has taken over every square inch of my brain.

This recipe just looked too good to not try. They are made with oats, chocolate chips, shredded coconut, and pecans. A perfect blend of salty and sweet. All things Griffin is.

Even though the music is turned up, I hear the bell chime over the front door, telling me a customer is here. Wiping my hands off with a dishrag, I push open the kitchen door to find Griffin standing on the other side of the counter with two coffee cups in his hand.

Speaking of cowboy...my mouth waters at the sight of him.

I don't think this man goes a day without a flannel, but it fits him. Today he's wearing a blend of checkered browns to match the deep color of the cowboy hat sitting on his head.

He lifts one cup in my direction before I round the counter to meet him on the other side. "I brought you a coffee. I didn't know how you take it, but Autumn told me what you normally get."

I take the cup from him, holding both hands over it to let the warmth seep into my skin as I sniff the aroma of caramel and vanilla.

"You didn't have to do this." I smile, even though my words are coming out nervously. "But it's very appreciated."

Suddenly, I'm feeling awkward. I don't know why because we've already had sex. He's seen me naked. He knows about my past. These new, stronger feelings I have for him make me terrified to mess this up.

He leans forward, pressing his lips to mine.

It's quick, almost like a habit.

As if he *could* do this every day with me.

"Good morning to you too," I say breathlessly.

His smile widens. "Good morning, sweetheart."

Okay, swoon.

I know it's not the first time he's called me that, but I still melt just the same.

"I was thinking about you when I was grabbing my coffee, so I figured I would grab you one too."

I bring one hand to my hip, cocking my head to the side. "You were thinking about me, huh?"

He takes a sip of his coffee, silence stretching between us as he watches me over the brim of his cup. The weight of his stare sends goosebumps across my skin.

"It's nothing new," he admits.

I avert my gaze to the floor, feeling embarrassed for whatever reason. These feelings today have me so on edge. It's a powerful thing to give yourself over to someone the way I want to give myself to him.

He uses the back of his fingers to lift my head back up.

"You're all I ever fucking think about, Blair."

"Feeling's mutual," I whisper, letting my eyes fall closed at his words, his touch, his presence.

He kisses me again with another quick kiss before moving his lips to the shell of my ear. "Good," he says and pulls away. "I have to head to work, but I will pick you up when my shift ends so we can head to the ranch."

I nod repeatedly in response.

Blair, chill out. There's no reason to be nervous.

He shoots me a wink before turning on his heel and retreating out the front door. But stops when Lily and Nan walk in at the same time. They all send each other a look before he continues walking, and Nan and Lily enter the bakery.

Lily's hands land on her hips in front of me, while Nan takes the stool behind the counter. Lily looks like she's ready to threaten me the way a little sister would be protective over her only brother. Except her features morph into something different. Her eyes widen as she scans me up and down. I follow her movements, looking down to see if there's something on my shirt.

"You're glowing today!" she shrieks.

"Alexa, play 'I Just Had Sex,'" Nan shouts, even though there's no device around to pick up on it.

I groan, turning to make my way into the kitchen again to finish making the batch of cookies I was working on. I feel Lily on my heel as if she wants to know more.

"Don't make me tell you why," I say over my shoulder.

She spins me around, facing her. "Now you definitely have to tell me."

"Lily," I say with a warning tone, letting my face tell her everything without saying a word.

Nan was right. I had sex with your brother. Happy now?

She releases her hold on my shoulders. "I take it back. Don't tell me."

I shrug, turning to face the cookie dough mix while I pick up the handheld mixer to get back to work.

We spend the next few minutes in silence, Nan not bothering to come back here. She works on paperwork on the other side of the kitchen, while I put a tray in the oven. Crossing the kitchen to bring the bowls to the sink to clean them, my steps falter.

"He's so gone for you."

I stand there staring at the sink, refusing to look at Lily after those words just came out of her mouth.

I hear her move, so I make quick work to keep myself busy. I can't say anything back because what do I say to that? I know he feels *something* for me. It's thick in the air between us when he's around.

"Do you know the last time he's been inside Batter Up?" Lily asks behind me.

My scrubbing slows momentarily, but I keep going.

"The day this place opened," she continues. "It's been over four years since my brother has been here."

"How? It's right next door," I reply into the sink.

"I don't have an answer for that. I mean…I know he doesn't do baked goods and treats. I can't believe I'm even related to someone like that." She laughs. "He's never had a reason to *want* to come in here."

I stop, turning to face her completely.

I'm still unsure about how I should respond to that.

He showed up this morning for me. He came here for the first time in four years…for me.

"He laughed," I finally say.

Nan takes this moment to come into the kitchen, the door swinging open as if she heard it too. "Repeat that again for the class."

Lily sucks in a sharp breath before her hand covers her mouth. "What?"

"He laughed, Lil," I repeat so it really sinks in for them. "I'm talking hands on his knees, bent over in a fit of joy."

Lily's eyes widen more before she paces the kitchen, deep in thought. When I turn to face Nan, she's got her arms crossed over her chest and a knowing grin plastered on her lips. Like she's content with the revelation. But when I look back at Lily, I can tell just by the look on her face the wheels are spinning, because not only did she see him in here after years of never stepping foot in the bakery, but now she knows he's laughing and smiling again.

She stops abruptly, facing me. "Did you have time to talk to him? You know, assure him you're staying?"

I shake my head. "I haven't had the chance. But I'm thinking when he takes me to the ranch this afternoon I will," I add quickly.

Her fingertips find her temples. "This is too much," she groans, before sitting down at the stool where she was just doing paperwork. She looks where I still stand. "He's taking you to the ranch?"

"That's sacred land," Nan interjects.

I nod. "He invited me last night. He told me he wants to show me something, but I'm not sure what."

"Jesus," Lily murmurs. "He never does that."

"Should I be nervous?" I ask skeptically.

She shrugs. "I don't know in detail what's going on between you two, and what you two have told each other, but knowing my brother, he hasn't had the courage to ask you the things I'm not afraid to ask."

"And that is?" Nan asks for me as if she knows it's where my mind was going.

Lily gives Nan a pointed glare before bringing her attention back to me. "I asked you if you were staying, and you said yes. But has he asked you?"

I shake my head.

"The questions he's too afraid to ask for fear of being hurt again. Since you've clearly fallen for each other, I'm sure you've opened up about things. But you need to ensure him you plan to stay if you haven't already done so. I know Griffin enough to know he will let you in more than he already has."

Hasn't he, though?

He's opened up to me enough to know parts of him I'm not sure he shares with others.

My mind spins, wondering if I've *actually* told him this.

I haven't. I haven't said a thing about me being here permanently.

I nod again, this time nervously.

She stands from the stool, moving to stand in front of me again before she places a hand on my shoulder. "I only tell you all of this because I love you. I love my brother too. The last thing I want is for either of you to hide your feelings or end up hurt in the process. You both deserve this type of happiness."

She's right.

If I want this to work, and if I want to fully know how he feels about me outside of a physical connection, I have to tell him my plans.

CHAPTER 35
YOU'RE GOING TO HAVE ME KILLED.

GRIFFIN

Exiting my truck, I round the hood to let Blair out.

Her eyes widen as she steps out, taking in the ranch. Likely because she's never seen it this close before. At least that I know of. Lily could have brought her here to ride one day for all I know. Either way, I'm treating this like her first time here.

Because it's her first time *with me*.

I interlock her fingers with mine, guiding her inside the open barn.

With every step toward the horses' stalls, my nerves heighten.

Of all my horses I've never let anyone near Storm before.

He's the one thing that's always been mine. The one thing no one can take from me, and that won't willingly leave me.

Once we reach the stall I let go of her, despite my body screaming to keep holding on, and I unlock the stall gate. Entering first, I turn to find her still standing there, staring at Storm with worry in her eyes.

"Come on"—I gesture to the horse—"He won't hurt you."

"Are you sure? He looks mean."

I shake my head, huffing out a laugh. "I promise."

Her head snaps in my direction, and I know those two little words hold more power than I meant for them to hold. Instantly my head swirls with ideas of her past and promises that she thought would remain true but ended up broken.

I move to stand before her, bending to level my gaze with her.

"I promise," I repeat the words that now hold more meaning.

She swallows before she nods and follows me into the stall. Storm lifts a foreleg, stomps his hoof in the hay, and shakes his head with a neigh.

She brings her hands up in defense as if he's about to attack.

"That's his way of saying hi," I tell her, before moving to put the halter on him and securing it in place. Once it's secure I give him a small pat on the head. I swallow past a nervous lump in my throat because I want her to know all of me. But it's scary to open up past a physical connection. "Storm has been in my life since my ex left. A light inside of me died, and I had a feeling I would spend the rest of my life alone. I needed an outlet. I needed some peace in my life and something that brought me an inkling of joy."

She remains quiet to let me continue.

"I want you to see that too. I'm not sure if you've ever ridden a horse before," I say, grinning as I turn my head to face her. "But I want to know if you want to give Storm a ride?"

"I…" She pauses. "I don't know, Griffin. From watching television shows, can't the horses tell if you're nervous? I really don't want to be thrown off a horse when I'm having a good day."

"You're having a good day?"

She rolls her eyes as if I should already know, but smiles. "Yes."

"Why?"

"For starters, I woke up aching everywhere." She winks at me. "The good kind of ache that makes me want more."

"Blair," I cut her off with a warning tone.

Just remembering last night sends blood straight to my cock. That was *not* how I wanted it to happen, nor was it my reason for taking her out there. But it happened and I don't regret it for a second. It was perfect. I know the reason behind that is the woman standing in front of me.

"And then this cowboy showed up at my work this morning to bring me coffee," she continues, the corners of her mouth rising painfully slow into a smile. "And that's when I realized I was having the best day. All of this to say, I'm not sure I want to be thrown off a horse today."

She laughs, and I just offer her a weak smile.

"I won't let that happen," I say honestly.

She stares at me as if she's trying to figure out if I'm telling the truth. I guide the horse out of his stall before making my way to the small tack room to grab his saddle. Taking the time to mount it on his back before making sure everything is in place and safe.

The last thing I would want is for her to get hurt. If I thought Storm would throw her off him there's no way we would be here right now.

It's a big deal to bring someone here, because this is my safe space. The one thing that's mine. Opening this part of me up to someone when I haven't heard the words I've wanted to hear is only opening myself up for the potential for heartbreak.

It's becoming a risk I'm willing to take with her.

Can I make her stay?

If she breaks my heart, then it's just another lesson I've learned too late.

I don't give her a choice before I interlock her hand in mine again and use my other to guide Storm out of the barn and into the open field. The skies are gray as if it might rain any minute.

I gesture to Storm. "I'll help you up."

She looks from me to the horse and back to me before taking slow steps across the tall grass to get on him. She reaches up to grab the pommel and hooks one foot in the stirrup. Standing behind her, I grip her waist to give her a little boost up.

She mounts the horse as if she's done it a hundred times before, like she's been riding all her life.

The idea of it excites me, while simultaneously turning me on. Riding is my life outside of the bar; and seeing her on *my* horse only ignites the feelings racing through me that have been growing for her. If I didn't want everything with her before this, I sure as fuck do now.

"How does it feel?" I ask, keeping the reins tight in my hand.

"This feels like nothing I ever imagined." She laughs. "I've never been on a horse before. It's scary. It's exciting. It's...can we go?"

This woman.

I nod, guiding Storm through the field at a slow walking pace. I'm unable to take my eyes off Blair as she looks forward. Every so often her eyes trail down to the top of the horse's head, making sure the horse is good. I can tell by her white knuckles that she's holding on for her life.

"I can see why you like this," she says. "It feels...calming."

"Most of the time it is. Other times it's exhilarating. When Storm and I need to blow off steam it's fast and wild."

"That sounds...wow. I hope to feel that someday."

I stop walking, which forces Storm to stop too. Turning my body to face Blair, I give her a look. *The* look in my eyes asking if she's ready for that right now, letting a grin form on my face.

"Oh no." She waves her hand around, keeping the other tight on the pommel. "You're going to have me killed."

I reach up, cupping the outside of her hand gripping the pommel, and pull myself up behind her. Swinging my leg around the other side of the horse until I'm sitting directly behind her in the saddle. My other arm reaches around, caging her in. She leans back, melting into me, and I fight the urge to just hold her up here. Not move or go anywhere. Just simply hold her the way I want to.

Bringing my lips to the shell of her ear, I pause, inhaling her scent. She smells like sugar from working today. The kind of sweet I want to devour.

"Are you going to be a good girl and hold on tight for me?" I whisper.

I want to regret the words as soon as they leave my lips, because now I'm more turned on than ever. With Blair, any filter I have is out the window. Her back stiffens, and I don't miss the way she sucks in a sharp breath before placing one hand on my thigh and adjusting her grip under my hand on the pommel.

She nods, before turning her head to the side, looking at me out of the corner of her eyes in front of me. "Let's ride, cowboy."

Pressing a kiss to her shoulder, I take the reins in one hand and wrap my other hand around her midsection to hold her against me while urging Storm to move quickly.

He takes off the only way he knows how with my command.

Blair's grip on my thigh tightens as we move in perfect rhythm through the field. I guide the horse onto an open trail, where we gallop at a steady pace until we reach the outside of the lake. She turns her head to take in the view, and I can tell she has a look of wonder in her eyes while she takes it all in. With her back pressed to my chest, I feel the worry drain from her body as she slowly inhales the crisp mountain air before releasing it.

For a small town, there's so much to see.

One lake, but fifty different ways to view it.

One woman in my arms, and a hundred different ways to love her.

Is that what this is?

My heartbeat pounds in my chest while my hold on her tightens. This feeling is stronger than ever. The need to tell her. I can do it right here and now. Whispering the feelings I have in her ear with just three little words.

But something stops me.

Blair lets go of the saddle and my thigh, bringing both arms out to the side as if she's a bird in the wind. Letting her head tilt up to the sky, she stays locked in that position as the rest of our bodies move with the gallop of the horse.

This is her letting go.

This is her feeling the freest she's ever been.

Without saying the words, I know that to be true because I once did the same thing on this very horse.

Once we turn back onto the trail, her hands come down as she holds me for the rest of the ride. I do the same, not wanting this to end, but also eager to spill everything on my mind.

We reach the open field outside of the barn and come to a stop. I dismount the horse first, reaching for her waist as she puts her hand on my shoulders and leans into me for support as I guide her off the horse's back.

"That was amazing." She beams. "I can't believe I was afraid of that. I felt so free."

I guide Storm to the wooden beam set up outside the barn and secure him to it. "It's amazing, isn't it?"

She answers me with closed eyes, tilting her head to the sky and deeply inhaling the moment. The smile that stretches her face tells me she's letting herself feel the peace and serenity that comes with the ranch.

I stare at her, unable to wipe the smile off of *my* face.

I'm in love with this woman standing before me.

If I questioned it before, there's no doubt about it now.

She turns to face me, and it's as if she can hear the words in my head when she grabs my hand and guides me into the barn.

She stops me in my tracks once we're tucked under the opening, spinning around to face me. She wraps her arms around my neck. I pull her into me, holding her body flush with mine. She reaches up to press her lips to mine.

She's claiming me with this kiss.

My hands find the small of her back to keep her pressed into me. She angles her head just enough to deepen the kiss. Another reminder of how everything she does turns me on.

Despite my hold, she leans her hips into me. I know she can feel what she's doing to me. I know she can feel my cock hardening in my jeans at just the press of her lips on mine.

"Blair," I say, pulling away from the kiss and letting my forehead fall to hers. "What are you doing to me?" I breathe out.

She smiles against my mouth. "I'm losing control with you."

I pull back. Her eyes twinkle in the dim barn light and like every time before this that I've stared into them, I find myself lost. In a complete trance.

I lift her in my arms, and she wraps her legs around my waist on instinct. Her lips are on mine in seconds as I walk her over to the little bunk room off to the side that never gets used.

I kick the door shut behind me, but I don't let her go. I spin her, pressing her back against the door. Driving my hips against her, she moans into my kiss.

"I'm not going to push this, but I want you, Blair," I say honestly, holding her up. She grinds her hips against me, chasing the pleasure. "You turn me on in the most unimaginable ways."

"Stop being a gentleman and fuck me, Griffin," she pants out. With her hands behind my head, she pulls my face to her with a searing kiss.

I let her feet stand on the ground. Both of us ripping at each other's clothes. As if we both can't wait another minute to feel this as our lips locked in a frenzied kiss for all of it.

To my surprise, she stops, taking a step back and letting her eyes trail my body. I reach for the hem of the T-shirt I had on under my flannel and pull it over my head. Bringing her bottom lip between her teeth, she stares at me with eyes that are begging me to claim her.

I have every intention of doing so.

"Blair," I growl, and her head snaps up to meet my stare. "I should warn you," I start before bringing my body close to hers, gripping her chin between my fingers and forcing her to look up at me. "I'm going to fuck you as hard as you just eye-fucked me."

She smirks. "I just didn't know how much muscle you had under those flannels all this time."

Moving fast, I lift her in my arms again and sit her down on the desk in the corner of the room. Hooking a finger in the side of her panties, I swipe a finger through her already wet pussy.

"Tell me," I breathe out. "Tell me how bad you want my cock, sweetheart."

"So bad," she moans.

Letting her head fall back, I trail kisses down her neck. My lips brush over her pulse pounding hard and fast just below the surface. "Your pussy is begging for me isn't it."

"Mm-hmm."

"Take it out," I whisper into the shell of her ear. "Take it out and show me."

She reaches between us, unbuttoning my jeans quickly before pushing them to the ground, my boxer briefs right behind them. Instantly her hands wrap around my cock and I can't help the moan I release against her skin.

"*Fuck*," I draw out.

She sits back on the desk, tugging her panties down until they are around her ankles, then kicks them to the side. She lifts a foot to wrap around my waist while reaching up around my neck to pull her to me.

Lining my cock up with her entrance, she sucks in a sharp breath, but my movements still.

"Wait." I pull back. "I don't have a condom."

She cups the sides of my face, her thumbs brushing the scruff that lines my jaw. "I want you, Griffin Barlow. I want all of you and nothing between us."

"Are you sure? I'm safe."

"I'm on birth control and I'm safe, too. I was tested twice after I found out about...you know, my past," she says, clearly not wanting to bring that up right now.

"I haven't been with anyone else in years," I admit.

Saying it out loud makes it feel that much more real. Blair is the first woman I've been with since my ex left town years ago. She's been the first woman to ignite something inside of me that isn't gloom or painful memories.

"I want all of you, Blair."

She pulls me into her again, the tip of my cock grazing her entrance. It's so hard that I don't even need to use my hands to guide it inside of her. With one thrust I bury myself deep inside of her. Her back arches and she falls back on her elbows.

"Oh my god," she cries out.

I position myself so I can rest both hands on the sides of her, driving in and out of her. Harder and faster until the only sound around us is the echo of wet skin slapping against each other, mixed with her moans.

"So tight," I rasp. "The way you stretch around me and take my cock like you own it. You're so fucking perfect."

"Griffin," she moans.

I slow my thrusts, but pound into her harder. "Say my name again, Blair." Another thrust. "Scream it."

"Griffin," she shouts again through labored breaths. "Harder. Fuck me like I'm yours. Only yours."

I give her one more hard thrust before keeping myself buried inside of her full hilt. I lean forward, grazing her lips with mine, our breaths mixing in the small space between.

"Let me make one thing clear," I say, my lips grazing against her cheek as they move to her ear. "*I'm* yours. You own me." I grind against her, not pulling out even an inch. Her mouth opens on a sharp inhale, the friction against her clit increasing. "You've owned me since the day you moved in, and every single time you got on my nerves after that."

"Yes," she moans.

"You have ruined every part of me," I continue, this time pulling out of her painfully slow until my tip grazes her entrance and then I slam into her again. "And I fully plan to ruin you for anyone else."

"Ahhh." Her moan mixes with a scream of pleasure. "Don't stop. Ruin me, Griffin. I don't want anyone else, only you."

The admission almost knocks me off my feet. Lifting my body up, I grip her sides again to give myself the momentum to fuck her hard. Hard enough that she can't stop the orgasm about to wash over her.

"Then come for me, sweetheart. Soak my cock with this tight, pretty cunt."

She bucks her hips into me, matching my steady pace. In seconds, her legs are shaking around me and her pussy pulses around my cock. She feels so good. It catapults me into my own orgasm right behind her.

My abdominal muscles tighten, and I grunt out a string of curse words under my breath because I don't think I've ever come this hard. Not even doing this with Blair before today. I know that these feelings in my chest for her are only making this one more intense.

The words spoken.

How she feels around me.

How it feels being with her.

All of it.

Once our breathing slows down, I pull out of her, looking around the room for something to clean up with. I find a towel hanging from the hook on the wall. Wetting it in the sink from the bathroom connected to the room, I return to help clean her up before cleaning myself up.

After we're both dressed, we stand there staring at each other. The feelings of words unspoken linger between us and I want to scream it, but something holds me back.

She has to be staying.

I need her to *tell me* she's staying before I do.

"Let me just get Storm back in the stall and then we can head out," I say, breaking the silence before guiding her out of the room and back into the barn. "Are you up for dinner?"

She hikes a thumb behind her. "After all of that, I'm starving."

We both laugh as I make my way to get Storm, who's standing where I left him against the wooden beam. For the next twenty minutes, Blair watches as I get him situated in the stall, brush him, and put his saddle away. She stays there, curious about it all, as if she wants to do it herself one day.

It would have been a perfect time to ask her about her plans.

I tell myself I will ask her over dinner.

Making our way to my truck parked by the ranch entrance, Blair puts her hand in mine. Confirmation I needed to bring up this topic in a little bit when we get back to my place.

"Griffin?" she asks, pulling me to a stop and positioning her body for me to face her. "There's something I've been wanting to tell you. I think now's a good time for it."

My nerves spike and I feel the skip of my heart before it goes into overdrive.

She grins as if she can feel the energy radiating off of me. Placing a hand on my chest, I'm sure she can feel the way my heart's thumping. "All good things, Griffin. Take a breath." She laughs.

I do, letting the corner of my lips twist up, feeling at ease already with her words.

"This thing between us…I want you to know that—"

Tires screeching along the asphalt have her words falling short, and both of our heads turning in the direction of the main road. An all-black, tinted sports car stops in the middle of the road. The way they stop feels like they are looking for us, but from the looks of the car, it could be someone lost and needing directions.

The car doesn't move from where it's stopped, but the front door opens, and I narrow my eyes. The man is in black dress pants and a white button-down dress shirt as if he's headed to a business meeting.

The grin on his face is mischievous.

"Can I help you, sir?" I ask.

He shakes his head. "You can't, but she can."

I turn to face Blair and her face is sheet white. A look of horror written across her features. A stark contrast to the smile she wore moments ago.

She pulls her hand from mine and my eyes bounce between the man and her.

Is this…

No.

The man comes to a stop in front of her, stuffing his hands in his suit pocket. "Hi, babe."

CHAPTER 36
THE TRUTH HURTS, DOESN'T IT?

BLAIR

This can't be happening right now.

I feel the color drain from my face the moment we turned to see the car skidding to a stop in the middle of the road. Because I would know that car anywhere. Not only does it not belong in this town, but it belongs to the man who drove me to leave the city in the first place.

So what the hell is he doing here now?

"Hi, babe." Theodore smirks.

It's a devilish smirk plastered on his face, like he's proud of the fact that he tracked me down.

"You lost the right to call me that a long time ago," I snap back.

He shakes his head, and his grin only grows. He takes a few steps in my direction, and I want to back away. I don't want this man near me. But I stay rooted where my feet are planted because I'm not the same person I was when I left. I'm stronger now and him being here doesn't change that.

I feel Griffin's eyes locked on me, but I refuse to face him.

Not that I don't want to.

I just don't want to see the pain written across his features.

"What is this?" Griffin asks. "Why is he here, Blair?"

I wince at hearing my name on his lips. It's laced with concern, and I don't blame him. I've assured him my past is in the past and that's where it was intended to stay.

Except, it's now standing in front of me.

I just had the most explosive moment with Griffin in the barn. One I didn't expect would happen when he brought me out here, but it did. I had every intention of using this day to tell him that I plan on staying. Hell, the words were getting ready to leave my mouth. Lily told me it's what I need to tell him to really allow him to open up to me.

But has he opened up to me already?

He told me he's mine, and that I own him.

He told me so many claiming words back in the barn. Words that made me eager to tell him everything, including how I truly felt about him.

"Blair," Griffin says, his tone louder to get my attention.

I turn to face him, and just as I suspected...pain.

"I'm sorry, Griffin. I need—"

"Don't," he cuts me off with a raised hand before giving Theodore a once over. "I'll give you two a minute." Then turns back to me, emotions void on his face. "You know where to find me."

Griffin moves to brush past me. I can't even find it in me to give him one glance because it hurts that he's probably thinking the worst. His knuckles brush mine at my side as he moves, and in the last second, he hooks a pinky finger with mine. So quick that if I moved, I would have missed it.

And then he's gone.

Leaving me alone with my ex-husband.

"What the hell are you doing here?" I bite out, stomping toward him.

He shrugs. "I heard you packed your bags and moved out here."

"How?"

"I hired a private investigator, babe."

"Don't call me that," I say through gritted teeth, pointing a finger in his face before turning around. Bringing my fingertips to my temple, I rub the ache away and will my heart rate to slow down.

Wait, did he just say he hired a private investigator?

I would have known. I would have noticed someone—

The man who's weirded me out on multiple occasions and no one seemed to know who he was. How could I be so stupid?

I spin around with narrow eyes facing him. "Why did you track me down?"

He reaches a hand out to rest it on my shoulder, but I shrug it away, not wanting his hands on me in any way, shape, or form.

"After you left, I thought I'd be over us. I thought I could move on, but I couldn't," he says. "I needed to find you to tell you how much I love you and that I'm sorry for how things ended."

"Sorry will never be enough for what you did," I say. "You didn't lie to me about taking out the trash, Theodore. This isn't something small I can ever forgive. You were sleeping with your secretary," I practically shout, anger bubbling up again. "I was justified in leaving you."

"I need you, Blair," he says in a begging tone. "I want to run for office again, but I can't do it without you."

"So that's what this is all about? You hired a private investigator and drove sixteen hours to beg me to come back so *you* can run for office again?" I can't hold back the laugh as the words roll off my tongue.

He can't be serious right now.

Since the moment I first drove away from San Francisco to come here, I always wondered about what it would be like to run into the man standing before me again. I put him so far in the rearview mirror that I thought it would be easy to see him.

But it's even worse.

It's hard because I have to tell him to his face that I don't want that. I want no part of being with him ever again. Now I have to tell him I don't miss him and that I've moved on.

I knew before I left that I moved on.

I knew before I left that I deserve better than that life.

"Yes," he finally answers. "I need you."

"Have you ever stopped to think about what I need? Better yet, what I *needed* for years when we were still married?"

My words ring in the air as I watch him standing there in silence.

"You never once thought about what I needed," I continue. "I realized so much after I walked away from you. I was molded into nothing more than a trophy for you to display. Nothing more than someone to show off so it looked like you were fit for office. And that's why you came out here again. You need to look fit for office to run again because it looks better on a campaign ticket when the person running is married."

"That's not the only reason," he cuts me off.

"I've moved on," I keep going, ignoring his lies as I make my way to stand directly in front of him. "I'm sure you thought I wouldn't, but I did. I've picked up every broken piece you shattered," I say, poking at his chest and fighting back emotions, knowing I can't let him see me fall apart. "I put myself back together again. I'm done hanging onto the past."

He gestures toward the ranch where Griffin went to give us some time. "Is that who helped you move on? Are you with him now?"

I stare at him in shock that he just asked that.

Contrary to what he assumes, Griffin isn't the one who picked up my broken heart. I did that all on my own before stepping foot in Bluestone Lakes. The last step for me was getting out of dodge and making a life for myself that I could be proud of.

Falling for Griffin wasn't in that plan.

Falling for Griffin happened when I least expected it.

I'm not about to admit that to my ex right now to set fuel to the fire.

"He's just a friend," I lie.

Theodore scoffs. "He didn't look like just a friend. I saw the way he needed to touch you when he left us alone here. Dumb ass. For even leaving you alone with me. You'll always be mine."

I narrow my eyes and feel a smoke cloud forming over my head. Theodore doesn't deserve his heart handled with care at this point.

"You know you miss me," he says, not giving me a chance to respond. All the while bringing himself closer to me and success-fully placing both hands on my shoulders to hold me in place. "Stop trying to play the victim here, Blair."

And I hate my name from his mouth.

I look deep into his eyes, trying to find the man I fell in love with all those years ago hidden somewhere in the irises. But it's long gone. It was gone years before I left.

"Not a single piece of my heart misses you," I admit without even a single blink of an eye. He doesn't move, and I don't push him off me even though his touch burns me. But not the good burn. "I didn't know then what I know now, and I deserve better. I *have* better. You might have been the one to put the ring on my finger, but those vows meant nothing to you. The same way your apologies and begging to take me back mean nothing to me right now."

I expect my words to force him to remove his hands from me, but they don't. He stares at me with such intensity. Hoping I'll change my mind or that I don't mean what I'm saying.

"You and me...we were never right," I continue. "When I'm in his arms, it feels the way it should. It feels safe, and it feels right."

He steps back, removing his hands from me and averting his gaze from the dirt around his feet.

"The truth hurts, doesn't it?" I add.

He looks up at me again, emotions in his eyes, but I will not let them affect me. Deep down I know the emotions don't stem from the love he has for me; it's the love he has for the office and his job. The future he won't have because I will never go back to him.

"You don't want this, babe. You know it. Don't listen to what other people have been feeding into your head. They are just telling you this because they don't like me. But you love me."

I rear back as if I've been hit.

Not physically, but definitely mentally.

Has—Is this what it's been like all long, but I was too blind to see it? Has he always played this narcissistic and manipulative game on me? I want to rage and blow up on him right now. But what good is it going to do with a man like this standing in front of me?

"Theodore," I say with a sigh. "All I ever wanted was to be loved by you, and you crushed me. You destroyed me. If the tables were turned, and you saw what I did that day in your office, I'm betting you would feel the same way..." I pause, watching his face as he winces. No doubt understanding that he would feel the same way. "I have too much pride in myself to let that happen again. What you did to me never deserves a second chance."

"So that's it? I drove out here for nothing?"

I nod, feeling the energy shift between us.

I know he's angry at everything I just said, he's ready to turn the tables and make this my fault some more.

"You wasted your time. Go home," I say quickly, not giving him the opportunity to throw more manipulation my way.

I turn around to make my way back to the barn, unsure if Griffin is even still here. Did he leave with Storm to go back out for a ride?

"You're going to regret this," he shouts from behind me.

I cross the arch leading to the ranch entrance, stopping my feet. I inhale a deep breath as I look up to the sky, silently praying he gets back in his car and goes home.

When I open my eyes, I read the words *Barlow Ranch*. Directly under it are small words I didn't notice until right now.

The best view comes after the hardest climb.

I suck in a sharp breath. The words mean more now than ever before. The words carved in the wood as if they weren't originally there. As if it was a thought someone had after the sign was already in place.

Griffin.

I turn around, grinning from ear to ear.

"Not a chance in hell," I respond to his jab. "You're going to regret the things you did for the rest of your life, Theodore. As for me, I'm going to live. Happily, in the bliss of knowing you lost the one thing you need to thrive in your job, and the one thing you will never get back."

Turning on my heel, I start jogging toward the barn. I make it halfway without another look back when Theodore's words stop me in my tracks.

"Fuck you, whore."

CHAPTER 37
BLAIR'S EX IS HERE.

GRIFFIN

Uneasiness courses through me.

My palms feel sweaty, and I can't bring my heart rate down to a normal rhythm as I make my way back to the barn to give them a minute. My boots in the dirt feel louder than they are with every step I take away from them.

Her ex-husband is fucking here.

I wanted to be true to my word and give them exactly one minute.

I don't know why my gut tells me not to trust him. Based on the things she's told me and his infidelity; he doesn't seem like a good person. For him to drive sixteen hours to come here. To do what? Win her back?

My head is pounding from everything that just happened. How the hell did it go from the most perfect day, an even better moment in the barn, to her past coming back into her life?

I scoff out loud as I pace the inside of the barn, kicking up dirt and letting each second pass in slow painful torture. Just as I turn around for another pass from my back and forth, something crashes inside the tack room. Running to see what the heck that was all about, I swing the door open to find Nan with a large brush to groom a horse in her hand, ready to fight.

"What the hell?" I say, narrowing my eyes at her.

"Oh, it's you." She relaxes. "Sorry, I was trying to make myself scarce here. I heard some cars and thought you two were leaving, but then I saw another fancy-pants car pull up and I thought, hmm, better not."

Bringing my hands to my hips, I just stare at the crazy old woman.

Even with the anger bubbling inside of me and being unsure of what's happening outside of the barn, my shoulders somehow relax at the sight of Nan.

She tips her head to the side in confusion as if she caught onto my body language. She steps out of the room and stands before me, placing a delicate hand on my shoulder. "You know you can talk to me anytime, Griffin."

Sighing, I close my eyes for a brief moment. Thinking about how to even explain something I can't even explain myself.

Thoughts swirl with the idea of her taking him back. All I can think about is her getting in the passenger seat of his car, and him driving her back to her place to pack up her things and go back to the city.

Maybe that was her plan all along.

Maybe I was just something to hold her over until he wanted her back.

"Blair's ex is here," I tell her, but wince as the words leave my mouth. Just saying it out loud makes it feel all too real.

"And?"

Shaking my head, I look down at my boots to avoid her stare. Of course, she wouldn't understand. While I didn't have a long relationship with Blair like I did with my ex, it stings feeling like the cycle is repeating itself with Blair. It just feels like the same thing that happened to me before is happening again.

This one hurts more because I allowed myself to picture a future with Blair when I shouldn't have. I feel like a fool because

I should have never left my heart open enough for this to happen.

Her past is back in the present.

She has a history with him. A big one.

I'm safe to assume they can work things out.

I close my eyes and release a long exhale. "I took her to ride Storm today."

Her eyes widen, knowing what *that* means to me.

"As we were leaving, a black sports car call pulled up as if they were looking for us, or someone. He got out of the car and told us he was looking for Blair. The moment I looked at her, I knew it was her ex-husband." I shake my head at the memory from not long ago. A moment that will be engraved in my head for days to come. "He called her babe."

Nan scoffs. "That means nothing."

I narrow my eyes in confusion at her.

"Did she send you back in here for them to work it out? Like, what did she say to you?"

I don't answer as I replay the interaction in my head.

I didn't give her a chance to say anything.

Regret churns in my stomach because I should have fucking stayed out there with them. No. I should have put her in my truck and drove us away from her past, leaving it where it belongs.

As if Nan can sense my uncertainty, she continues. "Listen, I don't know what happened or how everything played out, but I do know Blair cares about you. She's got this weird twinkle in her eye when she looks at you," she says with a chuckle. "And just because someone from her past showed up doesn't mean she's going to run back there. It doesn't mean she's ready to pack up and leave. She doesn't seem like the type."

I raise an eyebrow. "She ran here, didn't she?"

"She also *bought* the house," she rebuttals. "Not rented it. She showed up in town with every intention of staying."

Nan makes a very valid point.

But the part of me that has built these walls to protect my heart from the cycle of my life repeating itself, is struggling to come to terms with that.

"I feel like I'm being brought back to the past and reliving everything all over again," I admit.

She eyes me with consideration, realizing quickly that Blair means more to me than I've expressed out loud before.

These feelings have only grown stronger with every moment I'm with her, or think about her. The way she smiles and lights up every dark part of my soul. The way her contagious laugh has helped me remember how to laugh again myself. The way her kiss has made me feel things I told myself I would never feel again.

"Can I tell you what I think you should do?" Nan cuts through my thoughts.

"No, but you're going to tell me anyway."

"Yep," she says with a curt nod, placing both hands on her hips. "I think you're jumping to conclusions here. Which is justified, considering your past. You've been through some shit, only making you come out stronger in the end. The light may have been turned off for a few years, but it's time to turn it back on for good," she says with a pat on my chest. "However, you two have something that neither of you can deny. Maybe she's out there right now telling him to fuck off."

Just as the final words roll off her tongue, shouting forces both of us to snap our heads toward the open barn doors. I move before I even have a chance to register what's being said.

"Fuck you, whore," I hear him say to her.

When I turn the corner, I spot her standing halfway to the barn, as if she was on her way back here.

On her way back to me.

My chest feels tight, my head feels lightheaded. The only thing I can hear is my own heartbeat before I hear her ex-husband shout to her, "This was the biggest waste of time. You'll never be nothing more than a piece of shit."

My vision clears.

My feet move on their own accord.

Blair is still facing him, and neither of them notices my presence as I stalk toward the entrance of the ranch. He's already turning around to walk to his car when my feet turn into a jog to catch up to him.

Flying past Blair, I hear her gasp, but she doesn't stop me.

My focus is on one thing and one thing only.

Reaching him, my hand grips his shoulder so tight, that he startles in surprise before turning around to face me with wide eyes.

"What the fuck did you just call her?"

The asshole stares at me for a moment before he smirks and then continues to remain silent. There isn't an ounce of worry in his face, as if he knows he's going to get away with whatever he just said.

"I don't know how things work in the city," I growl. "But you're in my territory now."

"Is that supposed to scare me?" He gestures behind my shoulder to where Blair stands. "City or not, she's still the same girl she was. A fucking whore," he spits out.

"That's what I thought you said," I say calmly before I rear my fist back and drive it straight into his nose. He falls to the ground instantly bringing his hand up to cover it.

"Fuck! Did you just punch me?"

I tower over him, looking down at the piece of shit in the dirt. "I can do it again if you need confirmation."

The look on his face dares me. A sly grin, and a raised eyebrow.

Just as I'm about to rear back to give the man another shot of what he deserves, the cock of a shotgun echoes behind me.

I don't bother looking back.

It's fucking Nan.

He turns to face Blair. "This is where you moved?" he shouts, telling me she's still a good distance away. "These people are nuts. This is a good enough reason for you to get in the car and come home."

I hear footsteps in the dirt—multiple sets—but I don't turn around to see.

Blair comes to one side of me, while Nan rounds the other. Her ex looks between all of us towering over him. While he still shows no fear by keeping that stupid smirk on his face, I know he's going to get out of dodge quicker than he arrived.

"This is my home now," Blair says with a soft, even tone. She crouches beside him, bringing a hand up to check his nose. "I'm not leaving."

Her words hit me square in the chest and I feel the tension in my shoulders evaporate with three little words. Three little words that make the other three words want to pour out of my mouth.

While this isn't how I wanted to hear them, it's exactly what I need to hear.

"And if you think for one second I'll get in the car after you called me a whore—not once, but twice—then you've lost your ever-loving mind." She laughs, but it's laced with sarcasm. She lifts her hand from his nose, rearing back quick enough, and smacks him across the side of the face. It was so quick that even he didn't have a chance to respond. "Now get the fuck out of here."

That's my girl.

"And don't ever let me catch you in my town again," Nan chimes in.

Her ex scuffles back enough to allow himself some room to stand, brushing the dirt from his dress pants before mumbling profanities under his breath as he gets into his car and speeds off. His tires screech as he heads in the direction of the interstate.

Away from Bluestone Lakes.

CHAPTER 38
I'M NOT LEAVING.

BLAIR

I don't take my eyes off Theodore's car until it's completely gone from my line of sight. Nan does the same and then retreats back to the barn as soon as he's gone. I'm not even sure where she came from.

Only then do I turn to face Griffin.

The man who just stood up for me and protected me from the harsh words my ex-husband threw in my face. Words that aren't even true because *he* was the one who hurt me. But there's one thing I've learned in life...it's that hurt people hurt people. Theodore is hurting from the fact I won't take him back as easily as I probably would have in the past.

He didn't expect me to stand up for myself.

But there's never been a single second since our divorce where I thought of a future with him after everything.

Swallowing through the thickness in my throat, I stare at him. Unsure of what to say. I *know* there's something here between us. Something big.

Is it love?

I've never known a feeling like being around Griffin.

Letting my feet move, I finally step toward him, eager to feel his arms around me and tell him everything I was trying to tell him before all of this.

But he heard me say the words to Theodore.

It's time to say it to him.

"Blair," he breathes out. My name on his lips like a painful whisper.

Emotions rise and I can't hold back.

We stare at each other, silence stretching with each second that passes.

Only moments ago, I had so much to say. Now I can't find a single word. Everything has died on my tongue.

"Blair," he repeats, and I crumble. The tears in my eyes spill and I know with certainty he's thinking the worst. I open my mouth to respond, but he holds up a hand to stop me. "You're staying."

I swipe a tear from the corner of my eye before it has a chance to cascade down my cheek, and then I shake my head.

His body visibly relaxes before me. His shoulders fall and he releases a breath, looking down at the dirt around his feet.

"I'm not leaving," I finally say out loud. "I was never planning on leaving."

"But—"

"Him showing up here wouldn't be a reason for me to leave. He showed up because he wants me back. Except it's for selfish reasons. And any reason he could try to give me wouldn't ever be enough for the damage he's already done. What he did doesn't deserve a second chance."

He stares at me, blinking twice before taking a tentative step into me.

I can tell he's holding back despite my words.

His fears are all the same as I had. We've both been hurt so badly before that this whole thing is terrifying for us.

"I mean...look at how he just spoke to me. Why would I *want* to leave and go back to someone like that?"

"The way he..." He shakes his head. "I wanted to murder

him for that, Blair. I was ready to kill him for saying those things to you." He lifts a hand, brushing a stray tendril of hair behind my ear. "Are you okay?"

I nod, letting my body gravitate into him. Leaving a breath of air between us.

He doesn't take his eyes off mine. It's almost as if he's trying to memorize me, or he's waiting for me to vanish in thin air.

"Talk to me," I urge.

His forehead falls to mine and his eyes flutter closed. He's in pain. Not just from the physical blow he gave Theodore, but from this whole thing. It wasn't what he had planned bringing me out here to ride Storm.

"I'm not leaving," I repeat again against his lips, sensing that he needs that confirmation.

"Blair," he breathes out my name and closes all the space between us, wrapping his arms around my neck and holding me to his chest. As if he needed to touch me. Feel me.

"I don't know what made you believe this was temporary for me," I say against his shirt. "But I bought the house. I have no intention of leaving unless…"

He pulls back at the pause of my words. His eyes laser focused on mine as if to assess the next words out of my mouth.

A lopsided grin stretches my face. "Unless my grumpy next-door neighbor hated me so much that he wanted to run me out of town. A girl can't live like that forever," I joke with a laugh. It's light, but just enough that he pulls my body back into his.

He holds me. Tightly as if to say, *"I'm never letting you go."*

But he still says nothing, only tightening the hold. A heart-beat passes before his head falls onto my shoulder, pressing his lips to it.

"There's no way he ever loved you as much as I do right now," he whispers.

My head rears back, eyes widening at his admission. Suddenly feeling lightheaded, as my heart hammers in my ribcage. Did Griffin Barlow just—

"Or tomorrow," he adds with a shrug.

"You w-what?"

"I love you, Blair," he repeats, bringing himself eye level with me. "I love you and I'm no longer afraid to tell you. My mind is set on *you*. I wanted to tell you back at the ranch. Truthfully, I think I've wanted to tell you for a while now."

My lips part on their own, while my mind spins with the words he says. I have to remove my eyes from his boring into mine because both of us have been through hell and back in our past relationships. The word has been ringing in my ear myself, but I've been too guarded to let myself say it again.

Griffin brings his hand to rest under my chin, urging me to look at him. "I want to fight for you on all the worst days. I want to laugh with you on all your best days. I want to dance in the kitchen with you when there's no music playing and see the stars with you in the bed of my truck any chance we get. But most of all…" He pauses, swallowing past the emotions. "I don't ever want to give you a reason to need to give me a second chance."

I blink, and the dam behind my eyes breaks. Moisture gathers in the corners and I'm ready to break down completely in front of this man.

"I know the timing isn't right to say this after everything—"

"I love you too," I cut him off, hands coming to cup both sides of his face. "I didn't move here to find this. I came to Bluestone Lakes to find myself because I felt like I kept losing pieces of who I was deep down throughout my past. Tiny pieces being chipped away day by day," I say, shaking my head as if to remove the memory. "You were the most unexpected thing to happen, because, in the process of finding myself, I ended up finding home. In this town, and most importantly, in you."

He pulls me back into him before the final word leaves my lips.

My vision becomes hazy as the tears build up more and more.

"Never did I believe that the dreams I once had to build a life…build a home…with someone would be on the table again for me," he breathes out against my hair. "I put that dream in the past, buried it with the memories of things out of reach."

It's more real now than ever before.

Pulling out of his hold, he eyes me in confusion. I stare up at him, blinking and bringing my bottom lip between my teeth while I silently beg him to seal the deal.

His eyebrows pinch in confusion.

"Are you going to kiss me or not, cowboy?"

The smile on his lips tells me that's not what he was expecting. His hand grips my hips while his other reaches to cup the side of my jaw, allowing his thumb to caress the apple of my cheek. My head melts into his light touch.

"You should know by now, I'll give you whatever you want, sweetheart."

"Then you better kiss me," I say quickly.

His lips crash into mine with a searing kiss. Sealing the words we just spoke moments ago as the final piece to make everything real.

My hands grip his flannel, pulling him into me before they wrap around his neck and tangle in his already messy hair. Reaching up on my toes, he moves to lift me and I wrap my legs around him in a tight hold, not once releasing the kiss.

This kiss is messy.

This kiss is wild.

This kiss is free.

It's as free and wild as I want the future to be for us.

Panting against my skin, he sets me down on my feet. Griffin looks down at me, and I swear I stop breathing. A feeling I will never get used to looking at him, or the way he's looking at me. But something pulls his attention from the corner of his eyes. We both turn to find Nan standing outside of the barn. When she notices us looking, she starts clapping.

We both fall into a fit of laughter as he intertwines his hand in mine, guiding me to where Nan stands by the barn. His hand feels like it was made to fit mine and I want to stay in this happy bubble.

"Now if this isn't the picture of love," she coos.

Griffin's hold on my hand tightens, looking down at me and smiling from ear to ear. I don't think I will ever get used to *that* either.

"How long have you been here?" I ask her.

"Long enough to hear both of you screaming at each other before that twatwaffle started screaming at you," she scoffs.

"Huh?"

She rolls her eyes and groans. "Don't make me repeat what I heard, Blair. I thought those things were just stuff I've read in my romance novels, but Griffin here..." She points a finger in his direction. "Have you been reading my books?"

He holds a hand up in defense. "Not me."

Then it dawns on me...she's talking about hearing us in the barn before everything just happened. I feel my cheeks burn, no doubt turning crimson red with embarrassment. Bringing my lips between my teeth, I hide behind Griffin's shoulder to avoid eye contact with Nan altogether.

"Nan," he warns.

"All in good fun, kids." She laughs. "But in all seriousness, the two of you standing in front of me has never made me happier." I emerge from behind him, letting myself look at the woman who first greeted me when I moved here. She makes her way to stand in front of me, placing a hand on my shoulder. "I knew from the moment I met you that this place would change your life. You had this hesitation about you, but I knew you would open up here. I knew that tiny home on Barlow Drive would be the key to do so."

"Did you plan all of this?" I ask.

She shakes her head, her smile only growing. "Never in life

would I do that." She winks. "But I know this grumpy man enough to know that he needed a twist in his quiet life. He needed someone like you to shake it up a bit."

"You're an evil woman," Griffin draws out, shaking his head in disbelief.

Nan simply shrugs. "I'm not evil, I'm just smart."

Facing Griffin, I look up at him with literal hearts in my eyes. If that's even a thing. The man who's flipped my world upside down. I wrap my arms around his waist, and his hands find mine on his stomach.

He leans down and kisses me again.

Out in the open in front of other people. Well, in front of Nan.

I want nothing more than his lips to be the first thing I feel when I wake up and the last thing before I fall asleep at night.

"Let's go home," he says against my lips before pressing one more quick kiss to the corner of my mouth.

I nod, locking my hands in his as he guides me out of the barn.

"Anyone want to drive me back?" Nan asks behind us.

I reach into the pocket of my jeans, pulling out my slim key fob for the Mercedes-Benz, and tossing it to her. She catches them even though she's caught off guard.

"You can borrow that," I say. "But take care of her."

"Oh, it's time for some donuts." She beams, fist in the air.

"Whoa, whoa," I say, trying to stop her.

"Relax, Bubbly Blair. I'm talking about the kind you eat." She winks and scurries past us, jogging as fast as her legs can take her to my car. Opening the door, giving us an exaggerated wave before she peels off toward town.

"She will always be the most interesting character in Bluestone Lakes," Griffin says, dumbfounded, as he guides me toward his truck.

"I was thinking the same thing," I say as I jump into his passenger seat while he gets into the driver's seat.

With one more glance in my direction, he looks over at me.

My chest warms and I feel like I can breathe again. There's a comfort in his stare that tells me moving here was the best decision of my life.

"Take me home, Griffin."

He nods in response and puts the truck in drive.

CHAPTER 39
I THOUGHT YOU DIDN'T LIKE DOGS.

BLAIR

The nerves from hours ago are now a distant memory as we ride the dirt road back to Barlow Drive. I don't even want to think about what I would be feeling right now if things didn't go the way they did. If he didn't believe that I was staying.

Turning onto our road, the sky transforms instantly from day to night as a soft glow from the setting sun illuminates behind the mountains in the distance. It's magical how the sky can transform in an instant here.

Griffin pulls into my driveway, exiting the truck without turning it off and quickly rounding the hood to open the door for me.

Confusion washes over me as to why he didn't turn it off.

I stand there, wondering what his plans are.

Grinning and taking my hand in his, he lifts it to his mouth and presses a kiss to the back of my hand. "Get your stuff," he says.

My eyes narrow. "What stuff?"

"Whatever you want. All of it. Load it in the truck," he rattles off in rapid succession.

"Are you sending me a text message?" I laugh.

"A what?"

"It means you're making no sense, the way your texts make no sense."

He barks out a laugh.

I will never tire of hearing this man laugh. From believing he was just my grumpy next-door neighbor to this. It's a total one-eighty I will never get used to but crave. I want to hear him laugh, watch him smile, and everything in between.

Stepping closer to him, I keep my hand in his and bring my other to his chest as I lift my head to keep our eyes locked.

"I love you," I tell him again. It feels so good rolling off my tongue.

He leans down, pressing a kiss to my lips. "I love you too, sweetheart. Now go get your things."

"I'm still not understanding. Are you asking me to grab a change of clothes because you want me to stay the night at your place?"

His features soften as he removes my hand from his.

Cupping my cheeks, he angles my head higher to really look at him. His eyes bounce between mine as if he's making sure I understand whatever he's about to say.

"I want you to grab all your clothes, all your things." His thumb caresses my cheek. "I don't just want you to stay the night. I want you to stay for good."

I take a step back out of his hold, shocked at what he's saying right now.

"But my tiny home."

His smile widens. "We can keep it as it is, or we can ask Nan to put it back on the market."

"But—"

"I know this is rushing it. It feels weird for me too," he cuts me off. "But, Blair, listen to me closely when I say this..." He pauses, erasing the space I just put between us. "I love you. I know with certainty that I want you in my life until it's time to put me in the ground. I want you in my bed with me every night, because I want you close. I *need* you close."

My stomach surges with warmth and emotion.

Griffin has turned into everything I never knew I wanted.

He loves loud and bold with his whole chest.

"There's no way in hell you're living here, and me there," he says, gesturing with his head behind him at his house.

Looking over his shoulder, I take in his house.

This feels real. It feels…right.

"Yes," I finally say. "But there's just one thing…"

He raises a brow in confusion.

"Reginald."

The moment his name leaves my lips I hear a bark come from inside my house and we both turn our heads. It's as if he heard us talking about him.

Griffin laughs before turning his attention back to me.

"You think I'd ask you to live out your future with me and not include him?"

Shrugging a shoulder, I bring my bottom lip between my teeth. "I thought you didn't like dogs."

"I don't," he scoffs. "But that one's grown on me, and I kind of like having him around."

My eyes widen briefly before schooling my features.

Only Reginald can make a man who dislikes dogs…like them.

I press my body into his, placing both hands back on his chest. I feel his heartbeat thunder under my palm, forcing mine to pick up speed. Being around him just does that to me. It happens all on its own. It's confirmation that *this* is what love is supposed to feel like. Knowing you're with the person who will always protect your heart, wipe away your tears on the bad days, and laugh with you on the good ones.

A person who's been through what I have should have trust issues. I should question this and be weary of the cycle repeating itself. But there isn't a doubt in my mind that Griffin would do that to me. Looking in his eyes I see an honest future. I swear if hearts coming out of someone's eyes were a real thing, he would see it in mine.

"You really love me, huh?"

He leans down, lips brushing mine. "I think I loved you when your dog first peed in my rosebush."

I laugh against his mouth before lifting myself up to crash my lips to his in a searing kiss. Knowing I could, and would, kiss this man for the rest of my life and be the happiest woman in the world.

Bluestone Lakes not only helped me find myself.

But it's changed everything for me.

I'm a different person from the very first drive into town. A woman who was nervous about what the future would hold in a town with no friends and no family.

"Can we keep the tiny home for now?" I ask. "It holds a special place in my heart."

"Whatever you want, sweetheart."

He wraps one arm around my shoulder, guiding me into the first place that was all mine. I grab whatever I can and stuff for Reginald before we load his truck and make our way back to his place.

Once I cross the threshold, a new feeling overwhelms me.

It's large and spacious.

Even though it's not my first time here, it feels like it is. Because this time, I'm entering and staying.

Finding a new home with Griffin Barlow.

And it feels really fucking good.

EPILOGUE

FOUR MONTHS LATER.

GRIFFIN

"I know I say this every week, but this is my favorite night at the bar." Tucker beams, his body bouncing to the music.

Biting back a smile, I nod. "Mine too."

"Who would have thought," Tucker starts, nudging me with his elbow. "Griffin Barlow would permanently put karaoke night on the schedule and actually enjoy it. I'm digging this new version of you, boss."

Averting my gaze from the bar to Blair, the smile comes naturally. I watch as she helps Nan with getting people listed and what song they plan to sing. There isn't a soul in Bluestone Lakes that can carry a tune, but the laughs that echo through these walls tells me that this was the right move. People love this night and look forward to it.

Blair has changed me in more ways than one.

She's opened up a piece of me that I kept stuffed down away from the world.

As if she can sense me staring, she turns to face me. The twinkle in her eyes, mixed with the crinkle from her smile only makes my heart race. A feeling I will never get used to. I truly lose my breath every time.

"I'm taking five," I tell Tucker, not bothering to look at him.

"Take ten, boss." And I hear him laugh as I round the bar to make my way to Blair.

Her face morphs into a *come get me* smirk, and I shake my head because there's no doubt that this woman owns me.

My heart.

My soul.

Without wasting a minute, I wrap both arms around her waist, pulling her into me. I let my face fall into the crook of her neck and inhale the sweet honeysuckle scent as if I haven't seen or felt her in days.

"It's been all of twenty minutes, Griffin," She giggles against me.

"Twenty minutes too long," I say, pulling back just enough to look her in the eyes.

There it goes again, completely losing my breath.

Her arms snake around my neck before she pulls off my baseball cap with one hand and intertwines her fingers through my hair with the other.

"I missed you too." She grins, pressing on her toes to bring her lips to mine.

I kiss her as if there's no one else in the bar.

I wish there wasn't because every kiss with Blair is like coming home.

"Blair is supposed to be working," Nan mutters off to my side.

We both pull apart, laughing against each other's lips before turning to face her.

"I'm sorry, Nan," Blair says to her. "This neanderthal can't go more than twenty minutes without having his lips on me."

"I don't need to know all the details about where Griffin puts his lip." She wrinkles her face in disgust.

"Nan!" Blair feigns embarrassment and her cheeks flame to a rosy, pink shade.

I lean down, letting my lips graze the shell of her ear. "I'd love to put my lips all over you, sweetheart. Every square inch of this body is mine, and when the night is over I plan to do just that."

She pulls back, the corner of her lips twist and she raises a brow. "Is that so?"

"Every." I press a kiss to her lips. "Square." Another kiss. "Inch."

Her body shivers, and she steps out of my hold. "Not here," she whispers through gritted teeth. "You know how turned on I get when you talk like that."

"I don't see the issue." I smirk.

She swats my chest playfully. "Get back to the bar. Tucker needs you."

"Tucker doesn't need me." I laugh. "But I'll get back to work. If you insist."

"I do." She presses both palms to my chest, lifting up to give me one more parting kiss.

As I walk back toward the bar, her words ring in my ear.

I do.

After my first real relationship went down the drain, I swore I would never think of hearing those words from anyone else. I felt as if I was destined to be the grumpy bar owner in Bluestone Lakes for the rest of my life. Waking up to tend to the ranch, working my lunch shift, and then going back to the ranch. I poured my life and soul into both of those things because I never believed I was worthy enough for another chance with someone.

Blair saved me from myself.

She saved me from ruining every relationship I had with my friends and family by bringing me out of the phase of life I felt stuck in. Looking back, I'm shocked that my sisters and Tucker didn't give up on me and cut me from their lives for being as angry as I was for no damn reason.

It's only been four months, but I see the future with her more than just her living with me the way she has been. Despite her not wanting to sell the tiny home yet, I don't get the feeling she's going to run off on me.

I fully trust Blair with my heart.

It's a wild and freeing feeling because I never thought I'd be able to trust this way again.

Stepping behind the bar, I find Blair staring at me again. I shoot her a wink and smile, and she does the same before getting back to work with Nan.

I love her.

I love Blair with my entire existence and will make her my wife one day.

That much I know is true.

Wiping the counter, a man I don't recognize sits down in front of me.

"What can I get you?" I ask.

He looks around quickly. "What's all this about tonight?"

"This is karaoke night." I point toward Nan. "See that woman over there? She organized this whole thing a few months ago so we made it a weekly thing here."

"Nan," he says.

I raise a brow and turns back in his stool to face me. "You know her?"

He nods. "She's the one who gave me the keys to my new place."

"Ahhh." I grin.

The old me would have been annoyed as shit at someone new moving here yet again. The man sitting in front of me is dressed in jeans and a polo T-shirt. But looks to be hiding his face under the baseball cap sitting low over his eyes. I've learned to read people through this job, and he's without a doubt from some big hub city.

"Guess I should introduce myself then, huh?" I extend my hand across the table. "I'm Griffin."

"Dallas." He returns my handshake.

"Oh my god," Tucker says to my side, covering his mouth with his hand.

"Don't say it," the man warns Tucker.

I look between the two of them, confusion likely stretched across my face. "What am I missing?"

Tucker leans in, keeping his stare on the bar, but whispering behind his hand. "That's the head coach for the San Francisco Stags major league baseball team."

"Was," the man cuts in with a whisper. "*Was* the head coach."

"Nooo." Tucker winces as if hearing the news is painful.

I give Tucker a questioning glare. "Since when are you a baseball fan?"

"I root for the underdogs," he says, lifting his chin into the air. "And the Stags were…" He pauses to look at the man, before leaning in again to whisper in my ear. "They suck."

The man nods, lips forming a straight line.

"So, what brings you to Bluestone Lakes?" I ask, trying to change the sore subject.

"Your website is very welcoming," he says.

Tucker barks out a laugh, and I laugh under my breath because that's a far cry from the truth. There's like one photo on the website.

Before I can even respond, Nan and Blair make their way to the bar next to where this man sits.

"Ah, Dallas," Nan says, throwing an arm around his shoulders as if their old friends. "You found the best bar in town. Have you gotten settled in nicely?"

He nods but remains silent.

"Dallas?" Blair says loud enough for everyone around us to hear. "You're…you're the head coach for the Staghorns. I'm from San Francisco too. What brings you all the way out here?"

"Hell if I know," he answers, keeping his head down toward the bar.

Moving to grab my bottle of Foxx Bourbon off the top corner

shelf, I pour him a glass. "On the house," I say, sliding it across the bar to him.

"Thank you." He nods.

"You got it," I say. "And, hey, for what it's worth… Welcome to Bluestone Lakes."

Want more Blair + Griffin?
Head to my website and click <u>bonus content</u> to download the
Extended Epilogue
http://jennmcmahon.com

ACKNOWLEDGMENTS

I'm going to end up doing what I always do, list some incredible people who have made this book what it is. But I can't do that without heavily thanking **my readers**. It goes without saying that I wouldn't be here writing this, I wouldn't have the team I'm about to thank in just a few lines, and I wouldn't have the urge to *want* to write if it wasn't for you. You love my book just as much, if not more than I do and there is not a single word that I could use to share my appreciation for that.

You've made this what it is.

You've given me the drive to keep going.

Thank you. Period.

My husband and my kids — the ones who put up with my crazy writing schedule and my deadlines. This book was a challenge at the end as it creeped its way into the holidays. Thank you for putting up with me and supporting my dream.

Lauren Brooke — my assistant not just in this job, but in life. Thank you for being the sounding board when I needed to laugh, scream or cry about something. I would have canceled this book if it wasn't for you.

Caroline — I'm a hot mess for all of existence. And you haven't fired me yet. For that, I owe you everything. Thank you for letting me be me in all my glory.

Amy and Tabitha — the feedback given during edits of this book has truly shaped this into what it is. I loved this book in the first draft, and now I'm obsessed with every aspect. It's because of both of you and the eye you have for the story.

My sprinting girls — Victoria Wilder, Julia Connors, Ashley James. From the laughs, to the cries, to the celebrations we have. I mean this with my entire chest, I can't do this job without you.

My alpha, beta and content creators — I was so lucky to work with so many of you on this project. You girls know who you are and truly...THANK YOU. For reading early. For letting me give up control for the first time in my life with content. You've made the transition for me so smooth.

My bubbly girls — Tori, Cait and Moe. I've never met a group of girls who cheers for indie authors harder than you. Your support and encouragement through this journey has really brightened my life so positively.

If you've made it this far, is it weird for me to say thank you again? What's the word count on that? Too much? No. It's never enough for everything you've given me on this journey as an author. Buckle up, *sweetheart*. Because there's a lot more to come in Bluestone Lakes.

I hope you're ready.

ABOUT JENN MCMAHON

Jenn McMahon resides along the shore in New Jersey with her husband, two boys, and three fur babies. She has spent years engrossed in romance books, to now writing her own and sharing them with the world.

When Jenn is not writing, she can be found reading, watching reruns of her favorite TV shows (Scandal, Grey's Anatomy and Friends – just to name a few), or doing puzzles. She also loves taking trips to the beach with the kids, Atlantic City date nights with her husband, and thunderstorms.

Scan Here to access my socials, Facebook reader group, newsletter sign up and everything you need to stay connected.

instagram.com/jennmcmahon.author
tiktok.com/@jennmcmahon.author
amazon.com/author/jennmcmahon

Printed in Great Britain
by Amazon

60900368R00191